Don't Call Me Kit Kat

K. J. Farnham

More Books by K. J.

Click Date Repeat

Click Date Repeat Again

A Case of Serendipity

Visit kjfarnham.com for more information.

Dedication

For Jody and Jamie

Part I

Summer/Fall

Chapter One

"Are you ready?"

I look down and scan my body as I debate Anica's question. Sweat drips down the small of my back. I don't know if the perspiration is a result of the three layers of clothing I'm wearing, or because I'm nervous about getting caught.

"I think so," I say, certain that she can sense the fear in my voice. But I really don't care if Anica knows how scared I am because I'm pretty sure we are actually friends. I worry more that she might tell her other friends—the ones whose parents make more money in one year than my mom and stepdad have made in the past five. It is that money that allows them to live in the upscale Orchard Hills neighborhood. They are the friends who shoplift just for fun. They are the cool girls—the ones I secretly wish I could be friends with, the ones I want to look and dress like.

She tilts her head slightly and whispers, "Katie, are you scared?" When I don't answer, she drops her Forever 21 bag, which contains mostly stolen items, and begins to lift the large sweater swallowing her petite frame. "Let's just forget it then. If you look all nervous, we'll get caught for sure."

For a second, I'm relieved because she's offering a get-out-of-jail-free card. But during the other half of that second, I picture Amy Bowie—the most envied soon-to-be eighth grade girl at Frank Lloyd Wright Middle School—decked out from head to toe in name brands my mother and stepfather would never be able to afford. I want to do this. I need these new clothes. Plus, Anica and the other Orchard Hills girls have done it a million times and never been caught. "No, Wait. I'm fine." I take a deep breath and unlatch the dressing room door. "Let's go."

It's not like this is the first time I've ever shoplifted. When I was eight, I lifted a Heath bar from Snyder's Drug Store. While my mother waited at the pharmacy for her allergy pills, I poked around in the candy aisle. I knew she wouldn't buy the candy for me, mostly because she was always nagging me for being "a little chubby." She had warned me that I wouldn't be able to fit into any of the hand-me-down clothes from the neighbor girl if I didn't slim down. Then I wouldn't have any "new" clothes for the school year that was beginning in a few weeks. I pocketed the candy bar more out of spite than a desire to eat it. Two years later, I went on to steal nail polish from the same drug store. As I removed the small glass bottle from inside the waistband of my jean shorts, it slipped from my grasp and shattered on the sidewalk outside my house. My eyes welled up with tears as I looked down at my brand new flip-flops, which had been splattered with the pretty, pastel purple polish. I figured the accident was God's way of punishing me for stealing. And now, as Anica and I exit the Macy's dressing room, I wonder how I will be punished for walking off with layers of stolen merchandise.

Anica and I make a point of hanging several items in the reject area near the entrance of the dressing room. Then, as we exit, we discuss our disappointment over not finding anything we liked—rehearsed, of course. "Oh well. Let's go check out the Gap," Anica says loudly.

I'm supposed to respond, but suddenly I feel like I can't breathe. My torso is drenched in sweat and my palms are dripping. To make things worse, my shoes suddenly feel as though they are filled with lead. All I can do is focus on the shoe department up ahead, which is the last stretch of ground we need to cover before exiting the store into the hustle and bustle of the mall.

She nervously glances sideways at me. "Maybe we can stop at Auntie Anne's. You feel like a pretzel?"

"Sure," I murmur. I know that I am bombing in my role as an innocent, perky, just-hanging-out-at-the-mall thirteen-year-old.

We are so close to freedom when Anica stops to look at a pair of studded flats. "These are *so* cute!" She picks one up. "Don't you think?"

I breathe deeply as I pull my anxious eyes away from the relief that waits outside the confines of the store. I know that Anica is still playing her role. She wants to make sure no one is suspicious of us before we leave. I better play along, so I nod and say, "Yeah. I can *totally* see you in those."

She hugs the shoe to her chest and lets out an obnoxious groan. "I wish I had enough to buy a pair!" With that, she sets the shoe back in its place and tugs at my sleeve. "C'mon. Let's get pretzels."

I hold my breath as we step across the threshold, letting it out only when we are a good distance from the store. We look at each other and smile. Auntie Anne's is two stores away and we are about to make a beeline when the unthinkable happens: A security guard steps in front of us.

"You girls need to come with me," he says. Standing behind him is the woman who had been manning the dressing room in the Macy's Juniors section.

"Why? Is something wrong?" Anica asks, trying to sound confused.

I remain silent. Even if I could think of something to say, it would be impossible for me to form the words right now. The stream of sweat that was starting to dry up is again dripping down the small of my back into the waistband of stolen leggings.

"We know what you did. Let's not make this more difficult than it has to be. I need to take you to the security office where we will have to call the police and your parents."

"What are you talking ab—"

"Anica, just give it a rest," I whisper as a tear—masked by beads of sweat—rolls down my cheek. The tear is not a result of us getting caught; instead, it is due to the fact that my budding friendship with Anica is ruined. After all, this is all my fault.

She purses her lips and glares at me.

"Let's go, ladies." The security guard motions for us to follow him.

～

The room we are in is small, stuffy and musty. I wonder if they put us here as a form of punishment, as if being hauled away in front of dozens of shoppers wasn't torture enough. I avoid the death glare that Anica is giving me by closing my eyes and trying to imagine that I'm home in bed, curled up under the covers. Instead, I picture Amy Bowie with her long, perfectly shaped legs that make her look at least sixteen even though she's only thirteen. The Orchard Hills girls are thin in all the right places. But so far, Amy is the only one who has the fully developed Barbie-doll curves that make the boys stare. I open my eyes and look down at myself. Anica and I were forced to strip down to one layer of clothing, so the only thing I am wearing is a gray ribbed tank from The Gap and jeans. It was so embarrassing to have to remove the stolen leggings from under my jeans in front of the dressing room attendant. The rounded pooch that extends from my midsection makes me blush with embarrassment. I try to sit up as straight as possible, hoping for the fat to flatten out some, but it continues to jut out.

The door opens. "Well, ladies—the good news is that the store manager has decided to give you a break, since this is your first offense. As long as you pay for the merchandise you tried to walk off with. The bad news is that you are banned from shopping here in the future. Now, I could only get in touch with Anica's parents." The security guard focuses on me. "Do you have any idea where your parents are?"

"No," I say, returning my gaze to the floor.

"Can she come with us?" Anica asks.

Surprised, I quickly look up at her. *Maybe she isn't mad at me after all.*

"Nope. Sorry. A legal guardian's signature is required." He purses his lips and raises his eyebrows as he shrugs his shoulders at her—like this is just another day for him. Then he leaves the room again.

"Hey, Katie," Anica says.

"What?" I glance up at her.

"Let's not tell anyone about this. Okay?"

"Well, yeah. Of course I won't tell anyone," I say, dumbfounded that she even thinks she has to mention it.

"Hey," she whispers as she pulls something from the waistband of her leggings. "Looks like I get to keep a souvenir." She is holding a silver bracelet that still has the price tag affixed.

"Anica!" I whisper. "Are you crazy?"

She rolls her eyes and doesn't respond as she shoves the dainty piece of jewelry back into the small nylon pouch that is sewn into her pants.

I slowly shake my head and cross my arms. I like Anica. Or, I liked her. She's one of the nicest girls in the Amy Bowie clique, and I was starting to think I could trust her. Guess not. Although, I did just attempt to shoplift hundreds of dollars of merchandise, so if she's untrustworthy—what does that make me?

Not wanting to lose my friend, I search for something to say. I am about to ask her what her plans are for the upcoming week—our last week of summer vacation—but the security guard enters, followed by Anica's parents. The guard heads to a small desk in the corner while Anica's parents head straight for her. Anica's mom begins speaking swiftly in Croatian. Her voice is pained and she is near tears. I obviously have no clue what her mother is saying, but based on the way Anica looks up at me and then quickly breaks eye contact, I gather it has something to do with me. Anica responds by bursting into tears, but I can't decide if they are real. Then her father turns to me and says with a heavy accent, "Anica has never done anything like this before. She is no longer allowed to be your friend."

My face and chest suddenly feel like they are on fire and the profuse sweating returns. I look to Anica, mouth agape, willing her to make eye contact with me, but she doesn't. Then it hits me that her tears are, in fact, fake. She is going to let her parents believe that this was all my idea —that I am the serial shoplifter. I want to tell them the truth. I want them to know that their daughter has done this a million times with her other friends. I want to scream at Anica for letting them think that I am the bad influence. Instead, I stare down at the floor again.

The security guard has Anica's father sign several documents and then she is free. I remain seated, eyes on the stained industrial carpeting, as they leave.

"Well, I suppose I'll try your folks again," the security guard says as he grabs my T-shirt and oversized sweatshirt from his desk and hands them to me. "I'll be back in a jiff."

Being somewhat of a tomboy, I never really cared about clothes before middle school. Jeans, T-shirts and a pair of flip-flops—off brand, of course—were just fine with my grade school friends and me. But then we mixed with the kids from the more well-off side of town, and that's when I started noticing that I had no sense of style. Even if I did, my parents couldn't afford to buy me very many brand new things. In fact, most of my wardrobe still comes from the neighbor girl. Her mom is always giving my mom old clothes. And since Chelsea is three years older than I am, most of the clothes are outdated by the time I get around to wearing them.

I examine the plain, crew neck T-shirt and my sister's UW-Milwaukee sweatshirt on my lap, thinking to myself that she is going to be pissed if she finds out I borrowed it. Amy Bowie would not be caught dead in either of these items. She prefers more girly things like long tunics with belts, maxi dresses, chunky jewelry and make-up. I hate all of the above. So why do I even want to be friends with her? I don't know. I can't figure it out. I just . . . do.

My mind begins to wander back to my first week of seventh grade, when I felt like a very small fish that had been transported to a much bigger pond than I was used to. The pond was full of all kinds of fish, but just like when you are looking at a fish tank, the ones that caught my attention were the prettier, more exotic ones. I guess that was when I started caring more about my appearance.

"Katherine!" My mom rushes into the room, followed by the security guard and then my stepfather. She only uses my full name when she wants to strangle me. "What the hell were you thinking? Are you really this stupid?" She is crouched down in front of me with her face inches from mine.

"Mom, I—"

"You, what? You'd rather go to juvenile hall instead of back to school?!" She stands and turns to face the guard and my stepfather. "So, now what? Will this go on her permanent record?" The guard is about to answer, but she abruptly spins back my direction and wags a finger inches from my face. "And don't you think for one second that we're going to pay for the citation! You might as well—"

"Actually, ma'am," My mom turns her head slightly to glance sideways at the guard, clearly annoyed that he has interrupted her. "The manager on duty has agreed to not press charges, as long as the merchandise gets paid for. Of course—"

Before the guard can finish explaining the terms of the deal, my mom is back to scolding me. "You might as well say goodbye to all of that babysitting money you earned this summer! And you'll be donating the clothes to Goodwill! Honestly, Katie, I thought you were smarter than this."

"I know," I mumble. But she doesn't hear me because she is already back to talking to the security guard about how stupid teenage girls can be, assuring him there will be even more consequences for me to face at home.

My mother's reaction doesn't surprise me. I knew she'd be mad. But the thing is, she gets mad like this all the time. If I don't finish my dinner, if my room isn't clean enough, if I forget to take out the garbage —she goes from zero to sixty in an instant, even when minor things irritate her. Everything is a big deal because everything bothers her. Having my mom disappointed in me doesn't really matter right now, though. What does matter is the fact that I no longer have my foot in the door of the Amy Bowie clique. And I still have nothing new to wear on the first day of school. I know there is nothing adequate in my closet either.

After my mother signs the necessary paperwork, the guard tells me that I can go. As I walk past him, he gives me a look of sympathy, as if he knows that I'm the one who got roped into this. Or maybe he looks at me this way because of what my mother is now saying. "Honestly, Katie, you don't have the right kind of body to be wearing a tank top in public. Put on your shirt!"

As usual, my stepfather says nothing. He simply holds the door open for my mother and me with a look of exhaustion on his face.

The warmth of embarrassment quickly spreads through my entire body, but I still throw on Kelsie's sweatshirt in lieu of my T-shirt. My mom is right—I don't have the right kind of body to be wearing just a tank.

Chapter Two

"**K**atie!" my stepfather calls from downstairs. "Carly's here!"

I am busy going through my second-hand wardrobe, determined to find something that looks semi-new before stooping to the level of sneaking something from my sister's closet. "Can you send her up?"

"You're grounded, remember? You better come down and talk to her outside, just in case." He means just in case my mom comes back from the grocery store while Carly is still here. She is the enforcer in our house.

I examine myself in the full-length mirror for a few seconds longer. I feel like I am looking in a funhouse mirror—the one that makes people look squat. "Tell her I'll be down in a sec." I grab a tissue and quickly wipe away the lipstick I was experimenting with.

Carly lives across the street. We've been friends since the third grade, when she showed up at my door asking me to play catch. From that day on, we were inseparable. Although, things have been a bit strained between us since I started hanging out with Anica. I guess that's a non-issue now.

"Hey," I say to Carly as I step outside.

She has just thrown a softball into the air. She catches it in her baseball glove and tosses it to me. "Think fast," she says.

I laugh as I juggle the ball a few times before I can get a grip on it. "Thanks a lot. I don't even have a glove on."

"So, what's going on? Why are you grounded?" Carly takes a seat at the picnic table on our patio.

"It's a long story," I say, taking a seat across from her.

Her silence prompts me to fill her in on the unfortunate events of the previous day. She remains quiet while I talk, never interrupting with the questions that are surely on her mind. All she does is nod her head a few times. This is what I love most about Carly—she is an amazing listener. Maybe that's why we make such great friends; I'm a good talker and she's a great listener.

"So now I'm out about two hundred bucks because my mom made me buy the stuff I tried to steal. *Then* she made me donate it all. And as if that wasn't enough, I'm grounded until school starts."

She furrows her brow. "I can't believe you let Anica talk you into doing that. You're lucky they didn't press charges."

"Yeah. I know. Things could be worse. And just so you know, Anica didn't talk me into anything. I wanted to do it. She actually almost changed her mind right before we walked out of the dressing room."

Carly looks down at the softball in her hands and begins batting it back and forth on the table. Without looking up, she says, "Well, *bravo* for Anica." I start to say something, but she continues—this time meeting me in the eye. "And it was so nice of her to let her parents think you were the mastermind behind the whole thing." Carly has been leery but tolerant of Anica ever since January when Anica and I were assigned as lab partners. I clearly remember the conversation I had with Carly as we walked home from school that day.

"Guess who my lab partner is," I said as though I was about to burst. "Who?"

"Anica Slocjek!" I squealed, as if I was announcing a Teen Choice Award. "So what? Why are you so excited?"

"Carly, she's friends with Amy Bowie."

"Don't you mean Amy Boney?"

"Ha ha. Very funny. She's not that skinny."

"Are you kidding? She's a toothpick. I'm surprised she can even go outside on windy days. I hope she gets blown over flat on her face some day."

"Geez, Carly. That was harsh."

"Yeah, I guess. But you have to admit, Amy Bowie seems like a gossipy bitch."

"Well, making fun of her for being skinny is sort of like her making fun of you . . . or me . . . for being . . . not-so-skinny." At first, I was going to just say you. And I had an alternate word in mind for not-so-skinny. But I didn't want to risk hurting Carly's feelings. It's not that she's huge or anything, but she is what some would call *thick*. Her larger than average chest makes up for the extra pounds she's carrying elsewhere, though. At least, in my opinion. I wish I had boobs big enough to counteract the pudge around my middle.

"Katie," she responded, pulling me from my distracted thoughts. "I don't get it. Why are you excited about being lab partners with Anica? Just because she's Amy Bowie's friend? Amy and the rest of that Orchard Hills clique don't give anyone else the time of day."

"Exactly," I said, a smile plastered across my face. "Wouldn't it be kind of cool to be friends with them?"

"Why? All they're interested in is clothes, shopping, make-up and talking about which one of them is going to be prom queen someday. Bunch of snobs. No thanks."

I agreed with Carly about how shallow Amy and Anica's hobbies were, but I couldn't help but want to get to know them a little anyway.

In grade school, Carly and I were the "cool" girls. There were four of us: Selena Tropez, Darcy Watson, Carly and me. What made us popular was the fact that we were athletic and friendly with everyone. It also helped that we were the first to wear training bras. Turns out, middle school has a different set of standards because *all* the girls wear bras—most larger than mine—and there are way too many people to keep track of who plays what sport. It also seems like clothes, hair and make-up trump friendliness when it comes to determining who is popular now. Selena and Darcy, who are both very pretty and very nice, started dating a couple of boys who live on the shadier side of town. Rumor has it that their new group has been experimenting with cigarettes, alcohol and pot. Carly and I have never experimented with alcohol—just the occasional sip from our parents' wine and beer glasses—but we did have one encounter with smoking, if you could call it that. I don't remember whose idea it was, but we decided it would be fun to make our own cigarettes by rolling tealeaves inside paper. As soon as Carly held a lighter to the mock cigarette I was holding, it quickly caught fire and burned my fingers before I could put it out. I dropped it and we both started screaming and stomping on it. Luckily my mom still hasn't noticed the spot where I had to cut away the charred carpet. Anyway, Carly and I are still friends with Selena and Darcy, but we are no longer the least bit curious about any of that stuff. So I guess you could say we've all kind of distanced ourselves. Which leaves just Carly and me. It took being assigned as Anica's lab partner for her to sort of consider me a friend. I'm still a nobody to the rest of her clique though. And probably to her now, too.

"So, we can't hang out at all next week," Carly was saying, pulling me out of my thoughts. "That sucks."

"I know. I'm gonna go crazy having to hang out with my *mom* all day long."

Carly abruptly stops rolling the ball and grips it with both hands. *I am such an idiot,* I think to myself. Her mother passed away the summer before we entered sixth grade. Cancer. It will be two years next week. "Carly, I'm sorry. It just . . ."

"C'mon. Let's throw the ball around before your mom gets home." She is up on her feet in an instant.

I know the comment I made about my mom must have hit a nerve with her, but it's obvious she doesn't want to talk about it. So I do what any good friend would do, and I drop it. "I'll grab my glove. Be right back."

~

Carly and I only have time to throw the ball back and forth a few times before my mom shows up and squashes our fun.

"Katie! You're supposed to be grounded. Or have you already forgotten about yesterday?" She removes her hands from her hips and looks at Carly. "Sorry, Carly, but you're going to have to leave. I trust Katie has filled you in on what she did?"

I hate how formal my mom is with Carly. I mean, we've been best friends for like five years. Most moms I've met give me a hug or smile or speak in a pleasant voice when they see me, at the very least—and those are the moms of friends I don't even hang out with all that often. But my mom is not a warm and fuzzy kind of person. Not like Carly's mom was.

"Yes, Mrs. Clifton. She did," Carly says as she starts to walk toward the driveway. "See ya, Katie. Bye, Mrs. Clifton."

"I'll call you tom—"

"Oh, no you won't," my mother says over her shoulder as she hauls a bag of groceries toward the house. "You're grounded from the phone too."

I sneer in her direction, and then call to Carly who is already crossing the street. "I guess I'll see you on the first day! Be out here at seven!"

Without looking back, she waves her glove in the air in response.

Chapter Three

"Ugh," I say as I examine myself in the full-length mirror hanging on the back of my bedroom door. In each hand, I am gripping a roll of tummy fat and recalling something my mom once said about how if you can pinch an inch, some exercise would do you good. There has to be *at least* an inch of fat along my waistline. If only I could push some of it up into my chest, which doesn't seem to have grown very much since grade school. Am I destined to be an A-cup my whole life? Besides being on the short side and having this extra roll of fat on my belly, the rest of my body is okay—except my inner thighs meld together when I stand up straight. I hate that almost as much as my pudgy stomach.

I am about to turn to examine my butt in the mirror when there is a knock on my door. "Who is it?" I ask, knowing my mother would have just barged in.

"Just me," my sister Kelsie says as she opens the door and peeks inside. "What're you up to?" This is the first time I have seen her in three days. She's six years older than I am and sleeps at her boyfriend Kyle's apartment near the university a lot. She is wearing her work clothes: scrubs. She's not a doctor or nurse or anything medical related. Just a dietary worker at the hospital near our house. She worked at McDonald's all through high school, but the hours didn't work with her new college schedule. So she was forced to quit and take the job at the hospital.

"Just . . . trying on clothes, I guess." Except all I have on is a bra and underwear.

"Mom told me what happened." The way she crosses her arms in front of her chest reminds me of our mother. Besides sharing similar mannerisms, Kelsie is lucky enough to be naturally thin just like mom, but with ample boobage.

"Yeah, well, you're like the fiftieth person she's told." I sigh heavily. Then I throw on a T-shirt.

15

"So you're going to stop hanging out with that Anica girl, right?"

"It wasn't *all* Anica's idea. I wanted to do it too."

She squints her eyes at me and the corners of her mouth become pinched, as if she has eaten something sour. "Gimme a break. You might wear my clothes without asking sometimes—and I know you wore my sweatshirt, by the way—but you are not a thief. Why would you agree to do something like that anyway?"

I sigh again and sit down on my bed. "I don't know. I guess I'm just sick of always having to wear hand-me-downs. I mean, if I'm not wearing your old stuff, then I'm wearing Chelsea's. And your stuff is *always* outdated by the time it gets to me. Chelsea's stuff usually is, too."

"Why didn't you just buy some new clothes with all of the babysitting money you saved up this summer? Now you don't even have that option." She shakes her head, making me feel even crappier than I already do.

"I don't know." What I really want to say is that I sort of hate her for being the older one—the one who always had new clothes at the beginning of a school year and never had to pay for them herself, even when she was working at McDonald's. But I decide to bite my tongue because I kind of like the attention she's giving me.

"Or, you could have just explained to mom how you feel and asked for a new outfit."

Yeah, right. *Great* idea. Last year when I asked for money to go shopping for school clothes with Carly and Selena, my mom lectured me about how a new pair of jeans costs half a day's earnings for her. She went on and on about how I have plenty of clothes and they are just fine. Things became so heated between us that she ended up yelling, "Why don't you call your father and ask him? He has money!" So, I did, and it didn't end well. I was smart enough to figure out that my father would say anything to get out of giving me money for school clothes. He'd been working a lot of extra hours to pay for my half-sister's private school tuition. His car broke down. My stepmother's cat needed an expensive thyroid treatment. I ended up hanging up on him in tears. My mom was so sorry for suggesting that I call him that she tried to give me forty dollars, but I didn't take it. Kelsie doesn't know any of that happened though, and there's no need to tell her now.

"Okay, okay. Mom has already lectured me enough. *Trust me.* Can we just stop talking about it?"

We stare at each other for a moment. "We're supposed to be down for dinner in five minutes," she finally says as she backs out of my room, leaving the door wide open. "And don't forget to put on some pants!" she calls from her bedroom, directly across from mine.

~

"Bye, girls," my stepfather says, standing up and giving my mom a kiss on the cheek.

Gary works third shift at the post office, but he often heads out early to pick up extra hours. Today is one of those days. He grabs his lunch cooler and the Sunday newspaper off the counter before heading out the door with a final wave.

He's a good guy, but we aren't very close. I've liked him ever since I saw how happy he made my mom after my parents split. Plus, he has never once tried to discipline my sister or me, or take the place of our father—not that he'd have to do much. In fact, ninety percent of the time it seems like he isn't even around. Between work, sleep and reading his science fiction novels, I go days without hearing him talk. And most of the things he does say to me are just things my mother told him to say.

"Great lasagna, Mom," Kelsie says.

My mom smiles at her, and then glances at me as if she is waiting for my critique.

"Yeah . . . delicious," I say, shoveling another forkful into my mouth.

"I was worried it wouldn't taste right without meat, but it's a lot less fattening this way." She looks at me as she says this.

So, what are you trying to say, Mom? Instead of speaking my mind, I put down my fork and take a small sip of milk.

"Either way—meat or no meat—you make the best lasagna." There Kelsie goes again, always buttering Mom up. For what, I never know.

I am used to my mom making comments about my weight, shape or appearance in general. But lately, whenever she brings up my body, I feel uneasy. It always feels like she's comparing me to Kelsie.

"So, did you talk to her about that Anica girl?" my mom asks Kelsie, as if I'm not even there.

Kelsie's eyes widen a hair, and she glances up at me. "Um, a little bit, yeah."

"Why would you tell Kelsie to talk to me about Anica?" I glare.

"Because you don't listen to me when it comes to that kind of stuff, Katie. I told you months ago that that girl was bad news."

"You don't even know her, mom. In fact, you don't really know any of my friends because you never talk to them. Even Carly. She's my best friend and you still treat her like you just met her. She thinks you don't like her."

"That's nonsense. I like Carly. She's a good girl. A little overweight maybe, but a very nice girl."

I breathe out through my teeth and sulk. "I don't understand why you always have to say stuff like that."

"Stuff like what?"

"Stuff about how people look. Stuff about how I need to lose weight."

She shakes her head adamantly. "I never said anything about you needing to lose weight."

I sigh as I stand up and grab my plate, food barely eaten, and head to the sink.

"Where are you going? You're not going to finish your dinner?"

"Mom," Kelsie decides to join the conversation, "just let her be."

I head upstairs to my room without another word.

Then I turn on some music and lay on the bed as my stomach growls for the rest of the food on my dinner plate.

Chapter Four

This last week of summer vacation has been the worst ever. No friends. No phone privileges. Nothing remotely entertaining. I was forced to help out with the kids that my mom babysits for—without pay, of course—and I had to go grocery shopping with her. Twice.

I can't stand grocery shopping with my mom because she is the ultimate bargain hunter and coupon clipper. She keeps track of when and where items are on sale, so her grocery-shopping excursions might include up to four different stores. To make things even worse, she watches the little screen above the cash register like a hawk to make sure things scan correctly. If something rings up as more expensive than it is marked, she alerts the cashier immediately. I have seen cashiers close their lanes at the sight of my mother on several occasions.

Since I have not had a chance to talk to anyone, I have no idea what my friends plan to wear for the first day of school tomorrow. My room is littered with clothes and shoes. I have realized that I will probably never wear most of the items again, so I am thinking about throwing it all into one of the big black garbage bags from our garage. The outfit I have on is the current frontrunner, even though not one article of clothing is new. I am wearing dark Capri jeggings, a yellow dolman-sleeved top with a white tank underneath and colorful striped ballet flats—all hand-me-downs except for the shoes, which I bought from Goodwill. Before I make a final decision, though, I grab my yearbook from last year just to see what people were wearing. And by people, I mean the Orchard Hills girls.

The first picture I check out is Amy Bowie's, of course. Her long, blonde hair falls to her shoulders in perfect waves. I curled my hair a few times last year in an attempt to duplicate the look, but I could never get it to look natural. It always ended up too kinky. Amy has skin that always looks tan and a dainty nose that is perfectly angled at the tip. Sighing, I touch my stub of a nose before focusing my attention on her top. It's coral with lace trim of the same color and dips off one of her shoulders. Underneath, she has on a tank with spaghetti straps. Off the shoulder doesn't work for me because my shoulders are way too broad. My mother always says I got more of my father's stout German genes than my sister.

Next, my eyes wander back a few pictures to Laney Britt, who looks like she could be related to Kristen Stewart. Long, black hair. Porcelain skin. Laney plays volleyball and is the least girly dresser in her group. Still, everything she wears makes her look like a model because of her long legs and lean, muscular arms. In the photo, she is wearing a simple emerald tank top with a black scarf tied expertly around her neck. Her hair is in a sleek ponytail and she is wearing diamond stud earrings.

I decide not to look at Anica's photo. I can picture most of the clothes she wore last year after seeing her on such a regular basis anyway.

I am about to flip to Sloan Whitson when my mother throws open my bedroom door and enters like she is in the last leg of a race. Her arms are loaded with folded clothes.

"I went ahead and folded these for you since you need to get to bed earlier than normal tonight." A look of irritation forms on her face as she slowly scans my room. "Why in the world does your room look like this?"

"I'm trying to figure out what to wear tomorrow," I say as I shove a shirt on top of the yearbook and sit up on my bed.

She tilts her head slightly. "Is that what you decided on?"

"I think so." I stand and extend my arms out to the sides. "Does it look okay?"

"I like that color on you, but the style of the shirt makes you look like you have no waist." She quickly turns to put the pile of clothes on my dresser and then moves toward my closet. "What about that scoop-neck top your sister used to wear all the time? You look very nice in turquoise. Where is it?"

"Mom, I don't like that top. It's too plain."

"Well, Katie, it's not like you're appearing in a fashion show." She laughs through her nose, as if the fact that I want to wear something with a little more personality is ridiculous, and continues digging around in my closet. "I just don't understand why you care so much about what you wear nowadays. Your sister never threw clothes all over her room, and she never made a big to-do about what she was going to wear."

"Maybe that's because Kelsie always got to go shopping at the beginning of the school year. She never had to wear anyone's hand-me-downs." Not to mention, she looks great in just about anything.

My mother emerges with the five-year-old turquoise tee and holds it out to me. "There is nothing wrong with your clothes, Katie. Just think about wearing a different top with those pants. You certainly have plenty to choose from." She jiggles the turquoise tee in front of my face, so I grab it. "And please clean up this mess before you hit the sack," she says as she leaves my room.

As soon as she reaches the bottom of the stairs, I close my door and return to the worn spot of carpet in front of my full-length mirror. She's right. My silhouette looks fine from the side and from behind, but from the front, it looks like I am hiding something under my shirt.

I remove the yellow top and throw it on the floor with the other rejects. Then I stare at my reflection some more.

I never used to analyze my body in the mirror like this, but now it's all I seem to do when I'm alone in my room. My hair is brown and a bit wavy—not salon wavy like Amy Bowie's hair, but weird wavy like after you wear your hair in a ponytail overnight. My eyes are brown—not deep brown like Laney Britt's, but a plain, boring brown. And my body is shaped sort of like a boy's body, except for the small mounds across my chest. And then there is the roll of fat around my midsection, of course. My legs are okay, but my calves are more round than shapely and lean. Resolving for the millionth time that I cannot change the shape of my body, I go back to the task of choosing an outfit for the following day.

Chapter Five

The second my alarm sounds, I push snooze, roll over onto my back and stare at the ceiling. I wonder if I will be able to make it through the first day of school on less than two hours of sleep. Every time I managed to doze off, I woke up to find that only ten to fifteen minutes had passed. The only times I remember having fitful nights of sleep like this before were on Christmas Eves or on days before my birthday when I was little.

The big difference is that my inability to fall asleep in those instances was a result of anticipation. Last night was different. I couldn't sleep because I am nervous about eighth grade. Last year, I only had a little trouble sleeping, but it was because I was excited to start middle school and make new friends. What bothers me now is that the new friends I have made aren't close friends like the ones from grade school. How can anyone *really* get to know me when everyone is so busy getting to know everyone else? There is Anica, at least, but who knows if she will even talk to me after what her father said in the security office at the mall.

My alarm sounds again. I have fifty minutes before I need to meet Carly outside. I crawl out of bed, arch my back and reach my arms up high to stretch. Then I stand in front of my closed door and inhale deeply. *C'mon, Katie, get moving.* Instead of obliging the go-getter in me, I stand there, exhaling slowly. Two more deep breaths, then I open the door, ready to stick it to the anxiety I am feeling. Just outside the door is a large lavender gift bag. The tag reads: *Enjoy your first day of school. Love, Kelsie*

Inside the bag is a brand new black maxi skirt and a cute black and white striped scoop-neck top with three-quarter length sleeves. Squealing with delight, I hug the new clothes to my chest and barrel down the hallway towards Kelsie's bedroom. Her bed is made, and there is no sign of her. She must have stopped home late last night just to leave the gift outside my door and then left right away for Kyle's. I wish I had more time to call her to say thank you, but I need to get ready. At least now I won't need to look at myself fifty times in the mirror before going down for breakfast. The outfit Kelsie gave me is something I would have chosen myself. *And* it's something Amy Bowie would wear.

~

"Good morning," I say as I enter the kitchen.

My mom is mashing up some bananas for Kyle's six-month-old nephew, Brandon. Kyle's sister usually drops him off between 6:45 and 7:00 am every weekday. Shortly after Brandon arrives, three more children join him at my mother's in-home daycare.

"*Wow*. I've never seen you wear *that* outfit before." She only glances up for a moment. "That didn't used to be Kelsie's, did it?"

Gee. Thanks for telling me how nice I look on my first day of school. "No, but Kelsie did give it to me. She left it in a gift bag outside my door. Not sure when she put it there though. How do I look?" I spread my arms out and turn sideways, giving her my best runway pose.

"Very nice." She pauses long enough that I am surprised by her succinct, somewhat flattering response. The surprise wears off quickly when she adds, "But you know I've never liked you in stripes, especially horizontal ones. Hmm. I guess your sister has money to burn. Sure hope she doesn't come crawling to Gary and me for textbook funds."

My mom moves to the stove to make oatmeal and goes on about how my sister is always asking them for money.

I pour myself a bowl of Cheerios. I usually eat cold cereal with sliced bananas, but time is running out. Carly will be walking out her door soon, and I do not want to keep her waiting. I scarf down my cereal, grab a banana and my lunch from the fridge, and head toward the door where my backpack is hanging on a coat hook.

"You're leaving already?" Finally, my mom says something unrelated to Kelsie.

"Yeah. I told Carly I'd meet her outside at seven. We just want to make sure we don't miss the bus."

"But it doesn't come until 7:35! What do you two plan on doing until then?"

"I don't know. Talk, I guess. What's the big deal? I haven't seen Carly for a week. You know?"

My mom is about to respond when the door opens. It's Jane, Kyle's older sister. I retreat to the stairs, which are inconveniently located right next to the door, to give Jane room to get inside. She sets a sleeping Brandon, all snuggled up in his car seat, down on the kitchen table and then notices me putting on my backpack.

She takes in a sharp breath. "Katie. You look so good. I love, love, *love* that outfit. I knew it would look good on you." She gives me a wink.

"Thanks! Did Kelsie show it to you or something?"

"I helped her pick it out when we went shopping together a few days ago." She smiles broadly and looks at my mother, who seems annoyed—probably because Jane mentioned she had been shopping with Kelsie. My mother only charges Jane half of what she normally charges to care for a baby because Jane is a single mom. I have overheard my mom complaining about what an expensive favor caring for Brandon has turned into. I am certain she is wondering how much money Jane spent during the shopping excursion. "What do you think, Elaine? Doesn't Katie look cute?"

"Uh-huh. Very nice. But I hope the outfit wasn't too expensive."

"Well, I have to get going," I announce, already feeling awkward. "Nice to see you, Jane," I say, smiling at her. "Bye, Mom."

Across the street, Carly emerges from her house. I pause for a second before heading toward her when I see what she is wearing: jean shorts, the T-shirt from our softball uniform and flip-flops. Her curly hair is pulled into a messy, blonde ponytail.

"Kit Kat!" She yells the nickname my dad gave to me way back on my first Halloween, when I was one and discovering new foods. Apparently, I had gotten hold of a Kit Kat bar while my dad carried me from house to house as he watched Kelsie trick-or-treating. By the time he realized I had the candy bar, the wrapper was chewed open and my face was covered in wafer crumbs and chocolate. Ever since then, I've been Kit Kat to him and Kelsie. My friends picked it up from them. Only my mom hates the nickname, always has, so she has never once used it. I'm not too keen on it either, but it has stuck after all these years.

"Hey, Carly-Q," I say with a grin. "I thought your Aunt Leslie was taking you shopping for school clothes. What happened?"

"Nothing. She did." She starts walking in the direction of the bus stop and motions with her head for me to follow.

"Then why aren't you wearing anything new?"

"I don't know." She shrugs. "I just wanted to be comfortable. What's more comfortable than this?" She stops walking for a moment to face me, arms outstretched.

I laugh and shake my head at her as we resume our short trek to the bus stop. It doesn't surprise me that Carly opted for an outfit that she has worn at least two dozen times this summer. She doesn't really care about clothes—her own or other people's. I just wish she had considered wearing something a tad more fashionable today. After all, everyone is going to be standing outside scrutinizing what others are wearing. What will the Amy Bowie clique think of Carly's outfit?

I don't have much to say to Carly about my boring week, but she has plenty to talk about. She joined her father on a three-day trip up north. That's what everyone around here says when they go to their cottages, that they are going 'up north'. I'm not sure where Carly's family cabin is located exactly, just that it's somewhere north of Milwaukee County. Hence, 'up north'. Apparently, Selena joined them, which makes my stomach sting a little with jealousy. But Carly assures me that she would have invited me or wouldn't have gone at all had I not been grounded. Sometimes when her father goes up north, she stays home alone. My mother disapproves but reasons that it's better for Carly to stay home alone than be up north in the middle of nowhere alone while her father goes off to hunt and fish. Anyway, Carly tells me that Selena talked her into sneaking some vodka.

"What did it taste like?" I ask, enthralled that Carly had the guts to do something so risky.

"It was *so* nasty! But Selena kept drinking it, of course. She was sick the entire next day. My dad thought she had a stomach bug. Other than that, we did the usual. You know, play catch, swim in the pond, sunbathe, drive around on the four-wheeler, sit by the fire at night."

I silently grieve missing out on the fun. Carly seems to pick up on my envy, so she changes the subject. "Where'd you get the clothes? Did your mom cave and take you shopping?"

"No. Course not. Kelsie got them for me," I say, glancing at her sideways.

"Really? How cool. You look great."

"Thanks," I say with a grin. Even though Carly isn't much of a fashionista, the compliment still makes me feel good.

There are already two people at the city bus stop when we arrive. One is our friend Dominic and the other is a boy we don't recognize, probably new to the neighborhood. He has headphones in his ears and is putzing around on an iPod, so I don't really look at him too closely.

I smile and wave as soon as we are within a few feet of them. In her best homegirl accent, Carly yells, "'Sup Dominic?"

"Hey, guys," Dominic says as he gives Carly a fist bump. Then he pulls me in for a one-armed hug. I begin to back away, but he grabs both of my hands and holds my arms up high to get a look at what I'm wearing. "Look at you, Kit Kat." He whistles as he releases my arms.

"Knock it off," I try to sound serious, but I can't help grinning. And I can feel warmth spreading into my cheeks.

"Seriously, Katie. You look nice."

"Whatever," I mumble as I pull on the hem of my top.

"Hey, what about me?" Carly tries to sound like she cares what Dominic thinks. But we all know she's full of it. "Well?" She has one hand on her hip.

"Oh, sorry, Carly. Yeah. You too. Nice T-shirt."

Carly punches Dominic in the shoulder the way she has been punching him since he became our friend four years ago. We were all in fourth grade, and Dominic was a shy and chubby new kid. Our friendship began the day I noticed two fifth grade boys picking on him. I couldn't stand the way these boys bullied everyone, so I decided to do something about it. It just so happened that they were razzing Dominic at the time. When the boys continued to chant "fatty, fatty, two by four" after I asked them to leave Dominic alone, I lost it and punched them both, one in the gut and the other in the face. They never saw it coming. Needless to say, I ended up suspended for three days, but I also ended up with a new friend. Dominic has slimmed down a lot since then, but he could still stand to tone up a bit. Aside from riding a bike, he's not very athletic, so he says he is leaving it up to puberty to transform his body.

"So, are you gonna miss spending every day with your dad at the store?" I ask Dominic. He got busted skipping out of school a few times at the end of last year, so his punishment was to work most of the summer at his family's convenience store. The only times I saw him were when he managed to attend our softball games and when we saw a couple of movies together. Otherwise, I already had plans with Anica when Dominic asked me to go for a bike ride or to the local pool. I considered asking if he minded if Anica went too, but quickly decided that was out of the question since he pretty much feels the same way about her as Carly does. Plus, I'm not sure Anica would have been able to appreciate spending time with Dominic the way I do.

"No way. I'm so sick of stocking the shelves and cleaning that stupid Icee machine. People are such slobs." He makes a face that makes me laugh. Then he goes on. "What happened to you guys last week anyway? Neither one of you stopped in to say hi."

"I was up north with my dad. Selena went too." Carly looks at me with probing eyes. I know she is curious if I am going to tell Dominic that I was grounded and why. Dominic joins her in staring me down, as if he knows something big happened with me.

"I was grounded . . . Hey." I nod to the left. "The bus is here."

We all dig in our pockets for our passes and the conversation is forgotten when we see that Selena and Darcy are already on the bus.

The five of us catch up a bit and laugh about how sick Selena made herself by drinking too much vodka. It wasn't so much the fact that she was drunk that had us rolling, though. Instead, it was Carly's impressions of Selena slurring her words and stumbling around that had us in stitches. Carly has a way of making anything sound hysterical, even if it isn't really something to laugh about.

When Darcy and Selena begin telling us about two high school guys they hung out with at the state fair, I nod and smile at all the right times, but my mind wanders. I wonder what the Orchard Hills girls will be wearing, and then I take a good look at my friends. Darcy is wearing a frayed jean skirt with sheer black tights, a loose fitting, off-the-shoulder graphic top and ankle booties. Selena's look is similar, except she has on a belted, mid-thigh skirt. They both have a punk look that makes them seem older and more mature than the rest of us, even though their bodies still have just as much developing to do as mine. If it weren't for Carly's young and innocent demeanor, she would look older too, based on the size of her boobs alone. Dominic has a sporty look, even though he doesn't play any sports. He is wearing gray cargo shorts, a vintage

Brewers T and Chuck Taylor Converse sneakers. I consider for a moment that Carly and Dominic would make a cute couple if they weren't always bickering like brother and sister. But then I decide it would be kind of gross if they ever dated because not only do they act like brother and sister, they look it too, both with dirty blonde hair, sparsely freckled cheeks and hazel eyes—and both slightly overweight. Then there's me. I know my outfit is one that any of the Orchard Hills girls would wear, but for some reason, I suddenly don't feel comfortable in it. Maybe it's because I feel like the odd one out among my friends. Or maybe it's because I would probably feel much more comfortable in something similar to what Carly is wearing.

We get off at our stop and walk the two remaining blocks to school. Hordes of students are all around us, and cars and yellow buses are waiting to turn into the parking lot. Somewhere along the way, we lose Selena and Darcy when they stop to chat with a group of other punk-looking kids.

As we approach the front doors, my stomach is in knots. I scan the groups that are scattered on the lawn, but I don't see the Orchard Hills clique. *Where are they?*

"Katie? Hellooo?" Carly is waving a hand in front of my face. "Where are you going?"

Dominic is now standing on the outskirts of a group of girls who played softball with Carly and me over the summer, and Carly is clearly wondering why I am still walking.

"Oh." I shake my head. "Nowhere. I just spaced out for a sec."

We both join Dominic and the softball group. It occurs to me that Dominic could easily fit into most of the pods of people littering the school lawn because everyone knows him from his family's store. But he doesn't really have a "group." I admire him for being so friendly with everyone, but I also don't understand why he chooses to just float from group to group.

The kids I am standing with are all comparing schedules when I see them—Amy, Anica, Sloan and Laney are getting out of a Lexus SUV. I can't help but stare, and Dominic can't help but notice that I am staring. Luckily, he pokes fun at me privately.

"Talk about a lot of make-up. It's like a clown car. Are you enjoying the show?" he whispers in my ear.

A smile forces its way onto my face, even though I'm kind of annoyed. I happen to have on just as much make-up as they do, and if anyone looks like a clown, it's probably me. Putting on make-up is not something I am very good at, and no one has ever really showed me how.

He straightens up as the girls get closer to us. Before I can stop him, he yells, "Hey, ladies! Looking lovely, as always!"

"Dominic!" I hiss. My softball group briefly stops talking and looks at Dominic and me, but then they carry on, not even noticing the Orchard Hills girls.

Sloan Whitson narrows her eyes in our direction, but the rest of them just keep walking. Anica doesn't even glance at me, making my heart sink.

"Why did you have to say that?" I ask in a hushed voice.

"What? They actually do look lovely. Would you rather I told them they look hot?"

"No. I would rather you didn't say anything at all."

He looks at me suspiciously. "What's the big deal, Katie? I thought you were friends with Anica."

"I am," I say. Then I hesitantly follow up with, "Was." But the bell rings, drowning me out.

"What? I couldn't hear you," Dominic says.

"Nothing. C'mon. Let's go."

As everyone files toward the doors, I notice Anica and Sloan looking back in our direction. They quickly look away when I make eye contact, and Anica immediately whispers in Sloan's ear.

Suddenly, Carly's outfit is meaningless. And so is mine.

Chapter Six

After the morning announcements, I sit in homeroom and obsess over the way Anica and Sloan were staring. Then I try to imagine what Anica could possibly have whispered in Sloan's ear. Did she tell her that I was the reason we got caught shoplifting? Were they scrutinizing my outfit?

"Excuse me. Do you have a pen I can borrow?"

I look to my left and the boy from the bus stop is staring at me. A very cute face, complete with blue eyes and short, boy-band hair. "Uh, yeah, I do." As I unzip the front pocket of my backpack, I analyze the few words I have just spoken. *Uh, yeah?* Can you sound *any* stupider, Katie?

"Here you go," I say as I quickly turn to hand Blue Eyes the only pen I have.

"Thanks." He smiles. Without breaking eye contact, he takes it from my sweaty palm. "Hey, I think we take the same bus to school. I'm Hunter."

I fluster. "Katie." Instead of immediately furthering the conversation, I continue analyzing. Did my voice just crack when I said my name? Can he tell how nervous I am? How did I not notice this morning how cute he was? *Hurry up! Say something else!* "So, you're new?" *Obviously.*

"Yeah. We just moved from Vermont."

"Cool. My dad is from Vermont. How long have you been here?" *Am I sweating?*

"Three weeks. What part of Vermont?"

"Burlington. My grandparents both worked at UVM when he was growing up."

"Do they still live there?

"No . . . They passed away when I was little. I don't really see my dad anymore either. Not since my parents got divorced." *TMI, Katie, T. M. I.*

"Oh. Sorry to hear that." And he does seem genuinely sorry.

Before I can say another word, the bell rings and everyone is on their feet and rushing to the door, including Hunter.

"See you, Katie," he says as he looks back at me with a grin and heads out the door.

See you, Hunter.

~

The morning flew by: language arts, social studies, band and Spanish. Dominic and I have been in band together since sixth grade, so we chatted a little during class. I also get to see him in my afternoon math class. I don't have any classes with Selena or Darcy, but I get to see Carly during gym, which we have on Mondays, Wednesdays and every other Friday. We will also have family and consumer-ed class together during the second trimester. So far, Anica is in language arts and Spanish with me (in both classes, she pretended I wasn't even there), and I'm guessing we have science together, too, since we had it together last year.

With so much going on this morning, my brain took an involuntary break from trying to guess what Anica and Sloan were saying about me earlier. Now, as I make my way to the lunchroom, the obsessing has returned. The thoughts racing through my head have caused my heart rate to increase and my entire body to break out in a cold sweat. I know Dominic has lunch now, too, but Carly doesn't. I'm not sure about Selena and Darcy, but even if they do have the same lunch, that doesn't necessarily mean I feel comfortable sitting with them and the other group they normally hang out with. And who knows? Dominic could already be sitting with a group of guys.

It's not that there aren't other people I could eat with; it's more like I have this insane fear of being rejected that prevents me from feeling comfortable just plopping down with a group of people I normally don't hang out with outside of school. Even when people are nice to my face, I constantly wonder if they might really be thinking that they wish I would go away. I never felt this way before middle school, and even though I've tried, I can't figure out where these thoughts are coming from. Things were never this complicated in grade school. Sometimes I want to spill my guts to Carly or Dominic, or even to Kelsie or my mom, but I can never muster the courage to reveal my insecurities.

Standing in the entryway to the lunchroom, I scan the tables for Dominic first. Unfortunately, he's nowhere to be found. What's even more unfortunate is the fact that the Orchard Hills girls are standing at the end of the beverage line, where I need to be in order to get a milk. How the heck did they all end up with the same lunch schedule, anyway?

Instead of appeasing the inner voice that is telling me to go to the bathroom so that different people will be in line by the time I get back, I enter the line behind them. Anica (who is at the end of the pack) immediately turns and looks right at me. For a split second, I think she is going to say something—something normal, like "hi" maybe. But then Sloan elbows her and says, "Anica, look! There he is!"

I follow the eyes of their entire group and find myself looking at blue-eyed Hunter, who happens to be sitting with Dominic and four other guys.

"O. M. G. Sloan, you were *not* kidding. He's *gorgeous!*" Anica squeals. Laney nods in agreement but Amy rolls her eyes. Maybe Hunter isn't her type.

"Yeah, but why is he sitting with Dominic Riley?" A look of disgust crosses Sloan's face when she says Dominic's name, and that's when we make eye contact. "Oh. Sorry. I didn't see you there, Katie." Except I can tell she's not sorry at all.

I shrug. "For what?" I do my best to pretend that I have no idea what she is talking about. What Sloan Whitson said about Dominic bothers me, but I'm more upset that this is the first time she has ever spoken my name. Why does it have to be because she is pretending that she gives a crap about offending me for disliking my friend? Does she dislike me too, even though she doesn't know me?

She breathes a little laugh through her nose. "You really suck at lying." All four of them are smirking at me, even Anica. "And *you're* the reason Anica got caught."

I want to run. But since I don't want to draw attention, I stand there frozen and speechless, wishing I could disappear. Finally, I work up the nerve to turn and aimlessly walk away. Snickers trail behind me.

"Kit Kat!" I vaguely hear Dominic's voice through the loud pounding in my head. "Hey, Katie!" I ignore him and continue winding my way through the maze of large, circular tables. But then a hand is on my shoulder. "Katie, where are you going? I saved you a seat." His smile fades when I turn to face him. "What's wrong?"

I glance toward the beverage line and see that the Orchard Hills clique is at the cash register. Dominic follows my gaze. "Them again? What is with you? Did something happen with you and Anica? I thought you two were friends and that you'd be in with that group by now. What? You're not bitchy enough to join their club?" He chuckles.

"Something like that." I mask the emotions that are welling up inside of me by trying to sound disinterested. "Where are you sitting?" Of course, I already know, but I can't let on.

"Over here. C'mon." Dominic tugs on my backpack strap. "I want you to meet someone." And now I have to pretend I didn't see him sitting with Hunter.

We arrive at the table and Hunter immediately gives me a wide grin. "Hey, Katie. What's up?" I nod and smile back at him. Then I give the other guys, who I barely know, a friendly rainbow wave.

"You guys already know each other?" Dominic asks.

"We have homeroom together," I say as I unpack my lunch.

"Cool," Dominic says. Then he addresses the table. "So, anyway, who watched the Brewers game last night?"

Under different circumstances, I would have joined the conversation because I did watch the game. But instead, I'm distracted by Sloan and Amy staring in our direction from three tables away. Now, not only am I unable to contribute to the discussion going on at our table, but I have also lost my appetite.

～

After lunch, Dominic and I walk to math class together. Just before we are about to enter the classroom, his eyes lower to my top. "What's that?" he asks.

I look down and see a smear of raspberry jelly right under my chest area. "Dang it!" Even though the top is black and white, the blob stands out and I worry that it will stain for sure if I don't give it a scrub immediately. "I need to run to the bathroom. Save me a seat?"

"Got it."

I jog halfway down the hall to the restrooms and find all of the sinks occupied. One has a group of five or six girls standing around it, someone is leaning over the next to get a good look in the mirror as she applies makeup, and someone is at the third scrubbing something out of her own shirt. "Crap," I say to myself.

I turn and trot out of the bathroom and around the corner. A single bathroom is down the hallway that leads to the band room. Students aren't really supposed to use it, but people do sometimes anyway. I push against the door expecting it to open, but it doesn't budge. "Crap," I whisper again as I turn, prepared to accept that I will have to wait until after math class to deal with the red blotch. Then I hear coughing from inside the bathroom. I am about to head back to math when the coughing suddenly turns into a gagging sound, making me pause and look back. More coughing.

"Katie? Shouldn't you be in class?" It's Mr. Reynolds, the band teacher.

"Oh, hi, Mr. Reynolds. Yeah, I just needed a sink real quick." I hold out the fabric of my shirt to draw his attention to the stain.

He nods. "Ah. I see. Well, if you wait a moment, I can get you one of those handy dandy Shout wipes from the bathroom here." He leans in and whispers, "My wife insists that I have them with me wherever I go. Otherwise the laundry is full of stains that she needs to treat."

"Thanks, Mr. Reynolds, but someone is in there, and I have to—"

The door to the bathroom opens and out walks Amy Bowie. We make eye contact for a spit second before she drops her gaze and briskly walks past Mr. Reynolds and me. Mr. Reynolds doesn't even seem to notice her as he rushes into the bathroom and returns promptly with a Shout wipe in hand. "Here you go, Katie." I take it with an appreciative smile on my face and hurry off to class just as the bell rings.

I manage to slip into the classroom unnoticed as everyone is still getting situated. Dominic waves to me from the back of the room. Our algebra teacher, Mr. Beatty, is one of the most talked-about staff members at our school because people say he is more like a stand-up comedian than a teacher. I have been looking forward to hearing his first-day routine ever since I got my schedule in early August, but now I can't seem to focus. I keep picturing Amy Bowie as she walked out of the bathroom. Her face was pink and she looked like she had just finished running a mile. My first guess was that she must have been sick, but she looked perfectly fine during lunch. In fact, she looked radiant as ever. When we made eye contact, she didn't really look sick either. She looked more like she had been caught off guard to find Mr. Reynolds and me standing there, like a deer in headlights. Amy Bowie looked frazzled. My classmates are laughing, but I am too busy remembering the coughing and gagging sounds to enjoy the show. Then I wonder: Was Amy throwing up? Is that how she stays so thin? By making herself throw up after she eats?

"Katie?" Dominic whispers. "Why aren't you laughing? Isn't he hilarious?" I nod and force a smile.

Chapter Seven

"So? How was your day?" Carly is bubbly as usual, whereas I'm already dreading day two of eighth grade.

We both smile and wave as we walk past a small group of people gathered just outside the front doors. "See ya, Carly and Katie!" someone yells.

I shrug at Carly's question. "It was okay. But it totally sucks that we don't have lunch together." I want to tell her about the whole run-in I had with Sloan during lunch, but I'm embarrassed—even if it is Carly. Plus, I know she'll probably just ask why I even care what any of those girls think about me anyway.

Carly will smile at anyone who smiles at her, and she'll talk to anyone. And I mean *anyone*. It doesn't matter who they hang out with, what kind of clothes they wear or even if she has heard an unflattering rumor about them. But if someone is publicly rude to others or doesn't make any friendly attempts to communicate with her, Carly easily writes them off. I wish I could be that way.

I also consider telling her about Amy, but decide I have no business mentioning something that could have simply been a regular potty break.

"I know," she responds. "But at least you have lunch with Dominic. Speaking of Dominic . . . where is he?"

"His mom picked him up. He has to work at the store."

Carly nods and then picks up where she left off. "Hey! We have gym together tomorrow. I can't wait. I heard we get to play Pickleball!" Holding an invisible paddle, she stops walking and pretends to take a swing. She looks at me as if she is waiting for me to hit the imaginary ball back.

Feeling a twinge of embarrassment, I glance around to see if anyone is watching. No one is, but I still don't play along. Instead, I force a laugh and resume walking. "C'mon, ya dork. I have a ton of homework."

"You're no fun, Kit Kat. Why're you acting so blah?"

"Why're you acting so hyper?"

"Hyper? You think I'm acting hyper? I don't think I'm acting hyper. What's so hyper about the way I'm acting?" Carly jokingly strings her sentences together without taking a breath.

This time I laugh at her for real. She really is funny.

Instead of waiting for the bus, we decide to stop at the corner mart and get some snacks—Ranch Corn Nuts for Carly and pretzels for me —and then we walk the mile and a half home. Along the way, we discuss our classes—how hard we think they are going to be and who is in them—who we sat with during lunch, and Hunter. As usual, Carly's classes are easier than mine are, and she seems to have more of the chatty people as classmates. She had a lot more to say about lunch than I did, especially since I decided not to mention anything about Amy.

"So that new kid Hunter Davis sat with you guys, huh?" Carly asks, followed by a loud crunch.

"Yeah. Dominic already seemed pretty chummy with him. I swear, he is like you in male form, always making friends with everyone."

"Really?" She scrunches her nose and glances at me sideways. "I *guess* Dominic has come out of his shell a bit over the last two years, but other than him being kinda talkative... Anyway, tell me about Hunter. Your voice sounded funny when you said his name before."

"No, it didn't," I say defensively.

"Uh, yes it did, Katie. He's really cute. We have language arts and social studies together, and all of the girls were batting their eyelashes at him and asking questions about where he used to live. It was so annoying. Anyway . . . did you bat your eyelashes at him, too?" She nudges me in the shoulder.

"No, of course I didn't. Don't get me wrong. He's cute, but not *that* cute." Actually, he is that cute and I probably did bat my eyelashes at him when I officially met him in homeroom. But I feel stupid about it after hearing how the other girls reacted to him. What are the odds he would be interested in me?

"Ohhh-kay." I can tell from her tone that she isn't buying my act. "Do you have any classes with him?"

"Just homeroom and science."

"And lunch," Carly adds.

"And lunch. But I doubt that I'll sit with him every day. You know how Dominic likes to move from table to table."

"That doesn't mean you have to follow him! I don't get you lately, Katie. You're friends with just about everyone. Why do you act like Dominic and me are your only friends sometimes?"

"I am not friends with just about everyone." I honestly have no idea what she's talking about. I used to be friends with everyone, but that was in grade school. Sure, I'm friendly with most of the kids in our grade, but that's different than being friends.

"Is it because of Amy Boney and her followers? I swear, before you became Anica Slocjek's lab partner last year, you never looked at those girls any differently than you looked at anyone else."

Actually, I did. I just never mentioned it to you. "Of course not, Carly! I'm just not as outgoing as you are. I have no idea how you even think of half of the things you say to people. Yes, I try to be friendly with everyone, but that doesn't mean I'm friends with everyone. At least with you, Dominic, Selena and sometimes Darcy, I don't have to think so much before I speak." I take a deep breath, not wanting to fight over something so stupid. Then I add, "But yeah, Hunter is pretty cute." I can't help but grin.

"I knew it!" Carly yells. "Did you hear there's already a dance this Friday? Maybe you can dance with him." Her eyes light up like a kid's in a candy store.

I shrug. "Hey, speaking of dancing. Did you see all the flyers about cheer squad tryouts? They start tomorrow after school."

Carly has begun crossing the street to get to her house. "So?" She stops and turns to face me.

"Well, I was thinking of trying out."

"Really?" She looks as though she has just eaten something rotten. "But . . . you've never been interested in cheerleading . . . or dancing. In fact, I was sort of joking about you dancing with Hunter on Friday."

"Gee, thanks," I say with amusement. "Anyway, I was thinking it might be fun to try something new." I lie. I'm actually terrified by the thought of learning a cheer routine and performing it in front of the existing cheer squad members, but how hard could it be? I have to do something to make Amy Bowie and Anica think that I don't care what they think of me. I probably won't make it, but I need to do something so that they stop whispering behind my back. "What do you think? Do you want to do it with me? Just for fun?"

Her look of shock and disgust evaporates quickly and is replaced by a rosy grin. "Sure. Why not? Let's do it!"

"Okay, cool! I'll see you tomorrow morning. Seven again?"

"Yep. See you then."

As soon as I turn to walk up my driveway, it hits me that there is no turning back now. I am *really* going to try out for the cheer squad. My smile fades and my heart starts beating a mile a minute.

Chapter Eight

School flew by again this morning. Maybe it had something to do with the fact that I'm dreading tryouts this afternoon. It always seems like the more excited I am about something, the slower time drags. And vice versa.

In homeroom, Hunter and I started the day off with a discussion about who was going to make it to the World Series, which at least filled the pit in my stomach for a little while. We discovered a shared love for the Yankees. Being from Vermont, which doesn't have a major league team, my dad grew up a Yankees fan. I remember watching games with him when I was little. Kelsie was such a girlie girl when she was younger, so she used to play with Barbies and dance around in dress-up clothes while I sat next to my dad on the sofa, occasionally mimicking his cheers and groans. I still try to watch Yankees games on TV whenever I can, but I have yet to make it through one without imagining what it would be like if my dad never left.

My nervousness returned when I discovered that the entire Orchard Hills clique had gym with Carly and me this trimester. During warm-ups, they did a lot of whispering and staring in our direction until Carly sarcastically asked them if she had a booger hanging out of her nose or something. She was just trying to be funny, but of course, they all snapped their necks to look away. Carly responded by whispering under her breath, "Sheesh, what is wrong with those girls?" I was so glad to have her there with me, but also wished she wasn't quite so quick to draw attention to herself.

After that, everyone broke into pairs for Pickleball, and Carly and I didn't have to get too close to anyone in the OH clique again.

Now it's lunchtime, and Hunter and I have resumed our discussion about the Yankees, much to Dominic's dismay. "You have got to be kidding me. Another Yankees fan?" he complains as he slowly shakes his head, face contorted with disgust. He then proceeds to talk smack in an attempt to rile up the rest of the people sitting at our table, but no one is as passionate about being a home-team fan as Dominic, so conversation migrates on to the topics of fetal pig dissection and the dance on Friday.

When the Orchard Hills girls walk past our table, Sloan looks like a lovesick puppy as she gazes at Hunter. I can't tell from the way he glances at them whether he's interested or not. When it comes to that kind of stuff, I'm clueless. Dominic doesn't say anything when he notices me looking after them. Instead, he gives me a funny look that says, *what is with you and those girls?* Then he says out loud, "Hey, you wanna walk home together today? It's still kinda nice out."

"Um, I can't today." For some annoying reason, no one else at our table is talking at this moment.

"How come?" Dominic shoves some string cheese into his mouth.

No one is trying to listen to our conversation, but I'm certain no one is trying not to either. So I hesitate before answering. "Because Carly and I are going to the cheer squad tryouts."

"That's awesome, Katie!" Beth Grumley says from across the table. She is in band with Dominic and me. "I hope you make it. It's ridiculous how skinny those girls are. They all look like they belong in an Abercrombie ad. You know? Because they all look like they're starving?" She chomps down on a Dorito and everyone laughs, including me.

But my laughter isn't genuine. *Is she insinuating that I'm not skinny?*

Then the bell rings, cutting off any residual laughter. Everyone stands and goes their separate ways. Before Hunter takes off, he says, "Later, guys. See you in science, Katie."

Dominic follows me to the garbage can where I toss my half-eaten lunch away. Then we walk to math class together. "Cheer squad, huh?"

I nod. "I know. I can't believe I'm going to do it either."

"Why?"

"Why can't I believe it?"

"No, why are you trying out?"

"What do you mean? Is it really such a strange thing for me to want to do something other than play softball?"

"No. But you're just not like those cheer squad girls."

"What is that supposed to mean?" I narrow my eyes at him.

He puts his hands up defensively. "Nothing. Geez. I'm just surprised. That's all."

"Yeah, well, I'm surprised that I'm doing it too. I just want to try something new. Okay?"

"What do you mean, okay? Of course it's okay. Maybe I'll hang out after school and watch."

"Please don't."

Dominic grins at me and then turns to greet another student as they walk into math class together. I am about to follow but realize that my bladder is tingling. I only have a few minutes, so I bypass the nearest bathroom, which is always packed right after lunch, and head straight for the semi-secret one outside the band room. As I approach, I hear the same coughing and gagging sounds that I heard the day before when I came to wash out the jelly stain.

Could it be Amy again? It has to be. What are the odds that it's someone else?

I come close to knocking and asking if the person inside is okay, but then my hand drops to my side. If it is Amy, which it most likely is, she might think I followed her to the bathroom since I saw her yesterday, too.

Just as I turn to leave, the door opens. I consider scurrying off in hopes that whoever it is doesn't recognize me. No such luck.

"Katie, right?" a voice calls.

The bell rings.

I turn. It's Amy. Again, her face is flushed as if she has just stepped out of a sauna.

"Uh, hey. I was just . . . I really had to . . ."

"You were out here yesterday, too," she says without expression.

I point to my shirt—different from the day before, of course—and respond in a flustered manner, "I had a stain and—"

"Did you hear me?"

I stare at her, shocked, because I can tell from the expression on her face that I was right. She *was* throwing up.

"I just haven't been feeling well lately. You won't say anything to anyone, right?" she asks.

"No." I shake my head as I answer.

Then without another word, Amy brushes past me.

We are both late for class.

Chapter Nine

"First of all, we would like to welcome all of you to the tryouts . . ." Hands on her hips, Amy Bowie smiles sweetly and looks like the quintessential all-American girl dressed in her cheer squad uniform. No one would ever guess that she had been puking four hours earlier. Her hair is in low pigtails that hang uniformly over the front of each shoulder. The rest of the Orchard Hills girls are standing in a straight line behind her, along with four other cheerleaders who are in seventh grade and the two coaches—the mother of one of the seventh graders and Ms. Ditsch, one of the physical education teachers. There are four open spots on the squad.

". . . As the new captain, I am honored to have the final say if there is indecision among . . ." Amy replaced Mabel Harris as squad captain this year. Looks-wise, those who pay no attention to who's who in the world of cheer squad stardom wouldn't know the difference between Amy and Mabel—both tall and skinny with blonde hair and blue eyes—but that's where the similarities end. Mabel Harris was class president, an active chess club member and a clarinet player in the band. She crossed all sorts of social boundaries because she was smart and well liked by everyone, even sixth and seventh graders. Amy doesn't socialize with anyone in band, as far as I know. I tried to quit last year, but my mother wouldn't hear of it. *"We spent a lot of money on that flute for your sister so we are going to get our money's worth, young lady! Besides, what's wrong with being in band? Dominic still plays the saxophone, right?"*

". . . During small-group practice, the squad member assigned to your group will teach you two chants, an individual cheer and a group cheer. Ms. Ditsch and Mrs. Clausen will walk around and take notes. They'll be watching for . . ." I look around the gymnasium as Amy continues explaining procedures. There are approximately forty other girls trying out. About half are seventh graders and the rest are mostly sixth graders. Besides Carly and me, there appear to be only five other eighth graders. I am about to count again when Carly elbows me hard in the ribs. "... you might want to reconsider trying out."

"Ouch!" I say, but not quietly enough I guess because everyone is looking at me, except Carly who is staring straight ahead.

"Did you have a question?" Amy Bowie tilts her head slightly, and a look of confusion spreads across her face. "What was your name again?" Most of the squad members behind her snicker, causing some of the other candidates to giggle, probably because they are relieved that they are not being singled out the way I am.

"Gimme a break. You know her name," Carly says loudly. Gasps spread across the room like quick fire.

Amy opens her mouth to respond, but Ms. Ditsch touches her shoulder with one hand and grips the microphone with the other. Amy maintains her grip so that Ms. Ditsch has to tug the microphone away. "Thank you for explaining the procedures for today's session, Amy." With a warm smile, and as if nothing out of the ordinary has just happened, Ms. Ditsch looks out at all of us. "Before we divide you into groups of seven or eight, are there any questions?"

A few hands go up, but I can't concentrate on any of the questions because I am still in shock. I have no idea why Carly nudged me, and I don't dare ask her now after the embarrassing scene that has just occurred. I am busy wondering if Amy was trying to embarrass me when Ms. Ditsch labels me as a four and Carly as a five. Everyone is directed to a specific spot in the gym based on the number she has been assigned. Still shocked that Amy singled me out in front of everyone, I make my way to the area for the fours. Mixed emotions overwhelm me when I see who our group leader is: Sloan Whitson. She glances at me with indifference and then gets right down to business.

In addition to the chants and cheers, which I have no problem remembering, we are taught motions. The motions are much harder for me to remember, and I realize quickly that I probably look like a toddler doing Dance Revolution at the arcade for the first time. Even though we are being rated based on eight different criteria, Ms. Ditsch said the most important thing is simply remembering the cheers and the motions. If I can't remember the motions, I probably won't make it past today.

We are in the middle of practicing the group cheer when Ms. Ditsch and Mrs. Clausen pause to observe, pens and pads of paper in their hands. Everyone in my group does a left punch but I do a right. Then they all make a sharp turn to the right and do a high V but I am still facing forward. Sloan has a devilish grin on her face. I stand still, tears welling up behind my stoic eyes, as the others continue to move in unison. Finally, the routine ends along with any chance I might have had at making it to the second day of tryouts.

~

"I'm so sorry, Katie," Carly says.

We are walking over to where our things are up against the wall. Random squeals of excitement from girls who made it through to the next day of tryouts can be heard all around us.

"Really, it's no big deal," I say with a smile, trying to hide how I really feel.

"Well, I'm still sorry you didn't make it. And I'm sorry for elbowing you. It's just that Amy was saying something about people having to be good at remembering choreographed moves and then she switched gears really fast to something about 'those of you who don't seem to be paying attention'. She was staring right at you, so I panicked and nudged you."

Well, thanks a lot for drawing everyone's attention to me! "Seriously, it's fine. We both know I suck at learning new dance moves, so it's not a big deal. I figured I wouldn't make it. But at least you did!" Even though I am super jealous of Carly, I am still happy for her.

Shaking her head, Carly responds, "No. You're done, so I'm done. I'm not going to tryouts tomorrow."

"What? You have to, *especially* since I didn't make it. You have to show them."

"What are you talking about? Show who?"

"Amy, Anica . . . you know, that group of girls."

"Katie," she moans. "I don't care about those girls. The only reason I tried out was because you wanted to. I don't even want to be on the cheer squad."

"Come on, Carly. You have to." Carly is very coordinated and a great dancer. She used to take dance classes through the rec department when her mom was still around. But then when her mom died, that was it. She hasn't signed up for a dance class since. Odds are, she probably won't make the squad anyway because she's friends with me and doesn't exactly have the same body type as the girls on the squad either, but I still want to encourage her.

She takes a deep breath. "Fine."

I'm about to grab my bag from the floor when I feel hands on my shoulders. Carly is putting sweat pants over her shorts so she isn't paying attention to whoever it is. I turn to find Dominic standing behind me. And behind him is Hunter. I stare at them, mouth agape. What are they doing here? Were they watching the tryouts?

"Hey, Kit Kat," Dominic says.

Hunter laughs. "Kit Kat?"

"Yeah, that's what we call her."

"Oh, okay then. Hey, Kit Kat," Hunter says to me with a smile.

But I am too freaked out by the possibility that he saw what a fool I made of myself to enjoy his gorgeousness. And now he's calling me Kit Kat? *Gee, thanks a lot, Dominic.*

"Hey, guys. What are you doing here?" I ask.

"Yeah, don't you have anything better to do than crash cheerleader tryouts?" Carly interjects.

"Actually, no. We don't have anything better to do. Good thing, too, because that was *super* entertaining." Dominic laughs through his nose as he tousles my hair.

I put my hands over my face and lower my head. "Oh, God. You guys saw."

"Don't worry, Katie, I have about as much rhythm as a rock. You did much better than I would have done," Hunter says.

Dominic and Carly burst out laughing. I laugh too, of course, but I really feel like crying.

"Hiii, Huuunter." Sloan Whitson calls out as she approaches. The other OH girls are staring after her with grins on their faces.

Carly rolls her eyes as Hunter and Dominic turn to face Sloan. Shaken, I busy myself with putting on my sweatshirt and getting my things together, keeping an ear on their conversation.

"Hey, Sloan," Hunter says.

"Hiii, Sloooan," Dominic echoes her obnoxiously.

Out of the corner of my eye, I see her give Dominic a blank stare before focusing her attention on Hunter. "Are you going to the dance on Friday?" I imagine she is batting her eyelashes at him.

"Yeah, I think so. I take it you are, too?"

She giggles. "Of course we are. I'm wondering if you want to have burgers with us at this place called Brinkley's before the dance. They have the best burgers and custard in town."

"Dude. That's the place I was telling you about," Dominic says.

"Come on, Katie. Let's get going," Carly says. "It's getting late." Oblivious to the fact that I want to hear the rest of Hunter's conversation with Sloan, she starts walking. I don't want to make my eavesdropping obvious, so I follow.

"Hey, wait up. I was gonna take the bus home with you guys." Carly and I turn to see Dominic heading toward us, but Hunter is still talking to Sloan.

"Well, come on then. We gotta go!" Carly must be hungry. Her bubbliness fades when she's hungry. I can't help but laugh because it's rare for her to sound so gruff. "What?" she says a little softer. "We do."

"She's right, Dominic. The bus will be here in like ten minutes. If we don't hurry up, then we have to wait thirty."

He puts up a finger telling us to wait a minute and then yells to Hunter who is now surrounded by the entire Orchard Hills clique. "Dude, I gotta go! See you tomorrow." They all look over at Dominic, and then eyes shift to Carly and me. Sloan does not look happy.

"Okay. I'll see you tomorrow. See you, Carly. Bye, Kit Kat." Hunter waves. I hear Sloan, Amy, Anica and Laney begin to laugh.

"Thanks a lot for telling him that stupid nickname," I say to Dominic as we quickly walk to the bus stop.

He shrugs.

"*Katie.* Your nickname is *not* stupid," Carly says.

We all sit down inside the shelter before Carly is the first to speak again. "So, why was Hunter talking to Sloan and them?" she asks Dominic.

"Because Sloan has a thing for him."

Carly searches my face, but I'm doing my best not to react. Then she asks, "Does he like her?"

"I don't know! Don't care either. Why?"

"Well, I thought you were his friend. Aren't friends supposed to try to prevent each other from making mistakes? You know, like, shouldn't you warn him that Sloan isn't the nicest girl and she doesn't exactly have the nicest group of friends?"

"Are you serious, Carly? Guys don't talk about stuff like that. And Hunter is a big boy. I think he can figure out who he does and doesn't want to hang out with. I don't tell you who to be friends with."

"That's because I have really good taste in friends."

"I know. Me too," he jokes back. "Well, except for Katie over there. She's the only one I question."

"Very funny," I say.

"Finally, you speak! Why are you so quiet?" Dominic asks.

I shrug. "Just tired, I guess."

Carly playfully nudges my shoulder with hers. "Are you sure it's not because you have a crush on Hunter?"

"What?" Dominic looks at me wide eyed.

"I do not," I say defensively as I shake my head.

Dominic is still staring at me, eyes wider than usual, almost like he's searching for some cosmic truth in my face.

I widen my eyes and stare back at him. "What? Carly is full of baloney." Then I face forward and let my eyes fall to the ground. "Besides, if he had a choice between me and Sloan, or even Laney, Anica or Amy, I'm sure he'd be way more interested in one of them."

"Whatever." Dominic leans back against the shelter and butts his shoulder up against mine.

"You know what, guys? None of this matters. Because we all know Hunter has a secret crush on me anyway." Carly hops up onto her feet. "The bus is coming."

Dominic and I look at each other and laugh.

Chapter Ten

"Mooom! I'm hooome!"

"In here!" She calls from the living room. I remove my shoes and walk through the kitchen to find her dressed in a racerback tank and exercise leggings. A workout DVD is playing. "How was your day?" She asks without looking at me. She rarely lets anything interrupt her workouts.

"It was okay." I wait a moment, figuring she will ask about the tryouts, but she just continues working up a sweat.

"Sorry I missed dinner," I say, giving her another opportunity to remember where I was.

"Oh, no problem. I saved you a plate. It's in the microwave. Pork tenderloin with mashed potatoes and carrots. You have homework?"

"Yep."

"Alright. Why don't you go and eat?" She gestures with flapping fingers in the direction of the kitchen. "Then you can do your homework."

"Okay." *No, tryouts didn't go so well, mom. I didn't even make it through to day two. But thanks for asking. Nice talking with you.*

I set the microwave to ninety seconds and unload my homework onto the kitchen table. After completing a few algebra problems, something pops inside the microwave. *Dang. I forgot to cover it.*

"Katie? What was that?"

"Nothing," I say as I frantically try to clean the inside of the microwave before she comes to investigate. She is a total neat freak.

"What do you mean nothing? What popped?" *Too late.*

"It's fine, Mom. I just forgot to cover the food. I'm cleaning it up."

She wets a paper towel and nudges me out of the way. "Honestly, Katie. How many times do I need to tell you to cover food when you heat it in the microwave? *Especially* meat."

I take my plate to the table and start eating while I work on my homework. My mom harps about how no one in our house cleans anything except for her as she cleans the mess that I already cleaned. She does the same thing when I do the dishes and most of the time when I fold the laundry—always re-doing my attempts to help. When she finally closes the microwave, she folds her arms and says, "Why are you home so late, anyway?"

I look at her for a long moment as I debate telling her everything that went on at the tryouts: how I was singled out, how embarrassed I felt, how Hunter Davis saw me screw up and how Sloan happens to have a crush on him—the guy I kinda like.

"Well, where were you?" She's sweaty from working out, so I know she must be itching for me to hurry up and tell her so that she can hop into the shower.

"Cheer squad tryouts."

"Oh, my gosh! I totally forgot!" She smacks her forehead. "Well? How did it go?" Now she is leaning against the counter with her arms crossed. "I remember when your sister used to cheer. She was so good." Her eyes are pointed toward the ceiling as she recalls Kelsie's glory days.

"Eh. Not so good. I didn't make it."

"Well, I told you to practice, didn't I? If you don't practice something, how do you expect to be any good at it? You should have asked Kelsie for some pointers, too." I cringe, willing the lecture to be over, but then I feel kind of annoyed when she drops it so quickly. "Oh well. I have to take a shower." She heads toward the hallway that leads to her bathroom. A second later she yells, "Your dad sent you something, by the way. It's on the counter."

I look over to the spot on the counter where the cordless phone is stored along with a charging station for cell phones. A large envelope is standing upright in between the fridge and the charging station. Four years ago, I would have rushed over to find out what was inside, but things have changed.

I finish most of my food and complete my math homework. Then I pack up my backpack, wash my dirty dishes and make my lunch for the next day. The entire time, I try not to wonder what is inside the envelope, which I grab just before heading upstairs for a shower. Again, I contemplate opening it, but decide to get cleaned up and into some PJs first.

Standing under a warm stream of water, flashes of my

uncoordinated movements at the tryouts flood the back of my eyelids. Why is it that I can hit a softball farther than most boys my age and I can field just about anything, but I can't remember a simple cheer routine? Even if I had practiced like my mom suggested, I don't think it would have made much of a difference. I'm just not good at that kind of stuff. Then I picture the Orchard Hills girls with ribbons in their hair as they execute a perfect cheer routine. They are flawless in every way. In my imagination, Hunter Davis looks on and smiles . . . "Yeeeow!" I yelp and rush to turn off the shower when my thoughts are interrupted by a sudden surge of scalding water. I hear the faint sound of running water coming from my mother's bathroom just below mine and Kelsie's. She must have flushed the toilet. I hate when I'm in the shower and she does that.

Before getting dressed, I stand in front of the full-length mirror in my bedroom. I swear something about me looks different. *Have I gained weight in my cheeks?* I turn sideways. *Will my breasts ever stick out farther than my stomach?* I hold my hair in low pigtails, the kind Amy Bowie had today. Instead of looking stylish the way hers did, the pigtails in my hair make me look like a pudgy-faced kid. I release them and gently ruffle my medium-length, brown hair with my fingers. Even with my hair down, my face still looks rounder than usual. I scoff at my reflection and put on shorts and a T-shirt.

The envelope from my father rests on the corner of my bed. I suppose I have to open it sooner or later.

When I was four and my dad moved out, he sent Kelsie and me a letter every week. Sometimes he would even send a Kit Kat bar for me, and usually something cutesy for Kelsie, like barrettes. Sure, we got to see him on weekends, but it was still the highlight of my week when I would get home from school and there would be a letter from my dad waiting for me. Even if all he had to say was "how are you" or "I love you girls," just hearing from him was enough to fill my little heart with delight. Then when he moved to California for work, we started hearing from him less. His bi-weekly letters and treats (still Kit Kat bars for me, and girly items for Kelsie) became even more of a big deal, for me anyway. Then one day, when I was in kindergarten and Kelsie was in sixth grade, we arrived home to find an envelope bigger than normal waiting for us on the kitchen table. Inside was a letter from my dad explaining that he had gotten remarried and we would have a new baby sister soon. The letter had been accompanied by several photos from the wedding—the wedding we had not been invited to, the one we didn't even know about. Of course, there was a Kit Kat bar enclosed for me. I didn't eat it, though. Instead, I pounded on it with my fist until it was smashed to bits. The wrapper even ripped open along the seam. All my mom had to say about my fit was, "Well, at least you won't be eating it now." That night, I cried myself to sleep, not because I had a new stepmom that I had never met before, but because some other kid was going to get to live with my dad. That was also the night that I decided I would hate Kit Kat bars forever.

I grab the envelope and tear it open. There is a short note from my dad written on a medium, yellow Post-It.

Hey kiddos. How are things going? An eighth grader and a sophomore in college, huh? God, how time flies. We are looking forward to seeing you girls at Christmastime. Tell your mother that I'll make the flight arrangements soon.

Love, Dad

There is also a letter from my half-sister.

Dear Kelsie and Katie,

How are you? I started third grade this year. I think it's going to be a lot harder than last year! Do you guys remember being in third grade? I bet you don't since it was so long ago. Dad says you're coming to visit for Christmas. I can't wait! We will have so much fun. Please write back soon.

Love, Lily

P.S. I hope you like the picture I drew. It's us and my dogs. I know you like cats better Katie, but I think I'm better at drawing dogs.

P.S.S. I hope you like the pictures of me in my dance uniform.

I laugh at the way Lily has written "P.S.S." instead of P.P.S. I used to do that when I was little, too. Also inside the large envelope is a five by seven of Lily in her silver and maroon dance uniform. She has been enrolled in one dance class or another since she could walk, and she has been competing since preschool. In the picture, she is standing sideways with one hand on her hip, just like a model. Her hair is in a sleek, tight bun, and she's wearing makeup. At only eight years old, it's clear that she's going to be beautiful. She's definitely shaping up to be an Orchard Hills type of girl in the looks department.

There's also an eight by ten of my dad, my stepmom Connie and Lily —a beautiful family photo. It makes me nauseous. Why on earth would my dad send this to us? When I was little, I used to write him notes all the time begging for pictures of him and my new family members, but he never sent any. After the initial sadness I felt when he found a new wife and had another child, I started to think it was cool that I had two families. When my mom was too busy dating, or cleaning, or cooking to spend time with me, I would fantasize about living with my dad. Kelsie and I visited a few times after Lily was first born, but then it turned into only once a year when she started becoming more active with dance lessons, music lessons and playgroups. Connie filled up her schedule and my dad was always so busy working that neither of them had time to "entertain" Kelsie and me. By then, though, Kelsie was a teenager so she wasn't interested in being away from her friends during breaks from school anyway. I, on the other hand, would have loved to be involved in all of Lily's activities, just so I could be there instead of at home with my mom, a new stepdad that never really talked to me, and Kelsie who was too busy with her social life to pay much attention to me. At least I had my friends, though.

My stomach turns sour as I stare at my dad's most recent family photo. I love my dad and Lily—Connie is okay—but the picture makes me feel like an outsider. I feel like I'm looking at one of those generic photos that gets placed inside of a frame at the store, the ones where the families look so happy. You know they are just models posing as a real family, but still, you can't help but wish you were one of them. That's how perfect my dad's family looks.

Suddenly, I feel even more self-conscious about my performance at the cheer squad tryouts. Not only would Kelsie have been able to perform the cheer routine, but my little half-sister probably could have, too. It also bothers me that Lily seems to have the same thin, waif-like body type as Kelsie. How is that even possible? Why am I the only one to inherit my dad's stocky "German genes," as my mom so often puts it? I know looks aren't important, yet the disappointment I feel over my own appearance is overwhelming.

Looking more at the picture, I feel the pork loin I had for dinner making its way back up my throat. I jump up and run to the bathroom. When I get there, I immediately crouch down in front of the toilet, but nothing comes out. I rest my forehead on the rim of the seat and swallow repeatedly as acid burns my esophagus.

Would I feel any better if I did throw up?

I stand and come face to face with myself in the cabinet mirror above the toilet. "Maybe it *would* feel better," I whisper to myself.

I drop down to my knees and slowly insert a finger into my throat. I gag a little, but nothing comes up. So I try again, only this time I insert my finger so far that my teeth dig into my knuckles. Within seconds, the barely digested dinner that had been in my stomach is now floating in the toilet.

At first, I am shocked. *What have I done?* I quickly flush the toilet and rinse my mouth out with water. Then I brush my teeth to erase any remaining evidence of what just happened. It isn't until I glance at myself in the mirror, mouth full of foamy toothpaste, that I realize I feel better—much better.

In fact, I feel so much better that I crawl into bed and drift off to sleep effortlessly for the first time since Anica and I were caught shoplifting.

Chapter Eleven

"You look fine! Now, let's go!" Carly is standing in the bathroom doorway.

I turn away from the mirror to face her. "Are you sure I look okay?"

She lets out a long sigh. "Katie. It's not like we're going to a fancy ball or to prom or anything like that. It's just a school dance. The same exact people we see every day in school are going to be there. No princes. No movie stars. The same people we see at school *every day*. Who are you trying to impress?"

"No one . . . I just want to look nice, okay?" She's right about it being the same people we see every day, but her words still annoy me. Carly might be fine wearing the same jeans and sweatshirt she wore to school to the dance, but I want to wear something a little nicer. I know other girls—the Orchard Hills girls, in particular—will have changed their clothes. And then there's Hunter. If he does ask me to dance, I want him to notice that I put a little effort into looking nice, especially now that Sloan Whitson (of all people) is interested in him.

Carly is mid eye roll when Kelsie yells from the kitchen. "Katie! Carly! Mrs. Tropez is here!"

"You look fine, as always." Carly turns and heads for the stairs while I sneak one last peak in the mirror. Again, I blot an unsightly pimple on my chin with powder foundation.

Pimples started popping up along my T-zone last month. I did my best to ignore them until my mother made a comment one day. "Yikes, Katie. Looks like you got your father's oily skin. Why don't you start washing your face more than once a day? It might help get rid of those blemishes."

She didn't offer to take me to the store for face soap or for cover-up the way Selena's and Darcy's moms did—and obviously, I wasn't as lucky as Carly was to have a flawless complexion. I would have asked Kelsie, but she was rarely home during the summer. And when I did see her, she was usually with Kyle or in a hurry to leave. So, I went on my own. I settled on a Neutrogena face wash for acne-prone skin. Clearly, it doesn't work very well, but I don't have the money to spend on something else. I just keep hoping I'll wake up one day and all the pimples will be gone.

I am about to head downstairs when I hear Kelsie say to Carly, "Hey, I heard you made the cheer squad. Way to go!" I have no clue how Kelsie would know that because I sure didn't mention it. Maybe one of her old cheer squad friends told her?

"Yeah, no big deal. I really only tried out to support Katie."

"Well, you must be really good because my friend Stacey worked with her little sister for weeks and she didn't even make it."

Good doesn't even begin to describe Carly's individual tryout. She was amazing, and my insides burned with jealousy the entire time I was watching her. The looks on most of the judges' faces made it even more unbearable. Minutes into her performance all but the Orchard Hills girls started smiling and exchanging knowing glances. The Orchard Hills girls simply watched with mouths open in surprise at first. But by the end, they too were whispering to each other and nodding their heads. I can still hear Dominic whistling and yelling, "Way to go, Carly!" after she landed an impromptu flip at the end. I had no idea Carly even knew how to do a flip.

"Seriously, it's not a big deal, but thanks," Carly says, minimizing Kelsie's praise. "See you later. Bye, Mrs. Clifton!" Then the screen door closes.

"Katie! *What* are you—" Kelsie stops yelling as soon as she hears my footsteps on the stairs. She is looking at me from her seat at the kitchen table, textbook open in front of her. "There you are. What took you so long?"

"Nothing. I was just finishing getting ready," I say as I rub the throbbing pimple.

"All right, well, have fun. Don't forget, Kyle and I are picking you guys up at ten. Be right outside the gym doors. Okay? And stop touching that pimple or it's going to get worse."

I self-consciously hope that I didn't rub any of the cover-up off. "Yeah, okay. See you later. Bye, mom!"

"Have fun, Katie!" My mom calls from the living room. I imagine her sitting there watching TV.

~

Ten minutes later, we file out of the Tropez's minivan onto the sidewalk in front of school.

"You girls behave yourselves. Got it?" Carly and I know Mrs. Tropez is mostly talking to Selena and Darcy, but we answer anyway.

"Yes, Mrs. Tropez."

"God, Mom, what do you think we could possibly do to get in trouble?" Selena asks.

"Just watch yourselves." Mrs. Tropez wags a finger at Selena and then smiles at the rest of us before driving off.

Carly, Darcy, and I giggle as Selena mimics her mother under her breath. Then she looks around and motions for us to follow her toward a gathering of pine trees.

"What are we doing?" Carly asks, trailing a few feet behind the rest of us.

"Just come on!" Selena picks up her pace and again waves for us to follow.

As soon as we are all huddled together on the other side of the trees, Selena pulls a bottle out of the bag she always wears across her hip.

"What's that?" Carly asks.

"*Duh*, Carly. It's tequila," Darcy says with an eye roll.

Selena twists off the top. "Who wants the first swig?"

"I'm not drinking *that*." Carly puts a hand up in protest. "Isn't there a worm in it or something?"

Darcy grabs the bottle, puts it to her lips and tilts her head back. She does it too fast, and tequila trickles down her chin. She winces but then says, "Not bad." Then she hands the bottle back to Selena who takes an even bigger sip than Darcy. Selena and Darcy have obviously already tried tequila, but I have never even seen a bottle of it before.

I am busy debating whether I want to try it or not, but Selena hands the bottle back to Darcy instead of offering some to me. *Thank God.* Maybe they will just assume I don't want any.

"Where the heck did you get a bottle of tequila anyway?" Carly asks right before she goes into a wobbly handstand.

"My parents are having a party tomorrow night, so they stocked up on liquor today. These must have been on sale because there were four of them."

"Won't they notice it's gone?" Carly goes over into a sloppy bridge after another handstand attempt.

"Do you always have to act like such a goody-goody, Little Miss Cheerleader?" Grinning, Selena shakes her head and then takes another sip.

"It beats acting like a delinquent," Carly quips as she leans forward onto her hands again.

Darcy leans into me. "You wanna try some, Kit Kat?"

Selena holds the bottle out to me. Carly eyes me, but to my surprise, doesn't say anything. I take the bottle and hold it inches from my face as I look for the worm that Carly mentioned. There isn't one. I swear they can probably hear the valves of my heart opening and closing because it feels like it's going to beat right out of my chest.

"Well? Do you want some or not?" Selena peeks out through some branches. "A ton of people are showing up now. We gotta go."

I slowly bring the bottle to my lips and tilt a small bit of tequila into my mouth. At first, it tastes a little sweet. But then my mouth, throat and stomach are on fire. "Ack!" I cough while Selena and Darcy laugh. The nasty flavor lingers, causing my dinner to make its way up my throat. I swallow quickly several times to prevent a mess.

"Dumbasses," Carly says as she shakes her head.

～

The sun is dipping beyond the horizon by the time we emerge from behind the trees, making it difficult to people watch as we approach the illuminated entrance. A Rihanna song booms into the brisk night air every time the doors open. The four of us are about to enter when Brad Wilcox appears and starts gyrating against Selena's leg. Brad is with two of his stoner friends, Tyler and Jon. "Braaaad!" Selena squeals. They have been dating off and on since sixth grade.

The guys acknowledge Carly and me with nods and smiles. Tyler puts an arm around Darcy. Then he leans in and sniffs. "What's that smell?" He sniffs again, a little faster this time. "Wait, is that tequi—"

"Shhh!" Darcy has a finger to her lips.

Carly and I sneak a look at each other from the corners of our eyes as we follow Selena, Darcy and the guys inside. The hallway is crowded with people standing in line to pay the dollar admission and with people going in and out of the bathrooms. I look around nervously, wondering if the Orchard Hills girls have arrived yet. Then I remember Sloan saying something to Hunter about going to Brinkley's before the dance. I wonder if that's where they are and if Hunter is with them.

"Hey, there's Dominic," Carly nudges me.

I follow her gaze back to the entrance. Sure enough, Dominic is standing there in the same jeans and Adidas T-shirt he wore to school. His hair looks different, though. Surprisingly, it looks gelled. *He never gels his hair.* That's not what catches me off guard the most, though. Hunter is standing to his right, and just behind them I can make out Amy Bowie's perfect blonde hair. I don't even need to crane my neck to see who she's with because I already know. Hunter turns his head back a smidge then he smiles and says something to Sloan. *Both Hunter and Dominic must have gone to Brinkley's with them.* My heart takes a nosedive into my stomach.

"That's weird. It seems like he's with Amy and the rest of those girls," Carly says.

All I can muster is a shrug.

"Did he tell you he was going to the dance with them?"

"No." My voice quavers a bit, but Carly doesn't notice.

"Well, what's up with that? He usually shows up with his band buddies or by himself if he doesn't ride with us." Then she looks at me. "What's wrong with you? You look like . . ." Then a knowing look spreads across her face. "Oh."

"We'll see you in there. K?" Selena looks over her shoulder at Carly and me. Darcy has already disappeared into the strobe-light-filled gym with the stoner guys.

"Yeah, we'll find you," I say as she steps into the gym, making it a point to wiggle the fingers of her left hand just before it disappears after her.

Carly pays two dollars for our admission, and I thank her. Just as we are about to enter the gym, she looks back toward Dominic and Hunter, who are now out of line and waiting next to the girls' bathroom. "You wanna wait for them?"

"Why would we?"

"Because they're our *friends*?" She tilts her head and raises her eyebrows at me.

It occurs to me that she might not just be talking about Dominic and Hunter. After all, Carly isn't really friends with Hunter. Actually, neither am I. I wonder if she might be referring to the Orchard Hills girls. Maybe she feels like they are her friends now that she is on the cheer squad. The thought of Carly spending so much time with them turns my stomach even more than the thought of Dominic hanging out with them at Brinkley's before the dance. For a fleeting moment, I recall how calm I felt after making myself throw up the other night. *Would I feel the same way if I did it again?* "No, Carly, let's just go." I tug on the sleeve of her oversized Marquette University hoodie and silently hope that she follows without question. I cannot stand the thought of coming face to face with Dominic and Hunter when they are with those girls.

The dance floor slowly fills as "Best Day of My Life" starts to play. Carly and a girl from our softball team strut into the middle of all the other people on the dance floor. I stay put and listen to a couple of girls gossip about who they think is going to dance with whom when the first slow song comes on. These girls are both very nice, but I don't know them too well since we've never been in any of the same classes together. Carly is friends with them, though, so I stand there nodding, smiling and adding my two cents every once in awhile. For the most part, I am just working up a sweat as I keep my eyes on the door. At least ten minutes have passed, and Dominic and company still haven't entered. *Did they go back outside?* Besides wondering what happened to *them*, I question why I even came to the dance in the first place. I really don't like to dance, probably because I suck at it. Last year, I only attended two of eight school dances, using babysitting as an excuse five times and then claiming to be sick once. Why didn't I just tell Carly I wasn't feeling well tonight? Watching *48 Hours Mystery* with my mom would have been much less stressful.

A throwback jam comes on—Rob Base's "Joy and Pain"—prompting squeals all around. The girls I am standing with give me gentle nudges as they walk by, encouraging me to join them on the dance floor. I almost follow, but chicken out at the last second and instead stand awkwardly by myself. I am startled when hands suddenly cover my eyes from behind.

"Guess who." Dominic talks in a low-pitched voice, probably hoping I won't be able to tell it's him.

I can't help but grin. "I know it's you, Dominic. Nice try."

"Dang, Katie. How'd you know?"

I turn to face him, and again I am surprised by his styled hair.

"What?" He says, hands gently patting his new 'do. "Does it look weird?"

"Uh-uh. It looks good. What I'm wondering is who you're all fixed up for."

He lets one sarcastic breath escape through his nostrils. "Fixed up? Whatever, Katie. What about you? Why are you dressed all . . ." He motions with one hand from my head down to the floor. ". . . cutesy?"

"Cutesy? Gee, thanks. That's totally the look I was going for. Cutesy." I shake my head at him, but instead of firing back, he breaks into dance. I quietly chuckle, but do my best not to crack a smile for his benefit.

The banter between Dominic and me is normally all in good fun, but tonight part of me wants to snap at him. I can't help it. Why was he with them? And where were they now? *He's one of your best friends. Just ask!*

"So, Dominic . . ." He is moon walking in a circle at my side.

Suddenly Hunter shows up, dancing terribly on the other side of me. I'm not even sure I could mimic his level of crappy dancing if I tried. "What do you say, Katie? Wanna hit the dance floor with me?" he asks.

I look to my left at Dominic. Then I look back to Hunter on my right. "Uh, no. That's okay. I'll pass."

Dominic and Hunter both burst into laughter.

"Jerks! You guys planned that!"

"Dude, you weren't supposed to bust out your good dance moves," Hunter complains to Dominic as they bump fists.

"You call those good?" I ask.

Hunter laughs.

"So, when did you guys get here?" I ask, pretending I didn't see them earlier. Maybe they weren't with the Orchard Hills girls, after all.

"Fifteen minutes ago, maybe?" Hunter looks to Dominic for verification, but Dominic just stares blankly at him, as if he is trying to convey something through telepathy. "We were late because Brinkley's was a madhouse."

Dominic sighs. *He didn't want me to know.*

"Brinkley's?" I ask.

"Yeah, we went there with Sloan, Amy, Anica, Laney, and some other guys from school."

"Wow. Cool." I stare at Dominic as I say this. He sighs again.

"Is something wrong?" Hunter looks at me quizzically.

"No . . . nothing." I shake my head. "Joy and Pain" ends and people begin to leave the dance floor. Then "Roar" by Katy Perry starts and most of the people who were leaving turn back to dance some more. "I just didn't know you guys were going to Brinkley's tonight." I look at Dominic again.

"Hunter called me at the last minute and offered to have his dad pick me up. I was about to call you to see how you were getting to the dance when he called. Who did you come with anyway?"

"Carly, Selena, Darcy—Mrs. Tropez drove. Kelsie and Kyle are picking us up if you need a ride." I want to know more about Brinkley's, but then I remember Hunter is there and decide not to let my jealous thoughts turn into a scene.

Hunter laughs, "You two remind me of my sister and me. We argue *all* the time."

I laugh and sneak a glance at Dominic. He's only kind of laughing. Something is on his mind.

"Roar" ends and Carly returns with a group of girls shortly after. We are all standing in a large circle and talking when the Orchard Hills girls, and several of the "cool guys," form another circle right next to us. I have my ears on the conversation within our circle, but I am also keeping one eye on Sloan, who is standing back to back with Hunter. She keeps brushing against him, on purpose no doubt. Then she turns around and says to him, as if she didn't know he was standing right behind her, "Hey! There you are. We were looking for you guys." She smiles at Carly—a real one, too—and says, "Hey, Carly! We missed you at Brinkley's." Carly smiles and nods at Sloan, then glances at me before returning to the conversation she had been having with some of the girls from the dance floor.

Hunter turns slightly, so that half of his body is with our group and the other half is with theirs. Then he says something in Sloan's ear and she laughs.

"Katie! How are you? It's so cool that we have science together, isn't it?" Rebecca Winters, a girl I went to grade school with, squeezes in between Dominic and me. "Oh my God! Dominic! I haven't seen you yet this year."

After we both greet Rebecca, she proceeds to talk a mile a minute for at least five minutes straight. We mostly just smile and nod as she tells us about her summer. Dominic tries to say something once or twice, but Rebecca barely notices. She just keeps right on talking.

She has always been a talker. In fact, she used to get herself and others into trouble all the time in grade school for talking. I really don't think she can control it. She's like one of those small wind up toys that move really fast after you turn the little dial as far as it can possibly turn without breaking it, then you just let it loose. That's what I think of when I think of Rebecca—a wind-up toy. Horses also remind me of her. She used to gallop around the playground during recess, lost in her own little world. Sometimes she would even let out a loud whinny. Other kids made fun of her and avoided sitting next to her, but that made me want to sit next to her even more because I didn't want her to feel bad. As a result, Carly and I ate lunch with Rebecca a lot in grade school. Dominic too.

"Wow. Your horse won first place? That's awesome, Rebecca," I say, genuinely happy for her. With a grin that tells me exactly what he thinks of Rebecca's horses, Dominic tells us he has to use the bathroom.

"Thanks, Katie! Hey, when did you start hanging out with *them*?" She leans in close when she says this, but her eyes are on the Orchard Hills girls who are now pretty much standing in our circle—right in between Hunter and Carly. Sloan and Laney are talking to Hunter, and Amy and Anica are talking to Carly. *Carly is talking to Amy and Anica?*

I am about to tell Rebecca that we really don't hang out with them when "Party Rock Anthem" comes on. The hoots and hollers that follow are deafening. People flock to the dance floor, including almost everyone standing around me, even Rebecca. When I see that Carly and Hunter are about to follow the OH clique onto the dance floor too, I think about heading to the bathroom, but then Carly yells, "Kit Kat! Come on!"

"Yeah, come on *Kit Kat*," Amy jeers. She elbows Anica.

Then, as if Amy Bowie calling me Kit Kat isn't bad enough, Hunter hurries back, grabs my hand and leads me out to the dance floor. "I'm not making a fool of myself without you!" he yells. Sloan glares at me as she dances her way over to Hunter and me. Her moves make me feel like I'm watching a music video—she's that good. And so are the other OH girls. Carly fits right in too. But all I can manage is some awkward shuffling, head bobbing and swaying back and forth.

My face is red for sure, but luckily no one can tell because of the psychedelic lighting. Unfortunately, the bright flashing lights do nothing to mask my ridiculous moves, and to my horror, Amy begins mimicking me. She is followed by Sloan and then Anica. I can't tell if Hunter is copying me or not, because his moves are just as bad as mine. Carly is lost in her own world until she notices the three girls are making fun of me. Her mouth contorts into a frown and I think she is about to say something when the song ends and a slower one comes on, cutting the noise level in half. Amy, Sloan and Anica continue to chuckle softly. Laney is already dancing with a basketball player. Then people all around us begin pairing off. I make eye contact with Hunter who is smiling at me, but as much as I try, I can't make myself smile back. I am too dizzy with embarrassment. Instead, I quickly walk off the dance floor and into the hallway with Carly hot on my heels. Before I turn the corner to exit the gym, I glance back and see that Hunter is already dancing with Sloan.

"Katie," Carly calls after me. "Kit-Kaaat," she presses on.

I spin around to face her as soon as we enter the bathroom. Tears are trickling down my cheeks. "Please . . . stop . . . calling me that!"

A few girls are washing their hands. They exchange wide-eyed looks.

Surprised by my outburst, Carly jumps back a little. "Katie, they were just trying to be funny."

"Funny? Gimme' a break." I lower my voice, hoping that girls walking in and out of the bathroom can't hear me. "They were making fun of me."

Carly continues trying to console me, but I can't concentrate on what she's saying because my head is filled with visions of my awkward dance moves and the grins on everyone's faces, including Hunter's and Carly's. I feel stupid for letting their teasing get to me and ashamed for running off like a baby. Anger wells up inside of me and begins to seep through my pores.

"Why are you defending them? What, now that you're on the cheer squad, Amy isn't so *boney* after all?" This time I surprise myself and immediately feel guilty for speaking to Carly with such an accusatory tone.

She stares at me wide-eyed and speechless, long enough for me to know that there is some truth to what I have said.

"Forget it. I'm going to find Selena and Darcy. You hang out with your new clique. Dominic included."

"Katie, I . . ." Before she can get another word out, I storm out of the bathroom. As much as I want to look back, I don't.

I slip quickly into the gym and make my way to the top of the risers so that I can look for Selena and Darcy. From my vantage point, I watch as Carly joins Dominic at the edge of the dance floor. He leans down as she talks in his ear. As soon as he stands back upright, he begins walking slowly along the perimeter of the gym, scanning each group of kids. Carly follows behind him.

Instead of looking for Selena and Darcy, I take a seat and continue watching Dominic and Carly as they search for me. It's weird seeing the two of them together without me. They are my two closest friends, but they've never really hung out with each other without me. For some reason, as I watch them walking together, I feel like they are both drifting away from me. Or could I be the one who's drifting away? Carly reaches out and touches Dominic's shoulder. He turns to face her and leans back down to her level. Whatever she says to him makes him shrug. Then they begin walking back in the direction of Hunter and the OH clique. My heart sinks. They're definitely the ones who are drifting, not me.

I lean back against the wall and look around at the sea of bodies surrounding me. So many people are walking from group to group, and so many more are part of the collective mob on the dance floor, soon to include Dominic and Carly. Am I the only person who's all alone, just watching? Does anyone else feel as out of place as I do?

Shortly after I begin scanning the others who are sitting on the risers, I spot Selena and Darcy. Of course, they aren't alone. Darcy is sitting with Tyler and a few other kids. Tyler is behind her, and he is rubbing her shoulders. Selena and Brad are making out a few rows up. They are sitting low, where people normally put their feet to avoid being seen by chaperones. There are enough bodies in front of them to ensure this though.

Seeing Selena and Darcy with Brad and Tyler makes me think of Hunter. I laid in bed the night after I first met him and imagined what it would be like to kiss him. I imagined letting him put his tongue in my mouth the way I knew kissing was supposed to work.

I've kissed and been kissed before, just never with my mouth open more than a centimeter or two. Selena's cousin kissed me behind the swine barn at the Wisconsin State Fair two summers ago, and Nick Derillo kissed me during a game of spin the bottle in Darcy's basement just this past July. I could tell he was disappointed when the bottle pointed at me, probably because I was the only girl at the get-together who had not French kissed yet. I felt the wetness of his tongue touch my locked lips, but he didn't push hard enough to penetrate them. Part of me wished he had, though, especially now as I watch Brad and Selena enjoying themselves.

I want to know what it feels like. I was hoping Hunter might be my first French kiss, but now that Sloan is after him, I need to quit dreaming. It's probably for the best, though, because my mom says I better not even think about doing *anything* with a guy until I am at least fifteen. If she knew what Selena and Darcy have been up to, she would probably suggest I find new friends. While I have absolutely no desire to do most of the things Selena and Darcy have been doing, my mom's warning is still ridiculous. Kelsie was making out with guys in our garage when she was twelve and my mom knows about it. Why the double standard? Maybe it's because she isn't so wrapped up in worrying about what my father is up to anymore, now that the divorce is final and she has Gary.

Although, she would probably never find out if I did do something with a guy since she barely pays attention to my life anyway.

Deciding it's time to quit being such a loner, I stand up, intent on making my way over to Darcy and Selena. Then another popular song comes on and their group rises, almost as one, and moves to the dance floor. I watch as Selena and Darcy show off their MTV-like booty shaking and try to imagine my hips moving like theirs. The thought leaves a knot in my stomach, so I plop myself back down and sink into my thoughts for the last hour of the dance.

~

Before the dance officially ends, I sneak out a side door and make my way to where Kelsie is supposed to pick us up in ten minutes or so. I sit on the curb and lean back on my palms, looking up at the clear, starry sky. When I was little, I always wished on stars. *Starlight, star bright, first star I see tonight . . .*

"Katie?"

I jump. "Mrs. Ditsch, you scared me. Hi."

"What are you doing out here already? You know students aren't allowed outside until the dance ends."

"Sorry."

She cocks her head. "Are you okay?"

No, I don't think I am. Your cheerleaders have stolen my closest friends. "Yeah, I'm fine. It just felt a little stuffy in there. I think I might be coming down with something." I touch my forehead for effect.

She looks at her watch, and to my surprise, takes a seat on the curb next to me. Maybe she didn't buy my 'I'm fine' act and was going to press me about what was wrong. *Maybe it would make me feel better if I unloaded some of the frustrations and insecurities I've been feeling.* Instead she says, "It's a few minutes before ten. Who's picking you up?"

"My sister, Kelsie."

"Ah, Kelsie! I remember Kelsie. She was in eighth grade the first year I helped with cheer squad. Such a nice girl. Good gymnast, too."

"Yep, she's good at a lot of things. That's for sure."

Mrs. Ditsch gives me a knowing look. "Katie, don't let not making the squad get to you. After all, there were only four spots, dear." She puts her hand on my shoulder and then stands as the main gym doors burst open. "Say hi to Kelsie for me." With a wink, she begins directing foot traffic.

I stand with my back to the crowd, refusing to look like I'm waiting for my friends. The first to show up are Darcy and Selena.

"Kit Kat!" they call in unison.

I cringe as I turn to face them, a fake smile plastered to my face.

Selena's cheeks are red and her hair is a mess because of her make-out session with Brad—either that or she had more tequila. Darcy clearly has had more tequila, because she is walking unsteadily and her eyes are glazed. "You guys look like you had fun," I say, still smiling.

Selena hugs her hands to her chest. "I think I'm in love."

Darcy drapes an arm over my shoulder and hiccups once in my ear, releasing the nasty scent of tequila into the air. Then she giggles. "You guys better hope Kelsie doesn't smell—"

"Katie!" Dominic's voice booms from out of nowhere. Now we are standing face to face. "Where have you been?"

Beth Grumley saunters up beside him. "Hey, Katie."

I glance at her and say, "Hi, Beth." Then I turn my gaze back to Dominic. "Well, I was inside . . . and then I came outside." My voice has taken on an edge.

He shakes his head. "But we looked all over for you."

You call walking twenty feet looking all over for me? I'm not sure why Dominic would exaggerate like this, but it pisses me off. "Oh, really? Have you seen Carly?"

"Yeah. I was hoping to hang out with you a little bit. And yeah," He looks off into the distance over my head. "Carly's coming."

I shrug at him as Kelsie and Kyle pull up. "You need a ride?"

"Nope. We're going to Brinkley's," Beth says, as if I was offering her a ride too. Dominic looks at her funny and then confirms their plans. He gives me a quick hug, and the two of them disappear into the crowd just as Carly appears, looking sheepish.

Kelsie honks the horn.

"Come on. We gotta go," I say as I open the back door.

"Kit Kat! Let's go!" Kelsie shouts from inside.

Selena and Darcy climb into the back seat and Carly is about to climb in when Amy Bowie calls out to her, "Hey, Carly! Hang on a sec." Amy rushes in front of me, my hand still on the car door. "Aren't you coming to Brinkley's?"

"No . . . I . . . uh . . . I have to get home."

"Oh." Amy peeks into the car. "Well, don't forget about the thing at Sloan's house tomorrow night," she whispers. As she turns to leave, we make eye contact for a second, but I don't see the slightest bit of discomfort on her face for leaving Darcy, Selena and me out of the loop for tomorrow night. Nor do I see any recognition in her eyes. Does she even remember running into me outside the band room bathroom?

"Sweet Child O' Mine" blares on the radio as we drive Darcy and Selena home. Then "Sweet Emotion" plays as Kelsie makes her way back to our house to drop off Carly and me. Carly and I don't talk during the entire drive, but Kelsie and Kyle are too busy singing to notice. When Kelsie pulls the car up into our driveway, Carly and I slip out on opposite sides. I immediately rush to the door without even looking at her. When I get inside, I hear Kelsie and Kyle saying goodbye to her. Once inside my bedroom, I peek at Carly through a window. Arms folded across her chest, she slowly makes her way across the street. She stops in the middle of the street and turns around, and I am ready to run downstairs and meet her at the door to apologize for being such a big baby. But then she turns and rushes off, disappearing into her house within seconds.

Tears burn behind my eyelids, but I refuse to let any escape.

Not quite ready to go to bed after changing my clothes and washing my face, I plop down on the couch next to my mom. She looks away from the weather forecaster on TV just long enough to say, "How was the dance?"

I lean against her and lay my head on her shoulder. "Fine." I reach into the bowl of potato chips on her lap and grab a few.

"Just fine?"

I sit upright and turn to face her with one leg bent underneath the other. Part of me wants to tell her about the fight I had with Carly, but then again, I don't want to get into the whole thing about me being jealous of the Orchard Hills girls. My mother was an Orchard Hills type herself—pretty, popular—in fact, I think she still is. So, I decide she probably won't understand. "It was okay."

I grab more chips and this time my mother's gaze follows my hand from the bowl to my mouth. I can tell she is struggling not to say something. When I reach toward the bowl again, she quickly removes it from her lap and places it on the table next to the sofa.

"These greasy chips will only make that pimple worse. Honestly, I

don't even know why I was eating them. They go straight to the hips."
She pats my thigh then stands and stretches. "Well, I think I'll join Gary
in bed and read a bit before going to sleep. Do you want the TV on?"

"Yeah, thanks." I force a smile that vanishes as soon as she turns to
leave. Then I grab the bowl of chips that she forgot to take to the
kitchen on her way to bed.

Twenty minutes later, the chips are gone and I am staring zombie-
like at the TV as I flick through channels. My finger pauses when
Arianna Grande appears on the screen. I don't usually watch MTV or
music videos, but for some reason I watch this one. It makes me feel
embarrassed all over again. I think about the OH girls and their expert
dance moves, and I mentally compare their stick-thin figures to the girls
in the music video. I could never look like that. A sour pit develops in
my gut, so I flick off the TV and head upstairs. Enough torturing myself.

I am about to brush my teeth when my stomach gurgles, reminding
me of the bowl of chips I just ate. I look down at my body and decide
that even if I can't change my overall build, I can at least prevent my
stomach and thighs from getting any bigger. I carefully set my tooth-
pasted toothbrush on the counter and crouch down next to the toilet.
This time when I stick my finger down my throat, I don't gag as much
as I did the other day, but it still takes several tries before anything
happens. What comes up is mostly liquid, though, and it burns the back
of my throat. I can feel the partially digested chips just waiting to escape
and I am determined to make it happen. I grab my toothbrush from the
counter and remove the toothpaste with a square of toilet paper. Then,
even as I'm wondering what the hell I'm doing, I stick the handle as far
into the back of my throat as I can to make myself gag. It works, and
before I know it, I'm staring at every last bit of chip that was in my
stomach.

Not only does my stomach feel completely empty, but somehow, I
also feel like a weight has been lifted.

Chapter Twelve

Today is the kind of fall day that makes me want to stay in my PJs and eat homemade chicken noodle soup. Windy, dreary and overcast. I'm still in my PJs, but it's only ten in the morning, so I haven't had any soup yet.

Sitting on my bedroom floor, I'm surrounded by old photo albums. Most people create folders on their computers or use zip drives to organize and store pictures, but my mom is old school, so there are hard copies of every moment in our lives. Birthdays, lost teeth, sporting events, school programs, sleepovers, new shoes, hair cuts—think of any life event and my mom most likely has a photo of it. There is even a picture of me crying on the first day of kindergarten.

I'll never forget that day. My tears weren't because I didn't want to go to school, but because my mom and dad were on the phone arguing minutes before we left the house. She was upset that they weren't both dropping me off on my first day of school, but he simply wasn't able to make it. As I look at the picture of five-year-old me with pink, tear-stained cheeks and a forced grin on my face, my mom's voice echoes in my head. "Can you just stop crying long enough to smile for one picture? You can always call your dad tonight and tell him all about your first day. Please, just stop crying. Honestly, Katie, it's not that big of a deal."

I wondered why she needed to take a picture of me so badly if it wasn't a big deal. Why not give me a pass on one lousy picture? I run my fingers over the face of the little girl staring back at me from the picture and my heart aches for her. She just wanted her dad to be there to see her off on her first day of kindergarten. She wanted to see him holding her mom's hand and waving as she looked back one last time. Instead, he was in another state with a wife who wasn't her mother and a new kid on the way.

I blink back a tear and flip a few pages forward in the album labeled "Katie: Grade School Years – Album 1." I look happy in the rest of the pictures, and I remember being happy most of the time, too. There are photos of Selena, Darcy, Carly and me at various school events: track and field days, Halloween parades, concerts, and even ones of us playing at recess. God, teachers must have thought my mom was nuts when she would lurk around school waiting for a photo op.

Dominic isn't in any of the pictures until I get to "Katie: Grade School Years – Album 2." It occurs to me that I don't remember posing for so many pictures with Dominic when I was younger. He is pictured at my house on holidays, at my softball games, playing twister with Carly and me, sunbathing with me in our back yard (both of us with ample amounts of "baby fat").

The next album, "Katie: Middle School Years," is only half-full. There are still quite a lot of pictures of me with Carly and Dominic but only a few with Darcy and Selena. The last picture filed is of the five of us on the last day of seventh grade. Kelsie had driven us to school and snapped a surprise shot as we were all walking away from the car. None of us were prepared, so the looks on our faces are pretty telling, I guess. Carly's mouth is open because she was mid-sentence; Dominic has a pleasantly surprised grin on his face; Darcy has her hand up like she's getting ready to block her face from the photo; Selena looks annoyed to be caught off guard; and I am smiling from ear to ear. I can't remember the last time I felt as happy as I felt that day. I was surrounded by familiar childhood friends and was excited to be growing closer to Anica. I was certain that come fall, I would be hanging out with the rest of the Orchard Hills girls, too. Never in a million years would I have guessed that everything would be the way it is now—with all my grade school friends branching off into different directions and the entire OH clique (including Anica) making me feel like an outcast.

My eyes drift back over to Dominic. I am surprised by how much he has changed. He has gone from being a short, chubby-cheeked, freckle-faced kid to a guy I could see myself blushing over at the mall. I guess seeing him on such a regular basis has prevented me from noticing the transformation. Suddenly my cheeks feel warm, and I realize that the thought of Dominic being nice-looking makes me uncomfortable. For a moment, I ponder whether it's a good or bad sort of uncomfortable, but I can't figure it out, so I shrug the feeling away altogether.

I look at Carly again. Thinking about her tendency to talk

incessantly makes me laugh out loud, and I decide it's time to set my jealousy and poutiness aside and call her. But as soon as I stand, I hear the unmistakable sound of her father's truck roaring to life. I look out the window and see Carly climbing into the passenger side. Oh, well. My apology can wait until they get back.

I move away from the window, resolved to put away the photo albums, shower and be ready to run over to Carly's as soon as I hear her dad's truck pull into the driveway. But then, the phone rings. Once. Twice. Seconds later, it stops and I hear footsteps on the stairs. My bedroom door opens and Kelsie's head pops inside. "It's Dominic."

I swallow hard before taking the phone from Kelsie. She raises her eyebrows at me when I hesitate to bring the phone to my ear. "What?" I whisper to her, covering the phone.

She shakes her head and rolls her eyes, as if to say she couldn't really care less what is going on between Dominic and me. Then she disappears.

"Hello?"

"Whatcha up to, Kit Kat?"

I shrug, as if he can see me. "Nothing. What're you doing?"

"I just got done working the early-bird shift. I don't even know why we open so early on weekends. It's all old people until nine or so, and all they buy is coffee."

"What about doughnuts?"

"Yeah, that too, I guess. So, what are you up to this afternoon?"

"Why? What are you up to?"

"Wanna go to a movie?"

"Maybe. Depends what time, though. I need to talk to Carly."

"You haven't talked to her yet?"

"Uh-uh. I . . . I guess I kind of blew up at her last night."

"Yeah, I know."

"She told you?"

"Sort of. She didn't exactly say you blew up, but she did say that you were mad at her for making the cheer squad."

"What? You have got to be kidding me. That has nothing to do with what happened last night."

"Are you sure, Katie? You have been acting weird ever since those tryouts—since before actually, but even weirder since then."

"No, I haven't. Okay? But even if Carly making the squad did bother me, that was not what we argued about last night."

"Well, what happened then? Why did you disappear?"

"I don't know." *Talk to him, Katie. Tell him what's bothering you.* "I guess I was kind of upset that—"

"That what? That you didn't get to dance with Hunter?" There is a hint of sarcasm in his voice, but then he says more seriously, "Trust me, you could have if you hadn't run off."

"Yeah, right. Sloan was glued to his hip."

"Trust me, Katie, he would have danced with you." Dominic ends what feels like an uncomfortable silence by teasing, "Hang on, I know why you were upset. Because you were born with two left feet, right?" He laughs.

I almost hang up on him, but instead I sigh. "Very funny."

"God, Katie, I'm just kidding. Why are you so moody lately? It doesn't even feel like I'm having a conversation with my best friend. Is it girly puberty stuff?"

"Eww. As if I'd talk to you about it if it was! Anyway, what time's the movie? And what do you want to see?"

"Beth and I were thinking of seeing that new—"

"Wait. Beth is going?"

"Yeah. So?"

I think back to the night before when Beth sidled up next to Dominic. I see her arm brush up against his. "Hey, I don't want to be a third wheel. Thanks for inviting me, but why don't you guys just go?"

"Dude. Whatever. You would not be a third wheel."

"Look, Dominic, just . . . I just don't want to go. Just go with Beth. Okay? I have to talk to Carly anyway."

"Fine, but you wouldn't be a third wheel."

Maybe Dominic is right, but I can tell from the way Beth looks at him that she likes him. And I don't feel like being on the outs with any more girls at school.

～

"Katie, it'll take you forever to slice those if you keep doing it like that. Here, let me show you." My mom takes the knife from my hand and dices four carrot sticks at the same time. "Go slow. It takes practice." She hands the knife back to me but continues looking over my shoulder. I can't even think of a time that she didn't try to show me a "better" way to do something.

"I got it, mom. Thanks."

I am perfectly capable of cutting carrots more quickly, but half of my attention is on Carly's driveway. It has been three hours and they still aren't back. Carly and her dad normally go grocery shopping on Saturday mornings, but it never takes this long. She would have said something to me if they were going up north. *Where are they?*

I finish cutting up the carrots and move on to celery while my mom peels boiled chicken meat off the bones. When the phone rings, my first thought is that somehow, I missed the sound of Carly's dad's truck. I peek out the window, but it still isn't in the driveway.

"Katie, are you going to get that?"

"Oh, yeah," I say as I grab the phone and glance down at my dad's number on the caller ID. "Hello?"

"Hi, Katie." It's my half-sister.

"Hi, Lily. How are you?"

My mom tries to roll her eyes discreetly as she pretends to be concentrating on separating the meat from the bones. I didn't see her do it, but I know she rolled them because I've seen her do it a million times. Actually, she rolls her eyes, sighs heavily or slams cabinets anytime I talk to my dad, Lily or Connie. I'm not even sure she knows how much her demeanor changes. It's as if she's become so used to being angry with my father that she couldn't change her mental and physical reactions when it comes to anything or anyone that has to do with him if she tried.

"Great! Third grade is awesome. And I love my teacher! Her name's Mrs. Stanslewski. We call her Mrs. S. for short. And guess what!"

"What?"

"You and Kelsie are going to be here for my holiday concert at school! *And* one of my dance recitals!"

Every time I talk to Lily, I can't help but feel like a horrible person. She is the sweetest little sister a girl could ask for, but part of me will always resent her. I know it isn't her fault that my dad left us and ended up with her, but I just can't shake the nagging feeling I have deep down that tells me I should hate her. I try so hard, but I can't. Maybe it has something to do with witnessing the way my mom has always reacted to her. "Awesome, Lily. I can't wait. So, what're you up to today? It's about two o'clock there, right?"

"Yeah. We just got back from the beach. I built a huge sand castle!" I hear murmuring in the background. Then I think I hear Lily sigh before saying, "Did you get the pictures and the letters?"

"I did. I just love your dance picture. And the one of you and your mom and dad? Just awesome." I try to sound like I was pleased with the unexpected delivery, but I really can't even look at the pictures without feeling ill. "I meant to call and thank you, but I've been so busy with school just starting, you know?" My mom is shaking her head slowly as she eavesdrops on my conversation.

"My mom's the one who told me to ask you," Lily whispers. The way she lowers her voice, so Connie doesn't hear, makes me feel even worse for not loving her as much as I probably should.

I laugh. "I figured. I think all moms make their kids ask about stuff like that, Lily. Hey, is dad there?"

"Yeah, hang on. Daaad!" I pull the phone away from my ear. "Katie wants to talk to you!"

Mumbling from both my dad and Connie. "Hang on. He's coming."

"Okay, thanks." I feel like I should say something more to Lily since I can still hear her breathing, but I just don't feel like pretending today.

"Thanks, sweetie," my dad says softly to Lily. "Kit Kat?"

"Hi, dad. How are you?"

"Oh, we're good. How are you? Did you get the pictures and the letters? Lily has been asking every day if we'd heard from you."

"Yes, I got them. Thank you." *Thank you so much for the lovely, professional photo of your new family.* I feel tears forming, but my mom is now looking at me, so I work hard to contain them. She is leaning against the counter with her arms folded across her chest.

"Well, Katie, you know, it wouldn't have hurt for you to call to let us know. Not for Connie and me, of course. For Lily. You know how much she looks up to you."

School's just fine, dad. Thanks for asking. By the way, I made a fool of myself at cheer squad tryouts, and the cute new guy—the first guy I ever pictured kissing with tongue, by the way—happens to like Sloan Whitson. "I know. I'm really sorry. I've just been really preoccupied since school started."

"Alright, well, I hope you're not feeling overwhelmed. A lot of homework so far?"

I wish homework was my biggest worry. "No, well, more than last year, but not too much for me to handle."

"That's great, Katie. You've always been a good student. Yep, that's definitely something I never have to worry about with any of you girls. You're all extremely intelligent." He pauses, like he's waiting for me to thank him for the pat on the back. "Anyhoo, I assume Kelsie isn't there?"

"Nope. She's with Kyle."

"All righty, then. You'll let her know we called?"

"I will."

"Okay, love you honey."

"Love you, too, dad."

Just before the call is disconnected, I hear Lily yell, "Bye, Katie!"

Without a word, my mom goes back to picking the chicken bones as soon as I hang up the phone.

As usual, I can tell she's mad even though she doesn't say anything to me. At least a dozen questions linger in the air that separates us, causing me to feel uneasy.

She used to badmouth my dad and Connie all the time before Gary, but now she does her best to resist. Still, I have always been able to feel her pain and tension whenever she has been reminded that my father still exists, just without her by his side. She even has a hard time hiding her emotions when Gary is around. Sometimes I wish she would just speak whatever is on her mind. After all, her passive behavior isn't fooling anyone and I'm not the clueless little girl I used to be. I want to hear what she's thinking. I want her to tell me exactly why she's so angry with my dad. I know they used to fight, but I don't know why. I guess it shouldn't even really matter at this point, though, except I'm stuck seeing my mother like this whenever it concerns him. I hate it.

I open my mouth to say something, but then I hear a truck outside, prompting me to rush to the window instead. Carly is stepping down from the passenger side with her arms full of bags. Not grocery bags, though. Bags from the mall. *They went shopping at the mall?*

I bolt to the door, ready to run out and find out what's going on

(Carly hates shopping), when my mom stops me. "Where do you think you're going, Missy?" I can tell she's sort of joking, but know she's going to make me finish helping with the soup. After all, I'm the one who asked if we could make it.

"Carly's home. I was just gonna—"

"Carly can wait until we're done here. Okay?"

I peek out the window and see that they are no longer in the driveway, so I relent. "Fine. What's next?"

Once everything is chopped and added to the soup pot, I slip on some flip-flops and head to the door again. "Flip-flops? It's freezing outside today," my mom says. Then she responds to my silence by saying, "Don't be long. We'll be eating soon."

"Got it," I say with one foot out the door. I poke my head back inside and ask, "Is it okay if I invite Carly over for some soup?" Maybe we can hang out for a little while before she goes over to Sloan's. Part of me even wonders if she'll invite me. Not that I would go, but Carly is the kind of friend that would invite me knowing I would decline, just to be nice.

"Yeah, sure. That would be fine, I guess."

"K. Be back soon!"

When I get to the end of our driveway, a car pulls up in front of Carly's house. A Lexus SUV, to be exact. I watch as Amy Bowie hops out of the passenger side and heads to Carly's front door. I should have turned around and headed back inside the second they pulled up. Instead, I just stand there like an idiot, feeling sorry for myself. Then I realize that a face is staring at me from behind the tinted, rear driver's side window. Whether it's Anica or Laney makes no difference, because they're both likely in the back together waiting for Amy to return with my best friend in tow. *My* best friend. I slowly turn and head back up the driveway. My ears begin ringing, probably because they are talking about me. Before I step back inside, I glance back and make eye contact with Carly as she emerges from her house. She smiles and waves, but I pretend not to notice as I disappear inside.

"What are you doing back so soon? Where's Carly?"

I can't even look at my mom because the floodgates are about to burst open. In my very best fake pleasant voice I say, "Oh, they have company. I'll just see her tomorrow." Then I start up the stairs. "I'm going to grab a book and read a little before dinner."

"Sounds good."

Instead of going to my room, I head to the bathroom. In the back of my mind, a little voice is reminding me how much better I felt after I made myself sick last night. I stand in front of the toilet for who knows how long, looking at myself in the mirror as tears stream down my cheeks. I lick away a few that land at the corners of my mouth but let the rest drip from my jaw line onto my sweatshirt. The thought of Carly hanging out with the Orchard Hills girls is enough to initiate a gag reflex and suddenly I am down on my knees dry heaving into the toilet. All that comes up is small bits of carrot and celery. When the wave of nausea passes, I stand, flush the toilet and wash my face.

At the top of the stairs, I take three deep breaths and then descend, ready to put on a happy face. But when I get into the kitchen, my mom isn't there. "Mom?" I search the first floor of the house without luck. Then I make my way down to the basement where Gary spends a lot of time reading and playing games on his computer. As I am about to turn the corner, I hear my mother talking to Gary in an angry tone, so I freeze.

"I mean, *really*, a family photo? What do Katie and Kelsie want with that? What he should be sending is money for Katie to buy some of those clothes she wants so badly or money for Kelsie's books. God knows they have *plenty* of money."

I picture Gary shaking his head in agreement the way he always does.

"He treats Connie and that little girl like royalty and all Kelsie and Katie get is a portrait of his new family? That lousy son of a bitch never ceases to amaze me. Didn't even want me to have Katie and now he has that kid with Connie?"

"Elaine, calm down. Take a few deep breaths." Gary speaks to my mother as if he is trying to soothe a wild animal.

Dad didn't want to have me? I've never heard that one before, and it's my cue to sneak back upstairs. Gary will calm my mom down, and she will act like this conversation never happened the next time I see her.

Normally I love the smell of chicken noodle soup, but right now it turns my stomach sour. I can't imagine eating a bite of anything after hearing what my mother just said.

I look at the phone, wishing there was someone I could call. Kelsie would say mom is just mad or that it isn't a big deal. She might even make a joke about not wanting me to be born either. Dominic is at the movies with Beth. And Carly? She's hanging out with girls she never wanted to be friends with in the first place—girls she didn't understand me wanting to be friends with.

This truly has to be the worst day of my life.

~

"Kaaatie!"

My eyes snap open.

"Kaaaatiee! Time to eat!"

I remain motionless as I groggily attempt to piece together bits and pieces of the dream I have been jarred from.

I am performing on the stage of my elementary school. It's a dance routine for the talent show. I repeatedly try to get a certain move right. Muffled laughter travels through the crowd. My dad and Connie are sitting in the front row. They are covering their faces to mask that they are laughing at me. Then Carly is at my side. She touches my shoulder and directs my attention to her feet, as if it's all part of the act. Then she perfectly executes the move I couldn't get right. She is trying to save me from embarrassment. Everyone in the crowd stands and applauds. Carly takes my hand and raises it along with hers. She pretends that the applause is for both of us, but I know better. The Orchard Hills girls are on the floor in front of the stage in their cheerleader uniforms, complete with pom-poms. They are chanting, "Car-ly! Car-ly! Car-ly!"

"Katie? What are you doing?" My mom says as she opens my bedroom door.

I rub my eyes. "I must have dozed off."

"Well, it's time for dinner."

The thought of eating sickens me. "I don't think I can eat. I don't feel so well."

"What? We spent all afternoon cooking the soup you asked for. And I haven't seen you eat anything except carrots and celery since breakfast. You have to eat something."

"I told you. . ." The words come out with an unintended sassy twinge. "I don't feel good," I say more delicately.

She rests the back of her hand on my forehead. "You don't seem to have a fever."

I roll over to face the wall. "It's my stomach."

"Well, let me know if I can get you anything. Maybe you can try to eat something a little later? Gary got a movie from the Redbox. Some sci-fi action flick." I imagine her rolling her eyes and wonder what made them get married in the first place. They don't even like the same kind of movies. And that's just the tip of the iceberg as far as things they *don't* have in common. She pats my back a few times and then I hear my door slide over the carpet as it closes.

My stomach rumbles with hunger, but I ignore it and imagine Carly having fun with Amy Bowie and the others. The strange dream lingers in the back of my mind.

Car-ly! Car-ly! Car-ly!

Part II

Winter

Chapter Thirteen

The Red Owl grocery store is dead. I've only seen three other shoppers since I entered. Note to self: Saturday nights are no good for my shopping excursions.

I'm perusing Little Debbie products in aisle three with one of those hand-held baskets hooked over my left arm. The basket contains a half-gallon of vanilla ice cream and a package of Chips Ahoy cookies. It isn't enough, so I add a box of Swiss Rolls and mentally calculate whether I can afford anything else with the ten dollars in my wallet. Not likely, but I want the Nutty Bars too. My eyes jet left and then right. I take a deep breath, grab the Nutty Bars and shove them into the hobo bag resting against my hip. I eyeball the ends of the aisle again to make sure no one has seen.

Ever since my mom interrogated Gary, Kelsie and me about the missing pack of mint Oreo Cookies, I have made it a point to be more careful about what I binge on. The only way for me to continue doing what I've been doing is to buy things for myself. It started out with small amounts—like a few cookies and a bowl of ice cream in one sitting. Afterward I always throw up all the junk food along with whatever I had for dinner. My mom asked me last week why I'm suddenly taking showers at night instead of in the morning. I responded, "It isn't all of a sudden, Mom. I've been showering at night for the past three months!" That seemed to appease her.

The first time I stole food was a few weeks ago. I had been so nervous that I almost took the box of cupcakes out of my bag and handed it to the cashier, admitting my devious intentions. Instead, I did my best to purchase the rest of the junk food items in my basket without passing out from the fear of being caught. Then I rushed my way out of the store at two times the pace I normally walk.

I hate stealing, but my "habit" has become expensive, for a thirteen-year-old on a babysitter's salary anyway. After a few weeks of intentionally overeating, knowing that I would be throwing the food up anyway, it started taking more and more for me to feel stuffed. Not only is it easier to make all the food come out when I'm completely full, but the more food that comes up, the better I feel afterward.

Luckily, I've been able to pick up regular babysitting jobs on weekends. Without babysitting, I would feel even more worthless than I already do sitting home on Friday nights. It's been a long time since I've done anything with anyone. In fact, my friends hardly call me anymore. I just see them on the bus sometimes and at school.

Last night, I watched Kyle's nephew so that his sister Jane could go to a concert with him and Kelsie. I was at her place with Brandon until around one in the morning. When Kyle and Kelsie dropped me off, Jane looked at me and gasped, "Katie! Have you lost weight?"

I responded, "No, I don't think so." And that's the truth. In fact, I look at myself in the mirror every day, and I'm pretty sure I look like I've gained weight.

She cocked her head and walked in circles around me as Kelsie and Kyle waited impatiently. "Well, you look a lot skinnier since I last saw you. Has your mom stopped feeding you or something?"

"C'mon, Jane. We're gonna be late," Kyle insisted as he checked the time on his cell.

"Kit Kat, don't forget to lock the door as soon as we leave," Kelsie said as she checked her hair in the small decorative mirror in Jane's living room. "And remember, no friends."

I thought: *Are you kidding me? When was the last time I hung out with friends? Oh, wait, you're never around, so it's not like you know anything about my life.*

As they were leaving, Jane glanced back at me with what appeared to be concern and paused, as if she had something else to say. But before she could utter even a 'goodbye', Kelsie pulled her along. Not only did I close the door behind them, but I also closed it on Jane's obvious concern and suspicion.

I was glad that Jane was tipsy when she paid me—not because I was dreading her mentioning my weight again, but because I had done something horrible after putting Brandon to bed. I took five dollars out of the big glass milk jug she uses for spare change. I reasoned that I could make up for it by offering to babysit for free some night. Plus, my mom already gives her a deal for watching

Brandon during the week. But even after spending hours trying to justify my actions, I still felt like a total jerk when I came face to face with Jane at the end of the night, especially when she hugged me goodbye.

If I spend all my babysitting earnings on food, my mom will become suspicious when it comes time for me give her money to deposit into my bank account. So, I stole the change out of desperation, which left me feeling even more like binging. I went to bed last night feeling like the scum of the earth.

"That'll be nine fifty-two," the new Red Owl cashier says. He looks familiar but I can't figure out why. He is also smiling as if he knows me.

I hand him a ten and try to mask my nerves by poking at the displays of junk at the checkout counter while he retrieves my change. Gigantic lollipops, keychain flashlights, air fresheners for hanging on rearview mirrors. Even though I'm buying perfectly innocent items, I can't help but wonder if he thinks I'm going to eat all this stuff by myself. The thought embarrasses me, even though that's exactly what is going to happen. You would think I was a drug addict with the amount of guilt I am feeling.

"Here you go." He continues smiling as he drops the change into my hand. Our flesh touches for a second, and I feel an uncomfortable kind of queasy—not the kind I felt the first time I met Hunter. It occurs to me that most girls my age would feel queasy because the cashier is kind of cute, but all I can think about is being alone in my room and devouring the Nutty Bars that I am about to walk off with. I do my best to smile back before heading toward the exit.

"Hey, wait a second," he calls out.

Oh, no. Have I been caught?

I stop dead in my tracks and slowly turn to face him, expecting to see a customer standing at the counter ready to testify to seeing me shove the Nutty Bars into my bag. Thankfully, it's just the cashier.

"Aren't you friends with Selena? Kit Kat, right?" he asks.

I release the breath I had been holding since he stopped me, causing my chest to visibly deflate. "Yeah. How do you know that?"

"I'm a friend of her brother. I've seen you at their house a few times. Watched you guys play softball once, too."

That explains why he seems familiar to me, but as hard as I try, I can't remember ever seeing him at Selena's. Although, her brother Anthony is quite popular and regularly has friends over.

"I'm Nick." He reaches his hand over the counter.

I take a few steps toward the counter then lean forward a few inches to shake his hand.

"Well, nice seeing you, but I—"

"Wait, what's your real name, anyway?"

"It's Katie."

He smiles. "Katie. I like that much better than Kit Kat."

I shift my weight uncomfortably, wishing I could turn and leave without feeling rude. "Yeah, me too."

"You haven't been over to the Tropez's house lately," he continues. "Where have you been hiding?"

As cute as this guy is, I just want to leave. I'm no longer worried about getting caught, but I am concerned that the ice cream will be nothing but sugary milk by the time I get home.

"I haven't been hiding, just busy."

"Yeah? With what?" He doesn't strike me as a nosy person, just friendly. And maybe bored.

"Look, I really have to get going." I edge toward the exit and the door slides open.

"Oh, right." He removes his elbows from the counter and stands upright. "I guess I'll see you around?"

Smiling weakly, I say, "Sure. Sounds good." I am tempted to let out a scream of frustration when he addresses me again.

"Hey, Katie."

"Yeah?"

"Anthony is having people over and I'm heading over there when I get outta here. Any chance you have plans to hang out with Selena tonight?"

Selena had mentioned her parents were going to a wedding reception and that she was having some people over. She didn't exactly invite me, but then again, I have been making up excuses to avoid spending time with everyone lately. "No, not tonight. Maybe I'll see you there next time?" I force a grin.

He nods and turns his attention to a customer waiting to check out as I hustle out the door.

～

Before entering the house, I sneak into the backyard where I have stashed my backpack. I told my mom that I needed some things for the trip Kelsie and I are taking to California to visit our dad next week. She offered to have Gary drive me, but I told her I would be fine walking the eight blocks to the store. A teenage girl shopping at Red Owl on a Saturday night with a big backpack might make people suspicious. I quickly shove everything, including my hobo bag, into the backpack and throw it over my shoulder.

No one is in the kitchen when I enter, so I remove my backpack and seek out my mom and Gary to make sure they are occupied before I head up to my room.

"Hey, I'm back."

They are watching TV in the family room. My mom picks her head up off Gary's shoulder just long enough to glance in my direction. "Did you get everything you need?"

"Yeah, I think so." She used to always ask me to sit down and watch TV with them, but I haven't done that in months. Part of me wishes she would still ask. I know it wouldn't prevent me from going through with my nightly binge and purge, but it would still be nice if she asked. I feel guilty for all the sneaking around I've been doing. If only my mom would take a long, hard look at me, maybe she'd notice something was different.

"If you need anything else, add it to the grocery list. I'm going shopping on Tuesday," she says, her eyes still hooked on the movie she and Gary are watching. Then she mumbles, "God knows your dad won't . . . (grumbling) . . . if you forget something."

"Okay. I will." I wait for a few seconds to see if she will ask me to sit down with them. She doesn't, of course. "Alright, well, I'm going up to watch TV in my room."

"Yeah, okay. Night, honey."

"Goodnight, Katie," Gary says.

Before heading upstairs, I quietly grab a spoon from the kitchen.

～

It always starts out the same way. I eat the softer items first, the things that seem to come up easier. Then I move on to things that are more difficult to throw up. Peanut butter is the worst, so I avoid it unless there is absolutely nothing else. I eat slowly at first. As my stomach becomes fuller and fuller, the sense of urgency I have to get rid of its contents grows, so I start to eat faster. Most of the time I wonder why I am doing what I'm doing. I try to remember how it all started, but the only thing that comes to mind is standing face to face with Amy Bowie in the hallway that leads to the band room. Sometimes I wonder if she ever does the things I do. Does she eat until her stomach feels like it could burst and then release it all with one simple heave? Or does she simply throw up after regular meals? Whatever she does seems to be more effective than my habits, because my body looks the same (if not bigger) in places.

Sitting on my bedroom floor, I start in on the ice cream. It's melted to the point where it's the consistency of soft serve. I mindlessly shovel scoop after scoop into my mouth. With each bite, I become lost in my thoughts.

I wonder if Carly is out with her new friends. We still talk on the way to school and sometimes on the way home—on the rare occasion she doesn't have cheer practice—but not like we used to. Things just haven't been the same since she joined the cheer squad. Could this be how she felt when I was spending so much time with Anica over the summer? She has slimmed down quite a bit and seems to put more effort into dressing herself. Those aren't the biggest changes, though. Her attitude is different too. She used to tell me when she was missing her mom and when she was annoyed with her dad, but now, all she seems to talk about is reality television, music, and sometimes boys. She never mentions any of the OH girls, but when she tells me about something she did over the weekend and says "we," I know exactly who she's talking about.

Things have changed with my other friends too. Selena's brother got his license, so now he picks her and Darcy up from school most days. Selena has mentioned to me a couple of times that Anthony can give me a ride too if I want, but I always decline. Unlike Carly, who rarely asks me to do stuff on the weekends anymore, Selena and Darcy still do sometimes. Part of me wants to say yes, every time, but that part keeps getting smaller and smaller as weeks pass.

When I am down to about a quarter gallon of ice cream, I open the cookies. The first one tastes so good. It takes me back to when I used to look forward to having just two cookies for dessert after finishing my dinner. Two had always been enough. I never asked for more nor did I want more. Halfway through the cookies, I go back to the ice cream. Then I open a pack of Nutty Bars. Then another. Then another. Then I go back to the ice cream.

When I reach the desired feeling of fullness, a wave of guilt and the urgency to purge everything I have eaten overwhelms me. I quickly tie the empty ice cream container inside the plastic Red Owl bag and store them inside my backpack for disposal tomorrow. Then I hide the leftovers in my wicker hope chest. Robotically, I enter the bathroom and lock the door. I lift the toilet seat, bend over (crouching is no longer necessary) and give a little push. That's all it takes now, just one little push. Moments later, everything I have just eaten—including dinner from two hours earlier—pours into the toilet, sending splashes of water and bits of food up onto my face and the rim of the toilet bowl. I flush, clean the toilet off, and then give it another flush. Two flushes usually does it, but sometimes it takes three. Finally, I wash my face and brush my teeth.

I am ready to lie in bed and watch TV until I fall asleep.

Tomorrow will end the same way.

Chapter Fourteen

When my eyes flicker open on Monday morning, I wonder if I'm still asleep and just dreaming that it's time to start another week of school. My vision is fuzzy. I feel like I wouldn't be able to move a muscle if I tried. Then my stomach rumbles loudly, painfully reminding me that I'm alive and convincing me that I'm awake. The clock on my nightstand says I have fifteen minutes before it will scream for me to get up. I curse the thought of the sound it makes. I associate that sound with everything I wish I could avoid: my mom, my friends, teachers, the bus, pretending that there is nothing wrong with me. Life in general. And food. The funny thing about food, though, is that I love it as much as I hate it. I love that I can choose what to eat and how much to eat, or even not to eat anything at all. It's the guilt I feel after a binge that I can't stand. Because of the guilt, I sometimes find myself wondering if I control the food or if the food controls me.

My alarm goes off, but I don't move. I don't even push snooze. I just lay there wishing it would stop.

There are three quick knocks on my door. "Kit Kat? Are you getting up?" Kelsie says as she sticks her head into my room. She glares in the direction of my alarm clock, and I roll over to face the wall. I hear her shuffle across the carpeting and then there is silence.

I know she is standing there looking at the back of my head, but I don't move a muscle.

"Hey." She pushes the back of my shoulder. "Katie, get up," she says forcefully.

I moan and turn to face her. "I don't feel good."

"Again? This is like the tenth time I've had to come in here and get you up for school. What's wrong with you?" Now there is concern in her voice.

"Nothing. I told you. I just don't feel good."

"Well, if you've really been feeling sick for the last few weeks, then

92

you should tell mom so she can take you to see Dr. Crawford. You do look like you've lost weight. Is it your stomach that's bothering you?"

I don't understand why, but suddenly, I'm filled with rage. Why this sudden interest in my well-being? Kelsie is only around every occasionally, when she needs to come home to get new clothes or when Kyle has plans with friends. She has always been in her own little world and I have always been on the outskirts wishing I could join her—up until lately, that is.

I don't care anymore if we bond like other sisters—like Darcy and her sister. Selena even seems to have a closer relationship with her brother than I do with Kelsie. I used to care, especially when my mom and dad were in the thick of their divorce. Kelsie was older, so she was always hanging out with friends and sleeping at their houses. I remember crying myself to sleep some nights when my mom and dad were fighting or when my dad had moved out and my mom would send me to bed so she could cry in private. I used to wish Kelsie was there with me, either to tell me everything was going to be okay or to cry with me so that I would feel less alone. But she was never there. She got to go off into her own little world and pretend nothing was wrong at home. "My stomach is fine. And I have *not* lost any weight. I'm not *that* kind of sick," I snap.

"What kind of sick are you then?" She ignores my attitude.

I'm the "kind of sick" that makes you not want to go to school and fake being happy every day. The "kind of sick" that is caused by having your best friends practically disappear from your life—sort of like the way dad up and disappeared when I was little. The "kind of sick" that results from hearing your mother say that your dad never wanted you in the first place. The "kind of sick" that Orchard Hills types of girls with perfect families, clothes and bodies don't get.

"I don't know. I just don't feel good."

"Look, Katie. I get it. You're a moody teenager. I can relate. But you need to get your butt out of bed and get ready for school or I'm going to get mom." She threatens me with wide, demanding eyes and then turns to leave. I watch as my beautiful, skinny, smart, good gymnast/cheerleader sister walks away with a hop in her step. That's another thing about her, nothing ever seems to get her down. Even now, she seems to be in a good mood. There is no way she can relate to how I feel. Just when I think she's gone, she peeks her head back in and says, "And you better not be a drag like this when we leave for California on Friday."

It takes me another ten minutes or so to force myself out of bed after Kelsie leaves. I don't leave early for the bus anymore because Carly and I don't talk about things as much as we used to. Our relationship is different ever since she started spending more time with the OH girls. She still makes comments about them being shallow once and a while, but now she says things in more of a joking voice. I think she's really just trying to make me feel better, since she knows how much I wanted to be friends with them.

As usual, I spend way too much time examining my body in the mirror and picking out my clothes for the day. It isn't until I hear Jane saying goodbye to my mom that I realize I don't have much time left. I scurry into the bathroom, wash my face, and throw my long brown hair into a ponytail. Then I rush downstairs.

"Katie, you're late again. I swear, if you miss the bus, you're going to have to walk to school."

"Yeah, I know, mom. It's fine. I won't be late." I grab a banana just so she doesn't nag me about not eating anything.

All bundled up, I step outside into the cold. It's close to seven thirty, so there's no way Carly is still home. I start jogging up the block in the direction of the bus stop. When I turn the corner, a block of five houses separates me from the bus that has just pulled up to the curb. I am about to pick up speed, knowing that I can still catch it if I really want to, but then I just stop. Dominic and Beth (who normally doesn't even take the city bus to school) are sitting with their backs to the window. He has his arm around her. Carly is sitting opposite them, laughing. God, I feel like such an outsider.

My mom stares at me as if she's looking at a ghost when I enter the house. "What the hell are you doing home?"

"I don't feel well."

"Tell me the truth. Did you miss the bus?"

"No, well, sort of. I probably could have made it if I wasn't feeling sick."

"No, no, no, no, *no*. I told you that if you miss the bus you have to walk to school. So, get moving." She goes back to wiping Brandon's strawberry-stained hands and face.

"Mom, I don't feel—"

"Katie, I don't care how you feel right now. You have been moping around this house for weeks . . ."

I'm surprised to hear her say this because she never asked me if there was anything wrong. Not once did she even look at me sideways.

". . . I have tried to be patient, we all have. Yes, you're a teenager, so we expect some moodiness from you. But when you start wanting to miss school, that's where I need to draw the line. We both know you're not sick. Now get going."

Bitch.

Of course, I don't have the courage to actually call my mom a bitch, but I do ignore her request and head upstairs to my room.

"Katherine! *What* are you doing here? You need to go to school. Do you want me to cancel your trip to California? Because that's what I'll do if you don't get your butt to school!"

Be my guest. I don't want to see Dad anyway. And I certainly don't want to see Connie!

I throw myself facedown onto my bed.

"Katie!"

I hear the TV in the living room come to life with the sounds of *Curious George*—Brandon's favorite. Then there are footsteps on the stairs.

"What is going on with you lately? You have never just not wanted to go to school. I know you, Katie, and you are not sick. So, what is going on?"

I sit up to face her. "Nothing is going on! I don't want to go to school. Okay? I just don't want to go!" A tear streams down my cheek and I feel like a crazy person. No, it's as if I am outside of my own body watching myself behave like a crazy person.

My mom slowly sits down on the corner of my bed. "Katie. I know that you are at an age when hormones begin raging, but that is not an excuse to lose control of yourself. I'm sorry, honey, but you need to go to school. You can either walk now or wait for Ashley and Max to arrive and then I can drive you. I won't be happy about having to load the kids into the car, but I'll do it if that's what it takes to get you to school."

The only other time in my life that I have so openly defied my mom was on that first day of kindergarten when I wouldn't—couldn't—stop crying long enough for her to take the picture and I refused to enter the classroom. She eventually got what she wanted then, and she will get what she wants now.

Every ounce of defiance within me fizzles out and I stand, ready to do as my mother commands.

~

Instead of walking, I wait for the next bus. Either way, I'll get to school during the middle of first period. Or maybe I'll walk extra slow to avoid seeing Anica in first period altogether. Ugh. I hate having so many classes with her. Although, I can't remember the last time she acknowledged my existence.

By the time the bus arrives, my nose and toes are like ice cubes. The driver, who I don't recognize, sighs loudly when I have to fumble inside my bag to retrieve my bus pass, which frazzles me even more. Finally, I find the pass, scan it and stumble into the seating area. The front is full, so I set my sights on the back, where there are several empty seats. I am halfway to the back when the bus jerks forward, sending me toward the floor.

"Gotcha," I hear as someone leans out into the aisle to break my fall and steady me.

I look down at my gloves and bag on the floor and then up to meet Hunter's eyes. "Thanks," I mumble as I crouch to pick up my things.

He scoots himself all the way over to the window seat and gestures toward the now open aisle seat. One ear bud hangs over his right shoulder.

I plop myself down and wriggle as close to the aisle as possible so that not even our clothes are touching. My heart continues pounding in my throat, embarrassment over the whole previous scene. I don't think it will be slowing down anytime soon.

I haven't seen Hunter on the bus much lately. When he does ride it, he and Dominic talk mostly to each other. And ever since word got out that he officially started dating Sloan, I have avoided sitting near him in homeroom. Not that he seems to really notice.

I can feel him looking at me now, so I glance at him sideways.

I dread small talk, but to my surprise, he pops the dangling ear bud back into his ear and looks out the window. Relieved, my heart rate begins to slow and my body relaxes.

Halfway to our stop, I glance at Hunter again, wondering why he isn't talking to me. Did he move over just to be nice? Or does he still consider me a friend even though I've barely spoken to him in the last two months? His hair is poking out from under a striped gray-tone winter hat. He is wearing baggy jeans, a teal hoodie with a thick black down vest, and dark gray Vans. I sense the same feelings I felt the first time we talked to each other creeping their way back into my heart. The emotions surprise me. I have become so used to feeling nothing but numb, especially after my purges.

My eyes shoot forward when he removes his right ear bud again and shifts in his seat. *Did he feel my eyes on him?*

"I forgot to turn my alarm on last night," he says. "What about you?"

"Uh, I haven't been feeling well lately."

He nods. "Yeah, you look different than you did a few months ago."

"I do? Why?"

"You just look like you've lost weight."

Irritation quickly overshadows the tender feelings I was having only seconds ago. "Oh, well, I haven't," I say curtly. Who does he think he is, commenting on my weight?

"Crap. Did I just offend you? 'Cus you look offended. I didn't mean anything by that, Katie. Just thinking you might have some kind of stomach bug that's been making you barf your brains out or something. Plus, you just don't seem like the same girl I met in homeroom on the first day of school." He sighs and reaches for his ear bud again.

I cringe at the words "barf your brains out," but his tone convinces me that his comments are innocent. "Wait. No, I'm not offended. Like I said, I've just been feeling kinda sick lately."

He turns in his seat to face me. "Well, I hope you start feeling better soon."

"Thanks."

Leaning back against the seat, he sighs. "I'm so tired of this cold weather. You know?"

I look at him with scrunched eyebrows. "You're from Vermont."

"Yeah, so?"

"It's just as cold there in the winter as it is here."

He shakes his head. "I know. I hated the cold there, too. Someday, I'm gonna move somewhere warm. Like Arizona or California."

"My dad lives in California."

"Really? Have you been there to visit?"

"Well, yeah. He's been living there for like nine years now, so I've been there a bunch of times. But it's not like a vacation or anything when I go, because we pretty much just do normal things. Like shop, go out to eat and watch my little half-sister participate in all sorts of activities."

"Oh, that sucks. But at least it's never this cold there."

I'm not sure which part he thinks sucks, but I nod anyway.

"How old is your half-sister?"

"Nine."

"What kind of stuff does she do? Is she into baseball like you? My little sister does gymnastics and graduated from T-ball to softball last summer."

"Lily does gymnastics, too, and she dances. That's what their lives revolve around. Gymnastics, dance, dance and more dance." I roll my eyes. "She doesn't seem interested in playing softball or in anything related to baseball. Same as my big sister, Kelsie. She was a dancer, too. And a cheerleader. I'm the oddball, I guess."

"I think it's cool that you play softball and like to watch baseball." He playfully nudges my knee with his as the bus approaches our stop. "Can I tell you a secret?"

I turn my head a tad and meet his gaze. "What?"

"I'm an oddball, too. I can't even do the Macarena." I can't help but laugh when he starts flailing his arms around, like he's trying to do the moves to the popular dance. My giggles and his flailing continue as we step off the bus.

Walking next to Hunter makes me feel like a dwarf. He must be at least a foot taller than I am. And I feel something else besides just short next to him. I feel . . . comforted. And distracted from my usual self-conscious thoughts. Maybe it has something to do with the terrible dancing I just witnessed. Or maybe it's because our conversation this morning has been effortless ever since I stopped being such a defensive weirdo. Or maybe it's because it's been so long since I've talked to any of my friends. Whatever the reason, I don't want to have to stop talking to him.

So I say the first thing that comes to mind, desperate to keep our conversation going. "I always meant to ask, but never got around to it. What made your family move here, anyway?"

"My grandma is sick, and my mom needs to help my aunt take care of her."

"I'm so sorry." What else is there to say to that? We walk a block in silence before he responds.

"It's okay. She's been sick for a while."

"It must've sucked to move your last year of middle school. Right before high school, too."

He shrugs. "Nah, it's fine. I miss a few friends, but other than that . . . I'm just glad my mom can be here for my grandma. Despite what it might look like, I'm really not all that social. That's why I wanted to stay away from Amy and her friends at first, you know? Then this whole thing with Sloan got out of control. And now . . ." His voice trails off as we arrive at school. He opens the remaining unlocked door for me and then follows me inside.

What would make him want to stay away from Amy and her friends when he first moved here? And now? I expect Hunter to pick up where he left off before he opened the door, but he says nothing. *And now what?*

We both get late slips and then linger outside the office for a moment. He doesn't seem in any hurry to get to class, which is fine because neither am I. This is the first time in weeks that I've felt a connection to an actual person instead of food.

"I guess I'll see you in science?" he finally says.

We still have the same lunch schedule, but he sits with the OH girls now, sometimes stopping by to talk to Dominic. And I have spent a lot of lunch hours reading or in the bathroom lately. Sometimes I don't even make it into the lunchroom, if I can get away with sitting in a deserted hallway without being spotted by a teacher. I don't *really* see him in science anymore either, since Sloan and Anica are in there with us. But maybe . . . maybe today I'll say screw it and talk to Hunter. Whether Sloan likes it or not.

"Yeah. I'll see you then," I say, surprised at how anxious I am to see him during eighth period. Still, I know that by the time the end of the day rolls around, my heart will most likely have squeezed back into the hardened shell that now surrounds it.

Surprisingly, as I'm walking into eighth period, I realize I still want to talk to Hunter. In fact, I'm determined to go up to him and say "hi" or "hey" or whatever. Something. After thinking about it all day, I even convince myself to do it right away, so I don't lose my nerve.

Only, when I arrive in the science lab the lights are dimmed, hinting that it's going to be a video day.

So what? I can still say hi to him, right?

Instead of heading to my seat, I head toward Hunter, whose back is to me. I stop dead in my tracks when I realize Sloan has already switched seats with someone in Hunter's group, since Mr. Lentz doesn't care where people sit during videos. She's sitting next to him and staring right at me with a sneer on her face. It's almost as if she knows what I'm doing and daring me to follow through. I don't, of course. Instead, with heat spreading quickly throughout my body, I spin around and head in the opposite direction to my seat.

Sloan wins again.

Chapter Fifteen

The airport isn't very busy, but the security line is packed. I wonder how many other people are going somewhere warm like Kelsie and me. Who wouldn't want to escape the cold?

Kelsie gives Kyle another one of her dancing-finger waves and says, "God, I'm gonna miss him."

I roll my eyes behind her back. "Wouldn't it be easier if they just left? What's the point of him waiting until we get through security? So you can keep waving to each other?"

"Quit being such a brat." There's a hint of venom in Kelsie's voice. "Mom's the one who wants to stay until we get through, not Kyle."

"Make sure to call or text as soon as you girls get there," my mom yells for everyone at the security checkpoint to hear. Kelsie and I both look back through the winding maze of people to where she is standing with Kyle.

Kelsie says under her breath, "Yeah, I heard you the first fifty times."

Oblivious, mom yells out, "Okay! We're going, girls! Bye!" She and Kyle wave one last time before disappearing.

～

My eyes are closed, and the song "Demons" by Imagine Dragons blares through my ear buds. I have no idea what the song is actually about, but it reminds me of the demons I'm hiding. It ends and begins again for a third time because I have it on auto-repeat. This time, I plan to commit every word to memory. The chorus is about to start when I am jabbed in the ribs. My eyes flutter open and I find Kelsie and a slender male flight attendant staring at me. The flight attendant's lips are moving.

I yank my ear buds out just in time to hear him say, ". . . to drink?"

"What?"

"What can I get you to drink?"

"Oh, just some water please." I give him a thin smile and then glare at Kelsie, who is already back to reading a *People* magazine.

The flight attendant doesn't seem the least bit irritated. He hands me the water and then holds out a basket full of goodies for Kelsie and me to choose from. Kelsie takes a pack of M&Ms and some Cheez-Its.

"No, thanks," I say.

"What?" Kelsie looks at me wide-eyed and then back at the attendant. Reaching into the basket she says, "She'll take a banana."

She holds the banana out to me. "Mom says you haven't been eating breakfast. Eat it."

"I don't want a banana," I say, offended by her insistence.

"Katie. You look like you've lost a lot of weight over the last few weeks. And you can't possibly still be sick. Are you dieting or something?"

"I'm not dieting and I haven't lost weight. I just don't want the stupid banana." I move the fruit from my tray to hers.

"But you love bananas."

I stare at her and ponder whether she knows something. Has she heard me in the bathroom? Has she noticed remnants of food in the toilet?

She sighs. "Well, I guess you'll be extra hungry when they serve lunch then."

I am hungry. I am always hungry. But when I eat, the part of your brain that tells you you're full doesn't seem to work anymore. I can't even remember the last time I ate a meal and didn't want to eat as much as possible and then vomit everything up. There are days when I tell myself—promise myself—that I am going to eat a reasonable amount of food for each meal, but it just doesn't happen. Either that, or I simply don't eat anything at all. Since there was no telling the next time I would be alone today, I opted out of breakfast. Now, it seems I'm stuck having to eat something while on this plane. Kelsie won't have it any other way when they serve lunch. I hate that our tickets were upgraded to first class because of my dad's frequent flier status. At least with economy seats, we wouldn't have the option of a meal.

Kelsie goes back to reading *People*, and I go back to "Demons." I scan the pages of the magazine as she flips them. I used to like looking at magazines—*People*, *Entertainment Weekly*, all the various celebrity magazines dentists usually subscribe to. I used to love the "Stars, They're Just Like Us" section in *US Weekly*. Now all I think about as I look at the pages is how skinny most of the women are. I wonder how they look the way they do.

"How're you doing ladies?" The same male flight attendant who got our drinks and provided us with snacks is back.

"Great. Thanks," Kelsie replies.

I nod in agreement.

"Your choices for lunch today are a roasted chicken and red pepper Panini with pasta salad, or beef and broccoli stir fry. What would you like?" He looks from me to Kelsie and back.

"The Panini please," Kelsie says, then looks at me.

I have no choice. I need to order something. "I'll have the same."

"Katie, why don't you get the stir fry? Then we can share with each other."

I hate this about my mom and my sister. They always want to share food at restaurants—and on airplanes too, I guess. Not that I care this time, because I don't plan to eat any of my lunch, but it would be nice if I could order something just once without feeling pressured to share it. "Fine. I'll take the stir fry."

"Sounds good, ladies. Be back in a jiff with your food. Do you need anything else in the meantime?

Kelsie beams her beautiful, straight-toothed grin at him. "Nothing right now, thanks."

My stomach begins to rumble when the delicious smell of hot Paninis wafts through the air. Kelsie looks over at me, but I quickly lower my eyelids to make it appear as though I am on the verge of dozing off. When the food arrives, I pretend to be fast asleep, hoping that Kelsie will eat both of our lunches. But after a few moments, I hear her muffled voice. When I don't answer, she snatches the ear bud out of my right ear.

"Katie, food's here. Get up. You have to eat something."

I know there will be no dissuading her from nagging me about eating (when my mom gives her a task to complete, Kelsie does it), so I cut a piece of broccoli into tiny pieces and shove one into my mouth. I chew until it's pulverized into practically nothing. The intense flavor makes my stomach rumble, begging for a taste, but I am afraid to swallow. Kelsie places half of her sandwich on my napkin and then scoops half of my stir-fry onto the empty portion of her plate.

"So, what's going on with Carly? I haven't seen you with her lately."

Lately? She hasn't been to our house in weeks. "Nothing. She's busy with cheer squad."

Kelsie gives me a knowing nod.

Unless my mom told her, Kelsie has no idea I tried out. My decision to try out was so last minute that I never even had a chance to mention it to her. Then when I didn't make it, I was so embarrassed that I decided she didn't need to know.

"So, she'll be really busy until basketball ends. That makes sense. I thought maybe you guys got into a fight or something. I remember all the drama that went down with my friends and me when we were in middle school. That's when all the cat claws started coming out. Remember Jenna Beck? She became infected with a horrible case of bitchiness in eighth grade and never recovered."

Jenna used to make out with boys in our garage, too. I remember being shooed away whenever I tried to hang out with them. One time I was so mad when they wouldn't let me into the garage that I went and tattled to my mom they were "doing sex stuff" in there. My mom didn't care, or if she did she didn't show it. She was too busy crying over an argument she'd had with my dad.

"Yeah, I remember Jenna."

"What about Dominic? What's that little perv up to?"

"Would you quit calling him that, Kelsie? So he saw you in your bra and undies one time. I didn't know you were in the bathroom. I didn't even know you were home. It was an accident!"

"Well, he sure didn't act like it was an accident. Little pervert took a long hard look before asking if he could pee real quick. He didn't even look up at my face when he asked," Kelsie says, smiling.

It strikes me that this is the first "normal" conversation Kelsie and I have had in a long time. But then it strikes Kelsie that I haven't taken another bite of food, so she forgets about Dominic and hops right back on my case about eating.

"Aren't you gonna try the Panini? It's really good."

I don't want the normalcy to end, so I pick up the sandwich and take a bite. Before I know it, the entire thing is gone, along with every last bit of stir-fry that was on my plate. Then I eat a chocolate chip cookie for dessert and another when the flight attendant comes around to offer seconds. The moment the final bit of chocolate settles in my stomach, panic sets in.

Oh, God. What have I done?

I imagine the calories and fat from everything I just ate going straight from my stomach to my thighs. I imagine fat being deposited around my waist and on my butt. I feel fatter and fatter as I obsess over the food churning in my stomach. What is wrong with me? Why couldn't I just forget about this one meal?

"Katie, are you okay?" Kelsie looks at me with concern. "You're all sweaty."

That's my way out.

"I feel . . . sick. I wonder if it was something I ate."

"But I feel fine, and we ate the same things."

I clutch my stomach. "I think I have to go to the bathroom." I stand and crawl awkwardly over Kelsie's lap.

Once in the bathroom, I throw open the toilet seat and send a spray of food into the blue-liquid-filled bowl. In an instant, shame washes over me and I dread having to face Kelsie. Out of habit, I thoroughly clean the top and underside of the seat and wipe along the upper ridge of the bowl. Then I wash my hands, rinse my mouth out with water, and dab my lips and chin with a wet paper towel to remove any splotches of puke. The thought of the many other people who have used the toilet for normal purposes prior to me shoving my face into it turns my stomach. I feel like such a disgusting outcast because of this dirty little secret. When I open the door, Kelsie is standing outside with a furrowed brow.

"Katie, are you okay?" She wraps an arm around my shoulders and leads me back to our seats. "I heard you cleaning up in there. I'm guessing you threw up? How do you feel now?"

"Better, I think. But tired. I need a nap."

"Good idea. Maybe I'll join you."

~

The first person Kelsie and I see as we make our way out of the secured area at the San Diego airport is Lily. She is smiling from ear to ear and jumping up and down. If her legs weren't visible, you would think she was on a pogo stick.

"Kelsie! Katie!" Now she is jumping and clapping.

Kelsie reaches Lily first, enveloping her in a big hug and swinging her around in a circle. When she puts her down, Lily promptly turns to me and hugs me around the waist.

"You might not want to get too close to Katie, Lily. She's sick," Kelsie says.

Lily only hugs me tighter, making me smile and hug her tighter right back. After all the hugging commences, Kelsie and I both look around expectantly.

"Where's dad?" I ask Lily.

"He couldn't come because he had some important work to get done . . ."

Dad already working the day after Christmas? Go figure.

My mom used to complain all the time that he could never slow down. Of course, that's why he's as successful a sales person as he is. I'm sure that's one thing that keeps my mom angry at him, the fact that she stopped taking classes to earn a marketing degree so that he could fast track getting his undergraduate and master's degrees in business. Now some other woman is enjoying the rewards.

". . . but my mom is over there." She points toward a bank of charging stations.

Connie's cell phone is glued to her ear and her lips are moving a mile a minute. When she pauses to listen to whomever she's talking to, she smiles briefly and waves at us. Then she goes back to talking and begins pacing.

Kelsie doesn't seem nearly as annoyed with Connie's half-assed welcome as I am. She is already walking Lily over to a Starbucks for a Strawberry Frappuccino.

"You coming, Katie?" She calls over her shoulder.

"No, I'll wait here." I take the nearest seat, giving me a clear view of Connie to my left and Kelsie and Lily to my right.

A few girls who look around my age have gotten into line behind Kelsie and Lily. They look like typical California girls with bleach-blonde hair, waif-like physiques and a laid-back style of dress. What I envy most is the way they are smiling and laughing with each other. The way they all take turns talking animatedly reminds me of the way things used to be with my friends and me.

"Katie!"

I turn my head to see Connie standing next to me, arms outstretched as she waits for me to stand and give her a hug. She is not even close to being on my list of people I would worry about if there was ever a zombie apocalypse, so hugging her hello is the last thing I want to do. I stand anyway, smile politely and approach her for the anticipated hug. She pulls me in quickly and releases me with a few pats on the back. Then she holds my hands in hers and raises my arms out to my sides to give me a good onceover.

"Katie," she says hesitantly, "you look . . . different. Have you lost weight?"

I look down at myself and then back up at her, not even trying to mask my irritation. I don't understand why people are so focused on my weight lately, and I can't tell if Connie is asking because she is concerned or impressed. Either way, I am annoyed. I open my mouth to answer, but then Lily's voice interrupts.

"Mommy, you told me that it's not polite to talk about people's bodies."

"Oh, sweetie, as long as you don't mention negative things about the way people look, it's okay to talk about their appearance," Connie says as she walks over to Kelsie for a hug.

Lily takes my hand and whispers, "You look pretty, Katie."

I smile down at my sweet little half-sister and then back at Connie just in time to catch a concerned expression on her face.

～

The thirty-minute drive to my dad's house makes me wish even more that we'd never come. Kelsie sits in the front with Connie and the two of them jibber jabber like long lost pals. I don't understand why Kelsie is trying so hard to be nice to Connie. We used to talk about the role Connie may have played in our parents' divorce. At one time, Kelsie was adamant that it was all Connie's fault. She called her something like a no-good, slutty, home-wrecking mistress, even though we both knew our home was already in the early stages of destruction before my dad even met her.

While Kelsie and Connie bond, I am forced to listen to Lily tell me all about her wonderful, activity-filled life. She is spoiled rotten by Connie (and my dad by default), which makes me both envious and ashamed. Envious because since the age of seven, I wanted to be the one spoiled by my dad (or my mom). Ashamed because it isn't Lily's fault she gets everything most little girls dream of, including the luxury of living in an unbroken home.

By the time we pull into the circular driveway, all I can focus on is the desire that has been building up inside of me to stuff my face and then puke it all up. Anything to relieve this feeling of sadness I can't escape.

While we are unloading our suitcases from the trunk, my dad appears on the porch with Dill, Lily's Golden Retriever. "Girls, you made it!" Kelsie and I approach him, but Lily beats us to a hug, as if she doesn't get enough of his attention as it is.

"Hi, Dad!" Kelsie says as she hugs my dad, who is still holding Lily.

Then it's my turn, but as he lowers himself to me, I can feel his eyes scanning my body.

"Katie . . ." The look on my dad's face is a mirror image of Connie's when she scrutinized me at the airport. "Honey, you look a bit skinnier than the last time I saw you. More grown up, too."

He eyes me again and then glances over at Connie, who averts her gaze and quickly shifts into activity-director mode. "Well," she says with a clap of her hands, "let's get moving. We've got some Christmas presents to open and I should get to work on dinner. Busy few days ahead!"

～

We spend the rest of the day doing Christmas all over again. Kelsie and I both get some new outfits and gift cards. Lily opens gifts too. Apparently, she wanted to save some to open in front of us. It takes her longer to open her remaining gifts than it takes Kelsie and me to open ours. I cannot begin to imagine how many she opened the day before on Christmas morning.

DON'T CALL ME KIT KAT

After presents, Connie disappears into the kitchen and Kelsie follows her. Lily busies herself making friendship bracelets for Kelsie and me, leaving my dad and me sitting in front of the TV together.

"So, Katie, tell me what's been going on in your life."

"Nothing much. You know, school, homework. That's really about it."

"What about weekends? I remember when Kelsie was in middle school. She always had stories about going to the mall with friends, attending school dances and having sleepovers. All the cheer squad stuff, too. Oh, and the boys." He shakes his head and breaths a chuckle through his nose. "Come on. Spill it. What have you and your friends been getting into?"

I can see in my dad's eyes that he expects I am doing all the same things Kelsie used to do. This tears me up inside. It makes me feel like I am not living up to my father's expectations. Why wouldn't I be happy-go-lucky and outgoing like the rest of my family members? The way I used to be. Even after that first day of kindergarten when I knew my dad would probably never be there to drop me off at school—not because he was working but because he physically wasn't going to be living with us ever again—I managed to put on a happy face for everyone. Up until recently, that is.

"Okay, fine." I force a fake smile. "Carly and I have been hanging out at the mall a lot and going to movies. I've also gone to a couple dances. And there's this new guy—a Yankees fan—who I talk to a lot in homeroom. He's kinda cute." I shrug, ignoring the fact that Hunter is dating Sloan. And that I hardly ever talk to him. "Other than that, you know, Mom's always telling me to get off the phone. She's such a pain." *Does that sound normal enough for you, dad?*

"Well, that's great, Katie." He pats my knee. "Sounds like you're doing well. Looks like you've been exercising too. Maybe you could go out for track next year. That was my thing, you know?"

"Yeah, I know."

When Connie and Kelsie fill the dining room table with snacks, I remind everyone that I am not feeling well, and no one makes a fuss over it. But by dinnertime, I am starving.

"Here, Katie." Kelsie shakes a basketful of dinner rolls in front of me. "Pass the rolls."

I take it and pass it to Lily immediately.

"Don't you want one?" Lily asks.

"No, I'm still not sure I can eat."

"Don't be ridiculous, Katherine. Connie spent two hours preparing dinner. Be polite," my dad says. The way he uses my full name tells me he might be fed up with hearing me say I don't feel well. Even though we've only been here a few hours. When I was little, he used to make us sit at the table until every last bit of food on our plates was gone.

"Have you considered that you might not feel well simply because you haven't eaten anything since you got here?" Connie adds.

Kelsie huffs. "Try since yesterday."

"What?" Connie tilts her head. "Katie, you haven't eaten a thing today? No wonder you look so pale and sickly. You have to eat something." She plops a scoop of mashed potatoes onto my plate.

"That's not true. I ate on the plane," I say defensively. My heart rate increases as I watch Connie add a scoop of Brussels sprouts.

"Yeah, but you threw it all up, remember?" Kelsie says with a mouth full of food.

Connie adds a few more Brussels sprouts.

"Katie, you can't go an entire day without eating," my dad says as he adds a few slices of turkey to the growing pile of food on my plate.

Lily adds a roll, and Kelsie looks at me intently. So intently that I am certain she is becoming suspicious.

"I can't. I don't . . . I *told* you guys. I'm not feeling well."

My stomach rumbles loud enough for everyone to hear, causing all movement to cease.

"Katie." Kelsie's voice is shaky, as if she might cry. "I'm starting to worry about you. Can you *please* eat something?"

I look from face to face—all reflecting concern.

I pick up my fork. "Fine."

The first bite puts me in a trance. I chew slowly and consider spitting each bite into my napkin and feeding it all to the dog, like in the movies. But everyone is taking turns watching me eat. By the third or fourth bite, the mood seems lighter and Kelsie is talking about Kyle and her plans to move in with him. Instead of adding to the conversation, I methodically finish the rest of the food on my plate and picture myself in the bathroom throwing it all up.

Since I have zero privacy at my dad's house, I can't throw up in the toilet because Lily could walk in on me. Or someone might be standing outside the bathroom and hear me. The only safe place for me to get rid of the food I just ate is in the shower. No one will invade my privacy in there. I sneak a plastic bag from the kitchen into my toiletry bag, which I place on the ledge of the tub in between the two shower curtains. With the water running, I throw up into the bag as quietly as possible. Then I wrap my dirty clothes around the tied bag. Later, when everyone is asleep, I bury the bag in the kitchen garbage.

∼

For the next four days, I do my best to avoid eating anything for breakfast that might tempt me to binge. Cereal, for instance, is one of the most comforting things to devour and puke up. Same with pastries, like donuts. I stick with a piece of dry toast and orange juice, which is especially unpleasant coming up due to the acidity. I take the same precaution during lunch, except for on the two days that we eat out. I have no problem sneaking away to relieve myself in the bathroom after eating like a champ then. After I make sure the bathrooms in the restaurants are singles before indulging, of course. Then I use the same plastic-bag-in-the-shower technique each night to relieve myself of dinner. Everyone seems satisfied with my appetite, and I am certain Kelsie is no longer worried or suspicious.

On the last night of our visit, Kelsie, Lily and I decide to play German Shepherdopoly—the dogified version of Monopoly. Instead of buying properties, players purchase German Shepherds, and instead of the Electric Company and Water Works, players can purchase the Butcher Shop or Fire Hydrant.

Dad and Connie are in the kitchen cleaning up the dinner dishes. He's whistling—"Fur Elise" by Beethoven. The sound takes me back to when I used to follow him around outside when he would do yard work. He always whistles when he does work around the house. I am about to roll for doubles to get out of the Kennel when I hear Connie yell in a disgusted tone, "What the heck is *that*?"

The whistling stops.

My heart sinks, remembering she had just mentioned to my dad that the garbage was full. I hope and pray that her disgust isn't because she's found what I think she's found.

"Girls?" We all look up to see my dad standing in the doorway. "Can you please come in here for a moment?"

"But Daddy," Lily whines, "we're playing German Shepherdopoly."

"Sure, Dad," Kelsie says as she takes hold of Lily's hands and pulls our half-sister to her feet.

I say nothing, silently praying that they have not discovered my plastic bags as I follow my sisters.

When I set my eyes on the torn, leaking garbage bag, I almost pass out.

"Can any of you explain this?" my dad asks firmly.

"What is it?" Kelsie is leaning down close to Connie who is wearing rubber gloves and examining the contents of the garbage.

"Maybe Dill did it, Daddy." Lily bends down to search for her dog under the kitchen table. She doesn't understand that our dad is referring to the leakage, not the fact that the bag is torn.

Connie holds up the vomit-filled bag that is still intact for my dad to see.

"Is that . . .? Katie?" Kelsie looks up at me and everyone else follows suit.

My chest is visibly heaving and I have broken out into a cold sweat. They must know the answer based on my body language alone.

"Why are you guys blaming, Katie? She wouldn't rip the garbage bag apart. Dill did it, Mom." Lily moves to my side and grabs onto my hand. Then she looks up at me. "I know you didn't rip the garbage bag."

"Kelsie, take Lily to her room." My dad's voice is steady, but his face looks worn.

Kelsie does what he asks without question and without looking at me even for a second. As they walk out of the kitchen and through the living room, Lily asks, "Is Katie in trouble?"

Connie stands and heads to the cabinet for a new garbage bag. "I better get this mess cleaned up." Her personality is the opposite of my mom's. My mom would be hysterically firing questions at my dad and me, trying to dissect the situation. A lot of people say that opposites attract, but taking my mom and dad into consideration, that theory is crap. It occurs to me now for the first time ever that Connie is a much better fit for my dad.

My dad rakes the fingers of his right hand back and forth through his short hair several times before looking at me. His eyes are cloudy, either with tears or anger, I can't tell yet.

"Katie," he inhales deeply, "how long has this been going on?"

I know exactly what he means but I dodge his question. "I felt sick after dinner the last two nights, but I didn't want to hurt Connie's feelings if someone heard me get sick in the bathroom, so I—"

"Stop!" my dad yells. Now his chest is heaving.

Connie removes her gloves and rushes to his side. "Dale, maybe you should—" He waves her off without even looking at her.

"How *long* has this been going on? And you know damn well I'm not talking about this mess here!" He nods toward the vomit soaked trash on the floor.

My dad has never raised his voice to me like this before. Part of me is scared, but the little girl inside of me feels a certain sense of satisfaction. *His attention is all on you, Katie.*

"Look at you, Katie!" A few tears break free from the clouds and trickle down his whisker-covered cheeks. "Look at you," he whispers.

I know he is not literally telling me to look at myself, but I do anyway. I gather that he must think I've lost weight just like Connie, but I don't see it. I don't think I look any different than I did when school started.

It occurs to me that seeing my dad cry should make me feel bad. It should probably even make me cry. Instead, I feel nothing. No, that's not true. I still feel a small twinge of satisfaction. This realization is what causes the tears to start streaming down my own cheeks. *You are a horrible daughter, Katie.*

"How about if I make some tea and we all sit down at the table to discuss this?" Connie's voice is gentle and for the first time in eight years I feel like she's on my side.

"What is there to discuss? I'm feeling better now. I'm—"

"That's it." My dad grabs his cell phone off the counter. "It's time for me to call your mother."

"NO! Wait." I put my hands up as if I am casting a spell to stop him from moving another muscle. "I promise. I just haven't been feeling well. I'm better now."

I look to Connie with pleading eyes, willing her to help me stop my dad from calling my mom, but she just sighs and gives my dad a look that says she knows I'm lying and the hatred returns. My dad continues holding the phone, finger poised on the talk button, and looks from Connie to me. Then he puts the phone back down on the counter.

I let out a long, relieved breath.

"I'm going to trust your word here, Katie. But I intend to check up on you." *No, he won't.* "If Kelsie tells me you've been throwing up or that you've lost more weight, I'll have no choice other than to talk to your mother about monitoring you and your diet more closely. Understood?" I imagine this is how my dad must sound when he is making business deals.

Connie is staring at the floor and has a clenched fist to her mouth, as if it's the only thing containing her thoughts.

"Okay, Dad. I understand. But I really am feeling better." I want to believe that I can just stop doing what I've been doing. That I can will myself to just be 'better'. But I don't know if I can. Not anymore. My habit has become something I do day in and day out, like brushing my teeth or going to the bathroom. "I promise. It won't happen again."

Chapter Sixteen

I am tempted to kiss the ground the moment we step off our flight. Kelsie attempted several times to discuss my "food problem," as she referred to it, but I dodged the topic every time. She even forced herself to stay awake just so I wouldn't go to the bathroom without her. After eating lunch, I tried to crawl over her when I thought she had nodded off. But she got right up after me, even after my extra-careful maneuvering, and followed me to the bathroom. Her threat to listen with an ear to the door had been effective, so now I am dying to get rid of whatever is left in my stomach.

Before we step onto the escalator that leads to baggage claim, I feel Kelsie's hand around my wrist. She tugs, and I turn to face her.

"Katie, you can talk to me, you know? Always. Any time."

"I know," I say to the floor.

"Why won't you tell me what's going on? Have you really been feeling sick for the last few weeks? Is that why you've lost so much weight? Why you threw up at Dad's? Or is it something else? Do you have, like . . . an eating disorder or something?"

"Yes, I've been sick. Yes, I assume that's why everyone seems to think I've lost weight. Yes, I threw up at Dad's because I felt sick. And NO, I do not have an eating disorder." It's not a lie. I do feel sick. Just not the kind of sick I want her to believe I've been.

"Then you *have* to tell Mom. She *needs* to take you to the doctor."

"But I'm better now, remember?" I want to scream. Instead, I stand there. Willing her to drop the subject. *All of this over a leaky trash bag.*

Kelsie searches my eyes for a glint of truth that I know isn't there. "You're too skinny," she says before lowering her head, shaking it the way a doctor on TV would to indicate a patient hadn't made it. Then she boards the escalator to baggage claim, where my mom and Gary are waiting for us.

As soon as I see the look on my mom's face, I know this isn't over.

~

The interrogation begins as soon as Gary enters the ramp onto the freeway.

My mom takes a deep breath and lets out a long sigh. "I talked to your father this morning, Katie."

Kelsie's fingers freeze on her phone screen and she looks up. Apparently, she's more interested in whatever my mother is about to say than texting Kyle.

"Elaine, are you sure it's the right time to discuss this?" Gary eyes me nervously in the rearview mirror.

My mom looks over at him, eyes wide as saucers, "When do you suggest a better time would be? After she's withered away down to nothing but bones?"

Kelsie exhales loudly as she brings a hand up to cover her face.

"Elaine," Gary hisses.

"What? Look at her, Gary. I think now is the perfect time. We need to put a stop to this nonsense."

When my mom first said she'd talked to my dad, I was shocked. But now, as she discusses me with Gary as if I'm not even here, I simply don't care. Even something like this, something *about* me, isn't enough for her to include me in the discussion.

"Kelsie? Did you know your sister has been vomiting up everything she eats?" My mom unbuckles and turns all the way around in her seat to look at Kelsie. Not me, Kelsie.

"No, of course I didn't. I just found out just like you."

Finally, my mom looks at me. "When did this start?"

I think to myself, "I don't know," but the words don't come out. I simply stare at her.

"Katie! When did this start? How long have you been making yourself throw up?"

I hate you, Dad. You said you wouldn't tell her.

"Katie! Answer me!"

"Mom, quit yelling at her!" Kelsie barks. She is met with a cold stare from my mom.

"She's right, Elaine. That's enough for now. Let's just get home and give Katie a chance to collect her thoughts. We can talk later." Gary glances at me again, looking even more concerned than before.

As soon as the car comes to a stop in the driveway, I unbuckle and scurry to the door. The only thing on my mind is getting to a bathroom. Everyone knows now, so I don't even care if they hear me.

My mom searches for the right key as I impatiently watch Gary and Kelsie get our suitcases from the trunk.

I never imagined before how my mother would react if she found out about my vomiting. But now that she knows, it seems perfectly normal that she's angry. If she was the kind of mom to hug me and tell me how sorry she is that I'm so messed up, I might not even be where I am now. Sad. Sick. Angry.

As soon as the door opens, I shove past her and run upstairs to the bathroom.

"Katie!" she calls after me.

It has been a couple of hours since I ate on the plane, so it's difficult to get anything to come up at first. Bending over and giving a little push doesn't work after food has been in my stomach much longer than thirty minutes. So, I have to resort to shoving fingers down my throat. The memory of my mom yelling at me in the car mutes the sounds of her voice coming from the other side of the bathroom door. Even her heavy knocks are drowned out by my thoughts. I don't hear myself gagging either.

It takes several deep prods with two fingers before my gag reflex is tickled. I am disappointed when just a few chunks of apple come up, along with digestive juices that burn the back of my throat and leave my tongue and the insides of my cheeks numb. I try again. And again. Finally, my stomach is empty and I feel better. The only problem is that my mom is still knocking and yelling at me to open the door.

"Katherine! What are you doing in there? Katherine, open this door! NOW!"

With defiance boiling up inside of me, I pull the door open quickly and brush past my mom, clipping her in the arm with my elbow. She chases after me and slams her palm into my bedroom door when I try to close it in her face. Kelsie and Gary are hiding out on the stairs, probably afraid to get in my mom's way.

"Leave me alone!" I yell.

"Leave you alone? You just made yourself throw up in there." She gestures toward the bathroom. Then she continues in a less intimidating tone. "And you want me to leave you alone? Sorry, Katie, not gonna happen. You need to tell me what's going on." She waits a few seconds for a response that she isn't going to get. Then she reaches out, as if she wants to give me a hug, but I back away. Her lips tighten into an almost invisible line as any sign of compassion disappears from her beautiful face. "Tell me what is going on, right now!"

There's the Mom I know. The one who can't stand to not be in control. Maybe that's why my dad left. Because her love and kindness seem to be conditional, based on whether or not people do what she wants them to do. "Nothing is going on! I just felt sick, okay?"

My mom shakes her head and is ready to blow her top again when Kelsie steps into the room and puts a hand on her shoulder. Gary is leaning against the doorframe, eyes to the floor and hands in his pockets. I imagine he is probably wishing he could be in the basement playing one of his stupid computer games, but he knows my mom would be pissed if he didn't stand there and pretend he cared about what was going on.

"Katie?" Kelsie's voice is soft, as if she is speaking to a scared child.

"What?" I sneer.

"I believe you when you say you're sick. I just don't think you have the kind of sickness that goes away by itself."

For some reason, her statement hits me like a line drive to the chest. Or maybe it's the gentleness in her tone. I have a *sickness*. The kind that doesn't go away by itself. Suddenly, all the anger and defiance that has been building up inside of me deflates and I am sobbing.

My mom and Kelsie rush to my side and try to hug me, but I push their arms away and plop facedown onto my bed. Despite the emotional situation, the thought of being embraced by both Kelsie and my mom unnerves me. We rarely hug in my family, it would just be uncomfortable now.

I feel hands rubbing my back. One hand traces my spine and then my ribs, causing me to roll over and pull myself up into a sitting position. I hug my knees tight to my chest and realize for the first time how skinny I really have become.

Judging by the look on my mom's face, it was her hand that felt the bones protruding through my skin. Her glossy eyes are searching my bedspread for answers. "I need to make dinner," she says in a monotone voice, without blinking. Then she turns and leaves. Gary follows.

Kelsie slowly climbs onto my bed and sits facing me, her legs crisscrossed. The entire time her eyes are facing downward and she is chewing her left thumbnail—a bad habit that she'd broken years ago. Minutes go by before she finally looks up at me and calmly says, "Tell me why, Katie."

So, I tell her, purging myself of everything that I've been holding inside ever since my run-in with the Orchard Hills girls at the beginning of the school year. I tell her about how much I wanted to look and dress like Amy Bowie. How I would stand in front of the mirror wishing I could change the shape of my body. How much I envied her for being born with mom's physique. How embarrassed I was at cheer squad tryouts and how jealous I was of Carly. Then I go on about how much I hate myself for being jealous of Lily. And I almost tell her that I wished our mom and dad had never gotten divorced, but then I realize that that's not how I feel at all. It doesn't bother me that they're divorced. What bothers me is that neither of them made any attempts to make sure we were okay. It was all about them. Neither of them once asked me how I felt about the whole thing.

Kelsie agrees with me about that part and we both cry. For the first time in months, it doesn't take puking my guts out to feel a sense of relief.

When I'm done telling Kelsie about all the negative emotions I've been bottling up, she asks how the throwing up started.

"I don't know."

"Katie, please, it's okay. You can trust me," she says, as if I'm lying.

"I'm serious. I don't remember." It's the truth, I don't. But I do remember hearing Amy Bowie throwing up twice in the bathroom outside the band room. I can't tell Kelsie that, though. I said I wouldn't, and I won't, even if Amy and her friends don't like me.

"I don't get it. How can you not remember?" There's a twinge of irritation in her voice, causing me to stiffen.

I begin crawling back inside myself, and the urge to binge and purge creeps back into my brain. "I don't know. I just can't."

"Well, you're done making yourself throw up. I'll sleep at home until I'm sure you aren't doing it anymore. Okay?"

She thinks it's as easy as telling me I'm done. That I can just stop. For her benefit, I wish that it were. But based on the thoughts that are running through my head, even now, I just don't see how it's possible. "Okay," I say anyway.

Kelsie's phone vibrates for the umpteenth time. She pulls it out of her pocket and starts texting, as if everything is back to normal.

Chapter Seventeen

"Katie! Time to get up!" Kelsie calls from the bathroom.

She must have come home late last night. Funny how she vowed to sleep at home to keep an eye on me and then ended up spending most of the weekend off doing things with Kyle anyway. Does she think I make myself puke in the middle of the night? Wouldn't it make more sense to be around when I'm awake?

I reach over to turn off my beeping alarm clock just when Kelsie storms into my room with a towel wrapped around her body and a matching turban on her head.

"Oh, good, you're up. How are you feeling?"

"Okay, I guess." *Just dying to get out of the house and away from all of you watching me.*

Other than when I snuck off to pocket a box of laxatives while grocery shopping with my mom, the only time I've had alone since Kelsie and I returned from California has been when I'm sleeping. But even in my own bed, it isn't exactly private because my mom made Gary remove my bedroom door. The bathroom door, too. It's like I'm at a minimum-security prison.

What's even more annoying is that my mom has constantly been offering to make me something healthy to eat, even though I explained to her that when I eat, I have a hard time stopping—even if it's something healthy. I know she means well, but it's frustrating to have to keep telling her the same thing.

After Kelsie and I had our heart-to-heart, we went downstairs and I explained to Kelsie and my mom what it's been like for me. The way the binging and purging has become normal, like brushing my teeth. Or how after I eat, I can't think about anything but the food churning around in my stomach, just waiting to be absorbed by my body. I explained how it actually hurts. How my chest feels like it's going to explode if I don't get rid of the food.

My mom suggested that I simply eat smaller portions. She also invited me to work out with her the last three days in a row, to keep my mind off food. One time, Kelsie said under her breath, "Yeah, invite the bulimic who's already skin and bones to exercise. Great idea." That was the first time I ever considered that I might be bulimic.

We read a chapter about eating disorders in health class last year. That was it, one chapter. I'd forgotten about it until Kelsie mentioned it. I guess that is what I am, though—bulimic.

I know Kelsie never intended this with her comment, but reminding me of bulimia also reminded me about how we learned that some people use laxatives to purge their bodies of food. It was like a light bulb going on in my head. I knew that even though throwing up isn't an option anymore, I can still control how quickly food is flushed out of my body by taking laxatives. Finally, something I learned in school was going to come in handy.

The first time I used them, I was careful to read all the instructions. I took two capsules—the recommended dosage— shortly before dinner. Halfway through a plate of stir fry, my stomach gurgled loudly, causing me to panic. I glanced from my mom to Gary, expecting them to be looking at me suspiciously. But neither one seemed to notice, so I continued to fork bits of chicken and vegetables into my mouth.

Later, my mom seemed pleased as we loaded the dishes into the dishwasher. "Katie, I am so proud of you. This is the first time since you've been home that you've eaten everything on your plate." She hugged me tightly, and I couldn't help but feel bad for duping her—for leading her to believe that I was okay with eating the healthy dinner she'd worked so hard to prepare. In reality, I was focused on the quiet churning in my gut. I swear I could feel the food rushing its way through my digestive system.

By the time we had the kitchen cleaned up, I couldn't wait any longer. I clutched my stomach. "Mom?" I said, bending over theatrically, "I don't feel so good. I think I ate too much."

She followed me to the bathroom and waited in the doorway with her back to me as I sat on the toilet. "I suppose your digestive system needs time to readjust to taking in normal amounts of food." She peeked at me over her shoulder.

"Yeah, I guess so," I said, amazed at how perfectly the laxatives had worked.

After washing my hands, I continued clutching my stomach as if I was in pain, but I really felt fine. I felt as empty as throwing up always made me feel.

That's when laxatives became my new go-to when throwing up wasn't an option.

Later that night, I ended up working out with my mom. It felt good to do something with her, even if all I did was walk on the treadmill while she worked up a sweat on her Stairmaster.

We kicked off New Year's Eve with another workout session. Kelsie even joined us. Then Kyle came over and we had dinner and played cards. Afterward, Kelsie and Kyle took off, leaving me alone to wait for the ball to drop with Gary and my mom. Had I not downed two laxatives before dinner, it would have taken every ounce of willpower I had to not sneak off and throw up what little food I'd eaten that night.

In fact, if it weren't for the laxatives over the last four days, I would probably be ready to explode by now.

"So, you're going to tell Carly and Dominic today?" Kelsie looks at me with more concern than I'm comfortable with.

I sit up, swinging my legs over the side of my bed. My stomach sours at the thought of my friends finding out what's going on. But I also know telling was part of the agreement I made with my mom.

"Yeah, I guess so." I concede. "If I get a chance. Who knows when I'll be alone with either one of them, though. Beth is glued to Dominic's hip, and Carly is always busy after school now that she cheers." I realize that Kelsie is just staring at me, like a disappointed mother trying to get her toddler to tell the truth. "I really don't see what the big deal is." I continue. "You guys know now. Isn't that enough?"

Kelsie sighs. "I understand why you wouldn't want to tell them, Katie, but Mom is right. You need support. Your friends need to know what you're going through."

But what am I going through, exactly? Even I can't explain it very well. I just felt how I felt and feel how I feel now. Sometimes I don't even know how I feel anymore, because my mind has gotten so used to focusing on gorging myself and then getting rid of it all. Whatever feelings I happen to be ignoring at the time included.

"I think you're going to be surprised by how much of a relief it will be. Then they'll understand why you haven't been hanging out much lately. And why you've lost so much weight. They've gotta be wondering what's going on."

Rising to my feet, I sigh. Since when is Kelsie an expert? "Yeah, probably. Are you done in the bathroom? I have to shower."

~

Running to catch the bus, I nearly slip on a patch of ice. *Damn it, mom!* The banana she just forced me to eat is churning in my stomach and threatening to give me heartburn. And now I think I pulled a muscle in my crotch.

As I round the rear of the bus, I catch a glimpse of the last person boarding. Hunter. He hasn't ridden the bus to school for a few weeks, except for the one day before break when we were both late. I wonder if he'll be sitting next to someone or if the seat next to him will be open. Part of me hopes he is sitting next to someone, because then I won't have to deal with deciding whether or not I should sit next to him. Would he even want me to sit down next to him? Plus, my other friends will probably be on the bus. What would they think if I sat next to Hunter instead of one of them?

After scanning my pass, I make my way to the back where they all normally sit. I can't even bring myself to look up, so I gaze at the floor and out of the corners of my eyes at all the strangers as I pass. When I finally do look up, they are all there. Selena is sitting next to Darcy. Dominic is next to Beth Grumley—she takes the city bus all the time now that they are obviously dating, even though Dominic says they aren't. And Hunter is sitting next to Carly. They are all too busy talking to each other to notice me slide into an empty seat two ahead of Carly and Hunter.

Even though I feel invisible, relief sets in because I don't have to answer a bunch of questions about my trip to California. Would they even ask, though? I haven't had very many meaningful conversations with any of them lately. I don't even think the conversation with Hunter before winter break would have happened if we hadn't both just been in the same place at the same time. And the rest of them—my close, childhood friends—they don't ask me much anymore.

Sometimes I feel angry that they no longer ask why I never want to do anything on the weekends anymore. In fact, they have even stopped calling altogether. Now I just see them in school and sometimes on the bus. Other times, I remember that I'm the one who started telling my mom and Gary to tell them I was busy, even when I never was.

Carly and I never even talked about our argument in the bathroom at the first school dance. I tried to apologize for snapping at her and acting like a baby, but she just said it was no big deal and changed the subject. She doesn't seem as lighthearted anymore, and she's dressing differently now, too. More girlish. It's like she's transforming into a larger replica of an OH girl. She even wears her hair in the same low pigtails that Amy wears sometimes. And she's lost weight. Not as much as I have, but enough to get more looks from the boys. I've seen it and I'm jealous of her for it. For being on cheer squad. For being "in" with the OH clique, even if it's mainly for cheer squad stuff. And most of all, I'm jealous right now that she's sitting next to Hunter. Or am I jealous that Hunter is sitting next to her? I'm not sure. I just feel out of place and extremely jealous right now.

"Katie?" I hear Carly say, followed by a tap on my shoulder.

I turn and look over my shoulder. Hunter is sitting upright and leaning forward a bit. Carly is smiling and waving. "Hey, guys." My lips are smiling, but I am far from happy.

"We didn't see you get on," Carly says. "How was California? How's your dad?"

The grey-haired man sitting in the row behind me removes a reusable shopping bag from the seat directly behind me, the one separating Hunter and me. "Would you like to sit here so you can be closer to your friends?" he asks.

I must not answer quickly enough, because Carly answers for me, saying, "Thanks! That's so nice of you!"

The man nods and gives me a cautious grin, as if he has realized I probably don't want to be close to anyone. "Thank you," I say, as I take the seat next to him, with my legs out in the aisle and my torso twisted so that I can face Hunter and Carly.

"Look at that tan," Hunter says with a grin.

"Yeah, Kit-Ka . . . I mean . . . Katie, has always tanned easily. Not like me. I turn the color of a lobster after five minutes in the sun." Carly laughs.

I look down at my arms and shrug. "I didn't even realize I'd gotten that much color, but I guess I see myself everyday, so it's harder to—"

"Kit Kat!" Dominic yells.

Now they all see me.

"Hey, Kit Kat," Selena says.

Darcy and Beth smile and wave.

Selena and Darcy go back to talking to each other, but Dominic is out of his seat and asking Hunter to switch seats before I can blink.

So now I'm facing Dominic and Carly, and Hunter is trying to talk to Beth, who is sulking.

I give them a generic rundown of my trip to California, leaving out all the dramatic stuff—for now, anyway. And then I lie and tell them that I'm sorry for not calling them when I got back, but that I had to babysit on New Year's Eve and then my mom had me busy helping her with some organization projects around the house all weekend. Neither one of them seems to care much; they just go on telling me about the things they did over break. Carly talks about how they spent Christmas up north and how her dad's side of the family joined them there from out of town—Arizona and Texas. Dominic tells me he was stoked about the season pass he got to a local ski park. He went skiing and snowboarding several times, once with Beth. He also talks about how he would have gone even more, if he didn't have to work.

Sitting there, talking and laughing with them like this is all normal, I realize that I miss my friends.

"And what about New Year's Eve?" I ask. "What did you guys do on New Year's Eve?"

Dominic gives Carly a sideways glance.

"Oh, I just went to a small get-together at Laney's. It was no big deal," Carly says with a shrug.

She thinks I care. And she's right. I do. I can't help it. I wish I didn't, but I do. If she's still walking on egg shells around me whenever she mentions hanging out with her cheer squad group, then how will she treat me when she finds out about this whole eating issue I have going on?

"Oh, cool. What about you, Dominic?" I do my best to look calm and laid-back, but my chest feels heavy and I'm wondering if there's anything I can eat in the bathroom when I get to school.

"Well, Hunter and I . . . we hung out at that party for a while. Then, I went over to Beth's around ten. My mom and dad actually let me stay out 'til midnight for once. Can you believe it? Of course, my dad showed up to pick me up at like twelve 'o nine."

"What party? The one at Laney's?" I try to sound like I'm not that interested. Bile is creeping its way up my esophagus.

"Yeah. You know how Sloan's always wanting to hang out with Hunter. That was the only way I could hang out with him. If I went over there for a while, you know?"

I am about to tell them to stop worrying so much about telling me when they do things with those girls—mostly because it makes me feel like even more of an outcast to have them treating me like my feelings are too fragile to handle it—but the bus comes to a stop.

Hunter walks next to me as we walk the rest of the way to school. He tells me how good I look with a tan, "Not that you don't look good without one," he quickly corrects, before asking how my trip was. I give him a brief rundown, then he tells me about how his family had a movie marathon on Christmas Eve and Christmas day. We are laughing together, recalling scenes from *National Lampoon's Christmas*, when Sloan steps in front of us, cutting off our path. She's wearing a stiff, closed-lip grin. Her eyes roam slowly from Hunter to me and then quickly back to Hunter. The rest of my friends are still walking. I think about catching up with them, but Sloan's presence makes me so nervous that I stay put.

"I thought you were taking the school bus today?" she says to Hunter.

"Nah. I decided to meet Dominic at the city bus stop. Haven't seen him since Laney's party."

He seems irritated with her, which makes me wish I had cut out sooner.

"Dominic, huh?" She has a hand on her hip now, and she's glaring at me. "She sure doesn't look like Dominic to me. She's *way* too skinny." And then, under her breath, she says, "Gross skinny."

Gross skinny? My face is on fire, even though it's less than thirty degrees outside.

"Sloan," Hunter hisses. I imagine myself vomiting the banana I ate for breakfast right onto her UGGs.

At the same time, I hear Carly calling, "Hey! Guys! What's the holdup?"

The sound of her voice gets me moving. I accidentally brush against Sloan's arm as I scurry around her.

"Watch it!" she says. Her tone would make a dog whimper.

I hear Hunter say, "Why would you say something like that?" His voice trails off as I break into a jog to catch up to the others.

"Dang, Kit Kat. Quit running before you drop another pound," Selena says.

"*Selena,*" Carly looks at her with wide eyes.

"What? I'm just joking. But she's obviously lost a lot of weight." Her eyes lock with mine. "How much weight have you lost since school started, Kit Kat?"

I am so sick of being called Kit Kat!

I shrug. "Not sure. Five pounds, maybe?"

Dominic, Beth, Carly, Selena and Darcy all stare at me for what feels like hours without saying a word. Finally, Dominic takes a deep breath and opens his mouth to speak, but then the bell rings. Now it's so noisy that it would be nearly impossible to hear him.

As I enter the building, I peek back over my shoulder to look for Hunter. I'm met only with a cold stare from Sloan. She's with the rest of her clique, but Hunter is nowhere to be seen.

~

Hunter is leaning against the wall just outside our homeroom. He looks at me apologetically. "Hey."

"Hey." I walk past him into the room and he follows.

As soon as we sit down, he says, "I'm sorry about Sloan. She's really not that mean." He rolls his eyes to the ceiling for a moment, pondering his claim. "Well, most of the time she's not that mean."

I raise my eyebrows at him.

"Honest." He holds up three fingers. "Scout's honor. I just think she's jealous."

"Of what?" I couldn't hide my shock if I tried.

"Of you."

"Whatever."

"No, seriously, whenever I have plans with Dominic, she asks if you're going to be there."

"Well, have you told her that I don't really hang out with Dominic anymore? And why would she care if I was there anyway. You guys are like . . . boyfriend and girlfriend. Right?"

He shrugs.

"What does that mean?" I mock him with an exaggerated shrug.

"I don't have anything in common with Sloan. I don't care about shopping, clothes, Instagram, Pinterest. Oh, and Snapchat? What is that, anyway? So, I've told her a few times now that I think we should just be friends."

"Really? Well, I'm pretty sure she didn't hear you, because she seemed to think she's still your girlfriend."

"Yeah, that was awkward. Hey, can I ask you something?"

"Sure."

"What Sloan said earlier . . . about, you know, how skinny you are?"

"Yeah?"

"Well, after you left . . . she said you must have like . . . an eating disorder or something. Is she right? Do you?"

I let out a breath. Not a sigh, exactly. Just a slightly bigger than normal breath. The one I had been holding while I waited for him to spit out what he wanted to say. I realize I have been staring at the table but have no idea for how long. Could be seconds, could be minutes. I am too busy to pay attention to time, too busy wondering if I should tell him or not. I feel like Hunter might be someone I can trust. But then again, I don't want him to look at me differently. I don't want him to think I'm crazy.

"Katie?"

I look up at him and shake my head. "No, of course not. I felt sick for weeks, remember?" I won't binge anymore. I will get better. So, there's no reason to tell him. Maybe I don't even have to tell Carly and Dominic. Maybe I can convince my mom to give me a chance to prove that I can stop before she tells my friends and before she goes blabbing to anyone else.

Hunter lets out a huge sigh and his chest visibly deflates. He says, "That's what I told her. That you just had some kind of stomach bug for a while. So, tell me more about California. Did you do any surfing when you went to the beach?"

With each word, each smile, each laugh from Hunter, I start to feel better inside. Less self-conscious, less lonely, less like an outcast. Maybe getting caught wasn't so bad. Maybe I just needed my family to know that I didn't make it through all the fighting and feeling ignored without scars. Maybe I just needed my family to pay a little bit of attention to me, like when little kids do something naughty because they want attention.

As we leave homeroom, Hunter touches my lower back and grins at me before heading off in the opposite direction. My head and chest feel warm, and my stomach feels tingly, in a good way though. For the first time in months, food is the farthest thing from my mind. I just feel good all over.

Chapter Eighteen

I arrive late to gym class the next day because I want to avoid changing in front of anyone. On Monday, I could feel eyes all over my body. Every time I met someone's gaze, she would look away quickly. But even Carly looked a few seconds too long.

I never noticed the stares before the whole fallout with my family. I just don't get it. When I look at myself in the mirror, I still see the pooch, the rounded cheeks, the stocky legs and the way my thighs rub against each other. I've been dealing with the dislike I have for my body by covering it with clothes that are too big for me. Until I started getting the stares in gym class, I thought maybe the baggy clothes were what was making everyone think I look so skinny.

Last night, I got into an argument with Kelsie because my mom caught me sneaking food from my dinner plate into a plastic baggie on my lap. I've been using this technique when I'm low on laxatives. If I can't throw up what I eat or make my body crap everything out, then I'd rather not eat anything at all. Too bad I got caught.

Kelsie screamed at me when she found out. "What the fuck, Katie? I'm getting really tired of this shit." I assumed she must have had an argument with Kyle, because she hardly ever swears like that. When she realized that the harsh tone in her voice and the swear words had no effect on me, she dragged me upstairs to the full-length mirror in my room. "Look at yourself," she ordered.

So, I looked, but at my feet. "NO." She grabbed the underside of my chin, tilting my head up so that I was looking straight into the mirror. Then she kept a tight grip so I couldn't move my head. "*Look* at yourself. Look how skinny you are." I could see that I'd lost a little weight, but I didn't think I looked nearly as skinny as other girls at school.

Touching the exposed skin of my chest, she said, "Look at your bones." But all I could see when I looked at my chest was that my boobs were the same size as they were two years ago. *What bones?*

"You are *too* fucking skinny." Kelsie finally said. At that point, my mom showed up in the doorway. To my surprise, she told Kelsie to let it go. Then both walked out of my room. I was stunned. I had no idea what to think. Was my mom done policing me? Was she too disappointed to even deal with me? The next morning, she didn't even insist that I eat breakfast. She just said good morning and went about her business taking care of Brandon.

Everyone is already lined up for warm-ups when I step into the gym.

I can feel eyes on me as I hurry to my spot. Why do I always feel like someone is watching me? Am I just paranoid? Or is it because all this talk about how skinny I am has my brain paranoid that *everyone* has an opinion about my weight.

Or maybe everyone really does think I'm too skinny.

We are working on basketball skills today. Dribbling back and forth, doing layups, that sort of stuff. I suck at basketball, so I am less than thrilled. We number off and I end up in a group with Laney Britt. Carly is with Amy and Anica. Sloan looks pissed that she doesn't have one of her buddies with her. What a whiner.

Of all the possible scenarios, being in a group with Laney is one of the least threatening. The best would have been having no one I talk to or worry about in my group, but how often do things ever turn out the way you want them to? At least Laney is a star basketball player, so she seems to forget all about her friends when we're on the court. She is in let's-just-do-this mode. I can tell she couldn't care less *who* is in her group. She just wants to excel at the drills, and she wants others to do well, too. She's a natural born cheerleader.

When I accidentally kick the ball across the gym mid-dribble, Laney yells, "That's okay, Katie! Hustle to it! That's right! Hustle!" She's not the only basketball fanatic, either. A lot of girls are cheering for each other. When I bend down to pick up the ball, a foot flies in front of my face and it disappears back in the direction I came from. I bolt upright and come face to face with Sloan, who is waiting for her turn to dribble.

Stupid bitch, I think to myself.

"Oops. Sorry. Didn't realize that was yours."

I glance over at my group. Someone else has already started dribbling her way across the court. Laney is picking my ball up.

I picture myself slapping Sloan across the face, the way I remember my mom slapping Kelsie once. Then I picture myself hovered over a

toilet barfing my brains out, which calms me down enough to turn and
trot back to my group.

"Skinny bitch," I hear Sloan mutter.

Near the end of class, we get to scrimmage one of the other four
groups. My bad luck puts us against Sloan's group.

We all work up a sweat running back and forth, jumping, faking and
blocking. I know there are only a few minutes left in class, because I
have been checking the time religiously. So far, so good, though. Not
one encounter with Sloan. At least, not until she plows into me,
elbowing my ribs as she goes up for a layup. Clutching my throbbing
side, I drop to my knees.

Everyone but Sloan stops moving, and a few people crouch down
next to me to see if I'm okay. Sloan continues to dribble the ball, passing
it through her legs. She even dribbles down to the other end of the court
for another layup.

"Hey, that was a foul!" Laney yells to no one in particular.

"No, it wasn't," Sloan counters.

No one else says anything, probably because Sloan doesn't exactly
have a nice-girl reputation.

"*Yes*, it was." No one but Laney, that is. "You elbowed her for no
reason. She wasn't even blocking you."

Sloan rolls her eyes as Mrs. Johansen blows her whistle, letting us
know it's time to head to the locker room. Then she dribbles over to put
the ball away. Laney follows her, still complaining that the last shot
didn't count, oblivious to me still sitting on the floor. Anica and Amy
run to catch up with them. The rest of my group starts walking away,
too, but Becky Donovan and Sarah Whittle stay to help me up. Then
Carly appears.

"What happened to you?"

"Sloan elbowed her," Sarah says.

"You mean on accident?"

Sarah gives her a look that says, *are you kidding me?*

～

"Hey, Sloan!" My heart drops into my gut at the sound of Carly's
voice.

Sloan freezes with her hand gripping the dial on her locker and looks over at Carly. When she sees me, a smirk spreads across her face.

"What was that all about?" Carly asks.

I'm busy trying to spin in my locker combination, but I have to keep starting over because my hand is shaking. I know that everyone around us is surely listening, based on the hush that has traveled through the locker room.

"What was what?" Sloan tilts her head, as if Carly is a child who has just asked a silly question. Then she goes back to opening her locker.

"Why did you bump into Katie so hard? I heard she wasn't even blocking you." Carly looks around for Sarah and Becky, but they are nowhere to be found.

Sloan rolls her eyes with a huff. "I *did not* bump her. Besides, what's it to you?"

"For starters, she's my friend and I don't appreciate the way you've been treating her. And secondly, I'm sick of the way people walk on eggshells around you. Even the girls on the squad act like they're afraid of you."

"Okay, okay. That's enough." Amy steps in between Sloan and Carly. She has her arms outstretched and a palm facing each of them, clearly worried that something physical might happen. "It was an accident, right?" she says, looking at Sloan.

"That was *not* an accident. It was an intentional foul." Laney is still looking at the situation from a game standpoint. This earns her a dumbfounded look from Amy. Even Anica sighs heavily.

"Hey, it's not my fault she's such a skinny ragdoll. Maybe if she put on some weight, she wouldn't fall over when someone bumps into her." Her eyes scan Amy from head to toe. "She's even skinnier than you."

Skinny ragdoll. Her words remind me about Hunter asking if I have an eating disorder. Could Sloan know? Is it possible that Amy told her clique-mates that I probably make myself throw up? If anyone would be able to tell, it would be her. I glance at Amy, but she doesn't look too pleased with Sloan. No, she wouldn't tell them anything like that. Then they might wonder how she would know such a thing.

"I thought you didn't bump her!" Carly is pissed.

"Ladies! What's going on here?" Mrs. Johansen's voice booms. But instead of waiting for an answer, she taps her watch and says, "Let's get a move on. Bell's about to ring."

Sounds in the locker room go back to normal as people get back to freshening up and changing their clothes.

Amy whispers something to Carly. Carly responds loud enough for everyone to hear. "Whatever. I'm not gonna let anyone—not even Princess Sloan—treat her like that."

∽

Carly and I have to part ways now. I'm off to Spanish, and she's off to choir. People are moving all around us, hurrying to get to various classes.

"Thanks," I say.

She nods. "You know, Katie, just because I'm on cheer squad with Sloan doesn't mean we're friends."

Now that the door is open, I take advantage.

"Then why have you been hanging out with them so much? Even when you're not at a game or doing other cheer stuff?"

"Because I actually like the others—Amy even—and those girls come as a package. So, I do my best to put up with Sloan. Plus, you disappeared on me for a while there. Who was I supposed to hang out with? Selena and Darcy and all their new friends? When I saw you Monday on the bus, I got the feeling you might be back. Not back from California, but you know, back-back."

I want to tell her how jealous I am of her and those girls. I want to remind her how she used to call her Amy Boney. I want to try to explain why I have "disappeared" and how hard it is for me to be embarrassed like I was today and not feel like puking my guts out. I want to tell her that I want to be back, but I just don't know how.

But the hallway is starting to clear, and the bell is about to ring. So instead I just say, "I get it. I'll see you later, okay?"

A slight frown curls up into a cheesy Carly grin. "Yeah, okay. I got a game after school, so I'll see you tomorrow morning on the bus."

∽

"Hey, sweetie. How was school?" My mom still sounds like she's walking on eggshells around me. "And why are you home so late?"

"School was fine. I decided to stay for some of the basketball game."

Both lies.

"Really? That's great! I'm glad you're starting to hang out with your friends again. Have they been supportive since you told them what's going on?"

"Um . . . yeah." Worried that the hesitation in my voice might have tipped her off, I wait for a response. But she doesn't say anything, so I move toward the stairs. "Well, I'm going to get started on my homework. When will dinner be ready?"

"Fifteen minutes. Oh, and your dad left a message for you." She nods toward the phone, her hands holding alfalfa sprouts under the running faucet. It's almost as if things are back to normal. Maybe she really is done watching me like a hawk.

This is the first time my dad has tried to call since our visit. We've only been back a week. Normally, it would take him at least two to call. I guess he must still be concerned about me, since he made the effort to call sooner. Still, if he was so concerned, would he have waited an entire week?

Before I listen to the message, I run up to my room and quickly shove boxes of Twinkies, cupcakes, brownies and laxatives—three of which were stolen—into the gap between my bed and the wall. That's where I really went after school, to the grocery store. Nick was there again, but I wasn't nearly as nervous facing him this time. Just like last time, he flirted with me. But all I wanted to do was get the heck out of there. The sooner I could get home, do my homework and eat dinner, the sooner I could go to bed and relieve all the stress that's been building up inside of me over the last week.

He did stop me as I was about to pass through the sliding doors and asked if I planned to go to Anthony and Selena's party on Friday night. I had no idea they were even having a party, but was too embarrassed to admit it. So, I just said I wasn't sure.

My head is still swimming with snippets from the basketball court and the locker room, and my ribs are still kinda sore. I want nothing more than to tear into the snacks right away, but there's no time right now. Plus, my door still hasn't been put back up. It has to be after dinner, when everyone is busy getting ready for bed.

I don't argue when my mom loads my plate with an extra-large helping of veggie lasagna because I have plans to get rid of whatever ends up in my stomach tonight anyway. I can eat the snacks in bed while I pretend to read and watch TV. If I mute the TV, I will be able to hear someone walking up the creaky stairs. I can hide whatever I'm eating under the covers.

It's not really the binging that's the issue, though. It's easy to eat stuff without people noticing. Throwing everything up is the tricky part because more than one flush will be suspicious to my mom and Gary. It has occurred to me that maybe I could just puke in the sink, but I'm worried the sink will get plugged.

My mom is surprised when I have a second helping of lasagna. "Wow. That's the most I've seen you eat since . . . well, in a very long time."

Gary eyes me suspiciously, but remains silent as usual. If he thinks I might try to puke it all up, why doesn't he say something? Does he think it's not his place since I'm not his real kid?

Every bite fills the holes left inside of me, some created today by Sloan's insults and dirty looks. Some of the bites even fill the spaces that are beginning to widen once again now that my mom seems to be loosening up on me, almost like she's tired of putting forth so much effort to control my eating issues. Even though the constant attention she had been giving me was kind of annoying, part of me liked it. Having her eyes on me all the time reminded me of when I was a little kid, when she really cared. She always used to watch me and dote on me. Before my dad left, that is.

After dinner, I plow through my homework. I know I'm probably doing it all wrong. The only thing on my mind is my bloated stomach and the sweets waiting for me in my bedroom. It's times like this when I almost feel possessed. My thoughts are beyond my control and all I feel is an urge: an urge to purge. But not before I fill myself up completely—make myself whole.

I fake a yawn as I pack my math book and notebook into my backpack. "I'm gonna head upstairs to veg out for a while before bed. See you guys tomorrow."

"Yeah, okay honey. Night." She doesn't even look up from scooping the leftovers into a Tupperware.

"Night, Katie." Gary finally speaks, but he stares after me suspiciously, making me wonder if he is going to voice whatever he's thinking to my mom.

I rip off my dirty clothes and throw on sweats and a T-shirt. Then I quickly wash my face, turn on the TV, and climb into bed.

The box of cupcakes is under the covers with me. One by one, I unwrap them and shove chunks into my mouth. My bed will be full of crumbs, but my need to binge is stronger than my worry over making a sugary mess.

There's one cupcake left and I have a mouthful when Gary appears in my doorway, nearly causing me to choke. I can't say anything, because then he'll know there's something in my mouth, so I pretend to be asleep. The only lighting is the dim glow of the TV, so I'm hoping he didn't see that my eyes had been open.

Please don't look next to my bed. Please don't look next to my bed.

Gripping the almost empty box under the covers, I repeat the chant over and over until I hear him start down the stairs. It must have taken him a while to sneak up, because I didn't hear a thing. Oh, God. What if he heard the wrappers? No, he would have said something.

I am too scared to eat the last cupcakes, so I place the box back with the rest of the stolen desserts and then hide the bag in my wicker chest. Now, to the bathroom.

It takes me a good five minutes to get there because I have to tiptoe. If I make a sound, Gary might come back. *Why is he still off work, anyway?*

Finally, I am in front of the bathroom door. My plan is to throw up in the sink and then pour water from a hidden two-liter bottle down the drain to rinse it out. That way they won't get tipped off by the sound of running water.

I lean over the sink and give a push, releasing a stream of liquefied chocolate cupcakes. *A few more heaves, and I'll be done.* I prepare for another push.

The phone rings.

More cupcakes come out, but they are mixed with chunks of lasagna.

The phone rings.

I pour just enough water to clean the sides of the sink and rinse the chunks down. It's dark, but the light streaming in through the window allows me to see shadowy pieces of food clinging to the edges of the sink stopper. I pour the water a little faster to wash it down.

"Katie! Your dad is on the phone!"

Shit. Oh, shit. I forgot to listen to his message. Shit. I'm not done throwing up.

"Katie!" The hall light comes on. Footsteps on the stairs.

The two-liter bottle goes back under the sink. I pull down my pants and sit on the toilet.

"Katie, where are you?" The sound of my mom's footsteps is now heading toward me. "What are you . . . why are you sitting on the toilet in the dark? Wait a second . . . Get up!"

I do as she says and lean against the sink, hoping to block her view, just in case I missed any of the chunks. My mom peers inside the toilet, her face inches from the seat.

"There's nothing in there," she says suspiciously.

"I know. I'm . . . I'm constipated. Maybe 'cause my body is getting used to the changes I've made lately. With food, you know?"

She scrunches her eyebrows together and hands me the phone. Then she heads back downstairs.

I let out a huge sigh and then bring the phone to my ear. "Hello?"

"What was that all about?"

"It was nothing. Mom just found me sitting on the toilet and wanted to know why. That's all." I realize how ridiculous it sounds when I say it. Suspicious over me sitting on a toilet. It must feel weird to my mom to have to worry about such a thing. Then again, at least she doesn't have to wonder if I'm sneaking out of the house. Or worse yet, sneaking boys in like Kelsie did when she was my age.

"Why were you sitting on the toilet?"

"Uh . . ."

"Never mind, never mind. Dumb question. How are you, Kit Kat? You didn't call me back."

"I know. I got home late from school, and—"

"I know. That's great! You hung out after school at the game! Your mom told me."

Mom told him? So, they talked to each other? For some reason, this realization makes me feel a little less like putting my dad on hold to finish what I started. "Yeah, it was kinda fun, I guess."

"Well, good. You don't know how good that makes me feel. I worry about you Kit Kat. Connie and Lily worry, too. We want you to be happy and healthy."

"I know, Dad."

"Anyway, that's great. So, things are getting back to normal, huh?"

Yes—like magic—things are getting back to normal. If you say so, Dad. "Mm-hm. Getting there. I'm trying. Well, and I have no privacy, so that helps."

"Well, good. Good, good, good."

Right, good.

"So, I just wanted to check-in and see how you're doing. Oh, and I'm sorry it took so long. It has been a very busy week. You know, with the holiday and then with me not working at all those few days after Christmas?"

"I know. It's okay. I understand."

"Okay, Kiddo, well, I've got to get going here. Gosh, I wish you'd called us back earlier. Lily wanted to talk to you but she's in bed now. Being back at school after such a long break has really tuckered her out. So, anyway Kit Kat, I love you, and I'll talk to you soon. Okay?"

"Sounds good. Tell Connie and Lily I said hi."

"Will do, sweetie. Love you."

"Love you, too."

Phone still in hand, I finish throwing up every last bit of veggie lasagna. Then I turn the water on full blast to wash out the sink since my mom already knows I'm in the bathroom.

Sure, things are back to normal.

Chapter Nineteen

C ould there be something wrong with my mirror? Is it too high? Or maybe too low? Is it the lighting in my room?

No matter what I wear or which way I turn, my body still looks frumpy, and the flab at my midsection taunts me. Giving up, I throw on an oversized sweater and return to the mirror for another look.

"Katie! Carly's here!" My mom calls.

Carly? I throw a dejected look at my reflection and hurry downstairs.

"Hey, what're you doing here?" I ask Carly.

"We haven't walked to the bus stop together in a while. We should start doing that again. You ready?"

Throwing on my puffy silver coat, I smile and nod. Then I head to the fridge to grab my lunch.

"Hold on," my mom says, "You're going to eat something, right?"

"I'm good mom," I say, slipping my boots on.

"No, no you're not. You need to eat something. I'm sorry, Carly, but Katie will have to meet you at the bus stop. It's important that she eats at least a little something for every meal. You know, with her issue?"

I want to slap my mother.

"What issue?" Carly looks from my mom to me and then back at my mom.

"You didn't tell her what's going on?" Instead of apologizing for putting me on the spot, my mother seems angry.

"What? What's going on?" Carly asks, a frightened look spreading across her face. "Is something wrong with you, Katie? Are you sick? Is that why you've been avoiding me?"

"No, I'm not sick." I grab a banana from the counter and bore into my mother with evil eyes. "I'll just have a—"

"What do you mean you're not sick? You promised you were going to tell Carly about what's going on. You need the support of your friends if you are going to stop making yourself throw up."

Carly stares at me with huge eyes. "Making yourself throw up?"

"Yes, she's been throwing up everything she eats," my mom says, while I long to just run out the door. "For months. She was supposed to tell you and Dominic. She needs help. We thought having it out in the open might help. That maybe you guys could stop her from doing it."

"Let's go," I yank Carly out the door and slam it, my mom yelling after me.

"That's it! I'm making an appointment for you to see—"

"Katie, why . . . what—"

"Look, it's not a big deal. I was sick. I went through a few weeks where I felt nauseous every time I ate. I've been feeling better since I got back from California. My stupid dad told my mom I had an eating disorder. Like he'd know, even if that was the case." I barely recognize my own voice. It's as if my lips are moving on their own. My brain is on autopilot as it spews out these lies.

"When did it start?"

"What do you mean *it*? There is no *it*. I just explained to you that I wasn't feeling well. My mom is blowing things out of proportion."

"I know I'm not as smart as you, Katie. Book smart, I mean. But I'm not stupid. When did it start?"

We are directly across the street from the bus stop now. I hear the muffled sounds of Dominic and Hunter calling to us, drowned out by the thunderous sound of my heartbeat. Why does it sound like my heart is in my head?

I split open the banana. "I have to eat this before the bus gets here. And I know you're not stupid."

"*Katie*, when"

I ignore her and cross the street. The only things on my mind are the sound of my heart beating in my head and the bits of banana filling up my empty stomach.

Dominic and Hunter are busy discussing some X-Box game when Carly and I join them. I am grateful for the distraction. Carly even seems to forget about what my mom said, her furrowed brow loosening and a few laughs escaping as Hunter and Dominic tease each other about their user names.

When the bus finally arrives, I squeeze in next to Hunter in the second to last row. I will eventually have to talk to Carly, but it can't be right now. Not in front of other people and not right before school. Selena and Darcy are already in the very back row—the long one with five seats across—so Carly and Dominic sit next to them. No Beth today.

Hunter is telling me about his grandmother's upcoming eightieth birthday party. I'm trying to concentrate on what he's saying—something about his mom and aunt arguing constantly because they can't agree on anything and how this will probably be his grandma's last birthday—but one of my ears is listening to Selena. She's talking about the party at her house tonight, the one she still hasn't invited me to.

"Beth is fine. Just don't tell anyone else, okay? Anthony already told way too many of his loser friends about it."

"Cool. We'll probably show up after the movie then. You going, Carly?"

"I wish I could, but I already have plans with some of the girls from cheer. Unless—"

"Uh-uh. Don't even say it. You're not bringing those squad friends of yours to my house, Carly. No offense, but—"

"Fine. Forget it. I don't understand why everyone can't just get along." Carly has a little huff in her voice.

Darcy lets out a pft. "Really? We're supposed to hang out with girls who walk around with their noses in the air? And one of those biatches deserves a slap in the face for elbowing Katie in the ribs."

I had no idea that Darcy and Selena even knew about the elbowing incident. If they know, the whole school probably knows.

"That was *Sloan*." Carly says in a hushed voice. Probably out of consideration for Hunter, who glances over his shoulder at the mention of Sloan's name. He quickly turns back toward the window and blows on it, creating a steamy circle. "They aren't all like that. Amy is actually nice."

"Whatever," Selena says, "if you want to come, cool, but they're not invited."

"Hey, Kit Kat," Dominic says, squeezing my shoulder.

Cringing at my stupid nickname, I glance back at him. "What?"

"Are you going to Selena's tonight?"

I scan the faces of my friends, all of them waiting for me to respond. I haven't done anything with any of them in months, except ride the bus. Is that why Selena didn't invite me? Because she assumed I wouldn't want to go anyway? I can't tell from the expressionless look on her face.

"Uh, yeah, I think I'll be there."

"Really?" Selena and Carly say in unison.

"Yeah." My stomach knots up immediately. Why did I say I'd go? *Because you want to get better, Katie.* "It's been forever since I hung out."

Dominic grins from ear to ear. "Cool. Hey, you can come to the movies with Beth and me if you want. Hunter, you could go, too."

I catch Selena elbowing Dominic right before Hunter looks back in their direction.

"Nah, man, I have this family thing going on. My dad's boss is taking us out to dinner and then I have to watch my little sister while my parents go out after."

I didn't know Hunter had a little sister. The thought of him babysitting for her makes me feel warm inside. I want to ask about her when he turns back around, but the bus has arrived at our stop.

We all walk in a clump the rest of the way to school. Thankfully, Selena and Darcy are on either side of me and Carly and Beth are bringing up the rear when Sloan steps in front of Dominic and Hunter. Not a chance I'll be left behind to listen to their conversation.

Just before we move past them, Carly whispers, "Bite your tongue, Selena." Then in a normal voice, "Hey, Sloan."

"Hey, Carly," Sloan says, keeping her eyes on Hunter and ignoring the rest of us.

"Have fun, dude," Dominic says to Hunter as he joins us.

When I glance back, Hunter locks eyes with me. Then, of course, Sloan whips her head around to meet my gaze.

∼

"Okay, dude. Spill it. What's up with you and Psycho Sloan?"

Hunter chuckles. "Psycho Sloan. That's perfect. Says it all."

"Why don't you just break up with her?" Beth asks as she runs her fingers through her curly auburn hair.

I catch Dominic staring at her lips as she talks. Then our eyes lock and his cheeks turn pink, even before he has a chance to look away.

144

Hunter glances at the other two guys who are sitting at our table. They're discussing football and appear to be oblivious to Dominic's Psycho Sloan question. So Hunter leans in and says, "I tried, but she keeps acting like I never said anything. I even told her this morning that she's starting to creep me out. She laughed and just kept talking about how her mom said I could go over to their house to watch a movie tomorrow night. I'm starting to wonder if she needs a hearing aid or something."

"Sounds like you need to bust out your pimp hand, dude."

"What the hell are you talking about? Do you even know what that means?" Beth has an amused look on her face.

I grin, thinking about how it used to be me who would call bullshit on Dominic. Now it's Beth, almost like he has replaced me with her. My grin fades and I continue to do what I do everyday at lunch. I pick apart my sandwich, creating the illusion that I'm eating it. The only thing that goes down my throat, though, is water.

"Of course I know what it means!"

Dominic and Beth continue with their playful banter, and the topic of Psycho Sloan is nearly forgotten. Until Amy Bowie shows up at our table.

"Hey, Hunter, can I talk to you?"

"Uh-uh. Not right now."

I am shocked that he is trying to blow Amy off. Judging by her raised eyebrows, Beth is too. Dominic and the other guys are snickering though.

"It'll just take a sec."

"Fine," he says, standing with a huff.

They move over to a secluded corner, and I try not to watch.

"Those girls are so lame. As if it isn't enough that Sloan won't leave Hunter alone, now she's got Amy bothering him too. If one of them can't get what she wants, then all of the others have to jump in and try to help?" Beth looks at me when she says this, but I just continue to pick at my food.

"Who knows and who cares?" Dominic says. Then, rolling an apple into my torn-up sandwich, "So, what time are you going to Selena's?"

I shrug, not even sure I'll go at all. "Not sure. Around eight, I guess."

"Well, call me if you decide you want to go to the movie with us. Your dad wouldn't mind picking Katie up, right?" He asks Beth.

"No, of course not," she says sweetly.

Dominic looks back at me. "Call by six thirty if you change your mind."

It occurs to me that if I force myself to go to a movie with Dominic and Beth, then I won't have to show up to the party by myself. "Okay, maybe I will."

Instead of heading off to whatever class she has after lunch the way she normally does, Beth walks with Dominic and me all the way to our math class. She stays between us and even tries to hold his hand. When Dominic says, "C'mon, Beth, quit being all touchy feely with me," she gives me an embarrassed, angry glance, making me feel like it's my fault he doesn't want to hold her hand. *Great, now Beth has a problem with me, too?* I can't help but feel uncomfortable.

I am about to follow Dominic into the classroom, but Beth tugs on my backpack. "Hey, Katie."

"Yeah?"

"Could you do me a favor and not come to the movie with us tonight?"

"Uh . . ." Heat spreads up my neck and into my cheeks. "Yeah. No problem."

"Thanks." She does her best to sound appreciative. "See you at the party."

"Yeah, at the party," I say to myself because Beth is already hurrying off to her next class.

Chapter Twenty

"C'mon, Katie! If you want a ride to Selena's, we have to go now or we'll be late for our movie."

You don't have to go, you know. You can just stay home. And you'll be all alone, so you can . . . I turn my back on my own reflection and the thoughts that are racing through my head. I can't be alone. I shouldn't. It's too dangerous.

Hunter and I were the only ones on the bus after school. He filled me in on his conversation with Amy, where she tried to talk him into continuing to date Sloan. Beth had been right, I guess. None of them can take 'no' for an answer; not for themselves, or anyone in their clique. But Amy also got a 'no' from Hunter. He doesn't want to date Sloan anymore. "Period. Case closed," he told me.

Then he asked me if I wanted to see a movie with him tomorrow night. Oh my God, I swear that butterflies were going to explode out of my ears. Could this really be happening? Could Hunter really be asking me out?

The problem was, I had to say 'no' because I'm babysitting. The bigger issue was that all the butterflies were accompanied by fear.

I'm afraid to go out with Hunter because of Sloan and her clique. Those girls already dislike me enough. Going out with him would give them even more of a reason, on top of whatever else they hate so much about me. It scares me to think about crossing them.

I didn't want Hunter to think I'm not interested, though, so I told him that maybe we could see a movie some other time. He said he was going to hold me to that.

We sat there talking some more, and I started to feel like he might really like me. Then, when he proceeded to make me laugh with some teacher impressions, it hit me that what I'm most afraid of is getting closer to him and having him find out my secret.

There's no way he'd still like me if he knew.

"Kaaa-tieee! We'll be waiting in the car!" My mom screeches again.

I decide at the last minute to throw a long turquoise cardigan over the fitted black tunic I am wearing, and I switch from leggings to skinny jeans. I don't feel comfortable at all, but this is the kind of thing other girls wear. Maybe not the OH girls, but other girls who will be at Selena's party.

Gary pulls to a jerky stop in front of the Tropez's house. The entire drive, eight blocks to Selena's, my mom bitched about me taking so long. I wished that I had just walked.

"So, how are you getting home?" Gary asks.

"I think Mr. Tropez or Anthony can drive me." I am already standing on the sidewalk.

"No later than midnight. Got it?" My mom calls through the open passenger window.

"Got it."

With a beep, they are gone.

The sound of music coming from the house is faint. If I didn't know there was a party going on, I probably wouldn't even notice it. The front of the house is completely dark, too. All the action is happening in the kitchen, which faces the back yard, and the basement. The Tropez house is perfect for parties.

Halfway up the walkway, the motion light above the front door goes on. That's when I notice that I am wearing different colored boots. One brown and one black. Great. Just great. Instead of continuing along the walkway to the side door, I take a seat on the front steps and debate heading right back home. I can leave now, and no one will ever know I was here.

I sit there long enough for the light to go off. Five minutes, maybe ten. However long it was, it was long enough for me to decide that I'd rather be at home.

As soon as I reach the sidewalk, a car full of bodies pulls up and parks across the street. The driver is Nick, the cashier from Red Owl. He makes eye contact with me immediately and grins. Besides him, three guys and a girl emerge from the blue Ford Focus.

"Katie?" He calls out.

Guess I'm not going home after all. "Nick, right?"

"Good memory. Just getting here?" He looks up and down the street. "Did you walk?"

"No, my . . . I got a ride, but I was thinking about—"

"Hey, maybe you two want to talk inside. I don't think Anthony wants us hanging out here," one of the guys calls over his shoulder.

"He's right. We should get inside." Nick hooks an elbow around mine and pulls me along beside him. He's at least half a foot taller than I am, and he's wearing cologne. I inhale the scent deeply a few times as we make our way to the side door. It smells so good.

The music gets ten times louder when we walk through the door. The living room to our left is dark. To our right is the dimly lit kitchen that leads to the basement stairs. As we walk past the kitchen table, two of Nick's buddies grab handfuls of M&Ms out of a big red bowl. The table also displays several bags of chips, some dip, big red Solo cups and a few two-liters of soda. The innocent spread has me fooled until we reach the basement, where people are pumping beer from a keg into plastic cups. I can't see the keg, but I've been to enough family gatherings in the Tropez basement to know why people are hunched behind the bar.

Anthony rushes over to greet his high school friends, and then does a double take when he sees me. "Kit Kat?" The girl we walked in with giggles when he says my nickname. Before I have a chance to feel embarrassed, he lifts me into a brotherly bear hug. "Where have you been lately, girl?" He puts me down and forcibly turns me in a circle to examine my body. "And what the heck happened to the rest of you?"

Now I have a chance to be embarrassed. "Nothing. I've been . . . working out."

"Hey man, we're gonna . . ." One of the guys I don't know nods toward the bar, leaving me with Anthony and Nick. Anthony nods back.

"Working out? You need to eat more food if you're gonna be working out." He shakes his head. "Selena said you lost some weight, but not this much."

I glance toward the stairs and imagine myself running up through the kitchen and out the door, not stopping until I reach my house.

"Hey," Nick interrupts, distracting Anthony. "How 'bout we all get a beer?" He puts his hand on my shoulder, "You want a beer?"

I'm pretty sure Anthony knows I've never had a beer before, but he doesn't say anything. He is not the kind of older brother who tries to control his little sister or her friends. He's always been cool with us. But

I notice that he's continuing to scan my body with a look similar to the looks my dad and Connie gave me when they first laid eyes on me over Winter break.

"Sure, I'll have one."

"Cool." Nick turns toward the bar and Anthony is about to start in on me again when more people enter the basement.

"An-tho-ny!" A booming voice chants.

"Dudes!" Anthony howls at the three guys who just walked in. Then he looks down at me. "Selena and Darcy are in the other room with Brad and his friends. I'll talk to you later." He gives my shoulder a little squeeze and then he's gone.

Nick is still standing at the bar waiting for beer with the rest of the group from his car. Besides them, Anthony and the three who just showed up, there are two guys and a girl behind the bar, as well as a small cluster of people sitting in front of the TV playing video games. Realizing that I'm surrounded by high schoolers, I make a beeline for the utility room.

The click clack of an air hockey puck hits my ears before I even pull the long curtains apart. Darcy is too busy playing air hockey with some guy I sort of recognize to look up at me, and Selena and Brad are making out on the loveseat. That leaves only one of Brad's friends, who I hardly know, to notice me at first.

"Hey, Katie," he says, grinning and standing up straighter.

"Hey. What's up?"

Instead of answering, he takes a quick drag off the joint he is holding and hands it to me. I shake my head and put a hand up, waving off the pot. "No, thanks."

"Selena! Kit Kat's here!" Darcy drops her paddle onto the table and rushes over to give me a hug.

"So, you give up?" Darcy's opponent asks.

"No way," Darcy says over her shoulder.

Meanwhile, Selena is pushing Brad off her and getting up to greet me.

"You came." She has a lazy, pothead grin on her face as she approaches me with open arms. Suddenly, I am in a tight three-way hug with Selena and Darcy. "We missed you, girl," Selena says.

I missed you guys, too. I think it, but I don't say it for some reason.

Have I really missed them? Or do I miss who they used to be before they started hanging out with Brad Wilcox and his friends?

"Here's your beer, Katie." The sound of Nick's voice puts an end to our group hug.

"You're gonna drink a beer, Kit Kat?" The obvious shock in Darcy's voice tugs at my stomach for some reason. I don't know why, but I feel the urge to do something that I'm not supposed to do. And I don't want my friends to be shocked about it.

"Yep," I say, grabbing the red plastic cup from Nick.

Selena shrugs. "It's about time."

"Hold up, hold up." Brad shoves his way in between the girls and me. "This is the first time Katie has ever tried beer?"

Embarrassed, I glance at Nick.

"Yeah, so?" Selena says.

"Well, she has to chug it then."

Tyler nods in agreement.

I look at Nick again. Smiling, he takes a sip of his own beer and then holds it up to me. Hesitantly, I tap the rim of my cup against his and then bring it to my lips. I close my eyes and draw in the bitter liquid while everyone around me chants, "Chug, chug, chug, chug . . ."

～

"Lower?" Selena says. A seven is flipped on top of the ten. "That's three in a row!" she exclaims, looking at me. "Your turn."

I look down at the stack of cards. There must be at least eight in the pile by now. I can't remember the name of the game, but I know that if I guess wrong about whether the next card is higher or lower than seven, I have to take one drink for every card in the pile.

"Well? What do you think, Kit Kat? High or low?" Darcy asks.

Nick peeks at the next card and gives me a devious grin.

"I don't know, I don't know." I rub my forehead, as I work extra hard to focus. My head is spinning like I have just gotten off a Tilt-a-Whirl. *Seven. The next card has to be higher than seven.* I take a deep breath. "Higher."

Nick groans as he flips over a six on top of the seven. Everyone around me hoots and hollers. Tyler grabs the pile of cards and counts out loud as he slaps them one by one onto the table. By the time he gets to "Eleven," everyone else is counting with him.

"Go for it, Kit Kat," Selena says with a wink.

Or maybe she didn't wink. I'm not sure of anything right now. Everything is fuzzy, like I might be dreaming.

"C'mon, girl, chug it down," Brad says.

I take the first four gulps quickly, but then choke a little on the fifth. Beer dribbles down my chin and onto my top. Laughter envelops me.

Why am I doing this?

"Whoa, whoa, whoa," Nick takes the cup from my hand. "I think you're done."

"No way, man. That wasn't eleven sips," Brad says.

"Shut up, Brad!" Selena says, as she pushes hair out of my face and secures it behind my ear. "She's had enough."

Brad rolls his eyes. "Whatever. That's only like her fourth beer."

"Yeah, but she only weighs like eighty pounds," Darcy mutters.

"What did she say about me?" I mumble, as Selena and Nick help me to my feet.

"Nothing," Selena says firmly. "Nothing important, anyway."

As soon as I'm standing, my legs wobble like they're made of Jell-O. An arm wraps around my waist and my right arm is hoisted around Nick's neck.

An older girl I don't recognize asks Selena how much I've had to drink as I am guided through the main room to the stairs. The loud music and dim lighting cause me to feel even more disoriented, and I hear myself saying, "I have to go home. I just need to go home. Can someone please take me home?"

When I stumble on the stairs, Nick picks me up and I hear Anthony's voice, "What's going on?" I peer at him over Nick's shoulder. Then I am nearly shocked sober when I get a glimpse of Sloan Whitson grinning at me from the couch. *Is that really Sloan? Please, God, please don't let that be Sloan.*

～

"What are we gonna do? She can't go home like this. Her mom will *freak*."

"Katie . . . Katie." I assume Anthony is the one holding the glass to my lips. "Katie, you have to drink some water."

The bright light shining through my eyelids is painful. I open my eyes a teensy bit but then immediately squeeze them shut when I'm hit by the spinning walls of Selena's bedroom.

"It's only . . . what time is it, ten? Maybe she can sleep it off. What time does she need to be home?" Anthony asks.

"I don't know. Twelve? I'm not sure. She didn't say," Selena answers.

"Well, you need to figure it out," Anthony snaps. "I don't have time to babysit for your drunk friend." He sighs. "Look, I'm sorry. There's just too many people here. I gotta get back downstairs." The door opens and closes.

"I can stay with her if you want." Nick's voice. "So you can get back to your other friends."

"Are you sure?"

"Yeah, she's cool. I don't mind at all. Do you care if I turn on the TV?"

"No, not at all. But, are you sure?"

"Yeah, I'm sure. Go ahead. I'll keep trying to get her to drink some water."

"Ok. I'll be back in a bit to check on her."

The door opens and is left open this time. I hear Selena walking down the hall past the bathroom and through the kitchen. Then the TV goes on—loud at first, then just a hint of some sports announcer's voice —and the bright light goes off, allowing the pain in my head to fade. I open my eyes a crack. Nick is standing next to Selena's bed, staring down at me. When he climbs onto the bed and lies next to me, a nagging voice inside my head tells me I should feel uncomfortable, but I'm too out of it to listen.

"Katie," Nick whispers. He runs his fingers through my hair. "Katie." His breath warms my ear and neck, causing a vision of Hunter to enter my mind. "Hey, Katie," he says a little louder. It sounds like Hunter's voice. "Can I kiss you?"

Kiss me? I must not have heard him right. I mean to ask what he said, but before I can get a word out, his lips are on mine. Frozen, I struggle to figure out if I even want Nick to kiss me.

This *is* what I've been waiting for, isn't it? To really be kissed. To really kiss someone back. So I push my lips against his, and it feels as good as I imagined it would. But then I feel moisture from his tongue, and I panic.

"Stop." *Did I say it loud enough?*

"What?"

"Stop it," I say louder. "I don't . . . I feel . . . dizzy. My stomach . . . it . . . it hurts." My head is spinning again, and I'm trying to remember exactly where I am.

"Do you want some water? Or something to eat?"

"No, no, I can't . . . I can't eat."

"It might help."

I sigh heavily. "No . . . it won't. Eating never helps." *What am I saying?*

"How do you know? I thought this was your first time drinking."

A feeling of nausea rushes over me, and I have to swallow several times to hold back the beer that is inching its way up my throat. Turning to my side, I moan. Even with closed eyes, I see stars.

Nick begins stroking my hair again. It feels nice and makes me feel like I can trust him.

"Whenever I eat, I . . . I can't . . . stop. I just . . . eat . . . and eat. Then . . . I get rid of everything. But it doesn't . . . it never . . . helps."

He shifts next to me and stops touching my hair. "What are you talking about?"

"I throw up . . . when I eat. I think I'm . . . I think something's wrong with me."

I open my eyes wide. What *am* I talking about? Did I just tell him that I make myself throw up? I wait for him to say something. Anything. When he doesn't, I assume that maybe I imagined everything. Maybe I was asleep and he's asleep too. Maybe the kiss was part of a dream.

Footsteps. Voices. The hallway light goes on.

"What are you doing, Sloan?" Selena snaps.

Sloan?

Nick jumps, causing the bed to move and more nausea for me.

Sloan says something about the bathroom.

"You're supposed to use the one downstairs! Frickin' Anthony," Selena mumbles as she appears in the doorway along with two shadowy figures. When she flips on the light switch, one of the figures shoves past her.

"Why are *you* in here?"

Squinting to keep the light out of my eyes, I grin at Dominic, even though he seems upset and isn't looking at me.

Through zigzags of light I see Nick now too, and Dominic moving toward him.

"Hey, hey, hey! Knock it off! He was making sure she didn't puke all over the place," Selena rushes in between them.

"Yeah, I'm sure that's what he was doing," Dominic says as he turns his attention to me. "What were you thinking, Katie?"

"You guys . . . are finally here." I smile looking from Dominic to Beth, who is leaning against the doorframe.

He ignores me and looks back at Selena. "What else did you give her?"

"*Nothing*. God, Dominic. Why are you acting like such a jerk? I'm not the one who poured all that beer down her throat!"

"C'mon, Katie. We're leaving." Dominic pulls me up into a sitting position. "Beth, can you come and help me get her up on her feet?"

"No. I'm not leaving. I'm fine," I say as I slide off the bed onto the floor.

The next thing I know, Nick is on the floor next to me and Dominic is pulling Nick away. "Uh-uh. She doesn't need help from someone who just stood there and let her get wasted. Easier to take advantage of a girl if she's younger, huh? And even better if she's drunk, right?"

"Hey, that's not fair," Nick says.

"Dominic, this is all on Katie. So, you need to lay off," Selena says.

"Lay off and not say or do anything to help out my friend? You mean, like you?"

"Selena's right," Beth says. "Katie did this to herself."

"Shut up, Beth."

Someone gasps, but I have no idea who because my eyes are closed. The last thought that crosses my mind before everything goes black is that Beth probably hates me now, too. Just as much as Sloan.

Chapter Twenty-One

My tongue feels like it's coated with cotton. I open and close my mouth, smacking my lips together to create some moisture. That's when the nasty aroma and flavor of beer hits me. I need water, but I'm afraid to move.

Finally, I open my eyes, not sure what to expect.

I'm in my own bed, still wearing the same clothes I wore to the party. I peek at my alarm clock. Six thirty-five, around the same time I'm used to waking up for school. Then I recognize the smell of vomit, and everything rushes back to me. Everything.

Oh my God, oh my God, oh my God, oh my God. Stupid, stupid, stupid. What have I done?

The beer. The kiss. Dominic. Throwing up on the way home. My mom yelling at me.

What have I done?

If there was anything in my stomach to throw up right now, I would. But it's completely empty, because every last of bit of food I ate for dinner yesterday (which wasn't much) and all the beer I drank at the party got barfed onto the floor of Kelsie's car.

I remember Dominic calling her to pick me up. Then I remember sitting on Selena's front porch in between Dominic and Beth. I kept asking Beth if she hated me. Over and over I asked her. If she didn't hate me then, she has to now. When Kelsie offered to drive Beth home, Dominic was already in the back seat with me. I remember her glaring at me as she said she'd just get home on her own. That's when I barfed. All over the floor and all over Dominic's shoes.

I cringe at every memory that floods back to me. My pillow is soaked with tears within minutes. I need a tissue, but I don't know if I can ever get out of bed again. I don't even try. I just lay there staring up at the ceiling, thinking about how much I want to die. What is wrong with me?

I wake up again a little after eleven to the sound of dishes banging and clanking in the kitchen. This is what my mom does when she's angry; she takes it out on drawers, cabinets, pots and pans. I've always wondered if slamming dishes around is just her way of relieving stress or if she's actually trying to communicate with whoever has pissed her off—in this case, me.

I tiptoe down the stairs, listening, planning, trying to figure out what I'm going to say. I freeze on the second step from the bottom for a few seconds and then decide to turn around and head back upstairs, not yet ready to look my mom in the eyes.

"Katie?" Her voice travels from the other side of the wall. "I know you're there. Get. In Here."

I inhale deeply and then slowly make my way into the kitchen. Gary is sitting at the kitchen table reading the newspaper and my mom is leaning against the sink with her arms folded across her chest. They're both holding coffee mugs and wearing workout clothes. My mom and I stare at each other for at least a minute before Gary even looks up from the paper. But when he does, he looks at my mom, not me.

"Well, Elaine, are you going to talk to her or stare at her?" Now he looks at me. "What is going on in that head of yours, Katie?" He seems disgusted with me, and I don't blame him. I wait for him to continue, but instead, he gets up and leaves the room.

That's it? That's all he's going to say to me? Most teens would be happy with such a dismissive stepdad, but my heart sinks and more tears well up. I sort of got it when he didn't say anything to me about the puking. But getting drunk? Does he care about me at all? Does anyone?

"How could you, Katie?"

I glance up at her but don't maintain eye contact. "I . . . I don't know. I—"

"You made a fool of yourself, young lady!"

Now the floodgates are open, and I can hardly breathe because I'm crying so hard. "I know . . . I . . . I'm so . . . stupid."

"You got that right, missy! Making yourself throw up? Drinking alcohol? Making out with a Junior in high school? Who *are* you?"

Making out? She knows about Nick? "Wha—? Who said—"

"You're damn lucky Kelsie picked you up. I would have called the cops if Dominic had called me. That Selena is no good! I never liked her, ever since those sleepovers you two used to have. No nine-year-old should know such slutty dance moves! And those parents? Where do they get off leaving two teenagers home alone overnight?" She spins around, purposely sweeping a few dirty dishes into the sink with her arm. Glass shatters.

By the time Gary rushes back into the kitchen, my mom is in a heap on the floor, bawling into her hands. The scene is shocking enough to have dried up my tears.

"Elaine," Gary says softly, as he rubs her back.

I lift my foot off the floor slightly, ready to rush to her side, but then she whimpers, "Where did I go wrong? First, all that boy-crazy shit we went through with Kelsie, and now this?" She motions in my direction. "Is it because their father left? Do they blame me? Are they trying to punish me?"

"No, Elaine, no. This has nothing to do with you. It's what teenagers do."

My mom continues sobbing and whining about how she just doesn't know how to deal with me. And about how she never did any of this stuff when she was my age. How she was a good girl. A cheerleader. An honor student with nice friends.

After everything I've been going through and all the things I've done wrong, this is how she's going to deal with it? By feeling sorry for herself? By making it about her? Kelsie and I watched her feel sorry for herself for nearly two years after my dad left. It's always been about her. Suddenly, I am filled with the deepest darkest rage I have ever felt.

"You don't even care about me! All you care about is yourself!" I scream at the top of my lungs.

Gary and my mom look up at me, their faces filled with shock.

"I hate you!" I'm halfway up the stairs by the time I realize I want to tell Gary I hate him too. But I don't, because my mom is already scrambling up the stairs behind me.

"What did you say to me?" she yells.

"Elaine, please, just wait a little while before you—"

"Don't you *dare* walk away from me!"

If I still had a door, I would slam it. Since I don't, I scurry into bed and hide under the covers. "Leave . . . me . . . alone," I say through sobs.

The covers are ripped off me, leaving me feeling naked and helpless, so I curl into the fetal position with my hands covering my face.

"You think I don't care about you? How dare you say that to me! Why did I work so hard to stay here then? In this house, the one you came home to after you were born? Because I don't care? Trust me, if I didn't care, we certainly wouldn't still live in this house! Do you think I like being surrounded by memories of your dad! Who's the one who's always made sure you have food to eat and clothes to wear and that you always go to school and do your homework? Me, Katie! Not you father! Me!"

I hear her yelling, but it's as if I'm in a Lifetime movie. This can't be my mom. This can't be me, lying here all balled up, an angry screwed up teenager. What happened to happy wishing-upon-a-star Kit Kat? Where did she go?

I pick up my head and look over at my mom through puffy eyes. She is still screaming at me. I see her lips moving, but I don't hear her anymore. I just want to be a little girl again and lay my head on her lap while she reads me a book. I want her to hug me, to kiss my forehead and to tell me she's here for me. Heck, even one out of three might help me pull myself out of the pit I'm in.

Instead, I watch as Gary grabs my mom by the shoulders and forces her out of my room. "We aren't done talking about this!" She screams over her shoulder.

~

I wait for silence before tiptoeing back downstairs. I'm hungry, but today is a good day to avoid eating. No one will notice, and even if they do, I can say I feel sick from the alcohol. My rumbling stomach isn't what's on my mind anyway. It's Dominic. He has to be the one who told my mom about Nick. It's times like this that I wish I had a cell phone, or even a phone upstairs. But Kelsie had to wait until high school to get a phone so now I do too. What kind of sense does that make? Six years ago, not as many kids had phones. Now everyone has one—except for me, of course.

I'm pretty sure Gary took my mom downstairs for a workout. She'd pick running on her treadmill to relieve stress any day over going to a spa. I realize that I would pick a gallon of ice cream and a toilet, and the thought fills me with shame.

I sit on the bottom stair and lower my face into my hands. *I am a total freak.*

Finally, I muster the strength to reach up and around the corner for the phone. I don't even want to go into the kitchen in case my mom comes upstairs for water. If I hear her, I'll ditch the ancient, corded phone and retreat quickly to my room.

I try four times to dial Dominic but keep messing up on the third or fourth number. I swear I have dreamt about this moment. It was one of those dreams when you are trying so hard to get somewhere or accomplish something but you keep losing ground or messing up. You just can't get it right for some reason and you eventually force yourself to wake up because the frustration is overwhelming. Or maybe it's a sign that I should not be calling Dominic right now. But I push that thought away, *needing* to talk to him.

Finally, I succeed in punching in all seven numbers correctly. Dominic answers on the fourth ring.

"Kit Kat?"

"Please don't call me that."

Breathing.

"Hello?" I say.

"Yeah, I'm here. Are you okay?"

"No offense Dominic, but if you care so much about me, then why did you tell my mom I was making out with Nick? And how would you have known that?"

"What? Are you serious? You got so wasted that you passed out. Then you were stumbling all over the place and puked in your sister's car, and you're worried about your mom finding out you were making out with some guy?"

He's right. After the big fool I made of myself, why am I so worried about people knowing that I kissed someone? Especially when Kelsie was having sex at my age.

Maybe it's because there's no way I could have prevented my mom from knowing that I drank alcohol. But this? My virginity is the one thing I have that my sister doesn't. It's the one thing my mom has always seemed proud of me for. And now, if she finds out I was drunk and making out with some boy on a bed . . . I don't want her to think she doesn't have anything to be proud of me for anymore.

Either way, I'm pissed, and it's Dominic's fault. "Who told you I was making out with him?!"

"No one told me."

"Then why did you tell my mom that?"

"Katie, I didn't."

"Why are you lying? Tell me the truth! Why would you tell her that?"

"Katie, I swear. It wasn't me. It . . . it was Carly."

"What are you talking about? Carly wasn't even there."

"Yeah, but Sloan was there. Apparently, she's friends with some chick that Anthony hangs out with."

"Wait, what are you saying? I don't understand. How would Carly . . ." And then I remember. *What are you doing in the hallway, Sloan?* She must have been spying on Nick and me.

Oh no. If she heard us kissing, what else did she hear?

No longer mad at Dominic, I ask in a hushed voice, "How do you know Carly told my mom?"

"Because she called me this morning and wanted to know everything that happened. She was flipping out. Katie, Sloan told Amy and the rest of her friends everything. She even told them something . . . something she says she heard you say to Nick."

God, no!

I don't remember exactly what I said to Nick, but I have a guess. And the way Dominic is acting pretty much confirms it. "What? What did she say I said?"

"That you make yourself throw up . . . and Carly said it's true." Dominic must be holding his breath because the line goes completely dead for at least five seconds. Not a sound. Then he says, "Is that true? Did you tell Nick that?"

"Yes," I whisper.

Again, it is quiet for a few seconds. All I hear is soft breathing. I don't say anything because I'm too busy fuming over Carly confirming what Sloan said and telling my mom that I made out with Nick. How could she?

"I have to go," I finally say.

"Wait," Dominic says. "Are you going to call Carly?"

"Of course I am. I need to know why she would tell my mom something like that. She knows how my mom feels about that kind of stuff. I don't understand why Carly wouldn't want to talk to me first. I mean, how can she just believe Sloan?"

"Are you saying it's not true? Did Sloan make all that stuff up?" His tone is accusatory.

"Well, no, but that doesn't give her the right to go blabbing to everyone."

"So, you did make out with that Nick guy? And you've been making yourself throw up? Geez, Katie. Why is all this stuff happening? What's going on with you? Is it because of me and Beth? Or because Carly made the cheer squad and you didn't? That's when you started acting different, after she made the squad." His voice trails off when he says the last part, as if he's talking to himself.

"I don't know." I choke back tears. "I really don't know." At least it's the truth.

"Katie, I'm always here for you. You have to know that. I may not know anything about girl stuff, but I know you, and you're not acting like yourself. None of this stuff is like you."

But maybe it is like me.

"I know, I know. Look, I have to go. I have to babysit for the Andersons down the block, but I'll call you tomorrow. Okay?" I don't have to be at the Andersons' until five, but Dominic doesn't need to know that. I just don't feel like talking anymore.

"Yeah, okay. Tomorrow. But you can call me later, too, if you want. Okay?"

"Okay. Bye," I say, hanging up quickly before he has a chance to say anything else.

~

Stepping out of the shower, I jump when I see my mom sitting on the toilet.

"Mom! You scared me." My lips curve into a smile for a split second before I remember how angry she is with me. I pull my towel tight around my torso and lean against the wall, facing her.

"Katie," she says softly, "do we have to worry about you drinking?"

Her hair is pulled into a high ponytail, the way it always is when she runs, and her entire body is dripping with sweat. Her eyes are puffy, red and exhausted.

"No," I say without hesitation. But the truth is, I don't know.

"And what about the throwing up?"

"Mom, I haven't thrown up since I got back from visiting dad." My voice is so sincere that I almost believe myself, but her wrinkled forehead tells me she isn't buying it.

"I talked to Brenda this morning." She stares at me, waiting for a response.

"Okay." I shrug my shoulders. Brenda is our neighbor, the one who always gives me her daughter Chelsea's hand-me-downs. My mom talks to her all the time.

"Katie, Brenda is a therapist."

She wouldn't. Except, of course she would.

My heart starts racing, and I clench my teeth.

"Look, I *had* to talk to someone, someone who knows about these things."

"What things, mom?" My voice is unsteady. I am on the verge of yelling when I say, "What did you tell her about me?"

"Oh, Katie, don't get so upset. I needed some professional advice, and Brenda won't tell anyone."

"Well, I hope she told you that it will only make things worse if you go around telling people things that are NONE OF THEIR BUSINESS!"

My mom gives me a hard stare. It reminds me of the one she used to give me when I had fits as a little girl. It's a stare that says, "You are going to wear yourself out with an outburst like that."

"Actually, she said that young girls who develop an eating disorder are likely to harm themselves in other ways too, like experimenting with alcohol or being sexually promiscuous."

Sexually promiscuous? "Oh my God! So, I drank too much. It was my first time, you know! And so what if I kissed a boy? That's far from what Kelsie was doing with boys at my age."

"This has nothing to do with Kelsie and everything to do with the fact that you are nothing but skin and bones. It may have been your first experience with alcohol, but how many times have you made yourself throw up? Fifty? A hundred? Kelsie's actions didn't put her life in danger. Sure, I suppose she could have gotten pregnant, but she wasn't starving herself." My mom's hard stare remains, telling me that she isn't going to back down. "And now that you're starting to act out in other ways, it's time for us to get some professional help."

"I'm not acting out!"

"Katie," she tilts her head and looks at me with pity, "do you hear yourself? In thirteen years, you've only spoken to me like this a handful of times, and all of those times have been within the last few months." She sighs. "I'm making an appointment for you to see a psychologist."

"I won't go."

"Yes, you will."

And with that, she's gone.

I fall to my knees in front of the toilet, letting the towel slip to the ground. I push as hard as I can, trying to make something—anything—come up. But nothing does. Because there is nothing. I am empty inside.

Frantic to feel some sort of release, I shove three fingers so far into my mouth that my fingernails pierce the back of my throat and my teeth dig into my knuckles. Then I gag and begin to heave violently. Once. Twice. Three times. Still, nothing comes out. But at least now, I feel somewhat better.

Chapter Twenty-Two

"You're sure the Andersons are just going to dinner?"

"For the billionth time, yes!"

"So, what time should we expect you home?"

"I don't know. How long does it take for you and Gary to go out to dinner? Two hours? Why don't you call Mrs. Anderson and ask her?"

"You know, Katie, you're lucky we're even letting you babysit tonight after the crap you pulled last night. I expect you to come straight home. If you're not back by eight, I'm sending Gary over. Got it?"

"Fine. Whatever."

Even with the door closed behind me, I can still hear a drawer slam shut.

When I finally went downstairs after the most recent argument, it was clear that things were back to normal as far as she was concerned. Instead of looking all sad, my mom was back to her usual unemotional, hurried self. She was watching an online cooking tutorial. Some new low-fat recipe that Brenda recommended to her. When I reminded her that I had to babysit for the Andersons, she didn't even flinch. The only reason she gave me a hard time right before I walked out the door was because I'm grounded for getting drunk. And even though she didn't mention it when I was sentenced to two weeks, I'm guessing I'm grounded for making out with Nick, too. My mom has always taken grounding us very seriously. The difference for me this time is that I don't even care. She seems to have forgotten that she was the one who told me I had to start doing things with my friends again. Besides, who am I going to hang out with anyway? Dominic is with Beth, who hates me now, and Carly is all wrapped up with her cheer squad friends.

Carly. I still haven't talked to her. I snuck downstairs earlier and tried to, but I got their voicemail. I hung up before it even beeped for me to leave a message. I look at her house across the street as I walk down our driveway. The porch and living room lights are on, and I can see flickering lights from the TV. Carly's bedroom light is on, too. Were they really gone when I called? Or was Carly avoiding me?

I decide to call her as soon as Mr. and Mrs. Anderson leave, or at least as soon as I can get Zoe and Lizzie distracted.

The Anderson's only live ten houses down from us, so I'm walking up to their front door within minutes. Zoe and Lizzie see me through the kitchen window, causing squeals and quick footsteps from inside.

"Katie! It's good to see you, dear," a long and lean Mrs. Anderson says warmly as she expertly ties a fashion scarf around her neck. "The girls are supposed to be finishing up their dinner, but they are just too excited to see you I guess." While she talks, five-year-old Zoe and seven-year-old Lizzie tug at my arms until I hug them both. "What has it been? Four months since you last sat for us? No, no, no. It was in August, so five months. Anyway, how are . . ." She pauses midsentence and her eyes widen when I remove my coat. "things going?" Her eyes are scanning my body as she finishes.

Before I can answer, Mr. Anderson enters the room. "Oh, hey, Katie." He does a double take when walking past me into the kitchen.

"Hi, Mr. Anderson." I look back at Mrs. Anderson. "Things are good. School's fine. I visited my dad in California last week. Everything is fine."

"Are you sure, sweetie? Because you look kind of . . . pale. Did you get that stomach bug that was going around a few weeks ago?" I can tell she's nervous because she speaks more quickly than normal, eyeing me up and down the whole time.

"Yeah, now that you mention it, I was feeling kinda sick for a few weeks. I'm all better now though," I say as I pick Zoe up and give her another hug while Lizzie sets up Trouble.

Mrs. Anderson seems to relax a bit after I tell her I'd been sick. "Well, I'm glad you're feeling better," she says with a smile. Then she buttons up her stylish wool coat and puts on stripy mittens. "Hey, Dan! We need to get going. The reservation is for five thirty."

Mr. Anderson finishes up with the computer on the kitchen counter and turns, grinning handsomely at his wife. "Well, we best skedaddle then, honey."

"We won't be long, Katie. Shouldn't be much later than seven thirty,"

Mrs. Anderson says as she kisses the girls on their foreheads. "Be good for Katie, you two."

Mr. Anderson winks at us from the door as he holds it open for his wife. "See ya, girls."

The entire time the girls and I are playing Trouble, I am thinking about what I'm going to say to Carly. Why would she tell my mom what Sloan said without talking to me first? Is she embarrassed to be friends with me now?

Finally, Lizzie wins. "That was fun!" I say. "Good game, girls."

"Let's play again!" Zoe squeals as she begins moving her pieces back to Home.

"Yeah, again!" Lizzie yells.

"Um, you guys don't happen to have the movie *Frozen*, do you? I haven't seen it yet."

Lizzie's eyes widen to the size of saucers. "You haven't seen *Frozen*, Katie?"

I dishonestly shake my head and say, "Uh-uh. Do you have it?"

Both girls jump up and run for the DVD collection. Lizzie finds *Frozen* and loads it into the DVD player while Zoe runs back to me. "Can we make popcorn, Katie? Pleeease."

"Sure," I laugh. "Why don't you two sit down and watch the previews, and I'll make some."

While I'm waiting for the final kernels to pop, I'm tempted to pick up the phone to call Carly, but I need to make sure the girls are situated first.

"Here you go," I say, handing a bowl of popcorn to each girl.

"Why don't you have a bowl, Katie?" Lizzie asks.

"Oh, I just ate," I say rubbing my belly. "And I'm still pretty full." Lizzie is already back to looking at the TV before I finish my explanation. *Why can't my mom accept what I say this easily?*

Fifteen minutes into the movie, I sneak into the kitchen to call Carly. "Hello?"

"Hey, Carly-Q." The moment the nickname leaves my lips, I wonder why I said it. I'm mad at her, so why do I sound like everything is hunky-dory? Besides, I don't want her—or anyone—calling me Kit Kat anymore.

"Katie? I thought Mrs. Miller was calling me to babysit. Guess they called you first, huh?" She sounds disappointed. I just can't tell if it's because she would have wanted to babysit or because it's me.

"Yeah, I guess."

"So, what's up?" Carly does not sound like her bubbly self. She has to be upset that it's me. Wait a second, though. I'm the one who should be upset, not her.

"Well, my mom was pretty pissed this morning because someone told her I was making out with that Nick guy at Selena's party."

I imagine her shrugging her shoulders when she doesn't respond.

"I know it was you, Carly. Why would you do something like that? As if I didn't get in enough trouble for drinking? You had to go and tell my mom something you heard from Sloan?"

"Wait, who—"

"Dominic told me, Carly. He told me that you called him this morning and that you're the one who told my mom. I don't understand why you didn't call me to find out what happened."

"Why would I call you to ask if it's true that you got so drunk that you couldn't even stand straight and that you were making out with some guy you don't even know in Selena's bed? Gee, let me think about it. Oh, I know, maybe because you probably don't even remember what happened. Or maybe because the last time we talked, everything that came out of your mouth was lies." I feel like she just slapped me. I don't even know how to respond. But I don't have to, because she takes a deep breath and continues. "I'm worried about you, Katie. You're nothing but bones and you won't tell me what's going on! All those times you told me how you would never do any of the stupid things your sister did—the drinking, the smoking, the *sex*—and look at what you did last night. I'm sorry, I really am, but I had to tell your mom."

"I didn't have se—" I stop myself, remembering that Zoe and Lizzie are in the next room and continue in a whisper. "I didn't do *all* of that, especially the last thing. All I did was kiss someone. And I just wish I could have been the one to tell you about it instead of Sloan."

"Katie, you haven't shared anything with me for months. Sure, I've been busy with cheerleading, but not every single day. You never even call anymore. When I've called you, you don't answer. And if someone else answers, for some reason they always say you're busy. When I see you at school, you're so quiet or you act like everything is fine, yet you're the size of a toothpick!"

"Carly, what is the big deal about—"

"Katie? Why aren't you watching the movie?" Zoe asks, as she peeks into the kitchen.

I cover the receiver. "I will. Can you please wait for me in the living room? I'll be there in a second, okay?"

She smiles and nods before she turns to skip away.

"You should probably get off the phone and play with Zoe and Lizzie, Katie."

"*No.* I need you to tell me exactly what Sloan said and who all knows about last night."

"I don't know *exactly* what she said or who knows because she didn't tell me. She told Amy, and then Amy called to tell me this morning. She told her you could barely walk because you were so wasted and that she saw you in Selena's bed with one of Anthony's friends. She said . . . she said the guy was on top of you. Look, Laney and Anica slept over at Amy's last night, so they know too. And Sloan was with a few girls on the high school pom squad. I guess she knows them through her cousin in Anthony's grade. That's how she ended up at the party. Didn't you see her there?"

"No," I say quietly, "I didn't." At least I wasn't sure it was her, not until I heard Selena yelling at her in the hallway. "Was that all she told Amy? She didn't mention hearing Nick and me talking about anything?"

I already know Sloan heard me talking about how I make myself throw up, but for some reason, I want to hear it from Carly. I don't know why. Maybe I'm hoping Dominic was wrong.

"Well, yeah. She said that . . . God, Katie. I'm so—"

"Katie! Zoe is eating my popcorn!" Lizzie screeches. I rush into the living room to prevent an argument by squeezing myself onto the couch in between the two. Then I go back to talking to Carly. "Sorry about that. What were you saying?"

She takes a deep breath. "Just that . . . that I'm sorry. Because . . . because everyone is going to know that you've been making yourself throw up."

My heart rate increases. I want to crawl under a rock.

"Katie? Are you there?"

"Yeah, I'm here."

"Katie!" Lizzie wails.

"Maybe I'm glad the Andersons called you first." Carly says.

I laugh lightly, but it's just for show. I'm actually freaking out because everyone is going to know my secret. I also feel terrible about the way I've been treating my friends. "Yeah, these girls are getting antsy. Look, Carly, I'm really sorry I've been acting so weird lately. Can we hang out in a couple of weeks? After I'm finished being grounded?"

She hesitates for a moment, but then says, "Sure. I'd like that. And just so you know, I'm here for you. You can talk to me about anything. You know that, right?"

"I know. Same here. Maybe we can talk more tomorrow?"

"We're going to my Aunt Bonnie's for my cousin's birthday party tomorrow, but Monday for sure. Oh, and by the way, I think Amy called to tell me what Sloan said so that I could give you a heads up. She didn't say so, but I just have a feeling. It didn't seem like she was being gossipy, not like she usually is, you know? Anyway, I thought you should know."

"Thanks, Carly. I appreciate you letting me know. Talk to you Monday." I try to sound normal, but now all I can think about is Sloan and her big mouth.

I get more popcorn for the girls and plant myself in between them again. The scent of the buttery popcorn makes my stomach moan for a taste, causing the girls to grin and giggle at me.

"Katie, your tummy sounds hungry!" Zoe says. "You can have some of my popcorn if you want," she says, bringing a piece to my lips. Not wanting to disappoint her, I allow her to pop it into my mouth.

The moment I taste the salty sweetness, my mouth wants more. Or maybe it's my stomach that wants more. Or my brain. I'm not really sure what causes me to eat and eat and eat.

Either way, I help Zoe and Lizzie finish off their popcorn, and then we go into the kitchen to have some of the homemade chocolate chip cookies the girls made with Mrs. Anderson this afternoon.

"Just one. Okay, girls?"

"Aww. Why can't we have two?" Lizzie whines.

"Because it's almost seven thirty and you two need to get ready for bed."

"We got to stay up until nine on New Year's Eve," Zoe says proudly.

DON'T CALL ME KIT KAT

Lizzie nods in agreement. "Yeah, she's telling the truth. Do we still have to get ready for bed?"

"Sorry, girls. Please go brush your teeth." I am hoping that they will do this without argument. The urge I have to eat more is becoming painful.

As soon as the girls are out of sight, I shove another cookie into my mouth. The taste drives me to grab a plastic sandwich bag and fill it with four more, leaving only five in the Tupperware container. I know there's a chance the Andersons will question what happened to so many cookies tomorrow, but I don't care right now. Besides, is it abnormal for someone to eat six cookies?

When I slip the bag into my coat pocket, a sense of panic fills me because I realize that once those cookies are gone, there won't be anything else for me to eat. I check the clock, seven twenty-five. Mr. and Mrs. Anderson will be home soon. I peek into the bathroom to make sure the girls are still occupied. Lizzie is watching a sand-filled timer while she brushes, and Zoe is sticking foam letters to the mirror. I quickly tiptoe into the girls' bedroom and scan the room until I find what I'm looking for: a large porcelain cupcake bank. Lizzie had gotten it for her birthday in July. Looking back cautiously in the direction of the girls' voices, I carefully tip the bank over and pull out the black rubber stopper. Then I squeeze my fingers in to retrieve a couple of five-dollar bills. Two hours at eight dollars an hour won't be enough to buy food for the whole week. So, I need more, especially if I want to get a few things tonight. I will pay Lizzie back next time I babysit. "I promise," I whisper to no one.

"Hi, mommy!"

I nearly drop the bank when I hear Lizzie's greeting.

"Hey, girls. Did you have fun with Katie? Wait, where is Katie?"

I quickly replace the stopper, put the bank back on Lizzie's dresser, and grab the sets of pajamas that are lying out on the beds.

"Oh, hi, Mrs. Anderson," I say, trying to appear surprised to see her. "I was just getting the girls their PJs. Got caught up looking around at how cute their room is." I smile, and think about what a horrible person I am. Stealing a kid's money to buy food so I can binge eat. Don't drug addicts do this kind of thing?

"Thank you so much for watching them tonight," she says, taking the pajamas from me. "Jim's in the kitchen on his computer already. I'll finish getting the girls to bed if you want to just stop in there so he can pay you." She gives me a pink-cheeked grin that tells me she's been drinking, then turns to Zoe and Lizzie. "Say bye to Katie, girls!"

"Bye, Katie," they say in unison.

I give them both hugs and stop in the kitchen so that Mr. Anderson can pay me.

"Do you need me to walk you home, Katie?"

"Oh, no, of course not," I say, shaking my head. "I'll be fine. Thank you though. And thanks for the money." I hold up the fifteen dollars he's given me. I was expecting a little more, but I won't say anything, especially since I'm hiding cookies in my pocket and I just stole money from his daughter's piggy bank.

I leave the Anderson's house at seven forty-two. There definitely isn't enough time for me to go to the grocery store and be home by eight, but I'm willing to risk it.

I finish off the cookies I took from the Andersons on my way there. The only thing on my mind when I enter the store is getting more food and quickly getting home to eat it.

~

No one is at the front of the grocery store when I enter. This lessens some of the paranoia I'm feeling about what I'm about to buy. I can't help but wonder if people suspect the reason why I would buy so much junk.

The first person I see happens to be in the aisle I'm heading to. It's a woman pushing a cart with a toddler in it. The toddler eyes me suspiciously, as if he's afraid I might steal him. *Don't worry, little guy, I won't eat you.*

I pretend to read the ingredients on a box of Ho Hos until the toddler is pushed out of sight. That's when I quickly shove two boxes into my backpack. There's no time for me to be choosy right now. I'm already five minutes late. Next, I grab some of those generic Oreo cookies—the ones that are half white and half black—a six-pack of chocolate pudding and some Twinkies. My babysitting money is enough to pay for this stuff, so I can save the money from the cupcake bank for another day. The thought of the stolen money makes me hate myself even more than I thought possible, but my need to binge seems more important right now. I promise myself again that I'll replace Lizzie's money the next time I babysit for the Andersons, even if I have to risk taking it from my mom's wallet.

All I have to do now is pay and run home. Except when I exit the aisle, Nick is at the cash register. I think about ditching the items I'm holding and finding a back exit, but then he sees me and waves.

"Hey, Katie," he says warmly. Then he notices what I'm buying and his smile fades.

"Hi, Nick." I can barely make eye contact with him. I'm so embarrassed about the night before.

"Buying some snacks?" he says as he scans the Twinkies.

"Yeah, my mom—"

"Do you remember what you told me last night?"

I meet his concerned eyes and open my mouth to speak but nothing comes out. Probably because I'm panicking inside and I have no idea what to say. I remember everything now, and I wish there was some way I could take it all back.

"Katie? About when you eat?"

My eyes travel from the snacks on the conveyor back to Nick's eyes. I know he's trying to reach out—to help—but suddenly, I'm angry. Angry with myself, with Dominic, with that bitch Sloan and most of all, with Nick. My eating habits are none of his business. He had no right being in Selena's room with me anyway. Dominic was right; he was probably just trying to take advantage of me. I just want to go home and eat until I can't eat anymore. So, I shake my head and say, "Just tell me how much I owe? I have to get home."

Nick is quiet for a moment and then he begins putting my things into a plastic bag. "Eight fifty-two."

I pay and leave without looking at him again. I don't even say goodbye.

"Excuse me," I say to a man heading into the store, "Do you know what time it is?"

"Yeah." He checks his cell phone. "Eight twenty-five."

"Thanks," I say, already walking away.

I think about sprinting home, but I can feel the popcorn and cookies churning around in my stomach, begging to be released. So I open the box of Twinkies and begin eating those too. When the box is gone, I'm standing on the playground of my elementary school. I'm going to be in trouble anyway, so I might as well finish what I started before I go home.

As I make my way to the swings and tire tunnels, I look around and allow memories—all good—to flood my brain. I shake my head and sigh, part of me wondering why I would come to a place that represents such happy times in my life to do something so disgusting. I stop for a moment and consider turning around. My house is only three blocks away. I could be home in less than five minutes. Instead, my nearly full stomach calls to me.

Fill me up, Katie. You'll feel better if you do.

I climb on top of one of the tire structures and remove my backpack. Then I begin shoving Ho Hos into my mouth. While I eat, I envision the playground as it was when I was a kid. I see a large group of kids playing kickball. There was an equipment shed that all the good kickers aimed for. If you could kick the ball on top of the shed, it was an automatic homerun. I see Rebecca Winters trotting around like a horse, and I even hear one of her loud neighs. The same twinge of embarrassment that I used to feel for her when people would stare and laugh hits me as if I've traveled back in time and I'm there again. I see the box drawn on the side of the school. It was for a game called strikeout, but a lot of kids also called it the kissing box. If you stood in front of it, you were inviting the person you liked to kiss you. I think about how if Hunter was here with me, I would stand in that box all night.

When I reach the point of perfect fullness, the only thing left is the pudding and the black and white cookies. I put my backpack on, jump down and head for the bushes—the bushes that used to be loose enough for my friends and me to hide in. Now they are thick and overgrown.

After I bend over and give a little push, there is a loud splatter as Ho Hos spill onto the ground. I am about to give another push when I hear something, causing me to spin around.

Heading toward me is a group of kids. *Crap.* What if it's someone I know?

I have no choice. I run to the nearest opening in the fence surrounding the playground and don't stop until I am home.

～

Gary is in the kitchen when I enter. He gives me a hard stare and then yells to my mom. "Elaine! She's home!"

As I remove my boots, hat and coat, I hear my mom wrapping up a phone conversation. "Yes, she's home. Thank you, I appreciate you calling me back. Mm-hm, yeah, okay. Buh-bye."

As soon as my foot hits the third step, she starts in on me.

"Where were you?" I imagine a window breaking at the shrillness of her voice. "God damn it, Katie. It's nearly nine o' clock!"

I am so sick of being stared at, questioned, talked about and yelled at. I am so incredibly sick of it all! "I went for a walk. I needed some fresh air. Okay?"

"No, it's not okay. You were supposed to come right home after babysitting. We were worried about you! The Andersons were worried about you!"

My stomach gurgles, and I feel all the crappy food still left in my stomach sloshing around.

"And they're not just worried about you because we had no idea where you were. Mrs. Anderson mentioned how skinny you are, too. She has a cousin who's anorexic."

"Well, I'm not anorexic!" I scream and run up the stairs.

How dare she talk to another person about my body! Argh! I just want to screeeaaaaam!

I fall heavily to my knees, slam the toilet seat open and purge myself of everything that's left in my stomach. The last thing I taste is popcorn and a few bits of chocolate.

I rest my head on my arms across the rim of the toilet bowl. Normally making contact with the bowl would disgust me, but I'm too emotionally exhausted to care right now.

When I finally open my eyes, Gary, my mom and Kelsie are standing in the bathroom doorway. Kelsie is crying.

"See," my mom says with an I-told-you-so tone, "she's not getting any better. I knew it. I need to make that appointment with the therapist."

One by one, my family members leave. Kelsie is last. She glares at me and doesn't say anything. Then she slaps the wall so hard that the floor shakes and mutters, "Dammit," before storming into her room and slamming the door.

So, I'm left there on the floor, dizzy from everything that has happed since I got off the phone with Carly two short hours ago. Before anyone knew about what I've been doing, I felt so in control and good after I threw up. Now, I just feel guilty, crazy and out of control.

The house is silent when I finally pull myself to my feet and get ready for bed. I just want to crawl under the covers, close my eyes and fall into a deep sleep. Part of me even wishes that I could just sleep forever, but I've been wishing that for months, so I don't think it's going to be granted—not unless I do something to make it happen.

When I flip on my bedroom light, the fatigue I'm feeling is replaced by anger and an extra burst of energy. My room is in shambles. Drawers are open. My wicker chest is open. My closet is open. My blankets and sheets have been pulled to the floor.

I rush to my bed and shove a hand underneath the mattress. When I don't find what I'm looking for, I slide my hand all around until no space is left unsearched.

My laxatives are gone.

Chapter Twenty-Three

I *can't do this. I just can't do this.*

I hit the snooze button for the second time, but I'm no closer to being ready to get out of bed than I was the first time. I am dreading facing everyone now that Sloan has been running her big mouth. Even teachers will probably find out what happened on Friday night, if they don't already know. I don't know which is worse, that I was kissing Nick or what I said about always throwing up. A tear trails down the side of my face and into my ear.

"Katie! It's seven o' clock! You need to get up!" My mom yells from the kitchen.

At least it's not an angry yell, nothing like the way she yelled at me yesterday afternoon. Three hours. That's how long it lasted. It started out with my mom, Gary and I sitting down at the dining room table together to discuss the laxatives. I swore to my mom that the box they'd found was the only one I'd ever purchased, which was a lie for two reasons. I don't know for certain how many boxes of laxatives I've gone through, and I've never actually purchased one.

I received a lecture about over-the-counter drug abuse, which turned into a lecture about alcohol and sex—most of the same stuff she'd already said to me the day before. I thought about the cookies and pudding stashed in my room the entire time.

Kelsie had to work a ten-hour shift yesterday, so she wasn't there. She still didn't say anything to me before she left. She didn't even look at me. At first, her ignoring me made me feel bad, because I felt like I let her down. But now, I think she's just being a bitch. If she cares about me, why won't she talk to me?

Eventually, my mom made me call my dad to tell him what was going on. That was when Gary left the room. She made me admit that I'm still throwing up and that I need professional help. She even made me practice saying it over-and-over before calling: *I'm still making myself throw up, and I need professional help.* When I finally said the words to my dad, they meant nothing to me.

He reacted first with silence, then sniffling, and finally words of encouragement. Then he asked to talk to my mom, which resulted in a lot of yelling on both ends. I even heard my dad screaming a few times from where I was sitting, a few feet away from my mom. She would look really calm when my dad was yelling but then she would start yelling back. They went back and forth for nearly an hour like that, talking mostly about whose fault it was. The call finally ended with my mom telling my dad she'd call first thing Monday morning to make an appointment with a therapist. Then as soon as she was off the phone, my mom started complaining about how she's always been the one who's had to take care of things for Kelsie and me.

Then it was over. Problem solved—for my parents anyway. I would see a therapist who would fix me for them.

My mom and Gary went grocery shopping while I stayed home and binged on the cookies and pudding from the night before. Later, I walked on the treadmill while they worked out in the basement for two hours. Gary asked my mom at one point if she thought it was a good idea for me to be exercising in my condition. She said it would be good for me to tone up before I start putting on weight again. I guess even as skinny as she says I am, my body still isn't good enough for her.

Carly is waiting for me at the end of our driveway when I finally walk outside. She's wearing a black coat that I've never seen before and matching pink hat and gloves. If I didn't know her, I'd think she had always been part of the OH clique. That's how fashionable she looks.

"Hey, Carly. I like your new winter gear."

"Thanks," she says with a proud smile.

We start walking. The knot in my stomach becomes a little tighter for every inch we walk in silence. If things are this awkward with Carly after what Sloan told her, I'm sure it'll be ten times worse with the others. I feel like I'm going to throw up.

I can't do this!

Finally, Carly says, "So, is everything okay with your mom now?"

"Yeah, I guess. She's making me go to a therapist. My dad wants me to go too."

"That's good!" Carly's smile fades as soon as she sees the expression on my face. "I mean, if you're sick, then you should see a doctor. So you can get better. Right?"

I nod once and whisper, "Yeah." I haven't told Carly much about my issue, and she's acting like she knows exactly what I need.

"What about Anthony's friend? Did you and your mom talk about him?"

"Sort of. She lectured me about sex. And she was pretty much yelling the entire time."

Carly nods. "Mmm. So, I take it you're still grounded?"

"Two weeks."

"Darn. I was going to ask you if you wanted to go sledding next weekend."

I don't even bother to ask for any details. I can't go anyway.

We walk in silence for a minute, but then Carly starts talking about an assignment she's working on for English class. I realize she's talking like nothing is wrong. I thought that was what I wanted, but now it just feels weird. She thought my throwing up was such a big deal when she first found out, but now . . . what? Because my parents are forcing me to go to a therapist, she's considering me already fixed?

What would it even mean to be "fixed" at this point?

I am relieved when no one else is at the bus stop. The longer I can avoid seeing people, the better. But my relief is short-lived because I feel like a million eyes are on me when we get on the bus. To make things worse, the bus driver snaps at me when I don't scan my bus pass right away. "We don't have all day. Come on."

Carly curls her lip at him and pulls me to the back.

Selena and Darcy are in the very back row, as usual. Dominic and Beth are sitting in the two-person row in front of them. And Hunter is sitting by himself in front of Dominic and Beth. He has his back to the window and his legs are extended so that both seats are taken up. They are all watching as we approach.

"Hey, guys," Carly says when we're four rows away from where all our friends are sitting.

I smile but say nothing. I'm not even sure my voice would work right now if I tried to speak.

I hear a few heys and a hi. Dominic gives me a wave and Darcy smiles, but Beth and Selena don't even make eye contact with me.

Hunter smiles and removes his legs from the seat next to him. "Wanna sit here, Katie?"

Carly is already plopping herself down next to Darcy in the back row, so I nod and sit down next to him.

"How was your weekend?" Hunter asks.

If he knows anything about Friday night, he sure isn't acting like it.

"Um, it was okay. How about you? How was yours?"

"It was good. I told you how my dad's boss was taking us to dinner on Friday, right? Holy cow! I've never had such awesome food before."

"Where did you go?"

"I don't remember what the restaurant is called, but it's at the River Club of Mequon."

I shrug. "Never been there."

"Yeah, well, that's not the kind of place my family usually goes to either. But my dad's boss was treating, so, you know."

I nod.

Hunter continues, "Then on Saturday..." He nods his head toward Dominic. "we went to the Bucks game. I told Dominic we should invite you, but he said you were busy. What were you up to?"

My face reddens as I peek over my shoulder at Dominic and Beth to see if they're listening. Dominic raises his eyebrows and Beth glares at me.

"Um . . . I had to babysit for some neighbors. That's why I couldn't go to a movie. Remember?"

He nods and then says, "Are you babysitting this coming weekend? I mean, do you have time to see a movie yet?"

Yes, yes, yes, yes! Despite the insecurity I feel about getting too close to Hunter, my heart can't help but leap for joy—that is, until I remember I'm grounded and, more importantly, why. There's no way Hunter won't find out about everything that happened at Selena's. And there's no way he's still going to want to go to a movie with me when he does.

"Sorry. I can't," I say, shaking my head. "I have family stuff going on the next couple of weeks."

"You're not just saying you can't go because of Sloan, are you? Because Sloan and I are just friends." He quickly follows up with, "Not that you and I are more than friends or anything. I mean, I just thought it would be cool to hang out somewhere besides school and the bus. You know?" He smiles.

"No, of course it's not because of Sloan," I sort of lie.

Beth lets out a sarcastic snort, causing Hunter and me to both turn around.

"What?" She asks.

"What was that for?" Hunter asks.

Please, Beth, don't say anything about me being grounded or about the party. I plead to her with my eyes.

"Nothing," Dominic says firmly.

Beth rolls her eyes.

"Okay," Hunter mumbles.

We both turn back around.

"So, we'll see a movie after your family stuff is all taken care of? In a couple of weekends?" Hunter asks.

"Maybe."

"Alright, cool."

As the bus pulls up to our stop, I do my best to hide the deep breaths that I'm taking. Even though it's around twenty degrees outside, I remove my hat and unwrap my scarf because my nervousness is making me sweat like crazy.

As I walk next to Hunter, my eyes frantically dart from person to person as I watch for Amy or Anica or—God help me—Sloan. I have no idea what I will do if someone says something to me about Friday, especially if Hunter is around to hear it.

Luckily, I make it inside without seeing any of the OH girls, and no one seems to look at me funny at all. Besides the fact that Beth clearly can't stand me and Selena is ignoring me, maybe I'm making a big deal out of nothing.

~

"Hey, Katie! Wait up!" Dominic walks quickly to catch up with me.

I was planning to hide out in the bathroom by the band room, but now I have a feeling that won't be happening.

The good news is, so far, everything has seemed perfectly normal. Even in gym, none of the OH girls paid attention to me and Anica didn't look at me in language arts or Spanish either. Maybe I didn't have to be so nervous after all.

"Hey, Dominic." For the first time today, I smile for real.

"Where're you going? It's lunch time." He points toward the cafeteria.

"I was just going to ask Mr. Reynolds a question . . . about that band competition we can sign up for."

"He's not in there. I just saw him by the office. C'mon, let's go to lunch."

Dominic leads me to what has become his usual table. Waiting at the table are Beth (of course), Hunter and three other guys (Chris, Brett and Paul), who have also been sitting there all year long. I sort of feel like I know these other guys because we're all friends with Dominic and Hunter, but they never really talk to me directly. That's fine, though. I prefer to listen to lunch conversations anyway.

Beth smiles at Dominic as he approaches, but as soon as she spots me, her expression becomes a scowl. I sigh to myself as I smile at her and wave anyway. I've decided to be nice to her even if she continues wishing I would disappear. After all, she is Dominic's girlfriend.

Dominic sits next to Beth, and I take the empty seat between him and Hunter.

While Dominic chats with Beth and Hunter talks to the other guys, I take out a bag of celery sticks, a bottle of water and a Spanish worksheet that was assigned for homework.

"What're you working on, Katie?" Hunter says in my ear. I feel his breath on my cheek, causing a flashback of Nick from Friday night. I remember wishing Nick was Hunter.

Turning to face him, I pull my head away a couple of inches. "Peanuts?"

"You're working on peanuts?"

"No," I laugh. "Your breath smells like peanuts."

He breathes into his hand and makes a disgusted face, causing me to laugh out loud. "My breath does smell like peanuts! But I didn't eat any peanuts." He smiles and shrugs.

"It's Spanish homework."

He leans in close to me again to get a good look at the worksheet. "I'm taking German. But I do know some words in Spanish."

"Really? Like what?"

He looks up at the ceiling for a moment and then back at me. "Like bonita."

My cheeks become so warm that I have to look away from him. "Okay. What else do you know?"

Hunter is about to answer when Sloan appears next to us. Amy, Anica and Laney are looking on from a few feet away. They all seem like they're waiting for something to happen.

"What's up, Sloan?" Hunter asks, sounding uninterested.

I can barely breathe. What does she want?

"Actually, I have a present for Katie."

I look up at her in surprise. Her smirk is much bigger than usual. This can't possibly be good.

Before I can blink, Sloan leans in with a plastic bag and dumps something onto our table. I hear a mixture of gasps and laughter as I turn my head to find a huge pile of mini Kit Kat bars in front of me.

"For you next binge," she says coldly, before spinning around to leave.

I stare at the dozens of candy bars piled in front of me and am overcome by the all too familiar feeling of wanting to die. My head is pounding, sort of like when you first get done listening to really loud music, so I can barely hear what anyone around me is saying. I finally look up, and see Chris, Brett and Paul trying not to laugh. Then I turn my head back toward Sloan, my eyes meeting Hunter's for a split second. His lips are moving and he's placing a hand on my forearm, but I pay no attention. Sloan and Anica are laughing hysterically, but Laney and Amy don't look too amused. Laney rolls her eyes and Amy shakes her head. When she looks at me, I snap back around, stand, and shove my chair back in one swift motion. *I have to get out of here.*

I don't just walk out of the cafeteria, I run. And I don't stop when I find myself alone in the hallway. I keep going, out the door and to the sidewalk in front of school. I don't even have my coat, but I don't care. I had to get out of there.

I crouch down and watch as my tears drop to the ground. The pounding in my brain finally stops when my body realizes how cold it is. I can hear cars now. Cars and crows. Both sounds make me think of faraway places, and I wish I could be in one of those places. It could be the North Pole. I don't care. I just don't want to be here.

When my cheeks start to sting, I know I need to go back inside. Tingles travel through my legs and feet as I stand. My arms are filled with goose bumps and my teeth are chattering. As I slowly walk back to the building, I hear a door open and see Hunter when I look up. He's holding my backpack in one hand and my Spanish homework in the other. Dominic is right behind him, and Beth is holding the door.

"Come on, Katie. It's freezing out here," Dominic calls.

When I get close enough, Hunter holds my things out to me. "I got your stuff for you," he says.

If I was feeling more like myself, I would tease him for stating the obvious, but I realize he just doesn't know what else to say. "Thank you," I say as I take the items from him.

As soon as we get inside, the bell rings, but no one moves a muscle. We all just stand there staring at each other.

"I'm just gonna go home," I say to no one in particular.

"No." We all look at Beth. "That's what she wants. She wants you to hide and feel bad about yourself." She shakes her head. "I don't know. I guess making other people feel like crap makes her feel good about herself or something."

"She's right, Katie, you shouldn't go home. Who cares about Sloan?" Dominic gives me a reassuring look.

"How could you even like someone like that?" Beth asks Hunter.

He sighs heavily. "I don't know. She's . . . she's Amy's friend and . . . I don't know."

"So? What does Sloan being Amy's friend have to do with you dating her?" Beth says exactly what's on my mind.

Hunter looks at Beth with confusion. "You don't know that Amy's my cousin?"

"What?" Beth and I say at the same time.

"Dude. Amy Bowie is your cousin?" Dominic asks.

"Yeah, I thought you guys knew that. She nagged and nagged for me to go out with Sloan, and I didn't know anyone at first so I agreed. Then when I found out what she's really like, I couldn't get rid of her. I should have known better. Amy's always talking me into doing stupid stuff, ever since we were little."

"Dude. I can't believe you didn't mention that you were Amy's cousin." Dominic still seems shocked, but there's no way he's as shocked as I am.

"What's the big deal?" Hunter asks. "Amy's nothing like Sloan. You guys like her, right?"

"Let's just say we like her about as much as we like Sloan. You know, your *ex*-girlfriend, the one who's spreading the rumors about Katie?" Beth says.

Hunter shakes his head. "I know, I know. She's a total bitch." He looks at me. "I'm really sorry she's telling people all this stuff about you. But . . . is any of it true?"

"Does it matter?" Dominic asks defensively.

"No, just wondering." Hunter focuses on me again. "I know I've asked you this before, but . . . is that why you've lost so much weight? Because you have an eating disorder?"

"Hunter!" Beth snaps.

I close my eyes and wish I could disappear because now I know that Hunter has heard everything. Why is he still being so nice to me then?

"What?" He throws his arms up and brings them down with a slap against his thighs. "If it's true, then why wouldn't we talk about it? She'll need support from people to get better, right?" He looks at me when he's done talking.

Why does he sound like he knows from experience? Does he know about Amy?

"What are you, an expert?" Dominic asks.

Before Hunter can answer, we all turn our heads toward the sound of approaching footsteps. It's Mr. Donovan, the vice principal. "What on Earth are you kids doing? The bell rang nearly ten minutes ago." He seems angry at first, but then he sees the serious looks on our faces. "Is there a problem? Katie, are you okay?"

"I'm fine, Mr. Donovan. I'm just having some problems at home. You know, arguing with my mom a lot lately. My friends were just trying to make me feel better."

Mr. Donovan's face softens. "Well, I'm happy to hear that you have such good friends. But that doesn't excuse all of you from going to your classes. Come with me. I'll provide you all with late slips, but don't let me find you in the hall again when class is in session. Understood?"

We all nod and follow. Before Hunter and Beth break off into the

opposite direction of Dominic and me—since we have math together—
Hunter tells me he'll see me in science. And Beth gives me a hug. She
doesn't say anything, but I can tell from the hug that she's not mad at me
anymore. So at least one good thing came from Sloan and her games.

～

As I gather my things from my locker at the end of the day, I go over the
afternoon in my mind. It wasn't nearly as torturous as I thought it
would be.

Math and art seemed to last forever, but at least no one looked at me
funny or mentioned anything about the Kit Kat incident. Unfortunately,
science—which I have with Hunter, Sloan, and Anica—was another
story. Tomorrow we have a test, so everyone worked in groups playing
review games. At first I didn't notice it, but then someone in my group
said, "Hey, is someone throwing up?" We all looked around only to see
all the other groups quietly working together. But then I heard it, a
quiet gagging sound. I focused my attention across the room where the
noise had come from, but then I was surprised to hear it again coming
from the table right next to ours—the table where Anica sits.

Eventually, people started to realize that Sloan and Anica were
taking turns making the noises. They both had their groups giggling in
no time. Most of the kids in the other groups didn't seem to know what
all the laughing was about, though. I even heard one girl in Anica's
group ask if she was okay, clearly not up to speed on the big joke of the
day—me.

Near the end of class, Sloan walked to the pencil sharpener and
paused behind me to make a loud vomiting sound. I was shocked when
Hunter said loudly from across the room, "Would you just knock it off,
Sloan? My little sister is more mature than you. And *way* less of a brat."
Sloan's eyes grew to the size of half-dollars and she looked ready to
pounce. Everyone stopped what they were doing and looked from
Hunter to Sloan, prompting our teacher, Mr. Lentz, to ask, "Is there a
problem?" No one said anything, but at least that was the end of the
attempts to humiliate me further.

I could feel Hunter's eyes on me after what he said to Sloan, but I
couldn't bring myself to look at him. I was grateful for what he did, but

at the same time, afraid that it would piss Sloan off even more. Plus, I was too embarrassed to meet his gaze.

By the time the bell rang, I was ready to thank Hunter for standing up to Sloan, but Mr. Lentz asked to have a word with the two of them. As I made my way to the door, I risked the possibility of eye contact with Sloan by looking at Hunter. I mouthed "thank you," and he responded with a grin. Then I had no choice but to leave, even though I wished I could wait for Hunter, because Mr. Lentz began questioning them about the disturbance during class.

I'm still caught up in my thoughts when someone calls my name. Carly is wearing her cheer squad uniform and has her hair tied up into a super high ponytail with an obnoxiously large bow. I blink a few times as visions of pre-cheer squad Carly flash through my mind. She certainly doesn't look like a tomboy now.

"Hey, Carly," I say, forcing a smile. But then it registers that she isn't smiling back.

"I just heard about what happened. Sloan is such an idiot!" She stomps her foot like a child having a fit. "I swear to God, I'm going to let her have it after the game!"

People stare as they pass us in the hall.

"Carly," I whisper, my voice shaking, "please stop yelling. I'm embarrassed enough as it is."

"Oh, my gosh, I'm sorry." She puts an arm around me and walks with me toward the front doors.

"So, you had no idea Sloan was going to do that? None of the other girls said anything?" I ask.

Carly jerks her head back like she's been burned. "No, of course not! I don't think anyone knew what she was going to do. The other girls are getting tired of her snotty attitude. I can tell."

I nod in response. The problem is, it doesn't matter if Sloan's friends are sick of her. It won't stop her from bullying me, and it doesn't mean her friends will treat me any differently either.

Carly's eyes widen when she looks up at the clock in the hall. "I gotta go," she says as she begins walking backwards, away from me. "I'll see you tomorrow!"

I wave, but she's already hurrying down the hall.

I walk to the bus stop with my eyes on the sidewalk the entire time.

A few times, I think I hear my name coming from different groups of kids, but it could just be my imagination. Still, I can't help but wish Dominic was here, instead of getting picked up by his dad for work at the store.

Relief washes over me the second I step on the bus. *I made it.*

Now that the pressure of walking by myself through crowds of students is off, I wonder where Hunter is. He said he'd be on the bus. Did Sloan get to him? Did she somehow find a way to make him think that what she did wasn't a big deal?

Maybe it wasn't such a big deal. Am I being a big baby? Not just about the Kit Kat bars, but about my life in general? Is my life really so bad that I should be so angry and sad all the time? Is my food problem really something that I can't control? Or am I just using being sad as a reason to eat as much junk food as I want, and then throwing it all up for attention?

My mom never let me eat any of the stuff I binge on when I was little, partially because we couldn't afford it and partially because she didn't want my sister and me to become overweight. She used to look at me and say, "You must get that little pooch and bowed legs from your dad's side of the family." Then she'd laugh. As I got older and started developing, she didn't laugh anymore. Anytime she saw me naked or in a swimsuit, it felt like her stare was burning my skin. Long and lean Kelsie has always worn bikinis, but my mom always insisted that I get one pieces. I wonder what I'd look like in a bikini now. The pooch is still there, but I'm almost as skinny as Kelsie.

Moans fill the bus when it jerks to a stop after driving only a few feet. This happens whenever someone is late, causing the bus driver to stop and wait. When the door opens, Hunter appears. He spots me as soon as he's done scanning his pass.

I smile as he approaches, but have mixed feelings that he made it. I'm happy to see him (but I'm not) and I want to talk to him (but I don't).

"Hi," he says as he squeezes past me into the window seat next to mine.

"Hi," I say, turning to face him. "And thank you."

"For that thing with Sloan? Trust me, she had that coming for a lot of reasons. But, you're welcome."

We ride in silence for a while. I wonder if this is what's considered an awkward moment? Is everything he probably heard about me today finally hitting him? Is he starting to realize that I'm a total freak? Is it possible that he didn't know about Nick earlier, but that Sloan filled him in on everything after Mr. Lentz was done talking to them?

My thoughts continue to race until the bus pulls over at the next stop, blocks away from the hospital where Kelsie works. That's when I sense Hunter staring at me. I peek at him out of the corner of my eye at first, allowing my head to turn only when I am certain that he's looking at me.

"What?" I ask.

"Nothing. I was just thinking about when Dominic and I were dancing around you like dorks at the first dance." A small grin forms on his face. "You've changed a lot since then."

"Oh." My shoulders slouch a little at his response, and I straighten my head to look forward.

"You're quieter now. And you seem kinda . . . I don't know, sad. But . . . you're still the prettiest girl in school."

What? I turn my head to face him more quickly this time, my mouth open in shock. No one has ever told me that I'm pretty, not even my mom or dad. I've never been the pretty one, Kelsie is.

"So, do you still want to see a movie?" He asks.

"I . . . yeah, I guess. But, Hunter, why do you still want to go to a movie with *me*? You do know that your cousin and her friends . . . well, it's not just Sloan who doesn't like me."

He rolls his eyes and lets out a quick puff of air through his nose. "Katie, I don't care about what Amy and her friends think, especially Sloan. You and I are friends, right? I mean, I've secretly wanted to ask you to a movie since the first day of school. That whole thing with Sloan was sort of an accident, you know? And I know for a fact that Amy doesn't dislike you."

I want to ask how he knows, but instead, I just nod. "Okay, but, what about everything you heard about me today? The stuff that *everyone* was hearing. Thanks to Sloan."

He shrugs. "I didn't hear about any of that from you, and I wasn't there to see anything with my own eyes, so I don't really care what Sloan says. Plus," He squeezes his eyebrows together. "Those things don't matter to me for some reason. I like you anyway."

I think about telling him that I really don't have family stuff this weekend. But would he still like me if he knew that on top of everything else, I'm a big fat liar too? Plus, if I tell him that I'm grounded, maybe what happened at Selena's party with Nick *will* matter to him. Why would I be grounded if nothing serious happened?

"Friday or Saturday?" I ask.

"What?"

"In two weekends. Would you rather go to the movie on Friday or Saturday? I know there's a dance on Friday, so . . ."

"That's right, the dance. Do you want to—"

I begin shaking my head, knowing what he is about to say.

"Okay, okay." He laughs a little. "You don't want to go to the dance. Then let's go on Friday during the dance."

"Deal," I say, smiling to myself.

Chapter Twenty-Four

The earliest appointment my mom could get with the psychologist was for Tuesday at nine. I wake up that morning knowing I won't get to school until sometime during third period. Luckily, I have band on Tuesdays, so I won't have to walk in late to gym class and face having everyone's eyes on me.

Gary is going to have to drive me since my mom can't take a day off without giving the parents of the kids she watches at least a week's notice.

Ever since yesterday when Hunter and I made plans to see a movie, I have been feeling less down than usual. I still took two laxatives from my new stash (which I now keep in a pencil pouch in my backpack) before dinner last night, but I didn't feel as driven to try to sneak food from the kitchen once my mom settled onto the couch for the night. Every time I thought about him telling me he thinks I'm pretty, I couldn't help but smile.

"Hey, mom," I say as I pour myself some orange juice at breakfast.

"Mm hm?" She is busy washing and cutting up berries for the two toddlers she watches. Brandon is jumping up and down in an activity saucer.

"I think I might be okay now. I mean, I'll go to this appointment, but—"

"You're darn right you'll go!" She gives me a hard stare before going back to slicing.

The sadness—an ache that spans from my chest to my stomach—that I've grown so familiar with returns. What made me start feeling this way in the first place? Anica? My body? My dad? Or could it be my mom? I was feeling okay until just now.

"Katie," she pauses to hand the toddlers, Sarah and Mindy, each a bowl of strawberries and blueberries. "You are not okay. You might feel okay at times, but until you start gaining back some weight, you are not okay. Brenda says treatment could take months. Even years."

The mention of our neighbor makes me cringe.

"Gary!" My mom yells. "It's almost eight thirty! You and Katie have to get going!"

Then she grips my shoulders and leans in to look me in the eyes. "The more serious you take this today, the quicker you'll start getting better. Okay?"

I nod and mumble, "Okay."

~

Gary and I are sitting next to each other in the lobby of the Park Dale Clinic, which is in an office building next to the mall where Anica and I got caught shoplifting. Gary is filling out paperwork, and I'm eyeing a wall of pamphlets. Alcohol Addiction. Anger Management. Divorce. Domestic Violence. Eating Disorders. Grief. Obsessive-Compulsive Disorder. My eyes travel back to the pamphlet that says Eating Disorders in big black letters. I look over at the receptionist and catch her staring at me.

She quickly puts a smile on her face, stands and says, "Can I get you something, dear? Water? Tea?"

"No, thank you." I smile politely and turn my gaze to my lap. When she asks Gary if he'd like anything, I peek at the pamphlet again.

"A cup of coffee would be a real treat right now. Thank you," Gary says as he stands to return the pen and clipboard full of paperwork.

"Cream and sugar?" the receptionist asks. The nameplate at the counter says Dawn. She looks like a Dawn.

"Cream, no sugar. Thank you." Gary returns to the chair next to mine, and Dawn disappears into a little room behind the counter.

"Katie, your mother wants me to remind you how important it is for you to be open and honest with Dr. Abendi. The more cooperative you are with everyone, the easier it will be for you to get over this thing that's going on with you."

I stare at Gary for a second before nodding once. Then I say, "Okay," just as Dawn zips over to us, steaming paper cup in hand.

"Here you go, Mr. Clifton. Katie, are you sure you don't want some water? You can take it into Dr. Abendi's office when he's ready for you."

"I'm sure. Thanks," I say a little louder than the last time I declined.

"Alright then, Dr. Abendi will be with you shortly." Dawn gives me another smile, just like the first one after I caught her staring at me. It's a warm smile, but there's something else behind it. Does she know why I'm here? Does she pity me?

Gary sips his coffee as he walks over to the wall of pamphlets. He removes one of the Eating Disorder ones and holds it out so I can read the headline as he returns to his seat. When he starts reading the pamphlet, I think to myself that this might be the most interest Gary has shown in me in all the years he's known me.

"Katie?" Gary and I both look up to see a dark-complected man with salt and pepper hair holding a door open. The door has a window made of frosty glass, the kind that people can't see through. "I'm Dr. Abendi." Then he turns to Gary. "Would you like to be present during Katie's session today, sir?"

"No, no, that's okay." Gary pats my shoulder. "I'll wait for you here, alright?"

"Sure, see you soon," I say as I move toward the doctor who smiles warmly and gestures for me to go through the doorway.

He closes the door behind him and leads me down a bright hallway past four closed doors marked with the names of other doctors. When we get to his office, I glance at his full name as I walk in. Dr. Hiram Abendi, Psychologist, PhD.

He takes a seat in an emerald green chair with an afghan hanging over the back. It looks like one of my grandmother's. I stand awkwardly in the middle of the small room, not sure where to sit. There's a loveseat directly across from his chair and a chair that matches his to the right of the loveseat. His desk is off to the left of the door, so he must always sit in the chair he's in during sessions.

"You can sit wherever you feel most comfortable, Katie," he says as he removes a pair of glasses from his shirt pocket and puts them on. Then he taps the tip of a pen against the clipboard he's holding while he waits for me to take a seat. It isn't an impatient tap, just friendly and rhythmic, as if he's playing a song in his head to pass the time. I almost expect him to start whistling the way my dad always does.

Finally, I walk over to the chair and take a seat, shifting a few times before looking up at Dr. Abendi. He smiles and writes something.

"What are you writing?" I ask.

"Oh, I just like to note where patients sit during sessions. That's all."

"Why? What does it matter where people sit?" Actually, I'm sure it does matter. After all, I chose not to sit in the loveseat because it seemed like I'd be too close to him.

He smiles the same warm smile that I'm sure must be fake. How can someone smile like that all the time?

"It really doesn't matter, Katie. It's just an old habit of mine." He taps his temple. "Helps my old brain remember sessions more precisely."

I respond with a nod.

"So, tell me why you're here, Katie."

"You know why I'm here. Don't you?"

"I know why your mother says you need to be here, but I'd like to know why you think you need to be here."

"But I don't think I need to be here. My mom made me come. I tried to tell her this morning that I'm okay now, but she wouldn't listen to me. Instead, she's listening to our neighbor, who barely knows me."

"Your neighbor? How is she involved?"

"She's a therapist. She told my mom to take me to a psychologist. So here I am." I lift my hands out to the sides with my palms up and then let them flop down onto the arms of the chair.

"And why do you feel as though you don't need to be here?"

"Because there's nothing wrong with me. I mean, I was having trouble with food for a while, but I think I'll be fine."

"Okay. Can you tell me a little bit about school, Katie? Favorite subjects? Friends? Do you like school?"

Okay? That's it? "Uh, yeah, I guess school is okay," I lie. "I have some really good friends, mostly from grade school. And I like every subject. English is my favorite."

I leave out that even though I like science and gym, I hate going to those classes because of who some of my classmates are. I also leave out the fact that my best friend is now friends with girls who I wanted to be friends with, girls who she had no interest in before she made cheer squad—oh, and that Carly only tried out for cheer squad because of me.

Dr. Abendi goes on to ask more question about my classes and assignments, my relationships with family members, and how I feel about my mom and dad's divorce. Before I know it, the sound of water drops—*plip, plip, plip*—comes from his cell phone, marking the end of our session.

Except for right at the beginning when Dr. Abendi asked me why I was there, we didn't discuss my food issues again. We didn't talk about alcohol or sexual promiscuity either. The funny thing is, I actually feel okay when Gary drops me off at school. I debate whether I should tell my mom the truth about what we talked about, but decide I might not tell her anything at all. As long as I go to Dr. Abendi, my mom and dad will be happy, right? So why not go to a few more appointments so that they can forget about this whole eating disorder thing?

Chapter Twenty-Five

After changing my outfit for the third time, I examine myself in the mirror. First, I stand with my arms at my sides. Next, I turn to get a good sideways look at myself. Then, I turn so that my back is facing the mirror and look over my shoulder to see what my backside looks like. Finally, I return to facing forward. Sometimes I repeat this process thee or four times.

Tonight is my movie date with Hunter. I see him every day at school, so I can't figure out why I'm so nervous. Looking at myself in the mirror doesn't help, either.

None of my clothes fit right anymore. Tops are better than bottoms, unless I wear leggings, but even leggings look funny on me. Whenever I wear them, all I seem to think about is that people are looking at the way my inner thighs rub together when I walk. My bras fit funny now, too. Instead of providing a little lift like they used to, giving the illusion that my boobs were bigger than they really were, I now have nothing to be boosted. I don't understand how it's possible for my bras to still fit exactly the same around my chest, yet the cup area is nothing but loose fabric that caves in.

Finally, I choose the first outfit I tried on—dark gray jeans and a flowy white top with silver sparkles. The jeans are hand-me-downs from our neighbor Chelsea, and the top was a Christmas gift. Hunter has already seen me in this exact outfit, but today I'm going to add a floral scarf.

I turn again to look at my backside and notice that the jeans are sagging. How is it even possible for them to sag and still feel tight around my hips? I remember seeing Chelsea in these jeans. They fit her perfectly.

After tightening a belt around my waist to get rid of some of the sag, I look in the mirror again—this time from the front. Trying to look long and lean, I stand as upright as possible.

Ugh. I could lose another twenty pounds, and I still wouldn't look lean.

I haven't thrown up since my second session with Dr. Abendi—but that's partially due to the laxatives, too. We actually talked about my issues this time. He told me it was extremely important for us to figure out why I feel the need to binge and purge and then asked me a lot of questions, some that were difficult to answer, like do I remember the first time I made myself throw up and how do I feel right before I binge. I used up most of his tissues when I told him about the first time I made myself throw up, and I had a hard time explaining the way I feel when I get the urge to binge. I guess it's because I feel a bunch of different things before I start stuffing myself.

Sometimes it's like I'm a robot without a brain or emotions. I just do it. But I didn't tell him this last part because I felt like that could mean there's something else wrong with me in addition to my food issues. Something that can't be cured. My goal is to make him think I'm fine, that this was just a puberty thing or something. I don't need to see him to get better. I can get better on my own. During the last ten minutes of my session, Dr. Abendi asked my mom to join us. Based on the number of times he said bulimic and bulimia, I'm pretty sure that's what his diagnosis is. My mom cried, which made me feel sad, but I didn't feel that way for long because she ended up doing what she always does: She started asking Dr. Abendi whose fault it was. My dad's or hers? Then I was forgotten about while she went on about doing the best job raising us that she could, even if she had to do it alone, even if my dad was off starting a family with another woman.

Dr. Abendi gave her the same attentive stare that he gives me when I talk, and then he gave her a simple, one sentence answer: *These are things that we will certainly explore.* Then he cut her off and turned his attention back to me. That's when I decided I wouldn't fight seeing him next week.

He gave me homework. I am supposed to write down whenever I feel like I want to binge. I'm supposed to include what I was doing just before I started feeling that way and any specific thoughts that I'm thinking. He says I need to write for at least ten minutes and if I still feel like binging, I'm supposed to talk to someone, a friend or family member. When I exited his office, I heard him talking quietly to my mother before she followed behind me. I don't know what he said to her, but she didn't say a word to me in the car. It wasn't like she was giving me the silent treatment, but more like she was working hard to keep her thoughts inside. I silently thanked Dr. Abendi.

"Mom," I call from the kitchen, "it's almost time to go!"

"Okay. Hang on. Five minutes," she calls.

She's the one who insisted on driving Hunter and me to the movies, and now she's going to make us late because she *has* to work out at the same time every week day. It doesn't matter that she made a commitment to get me somewhere during that same timeframe. When she isn't babysitting, cooking, or cleaning, she's working out. Ever since I was little—even before my dad left—those have been her priorities.

While I wait for her, I look out the window at Carly's house. Her bedroom light is on. I know she's getting ready for the dance tonight because everyone was talking about it on the bus this morning. No one even asked me if I wanted to go. I would have said no anyway because of the plans I have with Hunter, but only Dominic and Carly know about that. While Carly, Beth, Selena, and Darcy talked about the dance—the songs they hoped the DJ would play, who's going to dance with who, and what they're wearing—Dominic asked Hunter and me which movie we planned to see.

Then, out of nowhere, he asked me when I was going to start gaining back some weight. It was the first time since we talked in the hallway that he mentioned anything about my weight.

I shrugged. We sat in silence for a few seconds, and then he started talking about some new releases that he wants to see. Instead of listening to him and Hunter, I thought about how worried I used to be that people might find out my secret. But now that people know, it isn't really any different. It's like people are afraid or too uncomfortable to talk to me about it, so they do their best to try to forget about my issue and act normal. Interestingly, Gary and my dad are the worst. Whenever they talk to me, all they ever ask is how I'm doing and if I've been eating enough food. People just don't get it. Even if I eat plenty of food and keep it down, it all ends up flushed out anyway because the laxatives have been working so great. I eat a "normal" amount of food just for show at school and to satisfy my mom at home, yet I'm still able to achieve that empty feeling I crave when the laxatives do their job. They are the perfect solution.

I understand Selena and Darcy not saying anything to me about the dance. Things are still weird between us because of what happened at the party. They say hi to me and acknowledge me in the hallway at school, but it seems like we're more like acquaintances now. Besides, Mrs. Tropez always provides rides to the dances. If Selena doesn't talk to me about the dance, then she doesn't have to feel obligated to ask if I need a ride.

But it bothers me that Carly didn't say anything. In fact, ever since she said she was going to confront Sloan about the Kit Kat prank she pulled, we haven't really talked. I wonder if she even said anything about it. Either way, not one of the OH girls has even made eye contact with me since last week, which is fine with me. It's weird how I wanted to be friends with them for so long, and now I just want them to pretend I don't exist.

~

The entire time we are driving to get Hunter, my mom lectures me. She starts by reminding me to maintain appropriate personal space while we are watching the movie. It's like I'm a little kid being told to keep my hands to myself. What does she think Hunter and I are going to do? Make out during the movie?

Then she cautiously mentions that I probably shouldn't eat anything, just in case. In case of what? In case I decide to binge on popcorn right there in front of Hunter and everyone in the movie theater?

Seconds after my mom honks the horn, Hunter is jogging down his driveway. He's wearing a hooded Yankees sweatshirt and a fitted navy and gray striped winter hat.

"He's a Yankee fan?" My mom sounds disappointed.

Ignoring her, I open the front door and hop out to meet Hunter.

"Hi," I say, smiling.

"Hey, you," he says. Then he waves at my mom.

I reach for the back door handle.

"What are you doing?"

"Uh, opening the door."

"Well, wait, you're sitting in front, right?" He reaches for the front door handle.

"No. Stop, stop. I'm sitting in back with you."

He shrugs. "Okay, but I still want to open the door for you."

When I slide into the back seat, my mom says, "Why are you sitting back there?" as if she's offended.

I shrug at her in the mirror and then introduce her to Hunter.

For the next ten minutes, my mom asks Hunter question after question. Where did his family move from? What brought them here? Do they have any family here? Are his parents still married? What do they do for a living? What made him ask me out? Is he friends with Dominic? Carly? Selena and Darcy? Doesn't he think I need to put on some weight? That last question made Hunter look at me with a sad *Did she just ask me that?* type of look. I break eye contact quickly because I am too embarrassed to respond, even if only with a tell-me-about-it look.

"Alright, well, enjoy the movie. I'm just going to run some errands and then I'll be back to get you. Stand right inside there," she points to the entrance, "and I'll pull up when I see you." The way she tells us exactly what to do makes my body tense up.

"Okay, okay. We'll be there."

"Thank you, Mrs. Mills," Hunter says.

"It's Clifton," my mom responds flatly.

More embarrassment.

"Oh, right, sorry. Mrs. Clifton. Thank you."

"Of course. See you guys soon."

As we stand watching my mom pull away, I wonder if Hunter is sorry that we're here together. When I was little, I once heard my father tell my mom that she was just like her mother. He said he should have known better than to marry her after he met her mother.

My mom's mom wasn't a very warm person—not even to Kelsie and me—not like my dad's mom was.

I wonder if Hunter, and every guy I ever meet, will decide they don't like me after they meet my mother.

I'm preparing myself for him to say something like *Maybe I shouldn't have asked you to see a movie* when he grabs my hand and gently pulls me inside.

We are about to walk into theater number six when Hunter stops and slaps his forehead. "I forgot to ask if you want popcorn."

"That's okay. I don't."

"You sure?"

"Yeah, but if you want some, let's go get some."

We return to the concession stand, and I immediately regret suggesting that Hunter get popcorn because seeing it and smelling it up close reminds me of the night I watched Lizzie and Zoe. Not only do I feel guilty about stealing more food from Red Owl and throwing up in the bushes at my elementary school, but thinking about the ten dollars I took from Lizzie's bank makes me feel even worse.

Thoughts of that night are stuck in my brain throughout the entire movie. They slowly trickle down into the pit of my stomach where only food can absorb them and make them go away. If it weren't for the guilt I'm feeling right now, I think I might be okay. After all, I've proven to myself (and my family) that I am still capable of controlling myself around food, but that's when I'm not feeling emotional. Every time Hunter takes a handful of popcorn, I yearn to have some too. But I know that one bite is all it takes to make me lose control with how I'm feeling. So, I breathe deeply and I imagine myself writing like Dr. Abendi said I should. I know doing it for real would be much better, but my thoughts are all I have to work with right now.

Finally, the movie ends.

"That was frickin' awesome," Hunter says. "What did you think?"

"It was good."

"Liar," he teases. "I saw the look on your face. You hated it!"

I smile. "Alright, you got me. I'm not a huge fan of sci-fi." That's not a lie. I usually don't enjoy sci-fi movies, but I really don't know if I liked this one or not because I barely watched it.

"Hey, Katie," suddenly, his face is serious. "You really wanted some popcorn, didn't you?"

"No, I didn't," I say, shaking my head.

"But you kept looking at it on my lap."

I stare at him, shocked that he noticed. *Why would he notice that?* I can feel my defenses going up like a drawbridge.

He shakes his head as he pitches the half-eaten popcorn bag into the trash. "I shouldn't have gotten it."

"Hunter, I wasn't staring at the popcorn, and I didn't want any. I told you that."

"Katie, someone in my family had bulimia."

I stop dead in my tracks. Tons of other people leaving the movie begin walking around us. We stand there in silence until the crowd thins out before I respond.

"Why are you telling me this?"

"Because I know what it's like. I've been listening to people in my family talk about it and argue about it for years. I know what my family member has gone through. She got skinny real fast a few years ago, just like you. Then she went through this treatment program at some hospital, but no one really knows if she's better or not. She says she is, but my mom doesn't believe her."

Is it possible that someone else in his family, besides Amy, has an eating disorder? Amy's mom? An aunt on his dad's side? No. He must be talking about Amy.

"Anyway," Hunter continues, "I just want you to know that I'm here for you if you want to talk about it."

I laugh nervously, but try to make it sound like I'm not nervous at all. "There's nothing to talk about. Really. Remember, I told you I was sick for a few weeks? That's why I've lost so much weight."

He stares at me as if he wants to believe me, but he just isn't sure if he should. The way he's looking at me—sad, unsure, caring—makes my heart skip a beat. Even though I'm lying, I want him to trust me. And the lie I'm telling right now isn't really going to be a lie in a few weeks, because I'm going to get better. I'll even work on not taking the laxatives anymore.

"There is something I should tell you, though," I say.

He tilts his head. "Okay. Go ahead."

"Remember when I said I couldn't go to a movie last weekend because I had family stuff going on?"

"Yeah?"

"Well, that was a lie. I was really grounded. For drinking at Selena's party." I lower my eyes to the ground, embarrassed for being grounded, for lying and because that's only half of the reason I was grounded—there was the whole Nick thing, too.

He nods. "I figured."

"I'm really sorry. I should have just told you the truth."

"It's okay," he says with a shrug. "It doesn't matter." Then his face lights up like we've time traveled to before we started talking about all this serious stuff. "Wanna play Marvel Super Heroes?"

I scan the parking lot. My mom's car is nowhere in sight. "Let's do it," I say, smiling. "But just one game. My mom will be here soon."

~

Hunter doesn't get out of the car right away when we pull up in front of his house. Instead, he turns to me and says, "I had a lot fun tonight."

My mom is eyeing me in the rearview mirror. If I know her the way I think I do, she is about to say something. All I can do is pray that she doesn't.

"Me too," I say. "Especially when I beat you at—"

But before I can get the words out, he kisses my cheek, taking my breath away and causing my mom to spin around in her seat.

"Bye, Katie," he whispers. Then he opens the door and as he's getting out says, "Bye Mrs. Clifton. I really appreciate the ride."

I'm expecting my mom to say something about how inappropriate is was of Hunter to kiss me, but she doesn't. Instead, she smiles at me before turning around and asking about the movie.

I know it was just a kiss on the cheek, but still, it was from Hunter.

I want to get better more than ever now. I know I can do it. After thirteen years of eating like a normal person, it shouldn't be a problem for me to stop worrying about what and how much I eat. I know I can control my urge to binge.

Chapter Twenty-Six

"Katie? Are you done in there?" Kelsie asks with a knock on the bathroom door.

I was so excited when Gary put the doors back up the other day. Finally, I could take a shower and sit on the toilet in private. But the rule is that I can't close any doors after I've eaten. It irritates me almost as much as not having doors at all, but it's better than nothing.

I pull the door wide open, releasing all the steam from the long shower I've just taken. Kelsie waves a hand in front of her face as if the steam were smoke. She's always been a drama queen. "You're home," I say. But what I'm really happy about is that she's talking to me again. It's been two weeks. My mom said that seeing me make myself throw up was hard on Kelsie, so she needed some time to process what's been going on with me.

"Yeah, well, I've been busy with work and the new semester starting. Mom told me you've had two therapy sessions already. How did they go? You like the doctor?"

"He's okay." I wish she'd asked about my date with Hunter last night instead.

"Do you think he'll be able to help you?"

I know Kelsie is trying to reach out here, but it feels like she doesn't really want to talk to me. She has this pained look on her face, like she is forcing herself to ask the questions. Is she only asking because she thinks it's the right thing to do?

"Honestly, I feel better already."

"Really?" She scrunches up her nose. "That fast?"

"Look, I don't know what happened. I wasn't feeling well, and then things just got out of control. You know? But I think . . . I really think I'm okay now."

"Well, good." She seems hesitant to believe me. "That's really good. Hey, Kyle wanted me to tell you he said hi. He's been asking me about you."

I feel a stab of anger when I realize she has probably told Kyle and Jane everything. Then again, I'm sure my mom has told Jane some, if not everything, too. "Cool. Tell him I said hi back and that I'm fine."

"Carly called while you were in the shower. She said she was calling to find out about your *date*." Smiling, Kelsie folds her arms across her chest and taps her foot a few times. "Who did you go on a date with?"

While I tell her about my date with Hunter, she follows me into my room so I can get dressed. I hear her take in a sharp breath when my back is exposed for a second, making my skin crawl. What does she see that I don't?

When I get to the part about Hunter kissing me on the cheek, she gasps again, only it's a good one this time. I've never talked to Kelsie about a boy before, and it makes me feel good to have her ask questions about how I feel and if I think we'll go out again sometime. I'm sad when she gets up off my bed and announces that she needs to get ready for work. I sort of wish she would hug me—even though we don't really do that sort of thing in our family—but she simply tousles my hair and says, "I'm glad you're feeling better Kit Kat," causing me to envision the pile of mini candy bars from Sloan's prank and deflating my good mood.

"Hey, Kelsie?"

She peeks back at me over her shoulder from the doorway. "Yeah?"

"Please don't call me Kit Kat. I don't really want anyone to call me that anymore."

"Really? Why?"

Because it's a stupid, childish nickname, and it makes me feel disgusting every time I hear it. "I just don't."

"Okay, but I'm so used to calling you that. You might have to remind me."

"Fine." *But if you really care, you'll remember.*

~

After I get done eating breakfast—half a banana, a handful of Cheerios and orange juice—I return Carly's call. She talks about the dance for at least ten minutes. First, she's telling me about things I don't care about anymore. What people wore, who danced with who; that kind of thing.

She even tells me about her and the OH girls doing a choreographed dance that they made up last week, and how people started joining in until half the gym filled with people doing their dance. I especially don't care about this tidbit and it sort of makes me angry that she would even mention it.

But then she switches gears and tells me about an argument that broke out between Dominic and Sloan. She claims it had nothing to do with me, and I don't ask questions because I just want to forget about Selena's party. But I have a hard time believing it didn't have at least something to do with what happened. Dominic isn't the kind of person to cause a scene.

Finally, she describes dancing with Brett Lester, an eighth grader on the basketball team. Her voice sounds all goo goo gaga as she talks. This surprises me, because Carly has never really liked a boy before.

After a while, I feel bad that she hasn't asked about my date with Hunter. Maybe she doesn't think it was a big deal because Hunter and I have been friends all year long or because we're always sitting next to each other on the bus? Maybe if she knew how much I like him, then she'd want details? So I'm about to share how much I think I like him, but my mom says it's time to go grocery shopping. Doctor's orders. So I don't even get a chance to tell Carly what I'm feeling.

Before we hang up, she asks if I want to sleep over at her house tonight. It has been forever since she's asked me to spend the night at her house, so of course, I say yes.

I'm supposed to go shopping for food with my mom every week to let her know what I feel comfortable having in the house. We're supposed to avoid things that tend to set me on a binge. Grocery shopping with my mom is usually annoying, but today she bites her tongue when I put things that I'll eat in the cart. I recognize the same determined look on her face that she had in the car on the way home from my last appointment with Dr. Abendi. She looks like she's biting her tongue the whole time.

At first it doesn't bother me because at least she isn't criticizing all my choices. But near the end of the shopping trip, her silence starts to bother me. What is she thinking? What did Dr. Abendi say to her to make her bite her tongue so hard?

By the time we get home, I'm so torn about how I feel about my mom's silence that I have a knot in my chest and I feel like throwing up to get rid of it. So after I help her put the groceries away, I go to my room and write in my journal. Then before I go down for lunch, I take two laxatives.

~

"You're here! Oh my God, it's been so long since you've slept over, or even since you've been over." The bubbly Carly I love jumps up and down as I remove my shoes.

"I know. It feels like forever."

I follow Carly through the back hallway and into the kitchen, where her dad is cooking some steaks. Probably venison. "Kit Kat! It's nice to see you sweetheart. Where have you been?"

"Dad," Carly's voice is stern. "Remember, I told you we aren't calling her that anymore?" He gives her a searching glance, as if trying to recall when they talked about it.

"It's okay, Carly. Hi, Mr. Jensen. Nice to see you, too," I say as I go in for a hug when he raises his free arm.

"What's going on?" He pokes me in the ribs. "You on a diet or something?" Mr. Jensen has always been a jokester.

I smile politely. "No. Just thinning out, I guess."

"Well, these steaks are just about done. Have you had dinner yet?"

I nod and pat my stomach. "Yep, but thanks anyway."

"C'mon Katie. I want to show you something," Carly grabs my wrist and leads me upstairs to her room.

"I'm makin' taters too, Carls! I'll call you down when everything's done!" Mr. Jensen calls.

"'Kay, Dad!"

I am shocked when I enter Carly's room. Walls that used to be a uniform jade green are now lavender and yellow. The participation medals for various sports, and posters of puppies, kittens, motivational quotes, and baseball players have been replaced by a full-length mirror, framed photos and cheerleading posters. And in addition to plain wood blinds, Carly now has colorful floral curtains.

"Whoa," I say with a fake smile plastered to my face as I stand in the center of her room, slowly turning to take in all the changes. *Whose room is this?*

"I know, isn't it great?" Carly squeals.

"It's so . . ." *Not like you*, I think, but instead I say, ". . . bright and flowery."

Carly moves over to her closet and opens the doors wide for me to see that her clothes—a lot of them ones I have never seen before—are now color coordinated. I immediately wonder if she bought the new clothes or if she's been shoplifting with the OH clique. Her dad would never know the difference.

"What's wrong?" she asks.

I didn't even realize that my smile had faded into an expression that must look like a mixture of shock and disappointment. "Oh, nothing," I quickly recover. "Where did you get all of this new stuff?"

After Carly gets done showing me her favorite new articles of clothing, she brings out a stack of magazines. "Let's take some relationship quizzes," she says, surprising me once again. Carly wants to take quizzes about boys?

"Sure, why not?"

The quizzes are called *How do you know if a guy likes you?* and *Is he more than just a friend?* We're about to score them when Mr. Jensen calls Carly downstairs to eat dinner, so I stay upstairs and grade them by myself. Carly is dying to know the result of hers, so she is back in less than ten minutes. "Well?" she asks, still chomping. It turns out that Brett might be just a friend, but as a true optimist, that doesn't dampen her mood. As for Hunter, the results said we have the potential to be more than just friends and he definitely likes me. I act like it's just a silly quiz, but deep down I'm jumping for joy.

We spend the next couple of hours painting our nails and reading about celebrities. It feels strange because these are the kinds of things that I would normally do with my mom and Kelsie, not Carly. Carly and I used to do things like play board games, watch TV and movies, do Mad Libs, or just sit and talk about life. She has changed more than I realized, and it makes me sad and jealous because I know that the OH girls, and the rest of the cheer squad, probably have a lot to do with her transformation.

I'm in the middle of reading an article about Taylor Swift out loud when a song that Carly likes comes on, causing her to howl like a maniac and crank the volume up until my ears hurt. Then she starts dancing all around the room, stopping several times to try to pull me up too. But I don't feel like dancing. Not now, not ever. "Come on, Katie! Dance with me! Don't you love this song?"

I do like the song, but dancing around like crazy teenage girls in a movie is another thing we've never done together. I try to act like I'm having fun watching her, but my insides are welling up with insecurity. The last time I felt this insecure around Carly was at the first dance of the school year, when all her new friends were making fun of my terrible moves. When the song finally ends, I am relieved until Carly says, "God, Katie. Maybe that's part of your problem. You've got to stop taking yourself so seriously and being so stuffy all the time. Live a little!"

That's part of my problem? I'm serious and stuffy? Suddenly I feel like Carly hasn't just changed a little. She's a completely different person. "Just because I don't like to dance doesn't make me serious or stuffy."

She rolls her eyes and lets out a little laugh. "Okay. Whatever. The only time I've ever seen you dance and enjoy it was in that video you showed me of you and your dad dancing around the house to 'Brown Eyed Girl.' What were you, like four?"

"Yeah, something like that." We have a lot of videos of me dancing when I was little. That one was from right before Kelsie and I found out my dad was moving out. Carly knows that, too, so I can't believe she would bring it up. "Thanks for bringing up such a happy memory for me and ruining my night." The words come out angrier than I intend.

"Why would that ruin your night?" She doesn't apologize the way the old Carly would.

"Gee, I don't know. How would you feel if I brought up a happy time you had with your mom?"

"What is up with you, Katie? Why are you acting so angry and defensive? Go ahead, bring up my mom. Memories of her make me happy, so talk about her all you want. Why would me bringing up your dad ruin your night? That's messed up. At least your dad is still alive and you can make more memories with him." Her eyes are filling with tears now. "But no, you're too busy acting all down in the dumps and feeling sorry for yourself all the time."

"Did you ever even say anything to Sloan about dumping all those Kit Kat bars in front of me?"

"What? What does that have to do with anything?"

"A lot! It has a lot to do with everything!" Now I'm ready to burst into tears.

"The Kit Kat bars were a joke, Katie. A *stupid* joke. Believe me, Sloan doesn't exactly have the best sense of humor."

A joke? She thinks something that made me want to die was a joke. "Just forget it," I say and crawl into my sleeping bag on the floor.

With a huff, Carly turns off the music and storms around her room putting things away. Then she turns out the light and crawls into bed.

I toss and turn, and so does Carly. I almost say something to her at least a dozen times. Maybe I am being a big whiny baby. Maybe. I also feel bad for bringing up her mom. That was a crappy thing to do. When I finally work up the nerve to say something, Carly lets out an airy snore. She's out. And when Carly is out, there's no waking her.

My stomach rumbles, and I try to ignore it.

I think more about my fight with Carly. I think about how I haven't talked to my dad in a week, even though he promised he would call every few days. I wonder if he talked to my mom about my appointment with Dr. Abendi. Does he know that I've been officially diagnosed with bulimia? Does he care? Or is he too busy with his perfect life in California to worry about all the baggage he left behind?

My stomach gurgles, and I try to ignore it.

I think about how different my mom has been acting since Dr. Abendi talked to her. And I don't know which mom I prefer: the one who criticizes everything about me or the one who bites her tongue. Is it better for her to keep her thoughts in, even though I probably know what she wants to say anyway? I think about Dominic and how much I miss him. I wonder why I don't really miss Selena and Darcy.

My stomach growls. *Feed me. Please. Just a little bit.*

I get out of my sleeping bag and open Carly's door a crack, peeking down the hall. Loud snores are coming from her dad's room. I step out into the hallway and quietly close Carly's door behind me. Then I tiptoe downstairs, pausing whenever a step creaks.

Brutus, their yellow lab, sits at the bottom of the stairs, dusting the floor with his wagging tail. He starts to whine when I get halfway down, probably because he thinks I'm toying with him by going so slow.

I put a finger to my lips. "Shhh." But this only makes him stand and start wagging even faster so that his butt is moving too.

"Brutus," I whisper. "Be quiet."

Finally, I get to the bottom, and he nuzzles my midsection with excitement. "Come on," I whisper, motioning for him to follow me into the kitchen.

I open the large pantry doors. I tell myself that a few pretzels will do, that any more is too dangerous. But the cabinet is stocked with so much junk food. I take a deep breath and reach for a bag of pretzel twists and then I see them: Little Debbie Zebra Cakes. As if driven by an invisible force, my hand changes course, and before my brain has a chance to process what my body is doing, I am unwrapping a black and white cake and shoving it into my mouth. Then another. And another. I am holding the last cake in my hand when the cloud lifts and I realize what I'm doing.

No, no, no, no, no! You're so stupid and disgusting.

But it's too late. There are already nine cakes in my stomach that need to be purged. So, I bite down on the last one.

The kitchen light goes on.

"Katie?" Carly is rubbing her eyes.

My eyes dart from the wrappers sitting on the cabinet shelf, to the Zebra Cake in my hand, to the floor where the empty box is lying.

"What are you . . ." Carly's eyes are wide open now. "You ate that whole box?"

My mouth is still full, but it doesn't matter. I couldn't make words if I tried. My chest feels heavy, like what I imagine it might feel like when you have a heart attack. Is it even possible for a thirteen-year-old to have a heart attack? Because if it is, I actually think it wouldn't be the worst thing right now.

"Is this a binge? Were you going to eat more? Were you planning to throw it all up?"

The hall light comes on. "Girls? What's going on?"

We both turn to look at Mr. Jensen standing in the doorway.

Embarrassed and horrified at being caught, I drop the cake in my hand and rush past Carly and her dad. As I quickly gather my things, I hear them talking in the kitchen. *Good. Maybe I can get out the front door without having to face Carly or her dad again.*

When I reach the bottom of the stairs, I hear footsteps coming down the hall. "Katie?" Mr. Jensen sounds upset.

But I don't answer. Instead, I unlock the door and rush outside. When I reach my driveway, the Jensens' door opens, but no one says anything. Before digging my house key out of my backpack, I bend over and vomit the Zebra Cakes into the bushes next to our house. It only takes a few heaves before my stomach is completely empty. When I stand, I hear the front door of Carly's house close.

The first thing I see when I open my eyes the next morning is that my bedroom door is gone again.

Chapter Twenty-Seven

"What time should I pick you up?" my mom asks.

"I'm not sure. Six maybe. I'll call you."

"Whose birthday is it again?"

"His grandmother's."

Staring at Hunter's house, she nods slowly and says, "I assume there will be plenty of adult supervision at this party?"

I stare at her. She just can't let my one screw-up with alcohol go. So, I'm thinking that maybe I should start binge drinking instead of binge eating, just to spite her. "It's a party for his eighty-year-old grandmother. There will be lots of adults there. Most of them older than you, probably."

She points a finger at me before I'm even done with my sarcastic response. "No sweets. I know those are the worst for you."

She knows this because she read my journal, which led to a huge fight and an emergency session with Dr. Abendi. When he asked her to explain her reason for reading my journal, she said she felt left out of my healing process because I never talk to her about anything. Then she brought up the night I got caught binging at Carly's and how embarrassed she was when Mr. Jensen called her the next day. Since I refused to talk about it, she decided to start reading my journal, just in case I mentioned it in there.

I wondered what her reason was for reading my diary when I was ten.

"I'll call you when I'm ready to come home," I say. Then I slam the door. I like how you can slam a car door without anyone really knowing you're slamming it on purpose, except I feel guilty as soon as I do it because it's probably passive aggressive—something Dr. Abendi mentioned when we were talking about my mom one time.

I look back at my mom through the windshield to see her shaking her head at me.

"Katie! It's so nice to finally meet you!" Mrs. Davis hugs me. She's so pretty. Not in a high maintenance kind of way, but in a beautiful on the inside shining through on the outside kind of way. She's wearing a floral sweater that my mom wouldn't be caught dead in, and khaki pants. She looks like a mom, and I like it.

The first thing I see is a table full of party stuff: punch, festive paper cups, finger foods, party hats, and gifts. "I didn't bring a gift," I say, embarrassed.

"Oh, Katie," She waves a hand in the air. "You didn't need to bring a gift. We're just glad you could make it. Hunter is downstairs playing air hockey with his cousins. Follow me." Mrs. Davis leads me toward the basement, stopping along the way to introduce me to her mother (the birthday girl) and a few other relatives.

I bend over into Hunter's grandmother's open arms to give her a hug. "Happy birthday. I'm so glad to be here for your special day," I say, trying to make a good impression.

"Ah, my dear, every day is special," she says smiling. "Why, you're as cute as a button. Isn't she Denise?"

I grin shyly, trying to hide how uncomfortable the compliment makes me feel.

"She sure is, Mom." Hunter's mom has the same warm smile and friendly demeanor as her mother. Being near them makes me jealous of Hunter.

The entire time I'm walking downstairs, I'm holding my breath because I wonder if Amy will be in the basement. I hear the click clack of the puck, laughing, and children's voices. To my relief, I don't see her.

When he sees me, Hunter lets go of his paddle to come over and greet me. The boy he's playing with groans. "Hey, Katie." He grins, peeking at his mother who is smiling that same warm smile she's always smiling. He gives me a hug. "Did you meet my grandmother?"

"Yeah, your mom introduced me to everyone upstairs." I look over at her—now talking to Hunter's dad and two other men, one who looks a lot like Hunter's dad. "She's so . . . nice." I secretly wish my mom could be more like his.

"Who? My mom or my grandmother?"

"Both." I sigh.

"Come on. I'll introduce you to everyone down here."

I meet five of Hunter's cousins—all boys and all younger—his little sister, his dad, and two uncles. One of the uncles is Hunter's dad's brother and the other is his mom's brother-in-law—Amy's dad. Two of the little boy cousins are Amy's brothers, and the other three are cousins from his dad's side. After all the introductions are made, I build Lego towers with the little ones while Hunter finishes the air hockey game he was playing. He tells me that I should play the winner. His dad and uncles are watching a college basketball game and drinking beer.

While I'm busy steadying a three-foot-high-and-growing tower, allowing his cousins to add Lego after Lego, I'm a wreck wondering where Amy is. Meanwhile, his cousins are giggling every time they snap a new Lego in place, because they know it will come tumbling down sooner or later. I also know I will have to face Amy sooner or later. After all, it's her grandmother too, and these are her brothers I'm playing with. I also think about how weird it is that I'm here with the family of the one girl I have wanted to be like since the first moment I saw her. She's pretty and a good dancer, and she has a perfect figure, the best clothes, an awesome family and a tight group of friends. The only things we have in common are . . . well, we only have one thing in common. We both throw up after we eat.

I vaguely remember thinking that it would make me more like her, body wise anyway, but I also thought it would give me the same kind of confidence she has. And maybe I sort of thought it might lead to us being friends. How stupid.

After a collective cheer from Hunter and his uncles, I realize that it's louder upstairs—more footsteps and voices. Then I hear them: light, tip-toey footsteps on the stairs.

That's when she appears.

Amy glances around the large rec room, her eyes eventually locking with mine. And then . . . nothing. She looks away quickly and heads toward the TV area, saying something to her dad and Hunter's dad. Then she heads back upstairs.

The TV goes off and Hunter's dad immediately says, "Okay, kids, let's go eat."

"Sorry. That was a never-ending game. We can play after we eat."

"Okay," I mumble.

"Hey, you okay?"

"Yeah, I'm fine. I just feel nervous about Amy."

"Pft. She's harmless. All that high and mighty stuff at school is just an act. It's because of her friends and . . . well, other stuff, too. But Amy and I used to make mud pies together and have bubble gum blowing contests. I didn't tell you that, though. Okay?" He grins and I can't help but grin back.

For the next two hours, there's eating—lots and lots of eating—talking, laughing, kids running around, a slide show of pictures of Hunter's grandma from baby to eighty-year-old, singing, cake and presents. The entire time, I am planted at a table in a corner with Hunter, and his three cousins who aren't related to Amy. Not only are there many more family members that I wasn't even introduced to, but there are also friends of Hunter's parents and his grandmother. Friends from work, from the neighborhood and from church. I can't believe how packed his house is.

My mother would never have a party like this at our house. She'd be too worried about crumbs and spills on the floor and smudges on the furniture. But Hunter's mom walks around with the same pleasant, care-free look plastered on her face. Even when she converses with her sister, Amy's mom, who seems the exact opposite, Hunter's mom still maintains a smile and speaks sweetly. And I can tell it's real.

The funny thing is, Amy's mom kind of reminds me of my mom—smiling at people one moment and then frowning and picking up garbage the second no one is looking. Except, she doesn't even pretend to smile at Hunter's mom, Amy's dad, or even Amy. I noticed Amy's mom whispering in her ear a few times. Each time, Amy runs off to do something—get her mom a bottle of water, help her little brothers eat, get a new fork for one of her brothers after he threw it on the floor, wipe up a mess someone made on the floor. One time, Hunter's mom told Amy not to worry about a spill on a table, but Amy's mom swooped in and said, "Amy will clean it. It's not a problem. Right Amy?" The "Right Amy" part sounds like a threat. And what was Amy's dad doing the whole time? As soon as he finished eating, he disappeared into the basement. Hunter's dad and other uncle didn't go with him. After seeing a look on Amy's face that I've never seen before, I started to think that maybe there is a lot more to her than I thought. Maybe everything isn't so perfect for her after all.

Maybe we have more in common than I realized.

I got worried at first when I saw how much food there was, but for some reason, the feeling to binge never came. I don't know if it was because I was with Hunter or because I was around so many happy, friendly people, except Amy and her mom. For the first time in months, I ate a "normal" portion of food without any crazy thoughts running through my head. Even when I eat for show in front of my family and kids at school, I usually have a hard time shutting off the voices in my head that tell me to keep eating. *Go on, just a little more. If you can't stop, that's okay. You can get rid of it later.* That weird voice that has come to live in my brain was quiet today.

After his grandmother finishes opening her presents, Hunter and I sneak downstairs to play a few games of air hockey. Then he gives me a tour of the house while coffee and other after-dinner drinks are served upstairs, and while the kids eat more cake.

He shows me their TV room upstairs, where the walls are decorated with sports paraphernalia. I freak out at the sight of a signed Derek Jeter poster. It's a blown-up Sports Illustrated cover; the one that highlighted his 3000th hit. My dad has the same poster, but it's not signed.

It's nearly six, so I call my mom to come and pick me up. Before we go downstairs, I ask Hunter if there's an upstairs bathroom I can use, since the one on the main level has been in high demand.

"Yeah, down the hall. Second door on the left." He points, and it feels good that there isn't a hint of suspicion in his eyes. "I'll wait for you in the living room."

The walls are covered with eight by tens of Hunter and his sister. I stop to look at each one as I make my way down the hall. As I get closer, I realize the door to the bathroom is closed and water is running. I am about to turn and head toward the stairs when I hear a few coughs followed by a splashing sound that I know all too well. I know I should get my butt downstairs, but something holds my feet in place. I just stand there outside the bathroom, waiting.

Amy opens the door, eyes facing the floor. Her eyes widen a little when she sees my shoes, and then she slowly raises her head until our eyes meet.

"What are you doing up here?" She asks. But then she shakes her head and says, "Never mind. I know why you're up here."

"You do?" Does she think I followed her?

"Yeah, the same reason I came up here. For privacy." She raises an eyebrow, and looks at me like we share a secret.

Actually, we share two secrets. One is hers, and one is mine. But unlike her, I'm not up here to protect my secret.

"No, I just have to use the bathroom. Hunter said I could use this one because everyone else is using the one downstairs."

"Yeah, okay." Anyone would recognize the sarcasm in her voice. She opens the door wider and steps past me into the hall.

"Hey, Amy?"

She looks back, but doesn't say anything.

"Hunter said that someone in his family had an eating disorder and . .." She narrows her eyes at me, but I go on. ". . . and spent some time in a treatment center. Did it . . . did it help?"

She crosses her arms, drawing into herself, looking timid like I've never seen Amy Bowie look before. "No. No, it didn't help. But that's because I don't need help."

The same thing I say.

Her timid demeanor disappears as quickly as it appeared. "I just do it to relieve stress. You know?" She says this with confidence, as if bulimia is a substitute for yoga.

I nod because I know exactly what she means.

"I have it under control. But it doesn't seem like *you* do, Katie."

"Why do you say that?" Of course, perfect Amy Bowie would say that to me. She's the bulimic who knows how to do it right. But me? Well, I'm the wannabe who can't even pull off being bulimic. She *would* think that.

"For starters, look how skinny you are. How do you expect people not to notice when you lose so much weight so fast? You can't throw *everything* up. You have to hold a little bit down. Otherwise you end up looking anorexic, and that's not a good look for anyone."

Hunter was right. She does have everyone fooled. And Amy is right. She does have it under control.

She's even the perfect bulimic.

"If I looked like you, Sloan would probably start giving me a hard time, too."

"Sloan hasn't been giving me a hard time because of my weight, Amy. It's because Hunter and I like each other and because she's a nosy witch who loves to spread rumors." I regret the last part, because now I've opened the topic of Selena's party.

But to my relief, she doesn't say anything about Nick. Instead, she just stares at me as if she's never thought about the things I just said. "Carly told me you two got into a fight."

I inhale sharply. Carly talked to Amy about me?

"She said it was about something that happened when you slept over at her house and that you won't talk to her about it."

I still don't say anything. How much did Carly tell her?

"You should talk to her about it. Carly is a good friend. You're lucky to have her as your best friend. Sometimes I wish I could talk to my friends about certain things, but . . . well, you know."

I'm so shocked at the things Amy is saying to me right now that all I can manage is a nod.

"Hey, Katie!" Hunter calls as he reaches the top step. "Oh, hey Amy. What are you guys talking about?"

"Just . . . nothing," I say as I walk past Amy.

"Your mom is here," Hunter says, handing me my coat. "My mom asked her to come in, but she says she's in a hurry, so . . ."

"Okay, well, I better get out there then." My bladder is burning, but at this point I'd rather wait to go to the bathroom when I get home. I glance back. "Bye, Amy."

Chapter Twenty-Eight

Things are different between Amy and I at school the next day. She waves to me in the hall before first period. Then she does it again in gym. No one saw, of course, because she kept her hand real low by her hip both times.

When I got home from the party yesterday, the first thing I did was dig my journal out of hiding. Ever since my mom poked her nose around in it, I've decided to keep it taped to the bottom of my wicker chest when I'm not writing in it.

One thing that Dr. Abendi keeps trying to talk to me about is what could have triggered my bulimia in the first place. Last week, I told him that I don't want to be skinny like the OH girls anymore, and since that's what probably started all of this (I still haven't told him about Amy), I don't think I need to see him anymore. He reacted by asking me if they're still skinnier than me. I told him that I didn't know, because I honestly don't. Even though people have been mentioning that I've lost weight, I still see the same me from back when school started. How can I not see what everyone else is seeing?

Anyway, Amy got me thinking about other things that might have caused me to become obsessed with food. I mean, she's always been skinny. I know, because I saw a picture of her as a kid at Hunter's house yesterday. She was born looking like a prima ballerina. So, what caused Amy to start throwing up? Doesn't she know how perfect she looks? She said it's a good way to relieve stress.

Stress.

I flip through my journal looking for all the spots where I listed how I was feeling right before I felt like binging. Most of the entries are about my mom. A few about my dad. One about Dominic and Beth. One about my fight with Carly. None of the entries are about me looking at my thighs or my pooch in the mirror.

I woke up today feeling determined. Determined to stop making myself throw up. Even if I really don't know why I'm doing it anymore.

Before lunch I normally take two laxatives, but today I decide to use up what I have left, just to be done with them once and for all. So, I take the last five, and I do something I haven't done since before school started; I eat a cookie—just one—from Beth, because it's her birthday today. I am fully aware of Hunter's, Dominic's, and Beth's eyes on me the entire time I'm eating it. But I keep chewing and repeating to myself:

It's just a cookie.

It's just a cookie.

It's just a cookie.

One cookie.

I try to calm myself by thinking about the laxatives, but I still can't shake the panic I'm feeling. When I first started binging, I felt so in control, but something has changed. It's like there's a crazy person living inside of me, constantly messing with my mind whenever I eat. *Listen up, crazy person! The laxatives will flush out the cookie.* I repeat this, and I defy the voice that is telling me I need to eat more and that I need to purge this

one

little

cookie.

"Earth to Katie." Dominic snaps a finger in front of my face.

I flinch and wave his hand away. "Good cookie, Beth. Happy birthday," I say, smiling.

"Actually, Dominic made them for me." She hugs his arm, causing his cheeks to redden.

~

"Are you okay, Katie? You look kinda pale," Dominic says while we're packing up at the end of math.

No. I'm not okay. My abdomen is on fire and cramping up; I feel nauseous. I can't tell him that, though. "I'm fine. I think I just need to use the bathroom." I pat my stomach. "Probably something I ate," I add. He punches me in the shoulder, knowing that I'm referring to his cookies.

"Well, you better go before your next class." He nods toward the bathroom. "But hurry up, okay?" Instead of heading to his locker, he leans against the wall.

"What are you doing?" I ask.

"I'll wait for you."

"Why would you wait for me? Go to class." I gently pull on his arm, putting distance between him and the wall.

He shakes his head. "Fine. But, make it quick, okay?"

"Yes. Okay. Go!" I say playfully, trying to hide the pain I'm in.

I end up on the toilet for all of seventh period. Normally, the laxatives just flush me out. It's like I'm peeing out of my butt, and then I feel empty and refreshed. Today, I'm left feeling crampy, nauseous, sweaty and dizzy. I try to get up several times, but the pains in my abdomen make me think more liquid will come out, so I'm back on the toilet.

I know it has to be because of the double dose of laxatives, but how long will this last? Would water help? I grab the water bottle from my backpack and force myself to take several gulps, but the only thing my body does is cramp some more and then crap it out. By the time the bell rings, I am seriously scared that something else is wrong with me.

Appendicitis? *Gary had his removed a few years ago. But I'm not even related to Gary. And appendicitis isn't hereditary anyway. Is it?*

Food poisoning? *I'm serious this time. Maybe my carrots were bad?*

Meningitis? *I know nothing about meningitis.*

No. *I screwed up with the laxatives.*

I spend all of eighth period in the bathroom stall too, trying to figure out what to do. Leaving early to take the bus home isn't going to happen. I'm too sick. And I can't call my mom, because she has the kids.

Finally, I come up with the best possible idea: I drag myself to Dominic's locker just before the bell rings and ask him if his mom can drop me off at home before she takes him to work.

I must look worse than I feel, because Mrs. Riley insists on helping me out of the car and into the house. As soon as we're in the house, I buckle over in pain and begin dry heaving, causing liquid to soil my underwear. My last thought before everything becomes a blur is that I should have saved the last three laxatives for dinner.

~

When I open my eyes, Gary is carrying me. My mom is ahead of us, talking on her cell.

"We have no idea what's wrong with her, Dale! . . . Why would we take her to emergency? So we can wait two hours before anyone even talks to us? . . . No, Dr. Crawford's receptionist said he'll stay late to see her . . . Well, too bad! You're not here, so you don't get to decide!" She snaps her phone shut and it rings immediately.

"Am I gonna die?" I mumble through tears.

"No, of course not, Katie." There is fear in Gary's voice. "Dr. Crawford is going to take care of you. Okay?"

"Yeah, I'll call you when we find out. . . No, don't leave work, sweetheart. . . Okay, I'll call you soon." My mom's phone snaps shut again just as we get up to the reception desk at the West Side Children's Clinic. I've been seeing Dr. Crawford here since I was a baby. I'm pretty sure he delivered me.

"Oh, my," Grace, the grey-haired nurse whose been working here as long as Dr. Crawford, says. "Why don't you folks come on back right now instead of waiting out there." She opens the door that leads to the exam rooms and we follow her into room number two, the one with a mural of Bambi and his friends painted on the wall. Gary lays me on the table as my mom begins filling Grace in on my symptoms. As soon as I straighten my legs out, I become aware of the moisture in my underwear. Tears fill my eyes as I stare at Thumper, afraid to check if anything leaked through onto my pants.

Dr. Crawford arrives moments later, prompting my mom to start over with the symptoms.

"Hello, Katherine. Can you sit up, dear?" Dr. Crawford says in a soothing voice.

I look at him with teary, puffy eyes and whimper because seeing his face makes me feel ashamed. His face reminds me of the little girl who was always happy to go to the doctor because she knew she would hear silly jokes and get a sticker and a sucker. Looking at him now, I am embarrassed about who that little girl has become.

"Grace, please help me sit Katherine up," he says, gently lifting my right shoulder as Grace rushes to help with the left. My mom moves in too to help with my coat. Once it's off, Dr. Crawford begins examining me. Grace sits next to me and continues to hold me up.

Dr. Crawford takes my temperature and my blood pressure, he looks at my eyes and in my ears, and then he tells me to open my mouth. When he presses down on my tongue with the tongue depressor, he sighs loudly. Then he uses his hands to feel the glands on my neck. When he lifts my shirt to place his stethoscope against my back, he gasps.

"What is it?" My mom asks.

"Grace, did you get Katherine's weight?" he asks, ignoring my mom.

"No, I didn't."

I recognize the looks on their faces. They are the same looks I saw on my dad's, Connie's, and Mrs. Anderson's faces. Except Dr. Crawford has tears in his eyes and he doesn't just look concerned; he looks angry, too.

"Mr. and Mrs. Clifton, how long has Katherine been ill?"

"Well, she just came home sick today after—"

"No, Mrs. Clifton. That isn't what I mean." He dismisses my mother and looks at Grace. "Let's get her on the scale."

Dr. Crawford and Grace help me up off the table and walk me down the hall to the scale. My mom and Gary follow behind. When my weight registers, even I can't believe what I'm seeing: 89.4.

"Eighty-nine pounds? Are you sure that's right?" My mom asks.

"Let's get Katherine back to the exam room," Dr. Crawford says. "Grace will stay with her while we go over a few things in my office."

Gary and Dr. Crawford help me back onto the exam table, and then I am left alone with Nurse Grace.

My first impulse is to turn onto my side so that I can more easily ignore her look of pity, but then I remember the leakage, which causes my body to shudder with shame and my upper lip to quiver. Before the first sob escapes, Grace is by my side holding my hand. This gray-haired grandmother always used to give me a sucker and a sticker after my appointments with Dr. Crawford. Now she's consoling me as I lay here crying with shit in my pants. At first, her touch is comforting. But as my tears slow down, I begin to wonder what she thinks of me. Is she holding my hand because it's her job? Does she think I'm stupid for taking too many laxatives? Is she disgusted by how I smell?

Just when I'm starting to feel uncomfortable being alone with Nurse Grace, Dr. Crawford returns with my mom and Gary.

"Katherine," Dr. Crawford is sitting on a stool and looking me in the eyes. "Have you managed to keep anything down today?"

"Yes," I whisper.

"Did you take anything that could have made you have diarrhea?"

He knows.

I start to cry again and whisper, "Yes. Laxatives."

"What?!" My mom yells, causing me to cry even harder. Gary puts an arm around her and pulls her close, which keeps her quiet.

"How many did you take, Katherine?" Dr. Crawford's voice is just as calm as it was at the beginning of the exam.

"Five."

"When was the last time you ate or drank anything?"

"Around noon."

"And when did you take the laxatives?"

"Just before lunch. Around eleven thirty, I think."

"And what did you eat? Only tell me the things you kept in your stomach."

"A banana, three carrot sticks, some water, and a cookie."

He pats my hand. "Thank you, dear."

"Mr. and Mrs. Clifton, I understand that Katie is seeing a psychologist for her condition, but I think this situation requires more than weekly therapy sessions. When I saw her in June, she weighed," he pauses to check a computer screen, "one hundred fifteen. She's lost nearly thirty pounds in nine months, and she wasn't overweight to begin with."

"Wha . . . What else . . . can we do?" My mom is crying so hard she can barely speak.

"I recommend that you consider in-patient treatment. There is a very good program over at St. Mary's Hill Hospital on the East side. I can have Grace send over a referral now."

"No!" I scream. "I don't want to stay in a hospital! Everyone will know then!"

"Katherine," Dr. Crawford returns to my side. "You must know how sick you are, dear. You need proper care for your body and your mind."

"Yes, please send the referral," Gary says, causing my mom to rush to my side. She leans down and places her head next to mine. Then we both cry even harder than we already were.

Chapter Twenty-Nine

I've been on the couch all day, nodding in and out of consciousness. I begged my mom to let me stay in my room, but she insisted that it would be easier to take care of me if I was downstairs, especially since she has three little ones to watch.

"You don't need to take care of me. I'm fine," I told her. To that, she responded with a pained stare that made me give in.

I continued to feel miserable last night after we got home from seeing Dr. Crawford. "I'm sorry, but there's not much that can be done to make her feel better," the doctor had said. "She'll just have to stick it out until the symptoms subside. Be sure she drinks plenty of water and give her several doses of Pedialyte to replenish her electrolytes."

Before we left his office, Dr. Crawford cupped my face in his hands and said, "You're a tough cookie, Katherine. I expect you to get through this." His loving touch made me feel like a child again, like I used to feel back when he would pull quarters from my ears and steal my nose, and the sad look in his eyes made me feel like such a disappointment.

My mom is busy changing a diaper when the doorbell rings.

"I'll get it," I say, slowly getting up off the couch. Wobbly legs and the sting of a couple of irritated hemorrhoids—a side effect of forced vomiting, according to Dr. Crawford—cause me to limp.

The sight of Dominic standing on the back porch makes my pulse pound, because I don't know if I want to tell him what happened or not. I need to tell him something, though, because I'm leaving for the treatment center tomorrow.

Opening the storm door, I say, "Hey? Don't you have to work?" I do my best to keep my voice steady, not sure yet what else I'm going to say.

"Yeah." He nods toward the driveway where his mom is waiting in the car. I return her wave. "But we wanted to see how you're doing. Are you feeling any better?" I don't really know what to say, so we stand there awkwardly for a second. "Oh, and I brought your math homework," he finally adds. "But I wasn't sure if you'd want me to go around asking for assignments from your other classes."

"Thanks, Dominic, I really appreciate this, but . . ." Before I have a chance to blink, tears start pouring down my cheeks. As I back out of the doorway and take a seat on the stairs, Dominic lets himself inside and crouches down in front of me.

Oh, God. I have to tell him.

"But what? Katie, what's wrong?"

I look up to meet his eyes. "But . . . I probably won't . . . be going back to school . . . for a while," I say between sniffles.

"What? Why not? Do you have something contagious?" He covers his mouth and nose with the crook of his elbow.

"No, of course not." I can't help but roll my eyes. He's such a baby when it comes to germs and being sick. "I don't think I'd be here if I was contagious." I swipe a sleeve across my eyes to dry them.

He cautiously lowers his arm. "Alright, then what's going on?"

It's time, Katie. Time for some honesty. "So, the reason I was so sick yesterday is because . . . because I took too many laxatives."

"Wha—"

"And the doctor told my parents that I should be in therapy because I've lost so much weight. Like, overnight therapy, in a hospital. So now I'm being forced to go." It all spills out like vomit, and I'm shocked by how good it feels to tell Dominic the truth.

"You lost all this weight from taking laxatives?"

"No." I close my eyes and shake my head, wishing there was some magic button I could push to make him understand. When I open my eyes his expression is the same, confused. "I'm bulimic, Dominic. What Sloan has been telling people is true. I want to throw up everything I eat, and sometimes when I eat, I can't stop, and I have no idea how it got so bad or how to stop it."

His look of confusion has turned to sadness. "How long will you be gone?" I don't know what I expected him to say, but that wasn't it. Maybe he doesn't really understand what bulimia is. At least he knows I need help though.

I shrug. "Until I'm better, I guess. I don't know."

"Well, how long does it take to get rid of bulimia?"

I want to tell him it's not like an infection that goes away after days of taking teaspoonfuls of that pink bubblegum stuff, but instead I shrug. "Hey, did Hunter ask if you knew where I was today?"

"Yeah, I told him you were sick, but that's it. Are you going to tell him? And what about Carly?"

"Yeah, I'll call Hunter tonight. But Carly and I haven't really been talking lately, so . . ."

"Okay, well, you know I won't say anything to anyone, right? Not even Beth. If anyone asks, I'll just say maybe you went to visit your dad again but I'm not sure."

"Thanks, Dominic."

Mrs. Riley honks the horn. Dominic stands and peeks his head out the door, shouting, "I'll be there in a sec!" Then he looks back at me. He has the same look on his face as he did when I was forced to spend two weeks with my dad in California the summer before fifth grade. I didn't want to go because I was afraid to be away from my mom and my friends for so long. "When are you leaving?"

"Tomorrow morning."

Then he says the same thing he said right before it was time for my mom to drive me to the airport back then. "I'll be here when you get back."

~

Later that night, Kelsie helps me pack my things. I need to be ready to go first thing in the morning because we're supposed to be at the treatment center by eight. My mom and Gary took the day off, and Kelsie is skipping her morning classes. My dad obviously can't be there, and my mom seems to hate him even more because of it. He called tonight to say he's proud of me for being so brave and that he loves me. It was one of his typical pep talks. Sort of reminded me of the conversations we had the night before my first day of kindergarten and the night before I started middle school.

I wanted to remind him that this wasn't my choice. How does hating the fact that I have to be away from home with perfect strangers for who knows how long make me brave? But I figured there was no point in trying to argue with him. If he wants to think I'm brave, whatever.

After we were done talking, my mom said she wanted to talk to him. Then I listened to them argue for at least an hour. Well, I couldn't hear my dad, but I heard everything my mom had to say.

Don't you think it's important to be here to support her? Don't you realize that your lack of attention over the years probably has a lot to do with this? Is Connie the reason why you aren't going to be here for your daughter? Do you know how expensive this is going to be? I certainly hope you don't think we're paying for half of the co-pay when you make so much more than we do.

Halfway through their conversation, I had already filled up two pages in my journal. Front and back.

I get why drugs, alcohol, lighters, matches and sharp objects like razors and compact mirrors are not allowed. Duh. Who would bring those things? But I'm a little surprised that jewelry, belts, shoelaces, cell phones, iPods, and other types of electronics are not allowed. What's even weirder is that I can't bring leggings, hoodies, or anything personal like pictures. So I pack just the basics: jeans, yoga pants, T-shirts, sweatshirts, socks, underwear, and a few bathroom items. Nothing special. Nothing fancy. Just plain, boring wear-around-the-house clothes. When my bag is finally zipped, I think about all the worrying I did over my body and clothes at the beginning of the school year. Was it worth it?

I start to cry and Kelsie holds me until her phone buzzes. "Kit Kat, I have to get going, but I'll be back tomorrow morning." Even after everything that has happened, she's still calling me Kit Kat. And still running off to be with Kyle.

"Yeah, okay. See you tomorrow," I say.

Not long after Kelsie leaves, my mom and Gary both show up to say goodnight—something Gary has only done a handful of times and something my mom hasn't done regularly for years. But instead of a simple goodnight, their visit turns into another pep talk about how good the treatment center is going to be for me and about how great I'm going to do. When my mom mentions that I might even make some new friends, that's when I stop listening. I'm being checked in to a treatment facility for girls with eating disorders, and they're acting like I'm going away to camp or some elite boarding school. Their complete obliviousness is just too much for me to handle.

After my mom and Gary both kiss me on the forehead and leave, I toss and turn all night long until I can see little specks of dust floating in the rays of sun streaming through my windows.

Part III

Spring

Chapter Thirty

Unlike most first days of spring in Wisconsin, today is sunny and above fifty degrees. Is it a sign? A sign that today is a new beginning for me? That inpatient treatment is going to cure me? Even if it is a sign of brighter days to come, I'm still a panicked heap of gloom and doom. I don't want to go to the treatment center. I don't need to go. I can get better on my own.

But it doesn't matter what I think. They're making me go, whether I like it or not.

What will people think if they find out? Hunter seemed to understand and didn't have a lot of questions, but what about other kids at school? What if Dominic breaks his promise and ends up telling Carly or Beth?

After being stuck in traffic for twenty minutes, Gary finally exits the freeway. The hospital is only a few blocks away. I think about jumping out of the car and running away forever.

The silence as we drive makes me feel like we're heading to a funeral. It's even worse as we make our way through the hospital to the inpatient psychiatric wing. Finally, we are standing in front of two large frosted glass doors labeled: St. Mary's Eating Disorder Treatment Center.

Moments after Gary pushes the blue buzzer on the wall, a voice says, "Good Morning, how can I help you?"

"We have an appointment to admit my stepdaughter, Katie . . . uh . . . Katherine. Katherine Mills."

There is a quiet buzz and the doors slowly swing open. "Please proceed to the waiting area to your left."

As soon as we enter, I see my dad. He stands and rushes over to hug me.

"What are you doing here?" my mom asks.

"What do you think I'm doing here, Elaine? I decided to hop on a red-eye."

"Well, no one said you *had* to be here."

"Goddamn it, Elaine! Give it a rest, would you? Our daughter is sick and that's what we need to focus on right now."

Gary steps forward and shakes my dad's hand. Kelsie gives him a hug. Then the lady behind the counter, says, "I'll need someone to fill out this paperwork." It was her voice that spoke to us through the speaker just moments ago.

"I got it." My dad quickly retrieves the clipboard covered with papers.

From that point on, things all kind of blur together.

The lead therapist, Tammy, came out to meet us. She told us her whole name, Dr. Tammy something or other, but then looked at me and said, "Please, just call me Tammy." Then she explained that phone calls were not allowed and that there were no visiting hours, unless required for family therapy sessions, which would happen twice a week.

My lower lip quivers the entire time I'm hugging my family members goodbye, and then I bawl as they begin filing through the frosted glass doors, one by one. I'm not sure what's going through my head when I make a run for it. I don't get very far, though, because Tammy wraps her arms around me from behind and holds me tight as I try to wiggle away. My mom and Kelsie watch in horror until the doors finally close, cutting me off from the outside world. When I can't see them anymore, I collapse on the floor and refuse to get back up. *What are you doing?* goes through my head several times, but there is no answer, because I have no idea.

Hours later, lying on a couch in Dr. Tammy's office, I think I finally know. I think it hit me that the little bit of freedom and power I had outside this place is still out there; I just don't have access to it anymore. I won't be able to continue eating—or not eating, actually—the way I have been, because I won't be able to fool anyone in here. And I won't have any privacy.

Tammy stops typing on her keyboard. "Are you ready to talk, Katie? We don't have much time left. Morning classes are almost over, and then it's time for individual therapy sessions. Since this is your first day, you'll go to an expression session."

"What's an expression session?" I ask as I sit up, wipe my eyes, and straighten my hair. Tammy stands and walks out from behind her desk. She's tiny—petite is what my mom would call her—and wearing a cowl neck sweater and dark skinny jeans with riding boots. She doesn't appear to be wearing any makeup, but she's still one of the prettiest women I've ever seen. She looks like an Orchard Hills type of girl, which instantly makes me leery of her. How could someone like this possibly understand how I feel?

"It's a block of free time that residents spend in the art room. You can draw, paint, sculpt—anything artistic. But after today you'll only earn expression sessions when you start making progress."

"So only if I do and say what you guys want to hear?"

"No, absolutely not." She shakes her head matter-of-factly. "Progress isn't telling people what you think they want to hear, Katie. Progress is owning up to the truth, whatever your truth may be. Once you figure out how to do that, you'll be much healthier on the inside and out."

I slowly nod my head once. I already hate this psychobabble B.S. "How long do I have to stay here?"

"As long as it takes, Katie. What do you say? Are you ready?" She claps her hands and interlaces her fingers under her chin.

"For what?"

"To start looking for the truth that's hiding behind your bulimia so that you can go home."

"Well, if that's my only way out of here, let's do it." What choice do I have?

~

During my first official session with Tammy, we talk about what I hope to accomplish while I'm in treatment. Just like my first session with Dr. Abendi, I feel like it goes nowhere, and I seriously start to wonder if this whole inpatient treatment thing is going to be a huge waste of time and money. I mean, all therapists seem to do is ask questions. Why don't they just tell me what I need to do to get better? It's like they're just fishing around for me to come up with a cure on my own, which I could just work on at home.

At the end of the session, Tammy gives me a folder that contains my daily schedule and some pamphlets on depression, bulimia and other eating disorders. I ignore the pamphlets and look at the schedule.

MONDAY – FRIDAY
6:30 – 7:30 GREET THE DAY
7:30 – 8:00 BREAKFAST
8:00 – 11:00 ACADEMICS
11:00 – 12:00 INDIVIDUAL THERAPY/EARNED EXPRESSION SESSION
12:00 – 12:30 LUNCH
12:30 – 1:00 JOURNALING
1:00 – 2:00 GROUP THERAPY
2:00 – 3:00 PHYSICAL WELLNESS
3:00 – 4:30 STUDY HALL/QUIET READING (DIETICIAN CONSULT T & F)
4:30 – 5:30 DINNER
5:30 – 7:00 FAMILY THERAPY/RECREATION
7:00 – 9:00 RECREATION
9:00 LIGHTS OUT

SATURDAY – SUNDAY
6:30 – 8:00 GREET THE DAY (7:30 – 8:00 CHURCH SERVICES *SU*)
8:00 – 8:30 BREAKFAST
8:30 – 12:00 SATURDAY FIELD TRIP OR GROUP ACTIVITY
12:00 – 1:00 LUNCH
1:00 – 1:30 JOURNALING
1:30 – 2:30 GROUP THERAPY
2:30 – 4:30 FREE CHOICE
4:30 – 5:30 DINNER
5:30 – 9:00 RECREATION

Some sort of therapy every day? Are they kidding me? I don't mind the individual therapy, but group therapy? I picture a bunch of girls who are much skinnier than I am sitting around in a circle staring at the floor. How will that help? Or will we trade secrets about how to sneak food and puke without anyone finding out?

"I know it's a lot to take in at first, but routine is good, and you'll adapt quickly," Tammy says as she leads me to a counter in what appears to be the recreation area. There's a large TV, several couches, a few computer stations, tables and chairs, a ping-pong table, an air hockey table, and bookshelves filled with books and games.

"Good morning, Tammy," a rosy cheeked woman with short, grandma hair says. "And who do we have here?"

"Good morning, Mary," Tammy says and then turns to me. "Mary is one of four nurses who rotate through the treatment center and work with Anne, our registered dietician. There is a nurse here twenty-four hours a day, so if you're ever not feeling well, Mary or whoever is on duty can look you over."

"Mary, this is our new friend, Katie. Katie Mills. She just received her schedule, so I was wondering if you could show her to her room and then give her a tour of where everything else is."

"I'd be happy to!" Mary links an arm around mine and picks my bag up with her other hand. "I'll give you the grand tour," she says with a wink.

When we arrive in the dining area at noon, I am exhausted and not looking forward to seeing the other girls. Mary drops me off in a line that's forming in front of a hole in the wall. The girl at the front of the line has her wrist under a scanner, sort of like the ones they use at Six Flags. When it beeps, the woman behind the counter disappears for a second and returns with a tray of food. "There you go, Britt. Looks like a good lunch. Good luck today."

Britt doesn't say anything. She simply turns and heads toward the long dining room table, looking at the floor the entire time with her black hair hanging in her face so I can't get a good look at her. She's not as skinny as I expected all the girls would be, but maybe she's been here for a while.

After two more girls get their food, I am finally up. I stick my wristband under the scanner, but nothing happens, causing a few groans from behind me.

"Aw, come on. Knock it off!" A girl with short spiky hair with streaks of purple grabs my wrist and twists my wristband so that the bar code is facing up.

She smiles at me when the scanner beeps and says, "You have to have the lines facing up like that for it to work. Oh, and be quick about it, otherwise these bitches will complain all day, every day." She nods behind me, causing an exasperated sigh from "these bitches." I want to look at them so bad, but I'm too scared I might come face to face with Sloan Whitson look-a-likes.

"Thanks," I say to the lady behind the counter who is carefully examining the label on my tray.

"You're very welcome, Katherine. I'm Sally. I work with Anne, the resident dietician. I believe you're to meet with her later this afternoon."

"Nice to meet you. And, it's Katie," I say.

"Katie," she repeats before motioning for the girl with the purple hair to scan her band. "Come on, Daisy Doo, let's see what you're having today."

As I walk to the table, I can't help but glance at the last two girls in line. I blink a few times just to make sure I'm seeing things right. The girls standing behind purple-haired Daisy are more than Sloan Whitson look-a-likes; they're twin Sloan Whitson look-a-likes. Great. Just great.

That makes seven of us, not including Tammy and two other adults I haven't met yet. Hair-in-her-face Britt pokes a carrot stick into some cottage cheese. The two girls who were ahead of me, one with long blond hair and the other with shoulder-length honey colored hair, talk to each other quietly while they take small nibbles of their ham sandwiches. The Sloan look-a-likes talk too, but they aren't whispering so I can hear that they're talking about their favorite contestants on *American Idol*. They're skinny, but not too skinny. They seem perfectly fine to me, just like Amy Bowie. I'm envious of them, of the way they can obviously control their bulimia, or whatever type of eating disorder they have.

Daisy is sitting next to me, making crisscross marks in her sandwich with a fork.

All the food on my tray taunts me. It says: *Go ahead. Take a bite. Show them you can do it*. A grilled ham and cheese sandwich, a small salad, 2% milk, a small bowl of cottage cheese, and a cookie. I thought the goal was to make me stop binging, not push me to binge.

"You have to eat it all. Just in case you were wondering," Daisy whispers. "See." She points at the label taped to my tray. "The number of calories is listed here by your name. They want you to start gaining weight right away. There is no easing into it." She goes back to mutilating her sandwich.

"What if you don't finish?" I ask.

"Then you don't gain weight and you stay longer than you would otherwise, I guess." She stabs a cucumber chunk and brings it to her mouth, revealing thick lengthwise scars on the inside of her wrist and forearm.

"How long have you been here?"

"Ten days," she says without hesitation. "But I'll be out of here soon. I wasn't as underweight as the last time I was here, so it won't take as long for me to gain it back."

"You mean, you've been here before?"

"Twice. My mom says this is it. I need to get better this time or else. Or else what, you wonder? Yeah, me too."

"Oh," is all I can muster, because I'm busy trying to get another look at her scars. I read somewhere that people who really want to commit suicide often slit their wrists wrong. Something like if you really want to kill yourself, you need to slit vertically, not horizontally. I wonder if Daisy knows this and if she is someone who really wants to kill herself.

After lunch, it's time for journaling. We have to sit in the lounge area to do this, and the rules are that we're supposed to jot down some thoughts about food to share during group therapy and that there's no socializing. If we think of something that we want to say to someone, then we're supposed to write it in our journals so that we can remember it for later. Most of the time I'm supposed to be writing, I try to think of a way to get rid of all the food I just ate. After going through every scenario I can think of, I realize it would be impossible, so painful thoughts invade my brain.

Stomach churning.

Calories absorbing.

Fat accumulating.

Losing control.

Starting to panic, I look from girl to girl and wonder if any of them are feeling the way I am. When my eyes lock with Britt's, I see it—the same sense of panic. I don't know how long we stare at each other, but by the time she looks away, the panicked feeling I had is gone.

During group therapy, Tammy formally introduces me to everyone

—the other girls, and the two other adults who ate lunch with us. Sully, a social worker and therapist, has longish salt-and-pepper hair and resembles a big teddy bear. From behind, he looks old because of his hair, but from the front, he looks like he could be in his thirties with wrinkle-free skin, like my dad. Corrie, a psychiatrist, is a tall woman in a sweater dress, tights, and suede shabooties. She has her highlighted brown hair in a French braid, and she's model skinny. My first impression is she could pass for one of us—if it wasn't for her height— but then she speaks and her crisp, monotone voice reminds me of someone on some news show. The phrase *don't judge a book by its cover* enters my mind.

After short introductions from everyone, we all take turns sharing something from our journals. Britt—still hiding behind her hair—and one of the Sloan look-a-like twins pass, but the other girls share things like how they felt while they were eating lunch, nightmares about binging on mounds of donuts and not being able to throw them up, and longing to eat something as simple as a potato chip and not feeling the need to eat the entire bag. I share that I don't understand how being in a treatment center is going to help me, which leads to a discussion about the importance of learning how to cope with the issues behind our eating disorders, the truths that we are denying or ignoring.

"I'm not hiding any issues," Daisy says matter-of-factly, crossing her arms and bringing her hand up to fidget with a silver cross hanging around her neck. "They're all out in the open, but it doesn't make any damn difference. One way or another, I still want to die."

All the other girls exchange glances, except for Britt—she simply moves her hair aside long enough to peek at Daisy for a second. And just when I think I'm going to find out what Daisy's issues are, Sully stands with one loud clap and says, "Who's ready for some line dancing?" The group session ends just like that, and we move into a room the size of a racquetball court. One wall is covered with floor to ceiling windows.

We're all lined up shoulder-to-shoulder facing Tammy, Sully, and Corrie who are standing with their backs to us. This is what we're doing for physical wellness? Dancing?

"Ready, girls?" Tammy says, smiling at us over her shoulder.

The twins nod like perky cheerleaders, and Daisy sarcastically yells,

"Giddy up!" Britt says nothing and looks as nervous as I feel, and the other two girls—Elsie and Lisa—mumble unenthusiastically.

Sully presses play on his iPod, which is attached to a speaker, and quickly gets back into position next to Tammy and Corrie. "Here we go."

It's an old country song that I've heard a few times, but even if I was offered a million dollars, I'd never be able to come up with its name.

The twins follow Tammy and Sully's moves to a T. Daisy dances too, but she's doing her own thing. The rest of us just stand there watching at first. But then Sully moves out of line and starts dancing around next to us and behind us. Even though most of us aren't moving a muscle, he looks like he's having the time of his life, and for a second I wish I could dance like that, too. Not that I wish I could move like him, but I just wish I could be free like that and be happy without worrying about how my body looks or what people will think. By the end of the song, Britt and I are the only ones who still haven't wiggled a muscle. But it doesn't matter; we still get high fives and hugs from Tammy and Sully. Then they start the song again and go through the routine four more times. I think I see Britt moving her hips at one point, but I could be wrong.

~

"Nine o' clock. Lights out girls." A new face peeks her head into the room shared by Daisy and me. Then she flips the light off as she says, "Sleep tight. Don't let the bed bugs bite."

"That's Phyllis," Daisy whispers. "She'll be here until around five, and then Mary comes back. I like Mary better." She sits up and faces me. "So, what's wrong with you. Are you strictly a puker?"

"Yeah, I guess you could say that. What about you? Do you make yourself throw up?"

"Sometimes. And sometimes I just stop eating, like for days at a time. And sometimes I . . . do other things."

I turn onto my side to face her. "So, you can eat without losing control if you want to?"

"Yes and no. If I eat something and can't stop, then I always throw it up. But if I can manage to not eat for an entire day, I get to a point where I don't feel hungry anymore and then it's not hard at all for me to be around food. If it's not one, it's the other."

"But you said you do other things too?"

Daisy doesn't say anything for so long that I think she's done talking. But then, as I'm starting to doze off, she says, "I only do other things when it gets really bad."

Chapter Thirty-One

Today started with a breakfast that made me cry. Oatmeal with sliced strawberries, a whole banana, 2% milk and orange juice. It was the entire bowl of oatmeal that did it. A few bites in, tears started pouring down my cheeks. Daisy, who was sitting across from me, told me to suck it up. But Britt? She inched her chair closer to mine and hugged me. Then one of the Sloan look-a-likes (Trish), who was sitting on the other side of me, hugged me too.

All seven of us managed to finish our breakfasts this morning.

∾

"Katie?"

Even though she says my name, everyone looks up at Tammy, except for Daisy who has fallen asleep on her life sciences textbook.

Tammy walks over and gently shakes her shoulder. "Daisy. Daisy. Come on. Wake up. You need to finish this." Daisy lifts her head and wipes drool from the side of her face.

"Yuck," Lisa says.

"Are you ready for your session?" Tammy's smile brings back the warm feeling I had this morning when Britt and Trish hugged me.

"Sure. I just have to pack all this up," I say, stacking books and notebooks. Then I carry the pile over to my book cubby.

Instead of sitting behind her desk like she did yesterday, Tammy sits in a big comfy chair. She's not holding a clipboard and pen the way Dr. Abendi always does. Instead, she has a big mug. Smells like coffee. "So, how are you feeling today?" she asks.

I almost say okay, but reconsider. "Good. I feel good today."

"Do you think you can talk about how you're feeling in terms of food?"

I was proud of myself for telling her I felt good, but now I feel like my answer wasn't *good* enough. "I don't know what you mean. I feel fine." *Less than good now, thanks to you.*

"Okay. I'll try to be more specific. Can you explain how you felt during breakfast? And afterward?"

"You know how I felt. You saw me crying. It felt crappy to have to eat that whole bowl of oatmeal. I wanted to throw it across the room."

My anger doesn't phase her at all. "But then how did it feel to have the other girls there to support you?"

I think about the hugs, and the way everyone took bite after bite together. Then I hear Daisy telling me to suck it up and I smile.

"Did it feel good to be understood and to have support?"

"Yes."

"Well, that *is* good!" She leans forward and pats my knee. When she is settled back in her chair, she says, "And did that feeling of being understood and supported carry over into academics? Were you able to concentrate on your studies? Or were you thinking about the food you'd eaten?"

I hadn't thought about this until now, but I didn't think about the food at all. I just did my work. I smile to myself, and that seems just fine for Tammy because she moves on.

"So, did you get a chance to look at the pamphlets that were in the folder I gave you yesterday? Or have you ever looked up information about bulimia online?"

I shake my head.

"That's okay. One thing we need to teach you here is what bulimia does to your body."

"Okay." I shrug and wait for her to continue.

"You obviously know that it can cause you to lose weight."

I nod.

"Well, there are other things that it can, and ultimately does, to a person's appearance. For example, bulimics often have swollen neck glands and cheeks, thinning hair, and extremely dry skin."

I feel my neck and notice that the lumps under my chin *are* kind of big.

"And their teeth will become stained and possibly corroded from coming into constant contact with stomach acid. Your gum line could even recede prematurely. Have you been to the dentist lately?"

"No," I say. Then I run my tongue back and forth across my teeth.

"But those are just the things you can see." Tammy pauses long enough to take a sip of her coffee. "As for the things you can't see, well, sore throat, low blood pressure, constant headache, dizziness. Have you had any of these symptoms?"

I scrunch my eyebrows together, realizing that I have experienced a lot of these things lately.

"There's also the inability to focus, insomnia, social anxiety, depression—leading to suicidal thoughts in some cases—and an inability to see yourself clearly, both physically and as a person. Sure, bulimics usually have some sort of psychological issue that causes the disease to manifest, but once the binge-purge cycle becomes habitual, the psychological issues only become worse. It gets to be like trying to put out a fire by dousing it with gasoline; the fire only gets bigger, obviously. Katie, the bottom line is that bulimia can kill you."

The first tear of many wets my cheek, but that doesn't stop Tammy from continuing.

"It could be one week, one month, or even a year. Heck, some people go years, decades even, living with this disease. But then there are the people whose bodies can't handle the wear and tear. The constant change in blood pressure. Low to high during a binge, high to low after the purge, when your body begins to starve."

"Okay, okay! I get it!" Tears are streaming now. "I understand," I whisper.

Tammy grabs a box of tissues from her desk and brings it over to me, but she doesn't go back to her chair. She sits next to me on the sofa and hugs me, making me cry even harder.

~

At the end of my session with Tammy, I feel like there's no way I'll be able to make it through the rest of the day. I think about going to my room, crawling under the covers and staying there no matter what anyone says. But Tammy leads me to the dining room, while I'm still gasping for breath, the way people often do after a hard cry. When I walk past the other girls to get into line, no one seems surprised by my puffy eyes and blotchy face. In fact, Daisy even says, "Hey, Katie. Rough session?"

At first I'm angry that no one seems to care, and I want to scream at Daisy for what she said. But then it hits me. They've all been where I am, many, many times. So, I had a rough session. So what? And I hear my Grandma Mills' voice. *I'm so sorry, Katherine. Life is rough sometimes, sweetheart. And it's hardly ever fair.* They are the same words she said to me when she held me in her arms as I cried about my mom and dad, way back when they first got divorced.

~

Family sessions are supposed to start at five thirty, but it's almost five forty-five, and no one has come to get me yet. With each minute that passes, my mood shifts from excited to scared to nervous. Then from sad to upset.

Daisy has a family session tonight too. We all got a glimpse of her parents as Corrie led them to her office. Daisy seemed happy to see her mom, but she wouldn't even look at her dad. When he went in to hug her, she looked stiff, almost scared. I made a mental note to ask her about it if she seems okay later.

"Katie, they're here." Tammy appears. I can hear my parents arguing, but I can't see them.

I jump up to follow Tammy. To my surprise, Britt says, "Good luck, Katie." I look back at her, wondering if I imagined it. But she has one side of her hair pulled away from her face, and I can see her smiling at me.

"Oh, Katie!" My mom rushes to me and pulls me in for a hug.

"Mrs. Mills, I know you're happy to see Katie, but we should really get to my office and begin the session. We're pretty behind schedule."

"Clifton, my last name is Clifton." My mother releases me and glares at Tammy.

Oh great.

"Well, you don't have to be so rude about it, Elaine. It's an honest mistake," My dad says as he moves in to hug me. "Hey there, Kit Kat."

Goosebumps begin to spread across my skin when he calls me Kit

Kat, and my mom snaps, "Would you quit with the juvenile nickname already? Don't you know she hates being called that?"

"Mr. Mills, Mrs. Clifton," I've never seen Tammy look upset before, but her face is turning pink and she's nervously looking around. "We need to move to my office. Right now."

Moments later, we are all seated in Tammy's office. Tammy is in her big comfy chair and my mom, me, and my dad—in that order—are on the sofa.

"Before we start, Katie, is there anything you'd like to share with your parents?" Tammy asks.

I think for a moment and then say, "Well, before I came here, I said I could get better on my own—"

"Oh, Katherine, don't you understand that—"

"Mrs. Clifton," Tammy says, her voice raised. "Please allow Katie to finish speaking before you respond. Go on, Katie."

I look at my mom. She's doing her best to keep a straight face, but I can sense her anger. She isn't used to being shut down like that.

Then I look over at my dad, and he looks glad that Mom was just scolded. In that moment, sitting between the two of them, I realize the truth behind my bulimia. I was created to save their relationship, but I wasn't enough. I'm never enough. I wasn't enough for my dad, so he left. And I've never been enough for my mom to think I was worth it. Never good enough, to be specific. The truth is, that's how I feel. Like I'm not enough. Like I don't matter.

I don't want to be skinny. I don't want to wear designer clothes. I don't want to be friends with popular mean girls. I just want to be enough for my parents.

"I know now that I can't get better all on my own. I need some help."

Both of my parents wait to make sure that I'm done talking. Then Tammy nods her head and my dad says, "That's wonderful, Katie. I'm so glad you're able to see that now."

My mom nods. "Good. Good for you, sweetheart. I knew they'd be able to help you here. What has it been like so far?"

"Well, everything is scheduled. There's a certain time when we can get ready in the morning. That's called Greet the Day. Then there are meal times, school, journaling, oh and physical wellness."

"What's that? Learning how to eat healthy?" My mom asks.

"No, it's like gym, I guess. The last couple of days, we did some dances."

"Dances? Like what?"

"Today it was the Macarena and the Electric Slide."

My mom laughs. "Well that must have been a sight. You doing the Electric Slide with your two left feet!"

I glance up at Tammy. She purses her lips but doesn't say anything. Why should she? She doesn't know that my mom says stuff like this to me all the time. "Yeah, I know. I didn't actually dance, but I still had to stand there with everyone and pay attention."

"So, what is the game plan for Katie, Tammy? How long do you anticipate she'll be here?" My dad asks.

"I wouldn't say that there's a specific game plan at this point. We're still getting to know Katie, and she's still acclimating to her new surroundings and her new schedule. One thing is for sure, though; she'll need to put on at least ten pounds before we can even consider discharging her. That makes her minimum goal weight at least one hundred pounds. But keep in mind that for her height and body structure, an optimal weight for her is somewhere around one fifteen. It could be two weeks, three. Maybe even four. Everyone heals at a different pace."

My dad coughs. "Four weeks?"

"Shame on you, Dale! I know what you're thinking. Shame on you for worrying about the cost! You know what? You're the one who caused this whole mess, so you should have to pay! And you should thank God that the payment is monetary and not our daughter's life!"

"That is not true, Elaine! None of it. If anyone is to blame, it's you and the way you always criticize Katie. The way you always criticize *everyone* around you!" My dad is on his feet now, and he's waving his arms around wildly.

I keep looking at Tammy. I'm used to my parents arguing like this, but I'm expecting her to be shocked and to put a stop to it. To my surprise, though, she just sits back and watches.

"How dare you!" Now my mom is on her feet.

Now Tammy decides she should intervene. "Mr. Mills, Mrs. Clifton, I need you both to take a seat. Please."

Like scolded children who aren't really sure if they want to cooperate, my parents grumble their way back into their seats.

"So, whose fault do *you* think this is?" My mom asks Tammy. "Don't kids develop eating disorders because they feel abandoned? Because they don't have a father figure?"

"Mrs. Clifton, I honestly can't tell you with one hundred percent certainty what caused Katie's bulimia. No one can. What I can tell you, though, is now that she has it, you and your ex-husband arguing definitely won't help."

With that, my mom sighs and her chest deflates, and my dad puts his head in his hands.

Then they listen to me. For the first time, in I don't know how long, they both sit quietly and listen as I answer the various questions Tammy asks. I talk about how hard the divorce was for me and about how I didn't understand why my dad had to leave. Why he had to find a new wife and daughter. This makes my dad shift nervously in his seat. When he tries to speak after I say how angry I was with Connie and Lily, Tammy says, "I'm sorry, Mr. Mills, but can you please let Katie finish?" This makes my mom smirk, sending me off on a whole new tangent.

"And I hate *that* too," I say, looking directly at my mother.

"What, Katie? What do you hate?" Tammy asks.

"I hate all of the eye rolling and smirking my parents do on account of each other. It's mostly my mom, but—"

"Katie, none of that has anything to do with you. Your father and I—"

"No! You're wrong! It has everything to do with me! Every time you make a nasty face when I'm talking to dad, every time you make some snide comment to Gary about him, every time you talk about how dad didn't even want me to be born. Every. Single. Time. *I* wish I was never born!"

My mom gasps. "Katherine! Don't say that!"

"What is she talking about, Elaine?" My dad's nostrils flare, like he's a bull ready to charge.

I glance at Tammy through tears to see if she's going to jump in, but she's sitting back in her comfy chair, hands folded in her lap and lips in a thin, straight line. Something in her eyes tells me it's okay for me to continue. That's the moment I feel a connection with her, like I can trust her.

My mom is suddenly sitting upright, as if there's a pole up her butt, and she's wringing her hands and clenching her teeth. "Katie, I'm not sure what you're talking about, but—"

I interrupt her. "When dad sent Kelsie and me that big picture of his family, you were in the basement telling Gary how he treats Connie and Lily like royalty and Kelsie and me like we're nothing. Then you said dad never wanted me in the first place. I heard you."

My mom starts to cry, and my dad just glares at her. The saddest thing about her crying is that I have no idea whether her tears are a result of me overhearing what she said or because she's just been outed.

My dad looks to me, leaning forward on his knees. "That's not true, Katie. The moment I found out your mother was pregnant with you was one of the happiest moments of my life, and the day you were born was another." He looks back at my mom who is dabbing her eyes with a tissue. "How could you say something like that, Elaine?" There is pain in his voice.

"I didn't . . . I don't remember saying it." Her shame-filled eyes glance up at mine. "I'm so sorry, Katie. Whatever I said, I'm sorry." Her eyes travel back down to her lap briefly, as if she's gathering the courage to say more. "Sometimes I get so angry that I say things without thinking, whether they're one hundred percent accurate or not. Whether they're hurtful or not. Your father wanted you. He still does. And he didn't leave because of you or Kelsie, or because he was looking for a new family. He left because he was offered a job—the job of his dreams—and I wasn't willing to leave Wisconsin. I was afraid, and I was stubborn. Every step of the way, I was stubborn. I just didn't think things would turn out the way they did."

With each word my mom says, I can feel tiny bits of the anger that consumed me just moments earlier slowly fade away. It doesn't all disappear, but I feel better. It's the first time my mom has ever said anything like this. It's almost as if she's admitting that the divorce was partly her fault. Up to now, it's always been all my dad's fault. It's always been because of Connie and Lily.

"I appreciate you saying that, Elaine. Thank you." After nearly a decade of not touching each other, my dad pats my mom on the knee.

I think for a minute, and then I realize I don't want to fight anymore. I tell my parents that I don't blame either one of them for the divorce and that I'm glad they aren't together, because usually all they do when they are is fight anyway. And it's true. My mom is much happier with Gary and my dad is much happier with Connie.

And that's when Tammy says the session is over.

After my parents leave, Tammy tells me how proud she is of me for speaking my mind. And for the first time in a long time, I'm proud of myself.

⁓

Even though we still have over an hour before lights out, I find Daisy already lying in bed. She's on her side, just staring into space, and she doesn't move a muscle when I enter our room.

"Daisy? Are you okay?" I slide onto my bed and lay facing her. Her eyes meet mine and the glistening sadness in them says it all. "Do you want to talk?" For some reason, the somewhat positive session I just had with my parents has me feeling more social than usual. Plus, it isn't like Daisy to be so quiet. I can't help but wonder what happened during her family therapy session to cause such a change.

"No, not really."

"Okay." I sit up and start to leave.

"Wait," she says, propping herself up on an elbow. "How was your session?"

I scoot back onto my bed until my back is against the wall and sit crisscross. "Surprisingly, it turned out okay. I mean, my mom and dad argued a lot at first, so I lost it. But things actually got better after that. I never imagined how good it could feel to just . . . let everything out."

"Well, why the hell do you think you make yourself puke? For the fun of it? Of course it feels good to 'let it all out.'"

Sometimes it's hard to tell if Daisy is trying to be funny or if she's trying to be a jerk. Giving her the benefit of the doubt, I laugh through my nose to let her know I'm not offended. After all, it's sort of okay if one bulimic jokes about throwing up with another one, right?

"What about you?" I ask. "How was your session?"

251

Daisy sits up and brings her knees into her chest. "It sucked, as usual."

"Are your parents divorced?"

She gives me the most pissed off eye roll I've ever seen. "I fucking wish."

"Why? Do they fight a lot? Mine fight all the time, even with thousands of miles in between them."

"No." Her voice is low, almost a whisper. "They don't fight. They act like everything is all rainbows and unicorns, but it's so fake. No one knows what a big lie they're—we're—living."

I think about the way Daisy stiffened when her dad tried to hug her earlier. "What do you mean?"

She gives me a long hard stare, like she's contemplating whether she should answer me or not. "I mean my big-time, successful, banker daddy is not who people think he is." The hard stare returns, making me uncomfortable this time.

What does she want from me? I can't tell if I should ask another question or if she's going to tell me more on her own. Since the topic of her family causes a weird vibe between us, I decide it's time to change the subject. "So, when do you think—"

"Katie, why do you make yourself throw up? Seriously." Daisy must have felt like we needed a subject change too.

"I guess . . . because . . . at first, I wanted to lose weight. But then, it stopped being about weight. I mean, I've lost so much, but I still see the same girl in the mirror that I saw before this whole mess started. So, I'm not even sure it was ever really about weight. God, I don't know." I pick at a loose thread on my comforter.

"So, you wanted to be skinny?" She looks at me like I'm an idiot. "I fucking wish my biggest problems were wanting to be skinny and divorced parents. You don't have a clue." With that, she lays back down, only facing the wall this time.

"Wait a second." I snap. "You don't get to insult me like that and then just roll over. What do you mean I have no clue? And I didn't say the reason for my problems is because I wanted to be skinny. That's not even close to what I said. I've been ignored by my mom and dad for years, because they're so wrapped up in themselves. And my mom has been criticizing me since the day I was born. Plus, some bitch at school has made it her mission to humiliate me as much as possible this year. What makes you so much more clued in than me? What's so wrong with your dad? He looked nice. You're the one who wouldn't give him a hug. I saw."

It takes Daisy a split second to turn over and jump up off her bed. With her face only a couple of feet from mine, she hisses, "Do nice dads crawl into bed with their daughters in the middle of the night?"

It takes me a second too long to figure out what Daisy is trying to say. By the time it clicks, she's already stormed out of the room. Now I don't blame her for thinking I'm a clueless idiot, and every reason I've pondered for why I make myself throw up seems a lot less important.

Daisy doesn't return to our room until nine o' clock on the dot, and she doesn't look at me or say a word. I feel bad for causing her to have such an emotional outburst. I have to say something.

"Daisy?" I whisper.

Nothing.

"Daisy?" I say her name a little louder.

"Jesus H. Christ. What do you want?"

"I just want you to know that I'm sorry."

There's such a long pause that I'm about to repeat myself. But then, Daisy says, "Don't be. Now, shut up. Okay?"

"Okay. Good night."

"Yep. Night."

Before I drift off to sleep, I can't help but think disgusting thoughts about Daisy's dad. I wish I'd never seen what he looks like, because being able to picture his face makes it harder for me to turn off the yucky visions running through my mind. Now that I know what Daisy's reason is for her eating disorder—and probably the cuts on her arms, too—my reasons seem so small. I feel like thanking Daisy for helping to pry my eyes open, but it will have to wait, because I hear heavy breathing, telling me that she's asleep. I wonder if that's another reason she's here for the third time. So that she can get a sound night of sleep, free from the nightmare that is her father.

Chapter Thirty-Two

It hasn't taken me very long to get used to the routine in the treatment center. The stuff we do is always the same, but I'm learning new things about myself every day.

We've gone on two field trips since I got here—to the Milwaukee Art Museum and to see *Disney's Little Mermaid* at the Milwaukee Youth Theater. Daisy said the play was going to suck and a new girl grumbled about how stupid it was that we were going to see a show for little kids, but everyone ended up loving it in the end. I used to watch the movie all the time when I was little, but haven't seen it for at least six years.

Today I finally get to have an expression session instead of individual therapy. I'm sure it's a result of my session with Tammy yesterday.

For nine sessions in a row we didn't talk at all about how I see myself. It's always been about how I feel and what I think about when I binge and purge. We talk about how I see other people and how I think other people see me, but never about how I see myself.

But yesterday, Tammy started the session with, "What do you see when you look at yourself in the mirror, Katie?"

I thought about it for a minute, and then I said, "The first thing I usually see is the way my thighs touch together. And then I see the fat on my stomach."

"So, you don't really ever look at yourself."

"You mean, like at my face? I guess sometimes I look at my face, but there's always a pimple here or there." I touched my nose and then my chin. "So I try not to look."

"No, I don't mean your face either. I mean your whole self. Do you ever look at all of Katie?" She asked.

"I don't know. I guess I don't know what you mean."

"Come here." Tammy got up out of her big comfy chair and reached out to me. Then she pulled me up and over to a double closet that I never noticed before. She opened a door to reveal a huge full-length mirror. "Look at yourself. What do you see?"

Shaking my head, I closed my eyes and said, "I told you. I see my thighs."

"Katie," she stood behind me and gently gripped my upper arms, "open your eyes and look at yourself. Look at both of us."

I did as she said and was shocked when I saw how much bigger Tammy's frame was than mine. She's only about three inches taller than I am, but the sides of her torso and hips were visible even with me standing in front of her.

"Katie, do you think my thighs and stomach look fat?"

"What? No, of course not."

"Well, then why do you focus so much on those parts of your body instead of looking at the whole picture?"

I pulled away from her grasp and rubbed my forehead. "I don't know. But I told you, I'm not trying to be thin anymore."

"I know, but you still need to try to see yourself in a realistic light. You're still about fifteen pounds underweight for your height, and if you can't see that, then you still might not be seeing other things as clearly as you think either. You've made a lot of progress, but when you leave here, you'll still have work to do. It took years for you to develop your eating disorder—not months, years—so two or three weeks here won't make it go away just like that. I need you to apply all the things you've learned about seeing other people clearly to the way you see yourself. I need you to see Katie clearly, too. There's more to you than hair and eyes and thighs and a rear end." Tammy returned to her chair, but I stayed planted in front of the mirror. This time, instead of looking at my thighs or my midsection, I looked into my own eyes. And after a minute or two, I tried to look at my whole self, as if I was looking at someone else. I tried to pretend it wasn't me in the mirror. For the first time, I realized exactly how thin and frail I looked, even though I've gained back eight pounds over the last two weeks.

Near the end of the session, Tammy said a big part of what I need to work on is the way I worry so much about how things look on the outside. She's said it's important for me to realize that people and things aren't always the way they appear.

An example she used was all the memories I have of my mom and dad fighting. She told me that I have to realize that the arguing has nothing to do with me—that they have a whole history together that I'll never really know about. So, I'm working on letting go of feeling like the problems they have with each other are about me. I understand that I need to do this, but it's a whole lot easier said than done.

What I can do for sure, though, is keep trying.

~

Britt and Lisa earned expression sessions today, too, but we all keep to ourselves, enjoying the break from having to be around so many other people, always being watched like a hawk or analyzed. Even during recreation or free choice time, a therapist or nurse is always monitoring. So it's nice to be able to do something without someone looking over my shoulder.

Britt chooses to paint, Lisa settles in at the sand art station, and I decide on the knitting/crocheting corner. My grandmother taught me how to crochet and cross-stitch when I was five. She and my grandfather spent a lot of time with Kelsie and me back then, when my parents were trying to work out their differences. And then after, when they decided to call it quits.

I haven't crocheted anything since I made my grandmother a scarf the last Christmas she was alive. That was when I was ten. I'm rusty at first, but crocheting is sort of like riding a bike, I guess. Once you know how to do it, your brain never forgets.

Even though I knew I wouldn't have time to finish it, I worked on a hat. I choose purple yarn, the same shade as Daisy's hair. If I ever get to finish it, maybe I'll give it to her. But who knows if I'll ever earn another expression session.

When our time is up, I gather what I've managed to complete of the hat, along with enough yarn to finish it. I know I won't get to keep it with me because everything needs to be turned in at the nurse's station for safe keeping. Not because someone would want to steal any of our artistic creations, but because some of the girls have a history of trying to hurt themselves in ways other than binging and purging. I can't imagine how anyone could hurt themselves with a watercolor painting, but I do understand how my crochet needles and Lisa's sand-filled glass bottle could be harmful.

"Did you enjoy your time, ladies?" Tammy asks as she locks the door to the expression session room behind us.

We all give her some form of 'yes' as we place our projects on the counter at the nurse's station and admire each other's work, along with Tammy and Nurse Mary. I'm most impressed with Britt's painting. I'm not the most artistic person, but I swear her work looks like it could be hanging on a wall in an art gallery.

"You're an amazing artist, Britt," I say.

"Thanks," she says shyly, her cheeks turning pink. "But—"

"You think that one's good? You should see some of her other paintings." Mary interrupts, turning to pull a plastic bin labeled with Britt's name from a shelf. Lisa and I stare in awe as she lays three more paintings in front of us. The first is the darkest of them all, with a black background and explosions of red, orange and yellow—almost like it's supposed to be a fire. There's an eyeball in the center of the piece, and if you look closely, you can see flames inside the eyeball too. Britt painted her name in the lower right-hand corner along with the date, which is from four weeks earlier.

Holy cow. Britt has been here for at least four weeks?

"They're all amazing," Tammy says, "but I like this one best." She smiles and points to the one Britt painted today. It's a sunrise or sunset —I can't tell which—and looking at it makes my heart ache. In a good way.

"I agree," Mary says, grinning from ear to ear.

Lisa and I nod in agreement.

Britt shrugs. "Thanks. But your artwork is beautiful, too," she says to us.

Lisa laughs with a snort. "Get outta here. I poured some sand into a jar. It's hardly art."

"Yeah, and my 'hat'," I use air quotes, "looks like a coaster," I say, causing everyone to giggle. "Britt, your painting is one of the most beautiful things I've ever seen. You're very talented."

"Thank you." This time she doesn't look shyly at the ground and she doesn't shift from foot to foot. She stares at her painting and her lips slowly begin to smile. "This one is my favorite too."

～

For the first time since I arrived, everyone—except Daisy, who's in a family therapy session—is hanging out together in the recreation area. Britt usually sits on the loveseat or in her room and reads. Trish and Stacey usually play cards or watch TV with each other. Elsie and Lisa seem to like messing around on a computer, either surfing the net or playing games. And I've just been floating around doing something different each night. Tonight though, we are having a ping-pong tournament. Even Sarah, the new girl who arrived two days ago, is watching.

"Fourteen to twelve. Game point," Trish announces as she serves to her twin. Stacey backs away from the rocket of a serve with her hands up, but the ball manages to nick the back corner of the table.

Stacey stomps her feet and drops her paddle onto the table as Trish does a victory dance. "Arg! How the heck are you so good at this game?" She looks around at all our laughing faces. "We've never even played ping-pong before."

"Okay, who's up next?" Lisa asks.

"Katie and Elsie," Britt says, looking at the chart we made. "Then Sarah and me." She smiles at Sarah. "You still want to play, right?"

The frail thirteen year old nods.

"Alright, Miss Katie, it's time for me to teach you how this game is played." Elsie repeatedly taps the ball into the air as she says this, never once taking her eye off the ball.

Elsie, a ping-pong pro, is beating me by eight points when Tammy enters the room.

"Hi, girls. Looks and sounds like you're having fun." Instead of just lingering near the nurses' station, like the therapists usually do during rec time, Tammy approaches me. "Can I borrow you for a second, Katie?"

I look over at Elsie who shrugs, and then scan the eyes of the other girls, who appear to be just as curious as I am about why Tammy wants to talk to me. Especially since she's usually gone by this time, if she isn't running a family therapy session. "Sure," I say, handing my paddle to Britt.

I follow Tammy, expecting to be led to her office or to the group therapy room. But instead she walks over to the couch, which is still within earshot of the others. She sits and pats the spot next to her.

"I have something for you." She reaches into her black leather bag and pulls out a large manila envelope. She lays the envelope on her lap and says, "I'm proud of the progress you've made, Katie, especially over the last few days."

A mixture of excitement and fear fill my chest. *Is she going to tell me that I get to go home?* No, there's no way. I haven't reached my goal weight yet. *But, what if?*

"Katie?" She waves a hand in front of my eyes.

"Oh, sorry. I was just . . . thinking."

She tilts her head slightly. "Don't worry, Katie. You're going to like what I have for you."

Not if it's my discharge papers, I won't. I surprise myself with this thought. It turns out, I've actually enjoyed my time here. It feels safe. Quiet. Calm. I'm not ready to leave.

"Okay." I adjust myself a little bit and sit up straighter. "What is it?" I ask.

"Well, your stepdad dropped this off for you two days ago. It's letters from your friends." She holds the envelope out to me.

I stare at the envelope. The part of me that misses my friends wants to grab it and tear into it, but the part of me that can't help but feel sad when I think about how much things have changed doesn't even want to see what's inside. "Why—"

"Why didn't I give it to you when Gary dropped it off?"

I nod.

"Because I wasn't sure you were ready. One of the hardest things for people with eating disorders is association. It can be hard for bulimics when they are put back into contact with people or situations that sparked the desire to binge. I'm not saying that your friends are the reason for your eating disorder, but they have been around you throughout its development, which I worried might cause you to associate them with binging and purging. But after some consideration, I don't think you will. If I'm wrong, then at least we know that it's something we need to work on. Right?" She smiles and holds the envelope out to me again, and I take it this time. Then she stands and gathers her coat and bag. "See you tomorrow," she says with a wink. "Bye, girls." She waves in the general direction of the ping-pong table.

I watch Tammy walk away and then look down at the envelope in my hands. My name is written on the front but there's no address underneath, and Carly's name is written above the return address.

Carly. My heart skips a beat. I never got to talk to her before I left. But wait, Tammy had said it was *letters* from my *friends.* I shrug to myself. Maybe she misspoke.

"Hey, Katie, what did she give you?" Elsie asks.

I look over at the other girls who all have their curious eyes on me. "It's a letter from my best friend."

"Really? How cool." Trish says.

Nods all around.

"Well, are you gonna open it?" Elsie asks.

I nod and rip an end of the envelope off. There are several smaller envelopes inside, and my eyes immediately become teary when I pull them out and see my name written in various handwriting—Dominic's, Selena's and someone's I don't recognize.

I start with the letter from Carly.

Dear Katie,

Surprised to hear from me? I thought you would be! (Sorry about that. Now's not really an occasion for exclamation marks, is it?)

Anyway, after calling your house five days straight and getting no answer, I finally went over to find out why you haven't been in school. Your mom told me you were visiting your dad again—which is what Dominic told me too—but I knew that was total bogus, so I told her I wasn't leaving until she told me where you really were. Then your mom started crying. I know, I couldn't believe it either. She still wouldn't tell me where you were, though, because she was crying so hard. So how did I find out? Gary told me. He said he felt it was the right thing to do. Please don't be mad him. Did I ever tell you that I like Gary?

I couldn't believe it when he told me you were in the hospital. But not because you're in the hospital, because you didn't tell me about it. At first I was mad, but then I realized that I don't blame you for not telling me because I haven't been there for you like a best friend should be.

I may not understand what's going on with you, but that doesn't really matter. I'm your best friend, so I should still be there for you no matter what. I wasn't there for you the night you slept over and I haven't really been there for you to talk about your mom and dad the way I used to be. I keep telling you I'm so busy with stuff, but busy is a lame excuse for being a dopey best friend.

I'm sorry, Katie, and I hope that when you come home, we'll still be best friends. I know things will never be the same, but nothing ever stays the same, right? Isn't there some saying about how things are always changing and there's nothing you can do about it? Well, I only think that's half true. If I could have one wish right now, it would be for us to continue being best friends. We can at least control that, right?

I miss you, and I hope you're starting to feel better. Please call me when you get home.

Love, Carly
BFFAA

By the time I finish Carly's letter, I am a blubbering mess. Why have I been shutting her out? Because of a little jealousy over cheer squad and Amy Bowie?

All the other girls are surrounding me now. I feel a few pats on my back, and Britt has her hand on my knee. Even the new girl is sitting in a chair across from me.

"Thanks, guys, but I'm okay," I say, sniffling.

Lisa hands me a tissue, and Britt says, "Do you want us to give you some privacy while you open the rest?"

"No, no, you don't have to. But you don't have to stay with me either. Really, I'm fine." When no one makes a move to leave my side, I reach for the pink envelope with Selena's handwriting on it. The outside of the card says *Get Well Soon,* and there's a picture of a cute puppy holding flowers in its mouth.

"Aww. Cute dog," Stacey says, peering over my shoulder.
On the inside, there's a short handwritten note.

We hope you're feeling better soon. Can't wait until you're back at school!

XOXO ~
Selena and Darcy

Next, I move on to the white envelope with Dominic's chicken-scratch handwriting on it. There's no picture on the front of the card. All it says is: *Hope your knee is feeling better soon!* At first, I'm confused and have to reread what it says, but then a chuckle escapes me.
"Your knee?" Britt says.
"It's from my friend Dominic. He has a bad habit of thinking he's funny."
The inside has two short notes: one from Dominic and one from Beth.

Hey Katie,

I'm sure you can probably guess who picked the card. :) Anyway, I hope things are going okay and that you're starting to feel better. Be strong. You can do it!

Love, Beth

Katie, Katie, Bo Batie, Banana Fana, Fo Fatie, Kaaatie!

Seriously, please get well soon. I miss you.

Love, D

The final card has a big dumbbell on the front and it says: *What doesn't kill you makes you stronger.* I laugh at first because of the dumbbell, but then my heart warms when I read the words again. Then when I open it, my heart heats up even more because I see Hunter's name.

Dear Katie,

I miss seeing you on the bus and at school, but I'd much rather have you be gone for a while so that you can get better.

Please call me when you get home.

Love, Hunter

I hug Hunter's card to my chest and then remember that I'm surrounded by the other girls, so I quickly lay it down on my lap. Then I glance around to see that everyone has dispersed into seats all around me, but the TV is on now, and they all have their eyes glued to it. So, I gather up Carly's letter and the cards from my friends and hug them all close. And that's how I sit staring at the TV, filled with hope and thinking about how there's nothing I want more than to go home and see my friends.

Moments later, we are all startled by yelling and stomping in the hallway.

"Daisy! You come back here! Daisy!" A loud male voice booms.

Daisy rushes past us toward the hallway that leads to our bedrooms, her dad close behind her.

"Mr. Flanders, please, you need to let her go," Corrie is hot on his tail. "You are not allowed in that area. Mr. Flanders!" She rushes to the nurses' station where Nurse Phyllis already has a phone to her ear.

"Security?" Corrie asks.

Phyllis nods quickly.

Seconds later, we are all herded into the group therapy room where we wait with Phyllis for the next twenty minutes. We hear yelling and lots of footsteps at first, but then things quiet down, and all we can make out are muted voices and crying.

By the time we're finally allowed to go to our bedrooms, it's fifteen minutes past lights out.

Daisy's bed remains empty.

Chapter Thirty-Three

The first thing I do when I open my eyes the next morning is check Daisy's bed. She's not in it, and it's still made.

I head to the nurses' station to get my shampoo and other bathroom stuff like I do first thing every morning. We aren't allowed to have these things outside of Greet the Day hour and the hour right before lights out.

"Good morning, Katie," Mary says, already reaching for my bin.

"Good morning." I lean my elbows on the counter. "Mary, do you know where Daisy is?"

Mary studies my face for a moment. She's about to answer when Lisa shows up, and Trish's and Stacey's voices travel down the hallway, letting us know that they are on their way too.

"Hey, Katie," Lisa says with a yawn. "Morning, Mary."

I think about asking Mary about Daisy again, but decide to just be patient. Daisy will show up sooner or later, right?

~

"So, where do you guys think Daisy is?" Lisa asks before taking a bite of toast. She chews the food slowly, the way she always does with a look of determination on her face. Sometimes I wonder what she's thinking about. Is she still struggling with the idea of eating something that she knows she won't be able to get rid of? Is she trying not to think about it? Or is she to the point when she no longer dreads every little bite? These are the kinds of things we talk about in group sessions, but Lisa has never shared.

Elsie shrugs sadly.

Trish rolls her eyes. "I'm sure she's fine." Stacey nods, agreeing with her sister. I stare at Trish, stunned and ready to fire at her for being so insensitive, but then she says, "I mean, we all know how she can go from normal to nuts in seconds. She's probably just cooling off in a padded room somewhere. Her stuff is still here, right Katie?"

She's right about how Daisy's mood can change in seconds. And she probably doesn't know about Daisy's dad, so I guess I understand why she thinks all the commotion last night was not that big of a deal. "Yeah, her stuff is still here." I respond. "But—" My thoughts are interrupted when Daisy enters. Corrie is at her side. Everyone's eyes follow mine, except for Britt's because she's being discharged in a few days and is having a meal processing session with Sully.

Daisy and Corrie talk in hushed tones as they wait for Sally to gather Daisy's prescribed breakfast.

"See, she's fine. I told you it was no big deal," Trish says to no one in particular. She goes back to eating her oatmeal, and the others begin following suit.

"What's up, girls?" Daisy says, placing her tray on the table between Lisa and me. "Would you mind scooting over, Lisa?"

Mid bite, Lisa lets the toast triangle she's holding fall to her plate and pushes all of her things over to give Daisy enough space to sit. "Yeah, whatever."

"Thanks." Daisy plops down in the chair Lisa had been sitting in and scans everyone's breakfasts. "Dang, Trish, you must not be plumping out as fast as Stacey. Why do you have so much more than Stacey?"

Daisy's observation is met with cold stares from both Trish and Stacey and a unanimous silence from everyone else.

While it isn't shocking for her to be so outspoken, she usually doesn't bring up food-related stuff during mealtimes. It's kind of an understood no-no.

"So," I glance over at the eggs and waffles on Daisy's plate, nervous to make eye contact. It's been a while since she's given me a hard time about anything. "You didn't sleep in your bed last night."

"What tipped you off, Sherlock?" she says sarcastically.

I glance up and am met with eyes that are twinkling with emotion. Sadness? Anger? A mixture of the two? Knowing what I know about Daisy, I don't feel the least bit like hurling any sarcasm back her way.

"Well, I just noticed that—"

"Relax. I'm just messing with you," Daisy forcefully stabs a waffle chunk and plunges it into her mouth.

"You know, Daisy, just because you had a bad family session last night doesn't give you the right to ruin everyone's morning," Trish says.

"What are you talking about? How the hell can I ruin your morning? If you feel like your morning is ruined, that's on you. I mean, isn't that what they're pounding into our brains here? That we're in charge of our own feelings and actions and we need to stop blaming them on others? Geez, Trish, how do you expect to ever get out of here if you don't get with the program?"

Trish stands, shoving her chair back in the process. Then she picks up her plate and walks to an empty seat at the end of the table. Stacey follows suit, leaving Daisy, Lisa and me to stare at Elsie. The new girl, Sarah, is eating by herself, a few seats down from Elsie.

"What's wrong with you today, Daisy?" I say quietly.

"Nothing," she says firmly, stabbing another piece of waffle and causing the table to wobble.

I turn in my seat and stare at the side of her face. "Look, if you want to continue being such a royal bitch to everyone, go right ahead. But you don't have to say such mean stuff." I continue staring at her, willing her to look at me. When she does, her eyes are watery and the anger is completely gone.

"They're sending me home soon. Corrie says I can only stay two more weeks, tops. Something with the insurance company."

My heart sinks, and a million horrible thoughts enter my mind. Shouldn't we be happy when someone gets to go home? Isn't it supposed to give the rest of us hope when someone reaches their treatment goals? We were all happy for Britt yesterday when we found out she was going to be discharged soon. But with Daisy, it's like the treatment center is a safe haven. A place where she doesn't have to face her worst demon of all. "I'm sorry," I say sadly.

She continues staring at me, blinking back tears.

"What are you guys talking about?" Lisa leans forward to see me, breaking the serious trance Daisy is in.

"Nothing," Daisy says, righting her posture and returning to eating. She's no longer stabbing her food now, though. Instead, she's carefully poking each morsel and chewing each bite as if it was her last.

We eat the rest of our breakfasts in silence, and Daisy is back to her usual sarcastic, yet not overly insensitive, self by the time we begin academics. I break the rules and try to find out more from her about her family session the day before, but she avoids the topic with a shake of the head and responses like, "It doesn't matter," "Let's just do our work, okay?" and "It's all good, Katie."

I know it's not all good, though, at least for Daisy. But the funny thing is, all the worrying I do about her leaves little time for me to worry about any of my own so-called problems. And now, a big part of me is wondering if I've ever had any real problems at all.

Chapter Thirty-Four

"Okay, ladies. This is your last chance to get a groove on for the next couple of days, because tomorrow we're playing some badminton." Sully announces every activity as if it will be the most exciting thing we've ever done. And I'm starting to like it.

"Ugh. Why can't we play badminton today? I'm so sick of dancing, and my days here are numbered. Now I'll never get to kick Trish's ass at badminton." Daisy sighs. Lately, whenever she complains, I laugh a little because she seems to complain about everything, even things I've seen her enjoy. Like the Hokey Pokey. She kept trying to hide the smile on her face when we did that one the other day.

"Daisy, you don't know what a treat you're in for!" People who don't know Sully might think he's being condescending, but the guy truly is this enthusiastic about nearly everything. "We're going to learn some dances from back when I was a hip cat. We're going back to the Sixties!"

Corrie starts making a swimming motion with her arms, and Tammy plugs her nose and shimmies to the ground.

"Lame," Daisy whispers in my ear.

Unless you count standing and just putting my arms and legs in and out without any additional movement when we did the Hokey Pokey, I still haven't done any dancing. I haven't been able to shake the pit I get in my stomach when people around me are busy shaking their bodies and I picture myself trying to do the same. It's not that I don't get an urge to dance, I just feel too self-conscious that my body is incapable of moving the way my brain tells it to.

So when everyone is lined up practicing dances like The Twist, the Mashed Potato, the Monkey, and the Funky Chicken, I sit against the wall. Up until a few days ago, Britt—who's going home tomorrow—always sat out with me. But now she's up there with the rest of the girls. Her hair is even pulled away from her face in a ponytail today. As I sit and watch, I wonder why Britt is finally brave enough to uncover her

268

face, but I still can't bring myself to wave my arms up and down and wiggle my hips a little.

Each time a new song starts, someone waves me over to join in, but I just smile and shake my head. Then I continue to gaze back and forth between the clock on the wall and the dance lessons.

Ten minutes before the end of physical wellness hour, the room goes quiet and everyone stands there wondering what's going on as Sully putzes with his iPod. Tammy and Corrie continue doing some of the dances everyone just practiced. They look like a couple of goofy teenagers.

"Is everyone ready?" Sully asks, ignoring a few groans. "We're just going to move around the room however our bodies feel like moving. You can move slowly or you can move fast. Just make sure you move like no body's watchin'!" He presses play and "Brown Eyed Girl" blares through the speaker prompting me to close my eyes and see visions of my dad and I dancing in our living room to the song when I was four. It's one of the most vivid memories I have from before he left. Kelsie had been painting her fingernails at the dining room table with kiddie nail polish that you can just peel off in one piece after it dries, and my mom was recording us. As if she's sitting right next to me, I hear her say, "Dance with daddy brown-eyed girl!" Then I feel hands gripping my arms. I open my eyes to see Britt and Daisy bopping to the music and trying to pull me to my feet.

"Come on, Katie. It's my last day. Dance with me before I go," Britt says with a shy grin.

"Yeah, get your ass up and dance," Daisy adds.

So I do. I allow them to pull me up, and I dance.

Chapter Thirty-Five

Just like when Britt was discharged a few days ago, I cried today when the twins, Trish and Stacey, went home. At first, they made me feel tense, because they reminded me so much of Sloan. But during the last two weeks of their stay, I started focusing on the way their actions made me feel. Turns out, they're really sweet girls who remind me more of Kelsie than Sloan.

Maybe that was part of the problem in the first place. I've always felt compared to Kelsie and so I've always wanted to be just like her, which would be impossible. We look too different and are just good at different things. So even though I love my sister, I've always kind of hated her too, which makes me kind of hate anyone who reminds me of her—on the outside anyway. Like the Orchard Hills girls and like Trish and Stacey.

This whole thing about Kelsie came up in yesterday's family therapy session, which Kelsie attended in person and my dad attended via Skype.

When Kelsie showed up, she hugged me harder and longer than she ever had before. Then she held me by the shoulders and pushed me back a couple of feet to examine me. "You look wonderful. Starting to look like the old Katie I know and love," she said.

"She's getting there," Tammy beamed. "I'm glad you could be here today, Kelsie. You're a very important part of Katie's life and will play a big role as she continues to deal with her eating disorder at home." She scanned my mom's and Kelsie's faces. "How about we move into my office? It's much more comfortable in there."

That was Tammy's code talk for *Look, we really need to move all this family interaction away from the other residents.* I've seen her and the other therapists move in on just about all the other residents when they first encounter their family members. Sometimes the reunions are happy, and sometimes they're not. Either way, families are always whisked away into privacy pretty quickly.

Tammy started the session with, "So, Katie and I have been making headway when it comes to getting to the core of her desire to binge."

Used to the openness of the family sessions, my mom nodded and Kelsie shifted nervously. My dad looked on in silence, his chin resting on a palm.

"We've established that it has quite a lot to do with her need to be in control of something, given her lack of control of anything and everything related to your parents' divorce. Another thing that we believe to be an underlying issue is her feelings of inferiority to you Kelsie."

"What do you mean?" Kelsie said, shocked.

"How could Kelsie have anything to do with this mess?" My mom asks.

"I think you need to stop referring to what's going on with Katie as a 'mess,' Elaine," my dad interjected. "Don't you think that's a little insensitive?"

I slumped in my seat, worried that the session was going to turn into a huge argument. But Tammy held her magic hands up and said, "Please, everyone. You all need to remember that no one is to blame here. We all need to work together to help Katie. So, can we all agree to keep our thoughts private unless they're directly related to the topic at hand?" She turned her gaze to me. "Katie, would you like to talk a little bit about how you feel when you're compared to Kelsie?"

"Sure." I swallowed hard and looked at each of my family members, pausing on my mom, who already looked like she was ready to jump up and start defending herself. "So, obviously," I began. "Kelsie and I look different. Not only that, but we like different things and are good at different things, too."

I paused to take a deep breath and dropped my gaze to an elastic hair band that I was nervously fiddling with. "Well, I've always felt like . . . like you guys . . . well, not really all of you, mostly mom, I mean . . . that you favor Kelsie. That you think—"

"Katie, nooo, that's not—" My mom started to cut me off, but then got a taste of her own medicine from Tammy.

"Please let Katie finish, Mrs. Clifton."

I had no idea whether my mom was hurt or angry, because I avoided her gaze. Instead, I just kept talking. "I've always felt that you guys are happier with the way Kelsie looks and with the activities she's so good at, like gymnastics and cheerleading. It's like she's always been the little princess of the family and I'm just a peasant. I hate that I'm expected to wear her old clothes, even though my body is way different from hers and things just don't fit me right sometimes. I'll never be petite like her. No matter how skinny I might be. Never." At that point, I looked up and met their eyes.

I don't know where the flash of courage came from, but I was ready to let it all pour out and ready to face their anger or disappointment or whatever they might feel over my words. "I know you and Gary don't have a lot of money, Mom, but if there was any way we could sometimes pick out a few things that fit me, not Kelsie . . . I'm not Kelsie. I can't be Kelsie. I can't wear the same stuff she wears and feel confident. I can't like the same stuff she likes, and I certainly can't do a lot of the same stuff she's able to do. I'm just not her! And I'm sick of being compared to her!"

"Katie," Kelsie started.

"No, wait. I'm not finished," I said calmly. Then I looked at my dad's face on the computer screen. "And it's not just mom, either, Dad. When I visited you over winter break, you brought up how Kelsie was always involved in activities and stuff with her friends and seemed to assume that I would be doing all the same stuff she used to do. Well, I don't. And I hate—*absolutely hate*—how Lily gets everything she wants, and then some. I love her, and thankfully, she doesn't act like a spoiled brat. But I have always had to listen to Mom complaining about how you have *so* much money, yet you never offer to help with money for clothes or extra-curricular activities for me. Is she right? Do you really think that none of that stuff costs money or that Kelsie and I don't need any of the stuff that you give to Lily?"

"Katie, honey—"

"No, I'm not done." I looked to Tammy for reassurance. She nodded without expression, giving me the go-ahead. "I'm not really interested in answers or comments from any of you." I shook my head. "Really, I'm not. I just want you all to know how I feel. I'm *not* Kelsie, and I don't want to be treated like I am anymore."

I quickly looked at Kelsie, and felt a little bad about the sad look on her face. "I know none of this is your fault, so most of the stuff I just said wasn't for you. But I want you to know that I've felt just as abandoned by you as I was by dad. You have to know how that felt, Kelsie. Remember when both of us used to cry ourselves to sleep at night, missing him? Well, after mom married Gary, I felt like you disappeared, too. Off into your world of friends and gymnastics and cheerleading. And now you're never around. You're always at school or working or with Kyle. I know it's not your fault, but I just wish you could make a little more time for me, even if it was just to take me to a movie or to come to one of my softball games." I looked back down at the hair tie in my hands. "That's all. I don't have anything else to say right now."

"Thank you for sharing, Katie. I'm proud of you," Tammy said. "Do any of you have anything you'd like to share with Katie?"

"I do," Kelsie said. "I just want to say that I'm proud of you, too. For telling us all those things. I didn't know how you felt about any of that stuff, and to be honest, it never occurred to me that Mom and Dad compared us. But I do want you to know that I will make more of an effort to see you and spend time with you when you get home."

I nodded. "Thanks, Kelsie."

After Kelsie was done talking, my parents attempted to put in their two cents at the same time. Surprisingly, my mom said, "Go ahead, Dale. I'll wait."

"I appreciate that, Elaine," he said. But then added, "I hope you don't take this the wrong way, but sometimes it's like you want everyone in your life to be someone else. I know that's not how you feel, but that's how it comes across with your criticisms." He looked to the upper left-hand corner of the screen. "Katie, I'm not trying to argue with your mother. I just want to make it clear to you and Kelsie that your mom and me, we're not perfect. Not even close. And high expectations is something that your mom has always had. It isn't just you, honey."

He paused for a moment, took a breath, and continued. "Like I said, I'm far from perfect. To be honest with you, most of Lily's activities are paid for by Connie's parents. We really don't have as much money as your mom thinks we do, Katie. And the cost of living in California is much higher than it is there. I know that's no excuse for me not kicking in half the cost of all the extra curriculars that you and your sister have participated in over the years, but I need you to understand that I've done my best. I really have."

I looked to my mom for her retaliation. But instead of the argument I was expecting, she just sat there, either confirming everything my dad said or biting her tongue just to prove that she wasn't too critical of others. Either way, it was the most shocking behavior I'd ever seen from her. She was quiet when she didn't have to be, for the first time in a very long time.

The silence made me hopeful. Hopeful that maybe it wasn't just me who was changing.

Chapter Thirty-Six

"So, are you ready for tomorrow?" Tammy asks.

"I think so."

"You seem a little worried. Talk to me."

"Okay, so, I know I'm ready. I know I can go without binging and purging because I haven't done either while I've been here. But . . ."

"But?"

"But it's not like real life in here. Once I'm home, I'm afraid that being there will cause me to feel the way I used to feel, before I came here. And I'm afraid that all the stuff I've talked to my mom and dad about will be forgotten and that my mom will continue to compare me to Kelsie and that my dad will keep forgetting to call when he says he's going to or he'll be too busy. What if that happens and I feel like I want to binge. Or what if I just feel like I want to binge and I don't know why? When I feel that way in here, there's always someone for me to talk to about it."

"Katie, if there's anything I want you to remember, it's that you're in charge of you. If your mom or dad slips up, then that's on them. You have no control over any of that, but you definitely have control over the things you do. If you slip up, then you slip up, you forgive yourself, and you move on. And you can always call me or any of the other therapists here any time if you need to talk. And don't forget that you'll go back to seeing Dr. Abendi once a week, at least for a while anyway. If you make it a couple of weeks without any major setbacks, then maybe you can scale the appointments back to every other week. Sound good?"

"Sounds good."

∽

Not only is it my last night at the treatment center, but it's Daisy's last night too. We're the only two remaining from the original group of girls that were here when I arrived. After Daisy and I leave, I'm sure two new girls will take our places.

"Would you go already?" Daisy asks. She is the most impatient person I've ever played Connect Four with, or any game for that matter.

"Sorry, I was just thinking."

"You're kidding, right? I mean, it's not like we're playing chess or even something that requires more than two brain cells."

Even though Daisy is mean and sarcastic, I can't help but like how real she is. It's nice to never have to wonder what she's thinking, about me anyway. "I'm gonna miss you Daisy."

"Yeah, okay. Now that that's off your chest, can you make your move?"

I drop a red piece into one of the slots. "Do you think you'll have to come back here again?"

"Probably. Or someplace else. My dad complains every time that these people don't know what they're doing, but then I end up here again."

"Don't you want to get better, Daisy?"

"Katie, there is no amount of therapy that will cure me. Now, if my dad went to therapy, or if my mom would divorce him, then maybe . . ."

"What? Then maybe what?"

"Just never mind. What about you, Katie? Are you gonna go home and have a private party with some Ding Dongs?"

I know she doesn't really expect me to respond, but I answer anyway. "No. I really hope I can do this, but I'm scared. I'm afraid that something will spark a bad memory or someone will say something rude to me—not rude like the things you say, but you know, bitchy-rude —and that I'll turn right to food to feel better."

Daisy shoves her chair away from the table and stands. Then she walks over to the stationary area and jots something down on an envelope. She drops the envelop onto the table when she returns. It slides in my direction and I catch it right before it falls over the edge.

"If anyone is bitchy-rude to you at school, call me. I'll kick her ass. Now go! And no more talking. It's almost nine."

I make my move, and then glance down at the envelope. On it is Daisy's name, a phone number, and a two big Xs.

"Thanks, Daisy. I'll call you even if no one is bitchy-rude to me."

With her lips slightly turned up at the corners, she says, "It's your turn again. Go!"

Chapter Thirty-Seven

I t's Sunday night, and I'm lying in bed with my journal. I'm supposed to continue writing every day, about food, about how I'm feeling, about how I'm getting along with my mom (or not), about anything and everything really. I have a five-hundred-word open topic essay due in English at the end of the quarter. I figure I might as well journal about my experiences in the treatment center and use the entries for the essay.

I was checked into St. Mary's Eating Disorders Treatment Center on a Tuesday, and I was discharged on a Friday. Two weeks and three days.

This is how far I get before my mind starts to wander. I hop out of bed and look out the window to see if there's any sign of Carly yet, but her house is still dark. It's been three days since I got home and left a message on her voicemail. They must be up north.

I look back down at what I've written so far.

I was checked into St. Mary's Eating Disorders Treatment Center on a Tuesday, and I was discharged on a Friday. Two weeks and three days.

I add:

That's how long it took them to "cure" me.

But my mind wanders again, and I replay the weekend in my head.

My mom thought eighteen days wasn't long enough, but Gary tried to reason with her that they needed to trust the staff at the treatment center. "We're not the experts. They are," he'd said. Then my mom went on to complain about my dad's insurance only covering the first two weeks, so Gary's insurance had to kick in to cover the rest but, "It'll be a miracle if it covers everything," she said. For a moment there, I felt like I'd never even been gone. It was back to the same old, same old. But then Kelsie nudged me and handed me a set of ear buds, so I popped those in and focused on the music blaring through her iPhone.

Kelsie was so happy I was home that she hung out with me the entire weekend. She had to work on Saturday and Sunday, but she came home afterward and we watched movies, played cards, and painted our fingernails together. She had a lot of questions about the treatment center at first, but none of them were about food or whether I thought I was really cured or not. Instead she asked a bunch of questions about the other residents and the therapists, and she wanted to know if I was allowed to take unsupervised showers and go to the bathroom by myself.

During meal times, my entire family seemed to be walking on eggshells around me. Did I want this or that? Did I need it cut in half? Was it okay for me to eat that? Did I mind if they eat this or that in front of me?

Finally, I put a stop to it.

"Look, I know you're all just trying to be supportive," I said calmly, "but all the hounding every time there's food in front of my face is driving me nuts. Can you please stop?"

After that, they tried harder to act "normal," but because I could tell they were trying too hard to be "normal," it didn't feel normal at all. Although, I have no idea what normal is anymore. Or if my life has ever been normal, for that matter.

On Friday night, I called all my friends. First, Dominic. He was so excited to hear from me that he wanted to run over to my house immediately, but I asked him to wait until I'd had a chance to call everyone else. To that he responded, "Okay, I'll be there in thirty minutes. That should be enough time, right? Get ready for two week's worth of American Idol!" After Dominic, I tried Carly, but like I said, there was no answer. Darcy and Selena were both at Darcy's house, so I talked to them at the same time. Instead of not talking about where I was, I decided to be upfront with them. To my relief, they were both cool about it. They didn't have a lot of questions, but I could tell that they were glad to hear from me. Our conversation was cut short because their boyfriends had arrived to watch a movie, though. They both promised to call me the next day, but I still haven't heard from either one of them.

On Saturday night, Kyle, Dominic, Beth, and Hunter came over for a movie. We picked out the third *Hobbit*, and Kelsie and Kyle watched with us. But Kelsie can't stand epic movies like that, so she fell asleep about a quarter of the way through.

After the movie, Kyle was cool enough to drive my friends home. Then he came back and slept over at our house with Kelsie. It's crazy to think that they like each other so much that they can't stand to be apart for one night. My mom wasn't happy about him sleeping over—she said it was setting a bad example for me—but she said it was better than having Kelsie leave and then having to worry about me upstairs all by myself.

Before treatment, I would have taken this to mean that she'd worry I was going to binge and purge, and I would have been angry with her. But now, I'm just happy to hear her say that she would worry about me.

The thing is, after only three days at home, I have been tempted to binge. I don't know why. Maybe it's because I haven't heard from Carly yet and I want to set things right with her. I know things will never be the same, but I'm hoping she can forgive me for being so distant for so long.

Or maybe I feel like binging because I'm scared to go back to school tomorrow and face people, especially Sloan. Or maybe—and this is the possibility that scares me the most—maybe I feel like binging just because I'm surrounded by all the people and things that caused me to start binging and purging in the first place. Like what Tammy said, the association thing. If that's the reason, will I ever really be able to control the urge?

I was checked into St. Mary's Eating Disorders Treatment Center on a Tuesday, and I was discharged on a Friday. Two weeks and three days. That's how long it took them to "cure" me.

I reread the last sentence and wonder if I'll ever really be cured.

Chapter Thirty-Eight

"Are you sure you don't want me to wake Gary up to drive you to school?" My mom asks.

"Yeah, I'll be okay." I go back to eating the breakfast she made for me: scrambled eggs, toast, strawberries and a glass of milk. "Thanks for making me breakfast again, mom."

"No problem, honey. All healthy stuff that you should have no problem keeping down."

Her comment causes a familiar unsettled feeling in my chest. After three days in a row of her laying food and snacks out for me, I'm starting to resent the fact that she's controlling everything I eat. I stare at the plate of half eaten food, and imagine myself throwing it across the room. But then I think about what Tammy said to me in my last session. *You're in charge of you. You're in charge of you.* Even if my mom makes me the food, I decide whether I eat it or not, and whether I keep it down or not.

As I'm taking the final bite, there's a loud knock.

My mom rushes to the door saying, "Why on Earth wouldn't Jane just let herself in?" Then, "Oh, hi Carly, come on in. Katie's just finishing—"

"Katie!" Carly rushes past my mom and throws her arms around my neck, causing me to dribble milk down my chin. "I wanted to call you last night, but we got home after eleven and my dad said it wasn't a good idea, that your mom wouldn't like it. Then I almost came over a couple of hours ago, but my dad said it was too early. I'm so happy you're home!" She stops talking a mile a minute to hug me again, and I hug her back this time. "Are you ready? I was thinking we could talk for a little while before the bus comes."

"Yes! Let's go." I put my dishes in the sink and throw on my sneakers and jacket.

"Bye, mom."

"See ya, Mrs. Clifton!"

"Bye, girls. Have a good day."

I haven't even closed the door all the way and Carly is already firing questions at me.

Are you feeling better? You look better.

I wish I'd known you were going to be away. Why didn't you tell me?

How many other people were there? Were there any boys?

What kind of food did they feed you?

Did you make any friends?

Did your mom and dad argue in front of your therapist?

Did Kelsie get to visit you?

Some of her questions make me feel like she thinks I was away at camp, but I get it. This is Carly's way of supporting me without making me feel like going away to a treatment center is the most shameful and depressing thing ever.

She's silent for a minute, and then she hesitantly asks, "Katie, what made you start throwing up in the first place?"

I try to think about my answer before responding. "It's kind of hard to explain because it was probably a lot of things."

"Well, isn't that why you went into the hospital? So they could figure it out?"

"Sort of, but also so I could learn how to change the way I think. So I know how to cope with stuff before I feel like I want to binge."

"What kind of stuff? What was it that night you slept over? What made you want to eat all those cakes?"

I take a deep breath. "I was mad because I thought you were taking Sloan's side about that stupid Kit Kat prank."

Carly stops walking. "*That* made you want to throw up?"

I turn to face her. "Well, that and . . ." I look away, partly to see if there's anyone at the bus stop yet, but also because I'm embarrassed to tell her how jealous I was of her and the OH girls.

"And what, Katie?"

"And, I was mad because I felt like you've changed a lot since you started hanging out with all the cheer squad girls."

"Katie, I'm still—"

"But you know what?"

"What?"

"You've changed in good ways. I'm the one who changed for the worse.

I was jealous. Jealous because I wanted to be friends with those girls so bad and I tried so hard to get into their clique by being friends with Anica. That had to be so annoying for you. The way I always used to talk about them and the way I hung out with Anica more than you last summer."

She shrugs. "Kind of, but it didn't matter to me. I knew we'd always be friends no matter what."

"Carly, I'm so sorry. I should have talked to you. I should have told you what was going on in my head. And you're not the only person I should have told how I was feeling."

"Don't sweat it. We'll always be best peeps, you know that." She flashes me a Carly grin that shoots straight to my heart, causing me to well up with tears. "What's wrong? What did I say?"

"Nothing. Just. Another big thing that I worked through in treatment is how crappy I've always felt about my mom and dad not being together."

"Well, yeah. Who wouldn't feel bad about their parents getting divorced? And anyone who would be forced to listen to your mom and dad argue would go cuckoo."

"No, I know. But I just feel so bad about bringing up your mom the night we got into that fight. You were right when you said I should at least be happy that my dad is alive. My parents might not be together, and they might not be the best parents in the world, but they're still here. I'm such a jerk for bringing up your mom. I'm sorry."

"Katie, you don't have to be sorry, but I accept your apology." She glances toward the bus stop. "We have to run. Are you going to be okay?"

I nod.

"Good. Race you!" Carly takes off running, and I take off after her.

When I finally catch up to her at the bus stop, it occurs to me that talking to Carly has given me the same sense of relief that I used to get from making myself throw up. I feel like a huge weight has been lifted.

When the bus pulls up, I'm all talked out, but that's a good thing because no one asks me anything about the treatment center. Instead, I get things like "Lookin' good, Kit Kat," "Did you watch American Idol last week?" and "Oh, my God, you won't believe who Anthony went on a date with!" It's like I was never even gone.

Life just kept on going while I was away. Selena and Darcy talk about hanging out with their boyfriends on Friday night and about a high school party they went to on Saturday. Carly talks about her trip up north with her dad and his new girlfriend. I've never seen her so excited about one of her dad's girlfriends before, which makes me happy. And Hunter tells me all about his dad's new position at work and about how they had to put his grandmother into hospice.

"Hunter, I'm so sorry. Why didn't you tell me on Saturday?"

"Because." He takes my hand and I get goose bumps from the way he looks at me. "You just got home. I didn't want to make you feel bad with everything you've been going through."

I shake my head in disbelief that he thinks my problems are more important than his grandmother. "Your grandmother is way more important."

I squeeze his hand as he lays his head on my shoulder and whispers, "I'm really glad you're back, Katie."

∼

Being back at school feels strange. Not necessarily bad or uncomfortable. Just strange. Just like on the bus, it's as if I was never gone. The same schedule, the same people.

So far, a lot of people have been smiling at me or saying 'hey'. A few people even asked where I've been. "Out of town for a family emergency" is what I decided on. It's not a total lie, at least. I was gone for an emergency.

But, I've only been to homeroom and first and second period so far. Now, I have gym, which scares me to death.

My hand grips the handle of the locker room door. I take a deep breath. Then I release my grip, and my hand falls to my side. I glance over at the vending area. My mom's voice echoes in my head. *Why do they need to have vending machines full of sugary drinks and crappy food in a middle school? Don't they know that childhood obesity rates are higher than ever nowadays?*

A few girls approach, breaking my train of thought. They smile as they walk by and enter the locker room.

I'm no longer scared to see Amy, Anica or Laney. It's Sloan I wish I could never see again.

Is there any way for me to avoid gym today?

"Katie, you're back." Amy Bowie appears out of nowhere.

"I am," I say with a startled grin.

"Were you . . ." She steps in closer. "Were you gone because of . . . well, you know." I figured Hunter would have told her, but I guess not.

I debate telling her what I told the others about having a family emergency. But then I think, *No, I can't lie to her.* If anyone should know the truth, it's her.

"Yes. I was gone because of . . ." I pause and look up as a few more girls enter the locker room. When the door is completely closed, I say in a more hushed voice, ". . . because of the bulimia. To a treatment center."

Amy covers her mouth for a moment, as if she wasn't expecting me to confirm what she had already guessed. "Did it help? I mean, how are you doing now?"

I think about the day of her grandmother's birthday party when I asked if treatment helped her and she said that it didn't because she didn't need help. Is she asking out of politeness now, or because she really wants to know? Is it possible that she's realized she really does need help herself?

"I think so," I tell her. "I mean, I've gained some weight." I pause to look down at my body, then I meet her gaze again and nod. "Honestly, the urge still comes and goes, but I feel like I can handle it better now. So, yes, it helped."

"Good. I'm really happy for you," she says.

"Amy?" We both look over and see Sloan standing next to the locker room entrance. When she realizes Amy is talking to me, her demeanor becomes stiff. "Why are you talking to *her?*" Her upper lip curls into a snarl.

Without another look in my direction, Amy shrugs and heads toward Sloan. "She asked if I had any money for the vending machine." I can tell from her tone that she's rolling her eyes. "Nothing important."

Sloan lets out an evil chuckle as she holds the locker room door open for Amy. "Guess she wants to get in a quick binge before class, hey?"

Every ounce of self-control that I've built up over the last several weeks comes crashing down the second Amy says we weren't talking about anything important. I'm left feeling like I want to binge, the urge stronger than anything I have felt since returning home.

I don't have anymore run-ins with Sloan for the rest of the day, but it doesn't matter, the damage is done. The only thing on my mind when the final bell of the day rings is getting home and scarfing down the snacks I bought from the vending machine outside the gym locker room.

～

Ever since Amy's dis and Sloan's comment, my mind has been in binge mode. Insecure. Plotting. Sneaky.

I tried to write in my journal several times, but I was interrupted every time by a classmate or teacher.

"Katie? Are you listening? You've missed a lot over the past few weeks, so you really need to pay attention." Mr. Lentz wasn't being mean or anything, but his words had the opposite effect of what I assume he intended. I stopped writing in my journal, but I couldn't concentrate anyway because I was so embarrassed by what he'd said in front of the entire class. For the rest of science class, the rest of the day, I thought about stuffing my face.

When the bell finally rang, I hid in the bathroom until I was certain the crowd in front of school had cleared. I just didn't want to see any of my friends.

When I arrived home thirty minutes later than normal, my mom was too busy talking to the parent of one of the kids she babysits for to grill me.

"Hey, mom." I said as I rushed through the door, past the kitchen, and straight up to my room. "I'm just going upstairs to do my homework real quick."

"Yeah, okay, Katie. I'll let you know when dinner is ready," she responded, barely looking at me.

That was easy.

The moment I close my bedroom door, I'm catapulted back in time to the days when I was consumed by urges to binge.

Unzipping my backpack, I drop to my knees and begin pulling out snacks. Two bags of Doritos, a six-pack of powdered donuts, a Snickers bar, and Oreo cookies.

I tear into the package of donuts and bring one to my mouth. The sugary temptation rests on my lips for at least a minute, then I lower it and sit staring at the spread in front of me. Suddenly, I feel dirty and ashamed.

I put the donut back into its wrapper and reach into my backpack for my journal. I flip open the cover to where I have the names and numbers of people I can turn to at times like this. My friends' names are all listed, of course, but only because I know they want to help, not because I believe they could. They have no idea what it's like, so what would they say?

My eyes navigate down to the bottom of the page where I have listed some of the names of people I met at St. Mary's. Tammy. Britt. Daisy.

Daisy. I'll call her.

As quietly as possible, I tiptoe downstairs and peek into the kitchen. To my relief, it's empty. I grab the phone off its base and head back upstairs taking two steps at a time.

"Hello?" The woman—Daisy's mom, I assume—sounds nasally, like she has a cold.

"Hi, is Daisy there?"

Silence.

"Hello?" I say.

Sniffles.

"May I ask who's calling?"

"Um, yeah. This is Katie. Katie Mills. I met Dai—"

"Yes, Katie, I know who you are, dear. Daisy mentioned you."

More sniffling.

It finally dawns on me that Daisy's mom might not be sick. That she might be crying instead. I feel warm and bile creeps up my throat.

"Um, is Daisy there?"

"I'm so sorry . . ." She's sobbing into the phone now. "Daisy's . . . she's not here. She's . . . she's gone."

Gone?

"Okay, well . . ." Sobs form in my chest as well, as I frantically try to think of a solution to this problem. This problem that I know can't be solved. "I can call back . . . or maybe—"

"No, Katie," Daisy's mom whispers, "I'm so sorry but . . . Daisy took her own life last night."

Shuddering, my body melts into the ground, and I let go of the phone. Tears run down my cheeks as I stare at the ceiling for who knows how long. For a while, I can still hear Daisy's mom's muffled sobs. But then the line goes silent and I eventually hear that incessant beeping that lets you know when the phone has been off the hook for too long.

I can't make heads or tails of the thoughts racing through my brain. All I can see is Daisy. I picture her spikey purple hair, her sparkly amethyst nose ring, and the range of facial expressions she always used, from irritated to sad and goofy to concerned. We only knew each other for a few weeks, but something made me feel bonded to her, more so than to any of the other girls.

I'm so angry with her for what she's done. Angry that she gave up. But I'm also angry with myself. Why didn't I call her sooner to see how she was doing? Why did I wait until I needed her? She needed me more than I needed her. Why was I so selfish?

The next thing I know, I'm sitting upright and shoveling the snacks into my mouth faster than I can chew. I gag a couple of times, causing the white powder from the donuts to fly out of my mouth, coating a corner of my lavender comforter. The choking doesn't slow me down, though. I finish off the donuts, and then tear into the cookies.

I'm about to rip open a bag of Doritos, when my door flies open. "Hey, Katie—"

Oh God.

My back is to the door, but I know Kelsie is still standing there.

I lower the bag, and slowly turn to face her.

She still has a hand on the doorknob, and her mouth is half open. I can see the disgust and disappointment in her expression.

"Kelsie, I . . . Daisy . . . she . . . " It isn't until tears start pouring from my eyes again that Kelsie rushes to my side and throws her arms around my shoulders.

"It's okay, Katie," she whispers. "It's okay."

We stay huddled together on the floor, listening to all the kids my mom babysits for being picked up. It must last at least twenty minutes. Kelsie slowly rocks back and forth, never loosening her embrace. I keep my eyes closed the entire time, not wanting to face the food that's still splayed out in front of us and thinking several times that maybe I'm dreaming. Maybe I really didn't talk to Daisy's mom? Maybe Daisy is okay. Maybe the food churning in my stomach is just a flashback from the days before I went into treatment.

Finally, Kelsie's voice snaps me back into reality. "Why are you doing this?" She peels her arms away and positions her head so that we are face to face.

I use a sleeve to wipe moisture from my cheeks and then meet her troubled gaze. "My friend—Daisy—a girl I met at St. Mary's, she . . . she killed herself." My lower lip begins to quiver, and my heart aches all over again, just like when I first heard Daisy's mom say the words.

She's gone.

Kelsie takes in a sharp breath and holds it. I wonder for a moment what words of comfort she'll throw at me. When she finally speaks, I'm shocked to hear her say, "So, you're stuffing food down your throat because of something that happened to a girl you barely knew?"

Glaring at her, I slide over a few inches so that our bodies are no longer touching.

"I didn't *barely* know her," I seethe. "We were friends. She probably understood me better than you ever will!"

Kelsie seems unfazed by my angry response. "You're right Katie, I don't understand this thing that you're going through. You know what I do understand, though? Growing up with our parents, in the same exact house as you, with the same exact issues."

I'm ready to storm out of the room because of how insensitive she's being about Daisy, but then her stone-like expression fades and a tear trails down her cheek.

"The divorce was hard for me too, Katie. I felt abandoned too. I just dealt with it in different ways. I drank alcohol. I smoked. I had . . . sex. And no one noticed. Not mom. Not dad. No one. So, I had to dig myself out of the big hole I was in. The one I threw myself into to deal with all the arguing and all the fear and loneliness that I felt. And I had to deal with all of Mom and Dad's issues by myself." She begins sobbing, so I return to her side. Now my arms are around her shoulders. "I'm so sorry, Katie. You were little. I should have been there for you. I figured you were okay."

It hits me that she's crying because, even though she is scolding me for not figuring this all out myself, she also feels guilty for not being there to help me.

"It's okay, Kelsie. It wasn't your job."

"No, it was. I'm your big sister. I should have made sure you were okay. I should have spent time with you instead of . . . instead of—"

"Uh-uh. It was Mom and Dad's job, not yours."

"Well, I'm still sorry. And I'm sorry about your friend, too. About Daisy. I need to know, though, why did hearing about her make you want to do this?" She motions toward the wrappers and leftover food.

I close my eyes and take a deep breath. "I don't know. I just feel so . . . helpless."

"But you were in treatment for three weeks. How can you still not know for sure why you would do this?"

"I don't know," I whisper, shaking my lowered head in frustration. "I don't understand it either. But what I do know is that there are things I can do to avoid going over the edge, like talk to someone. That's what I was trying to do when I found out about Daisy. I was trying to call her for support." I look up at Kelsie. "Daisy wasn't why I wanted to binge at first. Something happened at school."

"What happened?" she asks.

So I tell her about Amy and Sloan, but not just about what happened with them today. I tell her about everything, all the way back to the first day of school. I tell her all about how I wanted to be part of their clique and part of the cheer squad and how devastated I was when neither thing worked out. Then we talk about Carly and Dominic and Hunter and the party at Selena's, and I show her my journal.

"Girls! Dinner's ready!" My mom calls from downstairs.

Before we go down for dinner, Kelsie asks if anyone else knows everything. "Just Tammy," I tell her. "And Daisy. Daisy knew, too."

Then she says, "Katie, you don't ever think about . . . about hurting yourself, do you?" Creases form on her forehead and she holds her breath when I don't answer right away.

"No . . . I mean, not by doing anything other than making myself throw up."

Kelsie's chest deflates and she pulls me in for another hug. "Thank

God," she whispers. Her deep, relieved breaths warm my scalp for a few seconds. Then she says, "What do you say we get rid of all this stuff?"

Still hugging, we glance over at the empty junk food wrappers and leftover Doritos.

I nod, and we clean up the mess together.

Chapter Thirty-Nine

"Boot it in, Dominic!" Beth jumps up out of her chair, and Carly and I join her when Dominic scores the winning goal on the soccer field.

"I can't believe how good he is," I say.

"Yeah, tell me about it. He's the laziest video game nerd I know. It's amazing that Hunter got him to try out," Carly adds.

"Watch it." Beth gives Carly a fake evil eye. "It doesn't hurt that Hunter and him have been practicing nonstop. I love watching his games," she says as she stands. "I'm going to get some licorice for the road. Do either of you want anything?"

"No, thanks," Carly and I say in unison.

"I can't believe school is over in two weeks," I say. "I'm excited and scared at the same time, you know?"

"Katie, high school is gonna be just as awesome as this summer is going to be. We've got softball, we're going up north for the Fourth—your mom said yes, right?"

At first, my mom said I couldn't go because I had been caught throwing up a few days before I'd asked. It was only my second relapse —after the time Kelsie caught me binging in my room—but it was enough for her to drive me all the way back to St. Mary's and threaten to admit me again. We got all the way to those frosted glass doors before I collapsed in tears—I hadn't really believed she was taking me back until that moment.

Standing in front of those doors hit me hard. Then, while we were huddled together on the floor, she did something that I never would have guessed she'd do in a million years. She connected with my dad on FaceTime. Not as a punishment to tell him what I'd done, but so he could be there while we processed why it happened. So, for the first time in my life, I had a heart to heart with my mom and my dad at the same time.

It was hard to explain to them what happened. Sloan had snuck into my locker during gym and ripped a page out of my journal. Then she read it out loud during lunch that day. It was an entry about how easy it can be to hide an eating disorder if you really want to, and about how I wondered if any other girls in my school besides Amy and I had bulimia.

Clearly, Sloan didn't read it all the way through beforehand, because her eyes got real big as she read Amy's name. Everyone, myself included, watched as Amy stood and snatched the page out of Sloan's hand. I was certain Amy was going to yell at me, or at least give me a dirty look. But instead, she shocked everyone by calling Sloan the biggest bitch in the world. Then she walked over to where I was sitting, handed me the page from my journal, and left the lunchroom.

Even though Amy didn't seem upset with me, I felt so guilty for accidentally outing her that I slipped up when I got home from school. But since then, and since talking to my parents together, there haven't been any incidents. I think about binging less and less, mostly just when something upsets me or stresses me out. I've made it a habit to talk to someone when I'm feeling a moment of weakness, and then I process things even more by writing in my journal. But what helps me most is thinking about Daisy. I think about how easy it would be to just fall back into the same routine I was in before I met her in treatment, and I think about how I'd eventually end up just like my friend, even if it would be a slower form of suicide.

"Yep. And I can't wait."

"Oh, and then there's—dunna nana nana, you say it's your birthday," Carly sings.

I laugh.

"Are we gonna do something? Maybe a sleepover? Or are you doing something with Hunter?"

"I have to babysit for the Andersons that afternoon, but after that we can totally do something. It's so weird that they called me so far in advance. They never do that."

Carly shrugs. "Maybe they figure you need more notice since you've got a boyfriend now. Tell them they can always call me if you're busy. Because I *still* don't have a boyfriend." She pauses as Dominic, Hunter, and another guy from their team approach and then says with a grin, "*Yet.*"

Part IV

Summer

Chapter Forty

"Happy birthday to you, happy birthday to you, happy birthday dear Katieeeeeeee—"

"Hey! Stop it Zoe! You're ruining the song. Sing it right."

"I was singing it right. I was singing better than you!"

"Okay, okay," I say, interrupting the bickering girls. "That's okay. I loved it! Thank you, girls, for surprising me."

"So, can we eat our cookies now?" Zoe asks, a cookie centimeters from her lips.

"Katie has to take a bite of hers first, you dummy!"

"Lizzie! That's not nice." I frown at her until she apologizes, and then I pick up my cookie. Chocolate chip. I slowly take a bite. "Delicious. Best cookie ever. Okay, now you guys eat yours."

When I arrived at the Andersons', Zoe and Katie made me crouch down right away so they could tie a scarf over my eyes. Then the giggling girls led me to my special birthday surprise. They had set up a tea party with homemade cookies at the play table in their bedroom. The doorway and chairs were decorated with streamers, there were balloons, and they even took the time to make cards with glitter.

"Aren't you going to finish your cookie, Katie?" Lizzie asks.

"Of course!" I can't help but think about the last time I babysat for the Andersons—the day I ended up at the elementary school. It's weird how something as simple as a cookie can bring back so many memories and make me feel so many different emotions. I'm scared to take another bite, but both girls are staring at me, waiting. When I finally take a bite, they go back to gabbing with each other and sipping their tea with raised pinkies. As I continue to nibble on the cookie, my eyes wander around the room until they come to rest on Lizzie's cupcake bank. The sight of it makes me ill with shame, and I need to put the cookie down before I lose control.

Zoe and Lizzie are playing a Disney dancing game on the Wii when Mr. and Mrs. Anderson get home from their movie.

"Hey girls! Ah, Dancin' with Mickey, I see," Mr. Anderson says as he struts over to the TV and starts moving along with the girls.

"Good moves, honey. You still got it." Mrs. Anderson plops down on the couch next to me. "So, how was your party?"

"It was wonderful. Thank you for helping them set that up," I say as I stand to leave.

"They actually did most of it on their own. I just helped with the cookies." Mrs. Anderson digs in her purse and then hands me fifteen dollars.

I hesitate before slowly taking the money.

"Girls come and say goodbye to Katie."

Lizzie and Zoe turn and race to me, both trying to be first. After I hug them both, I crouch down so that I'm face to face with Lizzie. She wrinkles her forehead when I hold the ten-dollar bill that Mrs. Anderson just gave me in front of her face.

"What's that for?"

"Lizzie, I owe you this money. Remember the last time I was here babysitting for you and Zoe?" She nods. "Well, I borrowed some money out of your cupcake bank. No, that's not true. I took some of your money without asking. I'm really sorry, Lizzie. I shouldn't have done that, especially without asking. Will you please forgive me?"

"Of course I forgive you, Katie. You're my favorite babysitter." And with that, Lizzie grabs the ten and skips off to her room.

I stand and turn to face Mrs. Anderson, expecting that she won't be too happy with what she just heard. Instead, she pulls me in for a hug and says, "I'm so glad you're better, Katie."

～

I'm a block away from my house when I notice an unfamiliar car in the driveway. I figure it must belong to a friend of Kelsie until I get closer and notice that it has a rental sticker on one of the windows. I sift through my brain, trying to remember if my mom mentioned anyone coming over today. My friends and I have plans to go out to dinner and bowling, so hopefully it isn't some family member from out of town here to visit.

When I get inside, it's strangely quiet. My mom is usually making dinner at this time, and Kelsie is either coming home from work or heading off to Kyle's.

"Hello?" I head through the kitchen. "Mom?" I turn the corner into the living room and . . .

"SURPRISE!" Horns blow and confetti flies at my face.

The first person to give me a hug is my half-sister Lily. Then one after another, my friends and more family members line up for a hug.

Hunter is last. He hugs me and kisses me on the cheek. Then he steps aside, to reveal Amy.

"Happy birthday, Katie," she says, holding up a gift bag. "I hope you don't mind me being here." She glances at Hunter. "My cousin said—"

"Of course, I don't mind." I smile, taking the bag from her. "Thanks for the gift." I'm glad to see her, not because she's one of the popular girls, but because I realize there's more to her than just clothes and hair and a pretty face.

After the journal incident during lunch, Amy quit cheer squad and stopped hanging out with Sloan. She even sat by herself at lunch for a few days until Anica and Laney decided to join her. Of course, Sloan kept her nose held high and acted like it was no big deal, and she still had plenty of people to sit with.

"Open it," Amy says, pointing to the gift bag.

I remove several layers of neon pink tissue paper, reach into the bag, and pull out a purple journal with my initials embossed on the front cover.

"Hunter said you like purple, and he said you like to journal, so—"

"I love it, Amy. Thank you," I say, just as I notice Tammy waiting to talk to me next. I gasp when I realize Britt is with her.

Amy and Hunter follow my gaze. "Well, we'll talk to you later." Hunter rubs my arm and Amy gives me another genuine grin before they disappear into the crowd.

"Tammy," I say, hugging her tightly. Then I turn to Britt. "Oh my God. I can't believe you're here!" I throw my arms around her, hugging her even tighter than I hugged Tammy.

When I release her, she says, "Of course I am, thanks to Tammy. I know we didn't get to be as close as you and Daisy were, but . . ."

I shake my head. "I'm really glad you're here."

"I'm proud of you, Katie. You look healthy and happy," Tammy says, giving me another squeeze, with one arm this time.

"Thanks to you and everyone else at the treatment center. And my family and friends," I say, scanning the room.

"No, Katie, thanks to you. Don't forget to appreciate all of your own hard work too."

Britt nods. "Hey, I have something for you," she says. Tammy moves over to a portable speaker with an iPod attached to it.

"Okay . . ." I eye both of them suspiciously.

Seconds later, I hear it—"Brown Eyed Girl." Britt starts doing one of those goofy dances we learned from Sully. At first, everyone stares. But then, one by one, people start smiling, laughing and joining in, even my mom and Gary.

"Come on, Katie! This is our song!" Britt yells over the music. Then she leans in closer and whispers what Daisy said to me months earlier during a physical wellness session, "Get your ass up and dance."

So I do. I grab Lily's hands and dance like no one is watching.

When "Brown Eyed Girl" ends, "Into the Mystic" starts. Tammy is about to turn off the music, but my dad stops her. Then he extends a hand to me. "Katie, shall we?"

"Sure, Dad," I say with a grin, as I take his hand.

"Happy birthday, Kit Ka—" He covers his mouth. "Oops. Sorry, honey. I didn't mean to call you that. Force of habit."

"It's okay, dad. I don't mind. You can call me Kit Kat.

A Note from the Author

Thank you for reading Don't Call Me Kit Kat. Please let others know about your experience by leaving a review on the retail site(s) of your choice, Goodreads and/or any other book-related platform. Your support is greatly appreciated.

I love hearing from readers! Please connect with me on Facebook, Instagram, or Twitter. ~ K. J. Farnham

Afterword

Many Resources and treatment options are available for individuals who struggle with eating disorders. A multitude of services are also available for friends and family members of those with eating disorders.

If you suspect that you or someone you know may have an eating disorder, please consult a physical or mental health professional.

You can also refer to the following online resources for more information:

Eating Disorders Resource Center
   http://edrcsv.org/

National Eating Disorders Association
   http://www.nationaleatingdisorders.org/

Acknowledgments

I would like to thank my editor Leah Campbell for the amazing advice and encouragement she always provides. I could not have completed this book without her.

I am grateful for my wonderful beta readers: Abby, Alica, Amber, Chloe, Emma, Jamie, Kayla, Matt and Sue. Thank you from the bottom of my heart for taking time out of your busy schedules to read and critique this book.

And most of all, I thank my family for all of the support they have provided and for understanding how important writing is to me.

More Books by K. J.

Click Date Repeat

Click Date Repeat Again

A Case of Serendipity

Visit kjfarnham.com for more information.

About the Author

K. J. Farnham was born and raised in a suburb of Milwaukee. She graduated from UW-Milwaukee in 1999 with a bachelor's degree in elementary education and went on to earn a master's degree in curriculum and instruction from Carroll University in Waukesha. She then had the privilege of helping hundreds of children learn to read and write over the course of twelve years. Farnham now lives in western Wisconsin with her husband and three children.

Connect with K. J. at kjfarnham.com

CPSIA information can be obtained
at www.ICGtesting.com
Printed in the USA
FSHW011255091120
75747FS